Praise for Lizzy Barber's *A Girl Named Anna*

"A dark, addictive read, with a real heart at its core. I loved it."
—Amy Lloyd, bestselling author of *The Innocent Wife*

"Barber creates a fast-moving tale of good and evil, obsession and sacrifice—all in the name of love. This gifted storyteller is a writer to watch."
—*Publishers Weekly*

"A page-turning look at the aftermath of a ___ nightmare."
—*Kirkus Reviews*

"As convincing as it was ___."
—*Sunday Mirror*

"One of those thrillers in whi___ impossible not to flick ahead."
—Alison Flood, *Observer*

"Provides a clever, unexpected solution, by way of some fine writing."
—*The Times*

"It's the big emotions this book evokes that make you keep reading."
—*Good Housekeeping*

"Barber has created characters with sufficient appeal to fuel real suspense."
—*The Guardian*

"With well-judged interweaving narratives and plenty of rich description, this is an absorbing and promising debut."
—*Spectator*

"If you like compulsive psychological dramas with emotionally complex characters, make this your next read."
—*CultureFly*

Also by Lizzy Barber

A Girl Named Anna

OUT OF HER DEPTH

LIZZY BARBER

mira

ISBN-13: 978-0-7783-8644-5

Out of Her Depth

Copyright © 2022 by Lizzy Barber

Recycling programs
for this product may
not exist in your area.

For questions and comments about the quality of this book, please contact us at
CustomerService@Harlequin.com.

Mira
22 Adelaide St. West, 41st Floor
Toronto, Ontario M5H 4E3, Canada
BookClubbish.com

Printed in U.S.A.

For Marlowe, for making me live up to the challenge.

OUT

OF

HER

DEPTH

Before you judge me, remember this: a girl died, but it wasn't my fault.

I know that seems like a pathetic confessional. Even more pathetic because the confession itself has, until this point, never been uttered.

I've wanted to. Believe me, I've wanted to.

The words have formed themselves on the precipice of my tongue, palpitating with their ugly need to be heard, to make me part of the narrative. To declare to the A-level students when I see it coming up on their news feeds, languorously debating it, now, once more, as it has risen into public consciousness twenty-one years after the fact: *I was there.*

When they stumble in late to my lesson, less eager to talk of the *trapassato prossimo* than about who fucked whom at last night's social, and whether crimped hair really is making a comeback.

I was there.

When they blink at me from faces still etched with yesterday's makeup, reeking of the top-shelf vodka and menthol cigarettes that their house mistresses will studiously ignore.

I was there.

When they declare they "really struggled with this week's essay" so they only have notes, and they say, "About that C on the mock exam… Did you know my parents funded the library?" and they don't even bother to wait for the response as they pull out their laptops and glance at their watches, and they think to themselves, *Boring bitch has never lived.*

I was there.

I imagine each letter incubating in the saliva that pools in the side of my gums. I picture myself standing, drawing the blinds. An illicit eyebrow raise that will make them pause, look up at me anew, place their laptops on the floor as I edge toward them.

Screw Dante. Let me tell you a real story about Florence.

1

Now

I am just leaving for dinner when I hear.

People talk of remembering exactly where they were when great events happened: Princess Di, the Twin Towers, Trump. I know this isn't quite on the same scale, but I'll remember exactly where I was, all the same.

I've had back-to-back lessons all day, but now, at last, I have an hour to myself, the only person left in the languages office. I spend it working on my paper "Pirandello and the Search for Truth" for the *Modern Language Review*, barely coming up for air. This is the part of academia I enjoy the most: the research, the pulling together of an idea, the rearranging of words and thoughts on the page until they start to take on a life of their own, form arguments, cohesion. I'm hoping that this will be the one they'll finally agree to publish.

I am the only French and Italian teacher at Graybridge Hall, have been for the last ten years. When they decided to introduce Italian for the younger years, as well as the older students, I did suggest that perhaps now it would be time to look at hiring someone else. But Ms. Graybridge, the eponymous head—and third of that name to have held the position—reminded me that the school's ethos was "personal and continuous care for every girl." Which didn't really make sense as a rebuttal, but which *I* knew was shorthand for no, and which *she* knew—because of certain circumstances under which I assumed my position in the first place—I wouldn't argue with.

Not that I don't enjoy teaching. Sometimes. "Shaping young minds" and all that seems like it should be a worthy cause. When I was younger, much younger, I imagined maybe I would do a PhD, become a professor. I also thought about diplomatic service, traveling the world as a translator, journalism, maybe, why not? Instead I sit through mock orals on topics as ground-breaking as Food and Eating Out, Cinema and TV, and My Family.

My rumbling stomach is the first signal I have that evening is approaching, and when I tear myself away from my laptop screen to look at the darkening sky, I decide to ditch my planned root around in the fridge and be sociable instead. Wednesday is quiz night at the pub near school. A group of teachers go every week, the little thrill they get as their cerebral cortexes light up with a correct answer *just about* making up for a day spent asking the girls to kindly not look at their Apple Watches until break, and maybe not take their makeup out of their Marc Jacobs backpacks until class is over *just this once.*

I close down my laptop and do a brisk tidy of the room before slipping on my coat and scarf, and am just about to slide my phone into my rucksack when an alert catches my eye—

specifically, a name, bouncing out of the BBC News push notification, one I have avoided all thought of for a long while, as much out of circumstance as necessity.

Sebastian Hale.

I freeze in the doorway—phone clutched in my hand as preciously as though it were the Rosetta stone—and look again, not quite believing I saw it right, presuming perhaps it was just wishful thinking, a long hour of screen-staring playing tricks on my eyes, that could have conjured his name before me.

But there it is. That name. Those five syllables. The six vowels and seven consonants that have held more significance for me than any word or sentence written in my entire attempted academic career.

And next to them, three words that throw my whole world off-kilter, that see me reaching for the door handle and wrenching it shut, all thoughts of dinner gone from my mind:

Sebastian Hale Appeal Proceeds Tonight

I sit at my desk, lights off, face illuminated by the white glow of my phone screen, and read someone else's report of the story I know so well. The story I have lived. I place the phone facedown on the desk, snuffing out its light, and press my palms into the woodwork. The feel of my flesh rubbing against the desk's smooth surface grounds me, helps me process the report—think.

I knew there had been requests for appeals over the years, all denied by the Corte d'Assise d'Appello. A change of lawyer, probably hoping that new eyes on the case could find something that was missed. But they've all come to nothing. How did I miss this?

If he is retried, if there is any possibility that he might be released…everything would change.

After the initial trial, after my part was done and I could finally go home and resume the life I had worked so hard to live, I tried—I really, truly tried—to put it behind me.

That was what *she* did, after all, and I wanted to follow her lead. I have always wanted to follow her lead. But that time has never truly left me. Sometimes, it will take the smallest thing—the light filtering through a window just so, a particular kind of humid heat, walking past a patisserie and being hit with a waft of baked vanilla sweetness—and it all comes back to me with cut-glass clarity. The sound of our laughter ricocheting off ocher-colored walls. The clink of glasses and the taste of hot weather, raw red wine. The touch of sweat-dewed skin. The scent of pine. The giddy, delightful feeling of being young and happy and having the rest of our lives spooling out in front of us.

These are the good things—the things I want to remember. The bad things...those I have no choice *but* to remember.

And now, at the sight of his name alone, I am instantly transported: flying on the wings of a deep déjà vu, away from the cold late-autumn day and the dusty corners of my tired office and back, back, back to that time—that summer.

To those gold-tinged days and months that crescendoed so spectacularly into those final, onyx hours.

To the start.

2

Then

"You have to go, Rachel—it's the chance of a lifetime!" Ms. Moore, as prone to drama as she was to clichés, had caught me just as I was about to head home, beckoned me into the languages office with a palpable nervous energy and ushered me over to her desk.

Me, her favorite pupil. A shining example of what dedication and ambition could achieve in the drudgery of our ambitionless school. An offer for Cambridge, the only one in my year. Modern Languages—French and Italian, no less, despite the fact that the school didn't even offer the latter, and wouldn't, no matter how much Ms. Moore campaigned. I was her protégée, her project, her "See, I can make a difference." Her proof that she mattered. And in return, I felt I mattered too.

On the screen of the bulky white Dell computer, an email:

Dearest Nikki,
I have a favor to ask of you...

"I tutored her children for the year after university." She'd tapped the screen with a short, unpainted fingernail, next to an email signature that read, "Contessa Silvia Daniele." "She's looking for girls to work in her *pensione* over the summer." She snorted. "I say *pensione*—it's more like a luxury hotel. Very few rooms, *very* expensive. It's beautiful." I could tell she wanted to pull me to her, could see her hands itching toward my navy jumper, and then, remembering the propriety of her position, she flexed her fingers, and patted my wrist lightly instead. "She wants bright girls, Rachel. Polite English girls who can please her guests and give the hotel a sense of British charm. It's four months. Room and board in exchange for light housekeeping, waitressing, a bit of cooking. She'll even throw in language lessons. Oh, Rachel—" she'd turned to me, and I saw the memories wipe years off her face "—you have to do it. Florence—it's just magical."

Mum sniffed at it, didn't understand, when I put it to her that evening, judging my moment carefully between the last swallowed mouthful of chicken Kiev and her nightly delve into the box of Milk Tray chocolates: "Just one—I need a little something sweet."

"I didn't bring you up to be some rich woman's maid."

She cleared our dinner plates up with a loud clatter and wouldn't look at me.

But then Dad, later, stooping in the doorway of my room, in his temperate, monosyllabic way: "Go. Have a fun summer. You've earned it."

He pressed a check into my hands. Enough for a return ticket to Pisa.

★ ★ ★

A blast of heat smacked me in the face as soon as I walked out of the airport. I knew Italy would be hot, but I hadn't imagined this, this heavy thickness, the weight of it. Carried by a crowd of jostling voices toward the coaches bound for Florence, guessing, hoping I wouldn't end up in Naples. My phrasebook Italian slurred, cautious: *scusi, per favore*. The squat driver, beard glistening with sweat, helping place my suitcase in the hold.

Disgorged at Santa Maria Novella Station, I couldn't help a rush of disappointment. Pigeons. A McDonald's. I stared at the guidebook image of the basilica's green-and-white facade and wondered, *Is this what they mean by la dolce vita?* A man with roving eyes swung listlessly on a pole by the station steps, chewing methodically on a feather. When I walked past him, he bellowed a discordant "Bah!" that caused me to yelp and the woman next to me, a skittish pup in tow, to roll her eyes and mutter something incoherent. I thought of home.

But then I was in a taxi, and we were winding along the road, my carefully meted out taxi fare clutched in a sticky palm.

The driver's eyes had rounded when I gave him the name Villa Medici, and I saw him take in my jeans and crumpled T-shirt.

"Holiday?" He cocked his head.

"No, no...*lavoro*?" I failed to think of a mime to demonstrate, but he nodded knowingly.

"Ah."

The city peeled away in favor of green hills. Tall cypresses began to dot our peripheries, and a blanket of yellow seemed to descend, bathing everything in sunlight so thick that sound appeared muffled but for the faint calls of birds, the tinny rumble of the radio.

Eventually, we pulled off the main road and headed up a narrow path, where the unruly landscape brushed softly against the sides of the car. The taxi growled over the earth so deeply I felt the vibrations in my marrow. I glanced at the driver, looking for some sign of displeasure or annoyance, but he just turned off the now-staticky radio, soldiered on.

The air inside the car was stale, the wheeze of the air-conditioning providing little relief to the back seats, so that my T-shirt started to cling to me, sweat pooling at the base of my spine where it met the rough upholstery. I reached over to wind down the window, welcoming the instant coolness blowing against my face, but the driver grunted so sternly I froze my grip on the roller.

"*Pulviscolo.*"

"Sorry?"

"*Pulviscolo,*" he said again, firmer, whirling his free hand in a wide circle and then miming a cough.

I looked out the window at the clouds of dust choked up by the wheels. "Ah. Sorry."

"Hmm." He nodded, satisfied, then pointed to the air vents above the gear stick. "Is better."

I reached for my hair tie, scraped my ponytail tighter. At last, when we were so high I felt as if my breath were catching in my chest, we pulled up to a wrought-iron gate, and the car juddered to a stop.

"*Ecco là.*" He pointed. "Here she is. The Villa Medici." And there she was.

When I remember seeing that place for the first time, just thinking about it breathes within me the same soaring lightness I felt that first day, even now, even so many years later, even though darkness clings to the edge of the memory like the kicked-up dirt that clung to the sides of the taxi.

The majesty, the grace of the place. Its sheer facade, a faded deep yellow I would soon recognize as typically Tuscan. The arched windows and gently graduating steps picked out in the gray *pietra serena* sandstone, "the stone of the Renaissance." Bracketed on all sides by manicured gardens and impish nude statues winking into the sun. The smell of the roses, sweeter and stronger in the late-afternoon sun. The sound of a silver teaspoon hitting a china cup; the splash of a body hitting the pool water in a swanlike dive.

It was glorious. And, for four months, it would be home.

She's shut it up now, Silvia. One, maybe two years after it all happened. I found that out much later, when a nostalgic ennui led me to search for Villa Medici online. The reviews are still there—you can look them up—but they trail off after 2006. An online listing: "now permanently closed." Feverishly, I tried the telephone number, still engraved in my memory, was surprised to find it still working.

"No, no," came the answer. "La contessa, she moved permanently to Milano, where is her grandchildren. No, I don't have her number. *Dispiace.* I'm sorry."

Silvia did always like everything to be perfect. Unsullied. I wonder whether the thought of being part of everything that happened, even just on the edges of it, grew too much for her.

The car zoomed off in a puff of earth, leaving me to grate my suitcase over the roughed-up ground. He'd dropped me at the foothill of the estate, by the unmarked wrought-iron gate, and as I heaved it open, I couldn't help but feel I was intruding, every step I made, every drag of my suitcase clashing with the peace.

Gardens began to emerge as I clambered up the sloping dirt path, dotted with robust pine trees. Under the shade of one, a couple were stretched out—she, stomach-first on a sunbed, leg bent skyward at the knee; he, on a deck chair, reading the paper. He pulled it down as I passed, observed me over the top of his bifocals, resumed reading. I supposed, compared to the usual clientele, I was an uninteresting sort of person.

At the entrance, flanked by a marble terrace dotted with wrought-iron furniture, I hesitated. I had received no instruction as to where to go when I arrived; was there some servants' entrance? Some discreet, tucked-away door where I belonged?

"Hello?" Seeing nowhere suitable, I plunged forward, called into the cool silence, my voice catching on the stone walls. There was a small reception desk to my right, but no one manning it. I stepped farther in. "Hello?"

The clack of heels on marble made me turn to my left, peer through a set of frescoed living rooms to the figure approaching.

"May I help you?" the figure asked in liltingly accented English.

I was acutely aware of my appearance: sweaty from travel and, more recently, hot and dusty from dragging my suitcase. I subtly pressed my hand against the side of my jeans, wicking away the excess moisture, and held it out as she came toward me.

"I'm Rachel?" It came out as a question. Idiot. "Rachel Bailey. Ms. Moore's—Nikki's—pupil?"

"Ah!" She waggled her fingers in the air, and the hundreds of diamonds on them sparkled. "Rachel." She hardened the *ch*, lingered on the *l*, so my name became a song. "Please to meet you." And then, ignoring my outstretched hand, she kissed me firmly on both cheeks.

This was Silvia.

Most of the women I was close to up to that point could be marked out by their reserve: Mum, Gran, Mum's sister, Elaine. It wasn't due to any lack of affection on their part, but tactility was never their style. Mum was always prone to the pat on the shoulder, a stiff hug perhaps, if feeling particularly lavish, but she certainly wasn't one for kisses and cuddles. When Gran told us she had cancer, I'd shuffled to where she'd sat, dwarfed by Mum's overstuffed chintz sofa, tears stinging my eyes, and reached out for her. She, in turn, cleared her throat and patted me sharply on the upper arm. *There, there, dear, no need to get emotional.*

I soon learned that Silvia was the opposite of this, and more.

If Silvia was near you, she was touching you. A honey-colored hand resting on your upper arm to elucidate a point or cupping the point of your elbow to lead you where she wanted you to go, her fingers pressed to your back to announce her presence in the room you were in, the ridges of her heavily stacked rings digging into your flesh. She seemed to feed on the energy from the Tuscan sun, always ebullient, always moving, leaving behind her a jet stream of Chanel No. 5, the jingle of her jewels still ringing in your ears after she'd exited a room. She was once a model. Silvia Baroni, then. In the sixties. This, she told me nonchalantly that first day, breezing through the brocaded and gilded living rooms and pausing to show me the decadent portraits of her, hair bouffant and eyes smoldering, that lined the walls. Her career was brief, but prolific: the conte had fallen head over heels for her during a fashion show at the Palazzo Pitti and pursued her until she agreed to marry him. The demands of being a contessa—charities, fundraisers, children—caused the fashion world to slip through her fingers, but with the children now raised and living their own lives, and a team of staff keeping the rest of her affairs in order, "this"—and at "this" she swirled an elegant hand around us— had become her world.

"And you?" We had moved out of the main house now,

past the cypress-bound pool and toward a whitewashed, rectangular building obscured by a fence.

I squinted at her in the midday sun. Shunning her sixties, Silvia oozed the beauty and glamour of a woman half her age. Her face, tellingly smooth for a woman in her phase of life, was impeccably made up, her bosom elevated to show off her neat figure. She had probably seen things and been to places I couldn't even begin to imagine. How could I find anything interesting to tell her?

"I…" She waited. "I'm from Woking." I shrugged. "It's in Surrey?" Nothing. "Greater London?" *Ugh.* "I'm starting at Cambridge University in October." At this, I perked up—inherent pride. "Studying languages. French and Italian. Ms. Moore…she thought this would be a good way for me to kickstart my Italian. I…" The sunlight cremated my cheeks. "I'm afraid I'm nothing particularly special."

Silvia smiled kindly, nestled a finger under my chin, so that I was looking into her smoke-rimmed eyes.

"My dear, in Italy we have a phrase—*ognuno è artefice del proprio destino.* 'We are all the masters of our own fate.' I was a nobody from Calabria, the fourth of six kids. But I had brains and I had beauty and I put them to work. If you want to make yourself special, you *make* yourself special. No one else is going to do it for you. And now, *allora,* here is your room." She paused, clapping her hands together. "Let's get you settled in."

3

Now

Lamplight pools outside the languages office, and I still haven't left my desk. It's that odd in-between time for a boarding school: the dinnertime rustle of the cavernous Main Hall is over, but the younger students haven't yet been banished to bed, and the older ones aren't quite at the stage of sneaking out of their dormitories and through the windows of the neighboring boys' school. To which, for fees of fourteen thousand pounds a term, the school happily turns a blind eye. The grounds are quiet, speckled with the occasional navy uniform or giggle.

Silvia will be eighty now; her beauty and her brains, I am certain, will be no less diminished. I often wonder, if she could see me now, would she think I had taken her advice; would she think I was special?

Once, I thought she would. When I was standing in my black academic gown, waiting among the others in my year to matriculate. Those first few weeks, when I walked past the Backs to the Medieval and Modern Languages faculty, the shadow of King's College in my wake. Going through everything that had happened, and despite it all, setting foot in Cambridge, clinging on to the last threads of the girl I wanted to be, I thought, *Rachel Bailey, you've made it.*

But that summer changed me.

I should go home, leave the loud silence of the office. If nothing else, I am now starving. Already, I am picturing the ping of the microwave, the smell of yesterday's Sainsbury's lasagna, reheated, filling the corners of my flat. There's a bottle of wine in the fridge. And a baguette that's not unstale but will do. I could scroll through the myriad streaming subscriptions I possess and find some mindless made-for-TV American comedy, or maybe call Alex, who lives in my block and is usually in, see if she wants to come over for a glass.

But I can't tear myself away from the screen.

The sibilance of his name is like a whisper, calling to me through a corridor leading to the past.

Sebastian.

I have read every article I can get my hands on, but there's nothing much more that I can glean except for the plain, simple facts: the Italian Supreme Court of Cassation has agreed to an appeal, and he is being retried.

I haven't been called to testify. His lawyers haven't dared try since the first trial. The letters, the haranguing, after what it did to me, having to degrade, clearly it was starting to look worse on him than anything I could offer to the contrary. I can breathe a sigh of relief knowing my only involvement will be as an anonymous spectator.

On my laptop screen, there's the same picture in every article: taken on the boat, the day before it happened—perhaps the last existing image of Sebastian as a free man, frozen, forever twenty. Sun-drenched. Tanned limbs. The cerulean blue Ligurian Sea glinting behind him. Floppy hair and foppish grin. Navy polo shirt with that unmistakable horse insignia on the left breast. A young Hugh Grant playing at being an adult.

Whose lazy finger clicked it into being? Was it mine?

I press my finger to the screen now, trace his features.

Wonder how they would look, today.

Not that I don't have some idea. They have pictures of him from just this morning, footage of him entering the courtroom, arms held at either side by tight-lipped, blue-bereted policewomen. Neat in a blue suit his mother must have brought him, its sophisticated tailoring far from prison issued. Hair cropped, darker than I remember it. Body harder, wider than in his gamine youth. A jaw which, over twenty-one years, has grown more masculine, set. And in his eyes, a grayness, suffocating the life in them that once burned so brightly.

He is not the boy of twenty-one years ago, but a man who has been shaped and molded by the blows that life has dealt him. Like Michelangelo's *non finiti*, struggling to free themselves from the blocks of marble in the Accademia's high-polished hall, he has been trapped and unfinished, unable to become what he might have been. As I look at him now, it feels both like centuries have passed, and mere seconds. For it to possibly be over like this: a click of the fingers and he could be out, a free man. For my students to be reading about him, debating about him. For the *world* to be reading about him, debating about him. For him to be thrown back into public consciousness—even though a day hasn't gone by when he wasn't in my own, private consciousness…it is as though I too have been thrown, plunged into that crystalline sea, and have emerged twenty-one years ago.

I can smell the seawater drying on the wooden deck. I can hear the low thrum of the engine, the pop of champagne. I can see limbs: jumping overboard, rubbed with sun cream, tangled with others. I can remember that trip. I can remember that night. I...I can see her.

As always, however much I try to resist it, when my thoughts turn to Sebastian, it is she who overrides him.

Diana.

Diana with her red hair the color of expensive carved furniture. With a voice that Mum would call hoity-toity but in reality was low and round and tuneful, like a perfect note played on an oboe.

Her name—those three perfect syllables, the metric foot breaking her name into a sigh, Di-*ah*-na. The scent of the factor-fifty sunblock she slathered religiously over her pale skin. Her casual disregard for attempting any sort of Italian accent, when there I was, so slavishly determined to sound authentic that I took pains to master the guttural Florentine inflection even when ordering a soft drink: *"Posso avere una Chocha-Chola."* The tip her room quickly became—wading through clothes and magazines and clanking vodka bottles to reach her bed, where we'd lie after hours, tangled in sheets and more clothes, staring up at the ceiling fan and talking about Life, with all the overblown intensity afforded to those on the crest of adolescence.

Diana was like nobody I'd ever met. I was intoxicated with her, almost from that first moment, an intensity of feeling that perhaps blinded me to her other faults.

Whether that was for better or worse, honestly, even now, I couldn't say.

4

Then

I was there for a full week before she arrived.

The work wasn't mentally taxing, but it was long, and it was arduous, especially in the heat. The *pensione* only had sixteen rooms but, being June, it was peak season and already full, each guest bent on their particular and peculiar whim. Madame Bernard, a petite Parisian lady who Silvia told me booked every summer, all summer, liked to have breakfast served in her room at 7:00 a.m. every day: an Americano, orange juice, three pieces of toast and an egg boiled for exactly three and a half minutes, no more, no less. Tim and Sherry Knowles, the couple I had seen on the first day, kept the Do Not Disturb sign on their door until twelve o'clock, so that I'd have to double back, tidy the other rooms, help with the breakfast and then return to theirs. Mark English was writing a novel—he'd be out from early morning for most of the day, soaking up inspiration from the Florentine cobbles, spending the hours from dusk until dinner hunched over a notepad with a cup of tea that normally went cold before he finished it. He liked to relax on the terrace after dinner over a negroni and a cigarette too, his eyes lingering on the hem of my fitted gray uniform as I brought him his drink. I tried not to stay longer than absolutely necessary when Mark was there alone.

There was another girl, Marta, who helped out with the cooking and laundry, but she lived elsewhere, and between her lack of English and my nervous Italian we really didn't have much to add to one another, so I was largely alone. And then suddenly I wasn't.

It was a Sunday and I had the day off, spending the morning in the historic center, taking in Florence proper for the first time. I'd allowed myself to get lost in the winding streets, *Lonely Planet* clutched in my hands, stumbling upon one magnificent building after another and training myself to remember which one was which. The Duomo, the Uffizi, Santa Croce... I'd marveled at their scale and their beauty, even marred as they were by the shoving hordes of tourists who obscured their view. With rather calculated romance I had just started *A Room with a View*, and when I'd exhausted my feet, I took a spot at a café in Piazza della Repubblica and read with the sun beating down on my neck.

Returning to Villa Medici, I completely messed up the bus routes and ended up having to walk half an hour home, so that by the time I entered the annex where my room was located, my sundress was sticking damply to my back and all I could think of was a shower. I padded down the corridor to the bathroom at the end of the block and noticed for the first time that the door to one of the other rooms was open. Intrigued, I positioned myself at the door frame and looked in.

The room was identical to mine: a single bed pushed against one wall, a desk, chair and whitewashed wardrobe against the other. There was a suitcase on the bed, the contents of which were already starting to explode over the sheets and surrounding floor. A handbag was flung onto the seat of the chair, dripping a pack of Marlboro Menthol Lights, a circular tin of Vaseline and a passport in a gilt-edged leather cover. Next to them, a pile of clothes in a heap: jeans, a white thong, bra and T-shirt. I eyed the passport, considered having a peek.

"Fucking hell, it's hot, isn't it?"

I whipped around. A girl was standing in the doorway, naked but for a clamshell-colored towel, turbaned over her head. I felt myself blushing as I cast my eyes away from the neat triangle of russet pubic hairs that stood out against her milky white skin, and found myself stammering.

"I wasn't… I didn't mean…"

"No problem." She stalked across the room, swirled her hand through her luggage and plucked out a fresh pair of knickers. "I've already peeked into yours. Diana." She snapped the waistband at her hips in articulation.

"Rachel." I held out a clumsy hand, but she bridged the distance and pulled me in to kiss my cheek. I tried to twist my body, preventing my bare skin from accidentally grazing the side of a breast.

"Rachel." She winked at me. "How do you do?"

We became a team, Diana and I. *"Le bambole,"* Silvia would call us affectionately, as we trotted down in the early morning for breakfast service, arm in arm in our matching uniforms. *"L'inglese,"* Carla, the cook, would mutter somewhat more dispassionately, rolling her thick forearms into clouds of focaccia dough.

It was fair to say that Diana was different from me in almost every way that mattered. The confidence of her upbringing radiated through her. "Notting Hill," she'd told me when I asked where she was from, a specificity that presupposed she meant London. "But I went to School in Ascot." The implied capital on School indicating I should know which one she meant.

And she had an ease with the guests, a way of assisting them that somehow made it obvious they were in on the joke; she may be serving them, but really, she was one of them. I observed, and I followed. Held my back a little straighter. Wore a little more makeup. Took to wearing my one good piece of jewelry daily—a string of freshwater pearls my dad's mum had left me—when I saw that Diana was no stranger to adorning her uniform with trinkets.

"You shouldn't nod like that," she once told me quite sternly, when I slipped into the main house to arrange a pot of tea for Tim and Sherry.

"Like what?" I replayed the scene in my head but couldn't think of anything particularly out of the ordinary.

She hunched her shoulders together and bobbed her head. It looked ugly. My stomach twisted.

"Like that. Like you're flinching."

That night I faced myself in the wardrobe mirror, tilted my head to the side and whispered, "Certainly," the glimmer of a smile on my lips. Not quite Diana, but better.

There is a force to a friendship that is formed out of such proximity. Not being much of a joiner, I could only liken it to the time I agreed to stage-manage the senior school production of *West Side Story*, hoping it would give my university entrance form some much-needed flair. The cast spent unadulterated time in each other's company; we shared jokes that only we would get, we wore "stash"—T-shirts with the production logo on them—that made us feel as though we were above everyone else, part of some exclusive club. That's what it was like with Diana and me. An exclusive club of two. Raising an eyebrow at one another across the pool when purple-rinsed Lady Ashby droned on again to one of us about how she was really the first choice for Scarlett O'Hara. Making sure the other was never left alone with Mark English at night. Anticipating each other's ebb and flow so that even the dullest of tasks somehow seemed fun. And on the rare occasion that we had the same evening off, we'd head into town and guzzle cheap Chianti in a straw flask and share a beef tartare between two—"Try it!" she'd said, laughing as I'd stared down at the raw flesh for the first time—because I couldn't afford more and Di never seemed to eat much anyway.

I had never had a friendship like it, and it warmed the core of my soul more fully than any inch of the sunlight could. Whether it would have stayed that way—pure, unfettered—if Sebastian hadn't arrived is anyone's guess. It is perfectly likely that we would have hated each other before the summer's end, been ready to tear each other's eyes out like so many other relationships that have run their course. But arrive Sebastian did, and with him, the catalyst that changed it all. That shifted the narrative. And brought a shade over what might have been my perfect summer.

5

Now

I do leave the office, eventually. I knock on Alex's door, a floor beneath my own, but when she answers, she has an open bottle of wine in her hand, and I can hear a bubble of laughter floating out from behind her. Over her left shoulder, I spy a tangle of limbs around the kitchen table.

"Why don't you come in? Stay for some wine?"

"No, no. Honestly." I wave her away and am already half-way down the corridor. "I've got a load of essays to mark anyway. I'm only procrastinating."

The flat's cold. I turn on the portable fan heater and stick it by the sofa to warm my legs while the lasagna and baguette heat up. I pour myself a glass of wine, larger than I mean to, and eat with the plastic tray balanced on my lap, a tea towel protecting me from the heat. I resist the urge to turn on the news, knowing I'm likely to see more coverage of it. Photographs on a laptop screen are one thing, quite another to see him moving, walking, talking.

I flirt with the channels, land on a documentary about a maternity ward. Allow the violent screams of laboring women to flood my small living room and remind me how thankful I am I don't have children. I could, of course. I'm only thirty-nine. No sign of menopause yet. Besides, you hear of women giving birth in their fifties nowadays. I'd need a man, though, to do that. Not that I'm seeing anyone at the moment, but there have been men, a decent number, and I'm sure if I were desperate enough, I could entice an undersexed maths teacher to shove a fuck up me. I'm not unattractive, particularly when there is a certain amount of steam needing to be let off, being surrounded all day by nubile teenage girls.

But I like my life the way it is. The control of it, the reliability.

I'm not lonely. It's exasperating that people always seem to conflate being alone with being lonely, when they're not the same thing at all. I've been in rooms full of people—people I know, people I like—and felt far lonelier than I have here, with my own company.

Alex is different, hates being alone. That was how we got friendly in the first place: I bumped into her when she was moving into the building—literally, I was walking down the corridor and crashed straight into her carrying a cardboard box of cushions through the entrance—and she saw the opportunity, the fact that we're two single women of a certain age, living alone. She's always joining book clubs or exercise classes or pub quizzes in an effort to meet people, attempting with various degrees of failure to drag me along, but I prefer just being in one of our flats, a quick chat over a glass of wine or maybe something to eat if I'm feeling generous, before each retreating to our own, private headspace.

The television show finishes. The remnants of the pasta cool and condense in the black plastic tray, leave a hard, yellow frill of cheese around the rim. My thumb lingers on the remote, and then, as if it's not me but some external force in control of my body, I find myself switching to the nine-o'clock news.

I feign half an interest in the latest glum roundup about the state of the economy, take note that there's a cold snap on the way, raise an eyebrow at an in-depth feature about the rise in teetotalism in Gen Zs, which I can say certainly doesn't ring true of my students. But I'm not kidding myself, and there's no one else around I can fool: finally, I see the words flash across the screen, and my breathing sharpens as I turn up the volume.

BBC SPECIAL REPORT

A female reporter with a slicked-back ponytail and sharp-cut black suit addresses the camera with dead-eyed professionalism.

"Good evening. There is breaking news this evening from Florence, Italy. A verdict has been reached in the retrial of Sebastian Hale."

The image on screen changes to a courtroom, the reporter still droning on in voice-over as she catches the viewer up on the case. "Back in the late nineties…" Blah, blah, blah—I drown her out as I scan the crowd, searching along the front row in between the waiting police officers until I narrow in on the back of Sebastian's head. Smartphone generation that I am, I have a desperate urge to zoom in on the screen, to cut out the noise and the people so I can focus only on him. Instead I squint at the screen, try to read something in the tilt of his head, the position of his arms, that could give me some indication as to what he's feeling right now.

As if doing my bidding, the camera pans around, gives me just a glimpse of the side of his face. He is staring down, worrying the hands that are twisting in his lap, and I can see the minuscule tremble of his jaw, can feel the pressure biting at every part of him. I haven't felt this close to him in years.

The reporter is now speaking to a courtroom correspondent, who explains where the trial is at; that they're waiting for the judge to return to the courtroom to give the verdict. The correspondent helpfully tells the viewers to listen out for the word *reforma*, indicating that the case has been overturned. I can't help a reflexive twitch at his terrible pronunciation.

The camera homes in on the back of Sebastian's head, and I see him rake a hand through his hair, a gesture I remember as so distinctly his, a sign of when he's anxious or distressed. The reporter and correspondent chat back and forth, detailing the previous chain of appeals and rejections, but I don't want to hear it—I know it all, backward, forward, inside and out. I only have eyes for him. And then finally, something seems to be happening.

There's an energy on the screen, movement. The camera pulls back, revealing the whole width of the courtroom, and with a ripple effect, the court get to their feet, hands clasped at their fronts in an oddly religious gesture, as they turn to face the judge and the jury begin filing into position. Judge Bianchi takes the stand, clutching the piece of paper that everyone in that courtroom must be killing themselves to see— the piece of paper that will seal Sebastian's fate once more. Bianchi. I remember him from the initial trial. Pompous in a gold-braided robe, so gleeful when he looked Sebastian in the eyes—Sebastian who had personified exactly the sort of posh English party boy it was so easy to hate—and delivered that first, damning verdict. Now, he gives nothing away, his eyes locked on the paper as he turns his head toward the microphone and begins to speak.

"La Corte Suprema di Cassazione..."

"The Supreme Court of Cassation..."

Just as Bianchi starts to speak, an English translator talks over him, and I huff in agitation, my bilingual ear unable to train on one or the other. I feel sick, dizzy, as though I've been climbing a mountain all day with nothing to drink. My huff becomes the snatched breath of hyperventilation as I will Bianchi and the translator to hurry the fuck up and get on with it.

"In nome del popolo italiano..."

"In the name of the Italian people..."

They both drone on, mentioning articles and rulings I care little to nothing about.

And then. And then. *"Reforma."*

As if some Pavlovian response was created by the correspondent, my ears prick up at the word I have been waiting for, but never in a million years thought that I'd hear.

The room lurches around me as I reach for the remote control and turn the volume on full blast, still not quite believing that I've heard it correctly. The screen splits, and the female reporter is talking excitedly to the camera, but I can't make out a word she is saying, can only focus on the other half of the screen, where I see Sebastian, his head in his hands, crying and then hugging the man next to him, a lawyer in a tightly fitting gray suit. I feel wetness at my collar and instinctively press a hand to my face, realize I am crying too. The tears snake silently down my cheeks, and I give over to them, to this feeling of elation and hysteria and confusion, and the small, out-of-body thought of the absurd picture I would paint to a stranger: a near-middle-aged woman alone on her couch, crying into her lasagna over the nine-o'clock news.

The iconic red band begins to form at the bottom of the

screen, blocked white capitals scrolling across it, and I can finally convince myself I haven't misheard, that it isn't some crazy, wine-fueled dream.

ITALIAN SUPREME COURT OF CASSATION OVERTURNS MURDER CONVICTION OF SEBASTIAN HALE

The case is closed. Sebastian is free.

6

Then

The scream came from the kitchen.

I ran across the hall, a duster still clenched in my fist from cleaning the living room, expecting to find someone fallen over, dead, held hostage by a knife-wielding gunman. Instead I found Silvia, her back to a stove-top *cafetière* dangerously close to bubbling over, burbling in rapid Anglo-Italian and planting tomato-red-lipstick kisses over the cheeks of the boy in front of her.

I hugged the entrance, relieved, but unsure of whether to slink out or announce myself, when the boy caught my eye.

"Hi there." He stretched his neck away from Silvia long enough to give me a nod.

Even though I'd done nothing wrong, I found myself

pinkening, embarrassed. I held the duster in front of me like a barrier.

"Sorry, I didn't mean to interrupt—I thought someone had hurt themselves." I edged myself backward.

Silvia, turning to see me, let go of the boy's face but instead grabbed his hands beneath her fist, propelling him to the center of the room.

"No, no, no one is hurt at all! In fact, everyone is *wonderful!*" She kissed his knuckles with a loud smack. "This is my darling, darling Sebastian. My *figlioccio*—my godson, unofficially. Isn't he *meraviglioso?*"

Sebastian gave her a rumpled smile, waved his fingers through his hair and stepped toward me.

"I wouldn't go that far, Auntie Silvia." He winked at me. "Although I am pretty great. Pleased to meet you...?"

He held out his hand to mine, and as my fingers touched his, something deep in my core tightened.

It wasn't just that he was good-looking; he was *beautiful.* The faintest kiss of sun on his skin had brought out freckles on the bridge of his aquiline nose and streaks in his hair. Lean muscles protruded from the arms of his T-shirt and showed their shadow on his torso. His hand was large and soft and warm, covering my own with a confident squeeze. And there was something nonchalant about his manner, something easy and assured which seemed to emanate from his very soul. Not a single boy I had ever met, not a pale and spotty and arrogant one of them, could even come close to him.

In that moment, I think, I fell in love.

"I'm Rachel." He smelled of spring, fresh and clean and herbal. I swallowed, resisted the urge to bite the skin from the corner of my lip, an old nervous habit that left ugly ridges of broken skin. "I work here."

I felt the duster between my fingers and was instantly mortified, but he smiled at me kindly.

"You're English?"

"Yes."

"Me too. From London?"

"Woking?"

There was a pause in which I squirmed. I opened my mouth to speak but was saved by movement behind me, a low "Hell-o." Diana was at the door.

"Silvia, I didn't know you were hiring more help." The corner of her mouth twitched playfully, and then in one effortless movement she raised a hand to her head, tugged at her ponytail and let her red curls spill around her shoulders.

"Not exactly—" he laughed through his nose "—although I've been known to hang the odd picture or two, right, Silvia?" He stretched an arm around Silvia's shoulders and gave her a tight hug. "We're neighbors," he explained, although I failed to think of a house within striking distance. "My parents own the house down the road. My grandparents were Italian. We spend our summers here."

"Oh, is Mummy here?" Silvia pulled the spitting *cafetière* off the stove top. "I thought she wasn't coming until later."

"She's not." Sebastian began to move easily through the kitchen, helping himself to cups, milk, sugar. "She and Dad are in Greece but I came out early with some mates—done with uni for the summer, finally."

"Sebastian's at Oxford," Silvia said proudly, and I watched him give her a nonchalant shrug. "Your rival, Rachel."

Sebastian raised his eyebrows and I silently thanked Silvia for putting me back in the picture.

"Oh, are you at Cambridge?"

"Not yet." I couldn't quite bring myself to meet his gaze,

convinced he would read my attraction all over my face. "I start in October."

"Whoop-de-do, you're both geniuses." Diana minced fully into the room, her lips pursed into a pretty little smirk. "I'm sure I won't understand a word either of you are saying. I'm Diana, for what it's worth." And she stuck a hand out to Sebastian, the other planted on her hip, artfully exaggerating her small waist. "You look familiar—what's your surname?"

"Hale?" He cocked his head to the side, amused, presumably, by her bluntness.

"I knew it!" The tip of her tongue darted out of her mouth, wetted her bottom lip. "You're Hugh's brother, aren't you?"

Like the earth turning away from the sun, somehow this simple question unleashed a stream of conversation that dragged me further and further into the shadows. A torrent of words erupted, both of them rattling off names and schools and places that seemed to have been ripped from an Enid Blyton novel. I did my best to smile and nod like I was part of the conversation, but I was drowning in a sea of unfamiliarity. I had barely been in Italy long, stuttered my way through conversations in the native language, and yet I had never felt more out of my depth than now, hearing my own mother tongue. Even Silvia, it seemed, had more understanding of it than me, punctuating the conversation with recollections of Sebastian's friends or parents whose surnames she recognized.

I felt myself backing away from them, my silent exclusion deafening. When the tip of my elbow butted the door frame, I cleared my throat, swallowed.

"I should finish off the living room," I mumbled. I hadn't realized it, but I'd been clutching the duster so tightly it was sweaty beneath my palm. "Otherwise the bedrooms won't be finished until after lunch."

The three of them looked up as if they'd been interrupted

from a dream to see me standing there, shifting from foot to foot.

"Sorry, darling." Diana pressed a hand to her mouth, and I did hear a genuine note of apology in her voice. "This game of who's who is so silly. I don't know why we do it. It's the dullest thing on earth." She reached out a hand to me, and I was sure she didn't do it on purpose but it made me feel like a little sister being ushered away from the grown-ups. "Come on, let's get back to work."

Sebastian put his cup down on the sideboard and looked at his watch.

"I should be heading off too, to be fair. I've got a couple of mates arriving from Pisa this afternoon." He leaned toward Silvia and kissed her on both cheeks, then cupped her hands between his as he told her how lovely it was to see her again. She gazed at him adoringly. "Oh." He nodded toward us just before he turned to go. "I'm having a party at mine on Saturday night. You girls should come." He smiled indulgently at Silvia. "If that's all right with you, Auntie Silvia?"

Silvia shrugged.

"Bah. How could I say no to you? As soon as they finish their work, they go."

He pressed the tips of his thumb and forefinger together, touched them to his lips in a chef's kiss.

"*Perfetto.* See you Saturday."

Before he left the room, he turned back, gave us an insouciant wink.

I couldn't be one hundred percent certain, but I felt sure he was directing it at me.

Later, silently plumping cushions next to Diana, I chewed my thoughts around in my mouth.

"Sebastian seems nice." I inspected the brocade between

42

my fingers, but out of the corner of my eye I saw Diana's features morph into a smirk.

"You fancy him." I could hear the tease dancing in her voice. She coupled it with a neat little poke to my ribs.

I thought about denying it, playing cool, as I was sure she would do. But already knowing her as I did, I knew this wouldn't fly. So, I hugged the cushion to my chest, bit the corner of my lip, drew blood.

"I don't know...he's good-looking, isn't he? And he seems... friendly?"

Diana twisted a coil of hair between her fingers.

"If you like that type. I find it all a bit clichéd, really. Reminds me of all the boys back home. Give me an Italian stallion on a Vespa any day." She gave me a dangerous smile, though I couldn't help but think of their easy conversation, the way she had brightened when she met him. "So you definitely don't...like him like that?" I ached with the need to be her friend. I couldn't do anything that might endanger that.

She took the cushion from me and pressed my face between her hands. "Ab-so-*lutely* not. But if you like him, darling—" she planted a kiss on the apples of my cheeks "—we'll get him for you. I'll make you *la prima donna* on Saturday night, and he won't be able to resist you. With my help, he'll be eating out of the palm of your hand. Trust me."

And trust her I did. As awkward as I felt revealing my crush, in Diana I had a confidante. She was my only friend in Italy. My only friend, really, now that leaving school had severed whatever minor ties I had to the paltry group of girls I'd hung around with back home. And now the excitement of Sebastian sent trills rippling through me. I may have been clumsy and awkward and unfamiliar, but Sebastian was part of a world Diana knew.

With her help, she could make me a part of it too.

7

Now

Sebastian. Free. Walking among people. Made of flesh and blood, not the ink or pixels it has felt like his body has been formed of for the past twenty-one years. I instinctively curl into myself, hugging my limbs inward, as if expecting him to pop up from behind the sofa at any moment.

I keep the TV on, waiting hopefully for any remaining morsel about him, like a dog on its hind legs at the dinner table. But they've already moved on: missile tests in North Korea, some TV presenter sacked for racist comments, official photographs released from one of the royal babies' birthdays. Sebastian is nothing more than a bullet point on the agenda to them.

My eyes wander to the closed bedroom door, and as though I have some sort of special X-ray vision, I imagine my way through it, up to the farthermost corner of the topmost shelf of my wardrobe—the shoebox of letters, *his* letters, the ones I have dutifully stored and saved and tried but failed to forget about. I imagine the words whispering to me, flying off the pages and surrounding me like a fog of flies.

I never replied to them, the whole time he was in there. I couldn't—the thought of talking to him about it made me feel sick. I *was* sick, once, about six months after he'd been in there. Fuelled by a late-night lone drinking session in a corner of the college bar, I plucked up the nerve to call the prison, but as soon as I heard the municipal beep of the automated service—"*Grazie per tua chiamata.* If you know the extension you want to reach…"—I felt the hot bile rising in my throat and promptly threw up in the nearest bin.

That was the start of it all: the skipped lectures, the unfinished essays, the feeling, when I opened my eyes in the morning, that I was being pinned to the bed by a lead weight—no, an anchor; more fitting. The call to the dean's office and the suggestion made that perhaps Cambridge wasn't the right place for me at this time, for my own health. The bright, hot shame as Mum's car rounded the corner of Trumpington Street to pick me up. If it hadn't been for Diana, throwing me a bone even though by that point it was the last thing she wanted to do, who knows what I could have done? The calm reassurance in her voice when I called, begging—no, not for money, for *her*. The subtle increase in my bank balance that month, and all subsequent months, that helped me get on my feet, and out from under Mum's. "What about teaching, Rach? You've always loved learning." A prospectus in the post, a page folded down at the corner—"BA Modern Languages with Qualified Teacher Status"—plus the services of a highly paid doctor whose leather-scented Harley Street office I visited once a month for a year, with the implicit affirmation that I should *focus on the future, Rach, stop dwelling on the past!*

Diana has always known how to keep me on the right path, to shut out the voices in my head that try to tell me otherwise. What if this is exactly the excuse I need to swerve that path back round to her? I reach for my phone, already imagining her voice on the other end: *Rachel? Is that you?* Who knows, maybe she'll even be happy to hear from me, this unprecedented turn of events binding us together in a way only the two of us can appreciate.

The phone vibrates, making me jump, and for one heart-leaping moment, I think it's her, fantasize our mutual chuckle. *Your ears must be burning—I was just about to message.*

But of course it's not her. It's Mum.

Did you see the news?

I pick up the phone and call her. I can't face the wait between text exchanges, the slow death march of the three little dots on the screen that tell me she is one-finger-tapping a word a minute.

"Yes, I saw."

We're not ones for hellos.

I hear her turn down the TV, picture her on the floral-print sofa they haven't changed since my childhood, picture Dad beside her, dozing off halfway through his postdinner Bristol Cream sherry.

"Do you think you'll be contacted for anything?"

I know where she's going with this. "Me? No. Not now."

"No interviews, no TV pieces, or…?"

"No."

"Good." Neither of us says anything, but we don't have to. It's all there in the silence: her *I told you so*, her *You with your uppity ways, think you're too good for us*; me with my *You'll never understand*. Inevitably, she cracks. "Don't get involved, Rachel."

"I'm not going to, Mum."

"No, listen to me, Rachel." She raises her voice, and I hear Dad's disgruntled snort-snore in response. "Don't get involved with this again. It was hard enough the first time. The neighbors have just about forgotten you were mixed up in it all. Having to explain why you'd come home midterm. Hanging around the garden in your dressing gown like a madwoman. The snide comments in the supermarket checkout—'Shouldn't Rachel have gone back to Cambridge by now?' Don't go opening that can of worms again. Your father and I—we're private people. We don't want our names splashed about for anyone to know our business. I should have put my foot down twenty years ago and never let you go to that godforsaken country." There she goes, vocalizing her Brexit badge loud and clear. I barely listen to her final blow; I know it'll be the same tired argument she has brought up a thousand times before. I take the phone from my ear, my finger already paused on the red end-call button. "We're not like those people, Rachel." And there it is. "*You're* not like those people. No matter what you think, with your fancy job and your poshed-up accent. Stop trying to be. Stop trying to be something you're not."

When I put down the phone, the news is over, a quiz show in its place.

"Anne Boleyn," I say out loud. Anne of Cleves is the correct answer; it flashes up and the contestant does a fist bump.

I attack the screen with the remote, watch it fade to black. Sit in silence in my empty living room, listening to the rain starting up outside.

I know I can't call her. And of course she would never call me.

Sebastian is free. And I'm more trapped than ever.

8

Then

The day of the party, Silvia gave us permission to clock off as soon as the last guest turned in, and blessedly—given the balmy summer night—this left us free to go at ten.

Diana threw the window open in her room, allowing the resinous scent of pine and rosemary to soften the effect of the single, sterile ceiling light. She was all motion, kicking off her sleek but practical work heels and toeing them toward a corner, feeling for the zip of her gray linen dress and letting it pool on the floor. And then she was still, hands encircling the protrusion of her hip bones, assessing the contents of her wardrobe. She sighed, and I couldn't help but eye the rise and fall of her freckled breasts, the smooth skin rounding over the top of each bra cup. I turned my eyes to the ground. I was the one fully clothed, and yet I felt exposed, raw. With a deft hand she plucked out a piece of white material, shivering it over her head and down her body.

"Ugh, I'm so fat," she said, twisting her body in the mirror so her waist looked like a child's.

"You're not." By then I knew the game, Diana's need to have her reality validated back to her. "You look great."

She sucked in her cheeks and patted her nonexistent belly. "No. More. Pasta." She punctuated each word with a tap. Although I'd taken to counting, when we sat at the kitchen table during the staff meal: the most pieces I'd ever seen her eat in one sitting was ten.

"What are you going to wear?" She dismissed her reflection, mussing her hair so it frothed around her shoulders.

I hesitated, scratched my shoulders.

"I didn't really bring anything stylish with me. I've got jeans and shirts, or sundresses or…"

She was already back in the wardrobe, flicking through the rail as if she was turning the pages of a book, and emerged with two items aloft, one a pale cornflower blue, the other black.

"Hmm." She held each one against me while I surreptitiously tried to straighten my posture, already feeling as though I was spoiling her clothes just by looking at them. "This one." She decided quickly, whipping the hanger of the black one. And I was pleased, because if I was going to be coerced into wearing one of them, I somehow couldn't quite envisage myself in pastel.

Without asking, she reached behind me and started to undo the zip at my neck. Despite the heat, goose pimples formed involuntarily on the backs of my arms at the thought of being exposed. In the past few weeks, I think I had seen Diana naked or partially clothed more times than I had myself, but until now I had managed to get away with at least a T-shirt's worth of modesty.

"Where have you been hiding those?" Stripped, I instinctively crossed my hands over myself as Diana eyed my chest, protected, at least, by a bra.

"Nowhere?" I hunched my shoulders, remembering the giddy chants of preteen boys—*Do your boobs hang low, do they wobble to and fro?*—when it first became apparent that Rachel Bailey had tits. "Why?"

"Um, they're amazing?" she said with a Californian rising inflection. "I'd kill for more than these fried eggs." She shimmied her shoulders, making her pert little breasts dance. "Only..." She twisted her head to the side and I held my breath, feeling something was coming. "Don't take this the wrong way, but don't you have a better bra?"

Embarrassment flooded my cheeks. Using my own mother as an example, I'd never made it past plain supermarket-brand nudes. Diana's, I knew, were the embodiment of a 1950s idyll: frothy, lacy, candy-colored dreams that came in perfect matching sets.

She took the silence as my answer.

"Well, I don't think any of mine will fit you, but here's an idea." She rummaged around in the top of her chest of drawers, emerging with two half-moon, flesh-colored objects.

I was confused.

"Let me?"

I held my hands aloft, submitting.

Before I was quite prepared, Diana's cold little hands dived into my bra and scooped under each breast, depositing a semicircle into each cup. Then, reaching behind me, she hiked up each strap, so that my cleavage suddenly came into view beneath me.

"Now try the dress on," she commanded, holding it out to me.

"I look like a stripper," I concluded, once it was on and I

was angling myself in the mirror, Diana behind me. The dress was short and tight, clinging to my waist and thighs, without even the relief of sleeves to offer me protection. My breasts looked like two baby heads strapped to my chest. "Diana, I can't go out like this."

"What are you talking about, Rach? You look fucking amazing. Sebastian's going to cream his pants."

My chest, already constricted by its new scaffolding, grew tight. The thought of walking into a room full of strangers practically half-naked...of Sebastian seeing me...

"Rachel." As if anticipating my flight, Diana's voice grew smooth. "I promised to help you, didn't I?"

I nodded. She rested her hand on my shoulder, allowing our eyes to meet in the mirror.

"Then let me. You look *fit*. Own it. Just, maybe...don't let him in your pants until we've got you some new underwear, 'kay?"

I started to protest. The thought of even getting to the kissing stage was giving me hives; I was hardly intending to...

But she was already backing away from me, spritzing a cloud of rose-scented perfume into the air and twirling through it.

"*Relax*, babe. It's just a party. No one's asking you to suck his dick. But if you don't hurry up, someone else might be doing the job for you."

Before I could answer, she'd danced out of the door.

Sebastian's house was down the road, along the same dirt path I'd been driven up a few weeks earlier. The edge had come off the heat, but the humidity was still clinging to the air, heavy as dust in an antique shop. A film of mosquito repellent stuck to my skin, the smell agitating the corners of my eyes, protecting me from the savage munches that I knew would plague the rims of my ankles and the backs of my arms within seconds of exposing them to the naked night. Diana was, naturally, immune.

Holding our heels aloft, we picked our way over the small stones barefoot, rolling our feet from heel to tip to soften the impact on the fleshy pads of skin. As we got closer, we allowed ourselves to be guided by the growing thrum of music, the low and persistent bass mingling with the stars. Up in those hills, you could pick out the crystal pricks of starlight with ease, faultlessly ticking off Orion's Belt and the Big Dipper, but as we approached the house, floodlights polluted the sky and gave it a milky luminescence.

Eventually, an austere gray wall told us we had arrived, as did the letters painted on in elegant black cursive: Villa Allegria.

"*Cheerful* isn't the first word I'd use." I picked out the letters with a finger, translating the Italian, and raised an eyebrow at Diana, clocking the robust wrought-iron gates and multiple warnings about security cameras.

Buzzed in, we followed an avenue of cypresses to a set of polished marble steps, allowing us to take in the villa properly. Like Silvia's, it was gorgeous—vast, surrounded by verdant lawns—but there was nothing of the Medici's ramshackle charm; Villa Allegria was all smooth, clean lines and minimal foliage. Inside, the effect was even starker: white walls, white marble floor; even a white grand piano held court in the middle of the entrance hall like some sort of Elton John music video. Diana laughed when I told her that, but she patted my upper arm indulgently.

"I think it's very chic."

Stalking past the occasional limb draped over more white furniture, we followed the whomp of what I recognized as Smash Mouth's "All Star" into the garden. Instantly I could see that this was where the party proper began. A tangle of bodies crowded on the flagstones surrounding the pool, glasses and bottles in hand; cigarette smoke choked the air; voices muted the whistle of cicadas I knew the foliage would be thick with; pool lights smothered the last of the stars. Here, any hint of the natural world was suffocated, drowned by a sea of champagne and expensive perfume.

There was a vitality to it that tingled in my fingertips and made my chest tight: the laughter and the clink of glasses, and the occasional slap of a body hitting the water as they dive-bombed into the pool. I have never been good with large groups of people; the swell of voices around me, the pressure to do or say the right thing has always left me exhausted and unnerved, and here, the effect was overwhelming. And the people were not from a world I knew. It was obvious in the way they held themselves: the curve of the girls' bodies, a hand on hip placed just so; the insouciance of the guys, the ruffle of hands through hair or a gentle backslap. I had no business being among their designer clothes and their designer accents—at any moment, the crowd could open; a girl with a perfect blond blow-dry could point a French-manicured finger at me, call me out as the imposter I was.

I felt my palms grow sweaty, the nerves in the backs of my knees tingling as if readying themselves for flight. I pulled on the hem of my dress and tried to slink through the crowd as seamlessly as Diana, but my body felt all wrong, my gait awkward, the music and the voices pulsating in my ears like a warning cry telling me to get out of there, that I didn't belong.

But then something strange began to happen. Towed along by the loop of Diana's arm in mine, I found myself being swallowed deeper into the crowd. Someone handed me a drink. Champagne, cold and frothy, in an actual glass flute I was sure would get smashed by the end of the night. A girl smiled at me, asked me if she knew me. Someone else told me they liked my heels. I clocked a boy—nice-looking, with wavy hair and swimming trunks that had bright red lobsters all over them— sliding his eyes appreciatively over my body. And I realized, in that moment, that I didn't have to be me. No one here knew boring Rachel, who was friends with the teacher and always left parties early. No one here remembered the year-ten class trip to the Imperial War Museum, when I got my period on the coach and left a bloody stain on the seat, or that I once called my year-seven form teacher Mum.

I could be anyone. I could even be one of them.

And so I let the warm glow of inclusion envelop me, feeling my body articulate itself better, hearing my vowels soften, as if they'd been coated in butter.

"Diana!"

A small brunette in a tight red dress with a slash across the chest emerged from the throng and pulled on Diana's arm.

"Cecily! What on earth are you doing here?" Diana broke off to her left and pulled the girl into a double cheek kiss as they both let out a little involuntary squeal. I stood awkwardly, half turned between the group of people we were talking to and this new intruder. Somehow the group seemed to shift, re-forming itself without either of us in it, and so I found myself dancing at the edge of their twosome.

"Daddy got me a placement on an English-language paper in Rome for a few weeks." Cecily twirled a lock of hair in her fingers, blinking up at Diana with cowlike brown eyes. "He was at Harrow with the owner. I'm just here for the weekend." No, her eyes weren't cowlike actually, that would be too innocent—more blow-up sex doll. "I didn't know you knew Sebby!"

There was something silly about her voice—oddly high-pitched and infantile—which I was sure would appeal to a certain type of boy. I willed Diana to dismiss her, to find a way to end the conversation and pull us away from this irritating girl, but instead she seemed to adopt Cecily's body language, holding her weight on her left hip and dancing a red curl between her fingertips.

"We only met a few days ago actually, but I know his brother. I'm working down the road." Diana pronounced *working* as if in invisible air quotes, and somehow her voice seemed to get plummier and—could it be?—even more high-pitched. "It's quite fun really, this batty old socialite making a pretense at running a hotel. We're practically guests—we just do a bit of tidying here and there." At this, she seemed to realize that the other half of this *we* was standing next to her, and she fluttered a hand to her mouth.

"Sorry, have you met Rachel before?"

Cecily squinted at me with a misty half smile. "Hi, yes, I'm sure we've met at some party or another. You're from London?"

I parsed this carefully. "Nearby. You?"

"Chelsea."

"Ah."

Neither of us able to think of any suitable follow-up questions, the conversation flowed back to Cecily and Diana. I nodded and laughed in the right places but couldn't think how to inject myself into their chatter, fiddling with the stem of my champagne glass and taking cautious sips.

Then Cecily was knocking hers back and tilting her head at Diana's glass, asking if she "fancied a top-up." And then, I don't know quite when, or how, I found myself alone.

Diana, my shield and my confidence, was gone. I saw a flicker of red hair disappearing into the crowd, a candle snuffed out, and then, nothing.

It was a feeling akin to my early days in Florence; the un-fettered confidence of navigating the city center's main arteries only to take a wrong turn, and in a heartbeat finding myself in some forgotten tributary, the friendly familiarity of sunshine and tourists replaced by cool shade, and the faint smell of sewage.

I felt my own self returning to my body. And I didn't like her very much.

I glanced blindly around me at the little circles of acquaintances we had been speaking to before and tried to insert myself back into them, but I stumbled over their easy talk of school friends and skiing holidays, and conversations soon shifted, moved on without me.

Muttering unasked-for excuses about seeing someone or finding something, I skittered through bodies, my initial swelled pride deflating by the second. I found my way to the edge of the pool and removed the punishing high heels that by now were biting at my feet like the gnats pursuing Io, sinking my toes into the tepid water. Slumping into myself, I drained the champagne glass, casting my eyes around for a refill. On a table just out of reach, I spied a half-full bottle, groped it and let the bubbles fill my stomach and my loneliness.

"Cambridge, you came!"

A reflection marred the surface of the water. I looked up, and my heart swelled a thousand times. Sebastian.

"Hi!" I suppressed the impending horror of a burp, and attempted to rise to my feet, but he was already patting my shoulder, clambering down beside me. He swayed as he righted himself on the paving stones, clutching my upper arm for balance, and I noticed the musk of alcohol on his breath, the wide, dilated pupils I did not identify at that moment in time, but would soon come to recognize as a sign that there was something more than alcohol fuelling his celebrations.

But now my concern was not for how much he had drunk, or what he had taken; all I could think of was how to make him stay. A tyranny of thoughts flustered my mind, asking me, begging me, to find the perfect thing to say.

Instead: "Nice party."

Nice. The word circled on primary school essays.

Boring. Unimaginative. Rachel.

But to my surprise, he laughed, surveyed the garden. "Is it?"

His feet, circling in the water, lingered perilously close to mine, and I found myself tensing up, clenching my toes away from him.

"Everyone seems...very nice," I ventured, tilting my chin to observe the swell of bodies. "It's just...a bit much." As if to illustrate my point, a girl in towering stilettos and a tight red dress faux-wrestling with two boys squealed and leaped into the pool, fully clothed. One of them responded by shaking up a bottle of champagne, letting it explode into the pool as she arched her neck to catch the spray, mouth agape and tumescent tongue wagging. To be polite, I asked, "How do you know everyone?"

He paused a moment, taking in one clump of people after another. A group of boys in identical striped flannel shirts were racing to finish beers, tossing empty bottles at their feet or into bushes. Two girls with perfectly coiffed Jennifer Aniston blow-dries were bouncing on a sunbed, drinking from a bottle of designer vodka. A cluster of handbags kept each other company while their owners gyrated in a circle nearby.

He shrugged.

"I'm not really sure."

I waited, allowing him to elucidate. The water had splashed up to his knees, plastering the hairs down on his legs. I resisted the urge to rest a hand where his shorts ended and skin began. "There are some Italians," he continued, breaking my focus. "A whole bunch I grew up with over the summers out here. Most of them went to the American school here, or boarded in

England, and the majority are at uni in the UK or the States. That guy—" he pointed to a boy in a crisp white shirt, a cornflower blue jumper tied around his shoulders "—lives in a castle in the hills. He's as thick as two planks, but his parents were desperate to get him into a top American college. They donated a new library and now, guess what? He's an Ivy League man." He chuckled, saw the bottle of champagne next to me and reached across to take a swig. His arm brushed across my lap and I instinctively clenched my thighs. "Then there's the English lot. Most of them have houses on the coast—Portofino or Amalfi—or dotted around Tuscany in the hills. There are friends, and friends of friends, or friends of friends of friends. Someone gets word that there's something going on, and the pack mentality takes off. I know a chunk of them personally, but then as soon as you start talking to someone you haven't met, you realize you have at least one person in common, or your parents know theirs, or you went to the same prep school as their brother or...you know how it is."

I shook my head. "Actually, I don't."

He looked at me properly, so close that even in the diminished light I could make out the flecks of gray in his irises, the nick across his eyebrow that hinted at some childhood tumble.

"You're lucky," he said, a brittleness to his voice.

I felt my face flush, took the bottle back from him, drank deeply to disguise the silence.

"Why?"

"All of this—" he moved his head in a figure eight, encompassing the revelry surrounding us "—it's exhausting. People expect you to think and act in a certain way. Even if you dare to do or say something different, they just smile at you funny, pretend it hasn't happened. My parents are the worst. Mum has this superiority about having married an Englishman— she barely sounds Italian now, even when she's speaking the language. The two of them are so concerned with wearing the right clothes, and being seen in the right places, and saying the right thing. As long as Hugh and I went to a certain school, and played 'proper' sports, and behaved ourselves at the hunt ball once a year, they didn't really care what we did. I don't think it was even Oxford itself Dad was particularly pleased about, as much as the fact that it meant I could join the Bullingdon."

He must have seen me look blank, because he made a face. "Some stupid society full of other posh twats." He sighed. "I thought maybe it would be different there, but so far it's just more of the same. A fucking bubble. Even without meaning to, I've fallen into the same old clichéd friendships, the same old societies. Nothing's real, no one's genuine. It's just a never-ending circle of meaningless, self-aggrandizing bullshit and I just..." He mashed a fist into his hair, gripped it tightly. "Sorry. I really don't know why I'm ranting like this. I shouldn't drink champagne—it always makes me bitter." He shifted his body weight, leaning on a crooked thigh so that the point of his knee just touched my upper thigh. "You must think I'm a complete arsehole, sitting here complaining that my silver spoon is too big, and my diamond shoes are too tight. And we barely even know each other."

I blushed inwardly, feeling his acknowledgment of our unfamiliarity like a wrenching away. But something made me bold—the alcohol, or the warmth that clung to the air, or the churn of voices that surrounded us—and drowned out my awkward sense of self. And I rested a hand on his knee. Right there, where shorts met flesh, hot and sticky with evaporating pool water and sweat.

"I don't think you're an arsehole, Sebastian. I don't think you're an arsehole at all."

I let my hand linger, feeling the tiny bones and muscles of

my fingers and palm somewhere between relaxed and tense. He didn't move. He didn't move it.

And then: "Rachel!"

A voice: female, high-pitched. Ecstatic.

Diana lurched through the crowd, her limbs messy, her skirt hitched up a little higher than when she'd left me.

"Where did you run off to?" she asked rhetorically, snatching what was left of the champagne. Her tone was breathless, but when she turned to us her eyes were sharp and clear. "Hey, Sebastian, awesome party."

Sebastian stood, kissed her on both cheeks, a gesture I'd seen repeated ad nauseam this evening, and found totally odd among this group of almost adults. Our moment was gone, and now I was the odd one out, perched awkwardly between crouching and standing. All my previous desire to find Diana dissipated. Now she was in the way.

But she pulled me to her and kissed my cheek with a loud smack, and somehow, somehow, I couldn't help but glow at her affection.

"You've stolen my girl away from me," she accused Sebastian with a wagging finger, flinging an arm around my shoulder with a force that cuffed my earlobe. "And now I'm taking her back."

Sebastian held his hands up submissively, playing along.

"Hey, ladies, I'm not one to break up a friendship. I should probably check on the booze anyway."

He backed off—I felt my mood sink—but just before he turned to go, he smiled at me; a genuine smile that basked his face in warmth.

"It was really good talking to you, Rachel. Hope we'll catch up again soon."

"Don't pout." As soon as he was gone, Diana scolded me. "I'm helping you. You don't want to look too keen. Leave him wanting more." I nodded, needing her advice but still trying to eye his trail.

She pulled at me, sweeping us through the crowd and away from all trace of Sebastian. The party was ringing in my ears and the champagne had taken root in me, warm and fuzzy. The body count seemed to have doubled since I last looked, and I allowed myself to be manhandled through it, stopping when she did to mingle and talk and nod.

"Trust me," she murmured in my ear, when she saw me tracking him. "I know how these boys tick. You can't seem available. Just have a good time and let him come to you."

And so, I obeyed. And with each conversation in which I was a silent observer, I drank steadily from whatever glass or bottle I was handed. Until I couldn't have spoken if I'd wanted to. Until each limb seemed a separate entity, loose and flowing.

Until.

It was my own stupid fault. I caught sight of him, just there next to the door to the house, beside a lemon tree in full bloom. She was pretty, the girl he was with; tall and blonde with one of those figures that seems to slink naturally into just the right angle. And he was laughing. He was even more good-looking when he laughed. And looking at her like he hadn't looked at me, reaching to touch a lock of her hair and tuck it behind her ear. And I was looking at them, and not at where I was standing. Which was why I didn't notice that I was right by the edge of the pool.

It must have been a hairbreadth of a second, but in the moment that I was suspended I could sense everything: the change of weight, the rising smell of chlorine, my own impending humiliation. And then I was falling. Not gracefully, but like a wild animal: limbs flailing, dress hitched, a guttural cry ripping through me. And I heard the laughter start, and I was glad when the silence of the water engulfed me, knowing now it was all over, that they would see me for the imposter I truly was, ungainly, a fool.

Instinct forced me to break through the surface, gulping air noisily even as I awaited my ridicule, observing how, as if by some magnetic pull, the people who had actually *intended* to be in the pool fled to the side. The girls adjusted their bikinis, patted the tops of their heads to check whether I had disturbed their water-resistant updos. The boys posed in their patterned swimming trunks, watching the action.

I swept wet tangles of hair out of my eyes. My sodden dress clung to my legs, weighing me down. A sandal bobbed to the surface, dislodged when I fell.

But just as I readied myself to meet their taunting eyes, a war cry soared through the air, and I heard a body land with a loud splash next to mine.

Diana.

"Wahoo!" she cried, fist in the air, makeup running down her cheeks. "Go, Rachel!"

She pulled me into her, forcing my arm up to join hers, facing the crowd. Saving me.

I saw Sebastian notice us. I saw her notice him. And then she leaned in close, her body hot and wet and breathless.

"They want a show? Let's give 'em a show."

Before I had time to register it, she was stroking my hair back from my face, pressing her chest against mine. And before I had time to stop her, her lips were against mine, soft and clean and searching.

And before I had time to think, I was kissing her back.

9

Now

Those lips. The color of Florence's terra-cotta rooftops. The thought of them takes hold of me now, as the memory of that night washes over me. Always left unadorned, never kissed with lipstick or gloss. Wide mouth and flat lips. Everyone used to liken them to Julia Roberts's, which, back then, was the highest form of compliment.

It's been a day. A whole twenty-four hours since the news about Sebastian broke. So far I have been restrained, given myself a strict one-hour limit between checking for updates on him. Forced myself to avoid scouring the articles for any mention of her—not that there would be. Her parents made sure of that, a hefty sum to the right people ensuring that it would be in their best interest to keep her name out of it.

But now I am back in my office, lessons done for the day,

and at the thought of that one, singular part of her, the dam opens, and I am flooded with images of her whole.

Yesterday's narrow escape from calling her has flicked a switch inside me, and now the compulsion to look at her—just to look at her, only that—vibrates through my core like a live wire. Seeing that face—whose curvatures and crevices I once knew better than my own—is an exquisite pain I try to protect myself from. But now, with the news of Sebastian, the desire to see it burns inside me once more, and somehow the laptop is in my hands and I am typing "Facebook" into the search bar as if it is my fingers that control my mind, not the other way around.

I avoid the trite updates of old acquaintances—most of them on the cusp of middle age and clinging on to any small digital validation they can get—navigating quickly instead to the search tab. Scanning the screen for her name, I am momentarily crushed not to see it listed in the results—she has eluded me, finally, by removing herself from social media and therefore, seemingly, the world. And then a memory rises to the surface; the carefully worded announcement in the *Times*.

The engagement is announced between Diana, youngest daughter of Mr. and Mrs. Hugo Turner...

I type in her married name and there she is.

Diana Hogg. What an unlovely rechristening.

I fully expect the profile to be private, for the door left ajar for me to be no more than an inch-square photograph and the details of her employ, but by some sort of divine providence it is open, and I am in, scrolling and scrolling through pages of a play that once upon a time might have included me, at least among the supporting cast.

Diana Hogg née Turner is no less vibrant at forty than she was at nineteen. If anything, more so, enhanced as she is by the "hashtag no filter" era of high-quality camera phones, instead of the grainy digital camera printouts I can lay my hands on. In almost every picture she is laughing, head tipped back, surrounded by people. Looping her arms around a group of gorgeous but crucially not *as* gorgeous women. Kissing the cheeks of two boys who have inherited their mother's bloom of auburn hair. Cradling a little girl who will grow up to inherit her beauty. Allowing the arm of a handsome man with dark eyes to snake possessively around her waist, laying claim to her before the world. From these photos alone it is clear to see that she has lived a life unblemished.

That she has lived.

While Sebastian—

While I—

With more force than I intend to, I slam the laptop closed. The office feels smaller than it did an hour ago, suffocated by Diana's brief presence in it. I try to imagine what she was like when she was a student here, red hair tied in a neat ponytail, pale skin perfectly offset by the deep navy blue of the uniform as she roamed the halls, dominating them as she seems to dominate wherever she sets her foot down.

When this particular favor was first offered to me—*old girl, put in a good word*—I thought it would be a chance to feel close to her again. But it only made me feel further apart, demonstrating the gulf between our stations with each eloquent student and wildly imaginative extracurricular activity. In my first term, I would wander the halls, searching old photographs for her likeness. There was one: a cast photograph from 1996, the Upper School production of *The Wizard of Oz*. She is center stage, hair in plaits, blue gingham dress, a stuffed toy terrier clutched in her arms. Beaming with a genuine, youthful enthusiasm that was almost unrecognizable.

She'd never mentioned the production to me, not once, although she did talk of school, her friends, her exploits. Diana was always very good at only revealing the parts of herself she thought were entirely relevant to the role she was playing.

I leave the office, idly checking my pigeonhole before I go. There's a flyer about Mental Health Awareness Week from the Sixth Form Yoga Society; the fortnightly school bulletin, the *Graybridge Gazette*; next week's dinner menu; and a couple of essays, a week late, rolled together, tied with a pink hairband. Scarlett and Viola, tall, blonde, almost indistinguishable. Scarlett's father is the British high commissioner to Barbados, and for some very important yet undisclosed reason, it was necessary for both girls to escape the impending frost and spend last week there. I know both essays will be riddled with errors—at any other school they wouldn't have dared hand them in in the first place—but Viola's father is a theater producer and last year he paid for the entire West End staging of the lower-sixth production of *Little Shop of Horrors*, so instead I will painstakingly go through each error in detail, and then offer the girls an extension to have another go.

I'm about to chuck the whole lot in my bag when an envelope slips from between the pages of the bulletin and floats to the floor. I reach to pick it up, wondering—noting the formal, stiff cream—what wedding or christening I'm going to have the pleasure of sending my regrets to, but when I see the handwriting on the front I freeze, jerking my hand away as though the envelope is hot to the touch.

> *Ms. Rachel Bailey*
> *c/o Graybridge Hall*
> *Graybridge, Ascot*
> *SL5 7ZN*

There is nothing out of the ordinary in the content. The facts are all there, present and correct. I am Ms. Rachel Bailey. This is Graybridge Hall.

But the handwriting. The handwriting is as indelible in my mind as the ink it is written with. Its elegant, precise lettering has filled pages, addressed envelopes of a far inferior quality than this smart card, all of them unanswered, all of them filling the shoebox in the topmost shelf of my wardrobe.

I don't want to open it. I never want to open them, these untimely missives that I still keep, goodness knows why, in that shoebox. But I know I am going to all the same. I am compelled to, to feel each word rake across my skin like my own personal form of flagellation. I pick up the correspondence card with shaking hands, run a finger around the triangle on the back, trying not to picture how it has been sealed closed, draw out the simple correspondence card. Read.

Dear Rachel,
It's been a year since my last letter. How much everything—and nothing—has changed in that time.

Part of me doesn't expect you to answer. Part of me knows, like last time, and the times before that, you won't.

But there's still a part of me that holds on to hope. If there wasn't, I don't think I would have survived all these years.

Rachel, I didn't do it.

You know it, I know it. I think it's only fair to me that after all this time everyone else should know it too.

Please, once and for all, will you help me clear my name?
Yours, as always,
Sebastian

Still holding the letter, I stumble, straight lined, body rigid, to the first-floor girls' bathroom. I wrench open the door and yank the chain for the lights, plunging the room into stark whiteness.

"Hello?" I call, my voice ricocheting through the empty stalls.

I make my way to the sink at the far-right end, mash the palm of my hand against my mouth and scream into it.

It's your fault, I shout at the image in reflection. She smirks, corner of her lip curling, and I bash my fists against the corner of the sink. *Admit it—all of this is your fault.*

My fingers find the tap and I blast the cold on full, splashing my face with icy water until the heat leaves my body and I am finally calm.

When I look up, it's no longer Diana's face I see but my own.

10

Then

The day after Sebastian's party, I woke up alone. The length of my right arm was cadaver cold, and I worried for a heartbeat that I had suffered some form of extreme alcohol poisoning, until I realized that I had slept with my body pressed up against the cool white wall of the bedroom, numbing it completely.

I sat up, the blood immediately rushing through my inert fingers and foggy brain, making them pulsate with life, allowing the memories of last night to surface. Sebastian...Diana... humiliation...relief...pleasure. Confusion swirled around me like the turquoise waters of the Hale family pool.

I had wanted Sebastian. Did I want Diana? I closed my eyes and sought out the image of her chlorine-drenched lips reaching for mine, the impression of her fingers above my right elbow as she held me. But then, Sebastian: the vision of his sweet face in the heady moonlight, the unanswered promise of his skin touching mine, sending quakes through my body to my innermost thighs. No, it was Sebastian I sought. Diana, in saving me, merely clouded my senses.

I groaned, pressing my head back into the pillow, as the memory of my fall intruded on me.

The way they had stared at me, aghast in their pristine perfection, eyes fixed between horror and humor.

Diana's affections had lulled me into thinking I was invincible, when really, I had stumbled at the first hurdle over my own two inadequate feet.

I lay wallowing in the memories and my sweat-drenched sheets until a knock on the door jolted me into wakefulness.

Diana's angular face emerged in the doorway, the lack of makeup enhancing the smattering of freckles on her dewy face.

"I feel like shit." She strode through the room to plant herself facedown on the corner of my bed. I could smell acutely the pungent sweetness of the sweat on her skin, see the half-moons of her buttocks from where her T-shirt had ridden up to expose blue-striped chiffon knickers.

I wanted to retreat into myself, aware of the unspoken something that now lay between us as she coiled up beside me. I wouldn't be the first to mention it. "What do you want to do after the breakfast shift? We're not needed again until one," I asked instead, hugging my sheet around my knees as I pulled myself up against the pillows. "Besides die somewhere quietly..."

She stretched, catlike, twisting her body around so that she was gazing up at me.

"Mmm. First, coffee? Something involving pastry? Then go to Seb's and observe the cleanup job?"

It was only once we'd enacted two of these requests— slurping down cappuccinos and tearing open a croissant between us in the kitchen—that Diana paid any heed to last night's dramatic finale.

"You're a good kisser, by the way." She inspected a fleck of croissant the size of a fingernail, let it melt on her tongue. "Most girls get prissy with it, even though they know guys go nuts for it. Seb'll have had blue balls for sure."

I gazed intently at the brown sugar cube melting into my coffee, trying to mentally cool the redness I knew was now spreading across my cheeks.

"Thank you—for…" For what? *For saving me? For kissing me? For lessening my public humiliation but somehow heightening my own private shame?*

She dismissed me, took the spoon from my saucer and skimmed off a cloud of beige foam.

"What are friends for?"

If I had been expecting a scene of remorseful solitude, I was proved wrong almost as soon as we walked through the doors of Sebastian's villa. Party spoils littered every floor and surface—broken glass, discarded bottles, a sticky film of liquid pooling on the Carrara marble surfaces—but rather than the frantic military operation I had been anticipating, we walked through the empty house to find Sebastian lolled on a sunbed in the shade, sunglasses plastered to his face, a can of Coke clutched firmly in his hand.

"Hi," he croaked, seeing us, and I saw the heads of similarly supine boys rouse themselves from their fetal holds, taking us in. A white lace bra bobbed on the surface of the pool. The sun, now high in the sky, had burned through the champagne-soaked flagstones, so a smell of feet and cat sick lingered. I swallowed down a retch.

"We thought you…might want a hand?" I ventured, bending to touch the neck of a bottle that clinked against my foot.

Sebastian stretched, waved a lugubrious arm across his face. "The maids'll be here in an hour." And then, in a faux feminine, high-pitched drawl: "Let them eat cake." The group around him chorused a lazy laugh.

I waited, expecting the joke to end, expecting him to rouse himself. A hot breeze drifted through the garden, made the surface of the water ripple. Nothing. Was this really how people like him behaved?

My stomach tightened, and I felt acutely exposed against the white space surrounding me. The callous edge to his voice was nothing like the boy I'd spoken to last night, and his choice of words sliced through my skin. What was I, after all, if not a glorified maid at the *pensione*? Was that how he'd treat me, if he happened to be one of our privileged guests? And then a further thought, stinging me all over, as though I had stepped on one of the many patches of glass shards: maybe that was how he really saw me; maybe, last night, I was nothing more than a sounding board for his drunken musings.

I looked across to Diana for reassurance, but she had already flopped on a spare deck chair and was liberally rubbing sun cream into her exposed shoulders.

Without a word, I went into the kitchen, returning moments later with a roll of bin bags in my hand. Silently, I tore one off, throwing a bottle into it with such force that it hit the concrete and smashed in the bag.

A boy with sandy hair and bright red trunks pressed his palms to his ears. *"Jesus."*

Another bottle landed beside the first. Slam. Diana rolled her eyes. I wrestled a couple of champagne flutes from a flower bed and set them upright on a wooden table.

Energy seized me as I motored around the paving stones, cleaning and sorting with an ever-growing zeal. The sun burned off my hangover, all former sluggishness gone, and I

was consumed with the single-mindedness of my goal: to remove every piece of glass I could find. Why? Why this particular compulsion? If you had asked me at the time, I know
that I wouldn't have been able to fully collect my thoughts,
to understand why I was taking such issue with the glass in
particular, but with each clink of a bottle, each flute I set
straight, I felt the power coming back to me, a shield forming between me and Sebastian's hurtful words. It wasn't as if
Sebastian's comment was overtly shocking, or even directed
at me. It was something about the contrast of the scene—last
night's excesses laid bare, rotting in the sun—and their willful
ignorance of it all, the way they were happy to roll in it like
pigs in shit, to let other people clean up their mess.

"Rachel, what are you doing?" Sebastian called to me, as
I swept up beer bottles and drained their dregs in the gutters.

"Tidying up." Another champagne bottle landed in the
bag, cracking loudly upon making contact with its contents.

"Can you not tidy up a bit quieter, babe?" Diana pressed a
weary hand to her temple, lolled her right leg over left.

I ignored her, soldiered on. Beads of sweat began to form
along my hairline, the top of my lip, as I worked my way
around the terrace.

The other boys mainly ignored me, lost as they were in
their postexcess stupor. But I could see Sebastian gathering
himself, pulling himself to a sitting position and watching me
from the shade of the umbrella.

"Rachel," he said quietly, taking a swig of Coke.

"What." I couldn't look at him, my hurt now masked by
the fug of anger that coursed around me.

"You don't have to do this. Relax."

"No." I rounded up a handful of flutes, walked them
through the house and found the dishwasher. When I came

back outside, it took a moment for my eyes to adjust to the bright sunlight, for me to notice that his lounger was empty.

There he was, hovering by the edge of the pool, his fingers dancing on the neck of a bin bag, as if unsure whether to pick it up or leave it where it lay.

"Rachel, this is silly. We pay them to tidy up. It's their job."

I let out an exasperated hiss and pushed past him to lift the bra out of the pool. If whoever it belonged to didn't care enough about it to leave the party with it, she clearly didn't want it back.

"Come on," he tried again, cajoling. "We'll help you in a bit, but it's a million degrees out here. At least have a rest, grab a glass of water. You're probably dehydrated to fuck after last night."

I shook my head.

"Please, Rachel, just sit down for a second."

"Just leave me alone, Sebastian."

I snatched hold of a flute, stalked into the house. *"Ah!"* Too late, I saw the ragged rim of glass beneath my fingertips. A rivulet of blood was already snaking across my wrist.

"Gosh." Sebastian, coming in behind me, clocked the blood.

I cupped my cut palm with my good hand, shielding my body away from him. "It's nothing."

"Rachel." There was a gentleness to his voice that stilled me, and I allowed myself to be led over to the sink, to relax momentarily into the feel of his warm hand on the small of my back. "Let me see."

He took my hand between his fingertips, held it gingerly under cold water and then up to his face. "Well, I can't see any glass in it," he pronounced authoritatively. "But there's a first aid box under the sink."

I nodded, allowing him to take the lead, to spritz rubbing

alcohol on the now barely there line and hold his lips to it, to blow cool air across it when I winced.

"The operation was a success," he said, eyebrow raised. "No amputation necessary."

My lip curled into a smile, betraying me.

"Why are you cross with me, Rachel?" he asked, breaking the silence that followed. "I don't understand what I've done. Last night... I thought we had a really good time. Well, you and Diana certainly did."

I felt my cheeks redden, worse so when I saw the tease in his eyes.

"I'm not like one of those girls—really," I stuttered, wanting to disappear down the drain hole. "Diana was just messing around, trying to save me from the embarrassment of my own clumsiness. I—"

"Rachel. Why are you cross with me?" he said again.

"I—" I felt foolish now, standing in the bright light of Sebastian's kitchen, breathing in the tropical scent of his sun cream. Perhaps I was being childish. No one else out there seemed bothered about it, so why was I so consumed by it? I spoke slowly, chewing my words. "I just thought you were different. After the conversation we had last night. But the way you were behaving just now, you sounded like...like..."

"A spoiled brat?"

I looked down at my injured hand. Couldn't answer. He sighed, scratched a hand to his head.

"You're right. I wasn't thinking. I was showing off in front of my friends, like a child. I'm sorry, Rachel. I was being thoughtless. Let's go finish up now—I'll turf the boys off their sunbeds to help."

"You don't have to do that." I shook my head. "I'm hungover myself, and when you mentioned the maids and I saw you lying there like that, I just...overreacted."

Sebastian was silent. When I tilted my head, he was looking just over my shoulder, a distracted glaze across his eyes.

"When I was about five, my mother struck my nanny. Right across the face. She'd been cleaning out my wardrobe, found my christening robe and thought it needed a wash, didn't realize how delicate it was—passed down through the family—and completely ruined it. She tried to hide it, but Mum discovered it scrunched up in the back of a drawer, and went into a rage. Ripped the robe up in front of her and told her she may as well burn the thing. I was in the room, and it upset me terribly—I was very fond of her—but my mother told me the girl was just being disciplined, that it was good for her."

His eyes rolled upward, and I knew he was playing out the scene in his head. I pictured him as a little boy; delicate featured, big-eyed. I wanted to reach out for him, but held back, letting him relive the memory alone. Eventually he gave a shake of his head. "I always said I would never treat people like she did, like they were there to do my bidding. I forgot myself today, acting like her. But you've held a mirror up to me. You're a good person, Rachel. Promise me you'll always call me out, if you see me acting like that again?"

We went back into the garden, prodded everyone into some sort of action, and soon the conversation evaporated into the heat of the day.

But Sebastian's words lingered.

A good person.

All my life I had strived for some ineffable goodness. Good grades. Good behavior. Good morals. I thought that was the way of life: you worked hard, kept your head down, and eventually you achieved the things you wanted.

But here, with these people, none of that seemed to matter. They did what they wanted, and *whom* they wanted, and they gave little regard to the consequences because goodness didn't come into it.

The longer I spent in Italy, the more I saw that bad things happened to good people, and good to bad.

So, really, did it matter which any of us were?

11

Now

When my alarm goes off at 06:45 a.m., my head pounds. I stretch for a glass of water on the nightstand, fingers knocking, too late, a half-full bottle of vodka that has somehow found its way there instead. I watch it tip, fall. The bloom of liquid across the carpet won't stain but will leave a lingering sweetness.

The bed is littered with letters—*his* letters—the box they were contained in tossed clumsily to the floor. The writing squirms and dances before my bleary eyes, a school of tiny ants crawling across the bedsheets, making me itch.

Dear Rachel, please help me—

Dear Rachel, do you know something—

Rachel, you know it's not true—

Years and years of pleas. Years and years of my silence. Because I won't—I *can't*—give him what he needs.

And for two decades it hasn't mattered. His incarceration has been my preservation. But now everything is different, and I feel his words as keenly as though he were shrieking them into my face.

Help me, Rachel. Please.

"I can't!" I shout into the silence of the bedroom, my voice still clogged with sleep. "Why me? Why not her?"

The answer is easy, laced in gold thread.

"Does he ever contact you?" I asked her once, back when she would still speak to me.

"God no. My father's lawyers would have a field day if he did."

I wrench myself from the bed and parcel up the letters, the latest one's primness jarring against the prison-issued ruled paper. I should throw the box away—better yet, burn it—it's what Diana would do. But somehow, I can't bring myself to do it. Somehow, of all the many betrayals, that seems like the biggest one.

I force myself into the shower, make coffee strong enough to power a horse, but when I open my laptop to log in to my emails, there she is again, her porcelain features laughing at the grayness of my hangover.

The bookshelf—crammed with scholarly translations of Italian classics that mock my failed attempts to publish one of my own—calls to me from the corner of the room. I scan the spines for the slim, leather-bound volume I have almost forgotten but know is there, tucked away on the bottom shelf between Machiavelli's *La Mandragola* and a falling-apart copy of Marinetti's *Manifesto*. The plastic pages are almost stuck together, so long has it been since they were last visited. They unpeel with a satisfactory smack, revealing scenescapes of varying degrees of blur. Say what you want about this generation, at least they're not wasting their time queuing up at Boots to collect their thirty-four prints of out-of-focus churches and red eyes.

I navigate to the one I have in mind, loosen it from the plastic and hold the shiny paper between my fingers, breathing in the faint whiff of chemical processing that still clings.

The backdrop of the Ponte Vecchio is unmistakable, and I am sure unchanged even now. The wide shot takes in the edges of higgledy-piggledy medieval buildings, looking precariously like they could fall into the murky green Arno at a moment's notice. Tourists are frozen in motion, pointing in the direction of the Uffizi, posing for a photograph that may have been long discarded or that now lives in someone else's album, in someone else's living room. Between them, black railings festooned with silver metal that catches the sunlight and causes myriad flashes of white on the image like a hundred little starbursts. And among *them*, two figures. One red head, one brown. One holds the lock, caught in the act of attaching it to the railing, a naughty smile playing on her lips. The other, keys raised aloft, moments from hurling them into the river.

The Lovers' Locks.

Fix a padlock to the railings on the Ponte Vecchio, so the legend goes, then throw the keys into the Arno, and you'll always be connected to one another, and to Florence. Despite threats from the apparently Ferragamo-clad carabinieri police force, despite fear of fines or the knowledge that your lock will most likely be cut off that same night, your hold on Florence just a temporary gain, the tradition persists.

The memory of that day lifts me up and soars me back onto that bridge. I am among it, smelling the sweat of tourists, the oppressive musk of the leather glove shops; hearing the moaning "please, please" of the *zingari* women in their long peasant skirts, palms outstretched in supplication.

I stand beside those two girls and I can hear them, the laughter that masks just the tiniest arrhythmic quiver of their beating hearts as they ready themselves to perform the illicit act.

"Ready, Rach? On my count—one, two, *three*."

I want to reach through the passage of time, take up the position as the person I was then. So delighted to be part of the team, to be binding herself to that girl, and to that place.

Why? Why can't we be like that again? I find myself hurtling back through time toward the woman I am now, the need for Diana inescapable. Fumbling fingers find my phone and before I can stop myself, I am scrolling through the contacts, pressing hers.

"No!" I jam my thumb down to end the call before it connects, throw the phone from my person as though it's hot to the touch.

Calling her is no good. She won't answer; she never does anymore.

But I can't just sit here and do nothing. Whether she likes it or not, because of Sebastian, because of that summer, Diana's life is intertwined with mine. Perhaps she just needs a reminder.

I check my schedule for the day—full as always—then dial the number of the school secretary, delighted that at this time of the morning, I'll hit voice mail.

"Miss Shaw? It's Miss Bailey." I thicken my voice with a groan for good measure. "I'm afraid I've come down with a stomach bug. I'm worried it might be norovirus and I don't want to risk passing anything on to the girls, especially before mocks. Please would you inform Ms. Graybridge? I'll ask the languages department to cover my classes for the day."

A follow-up email to the other languages teachers:

Guys, I've been throwing up since 2:00 a.m. Would you mind covering my classes today? Round on me at the pub next Wednesday.
Cheers,
Rach

I can do friendly when I need to.

Brush my teeth. Change. Where's my bag?

It's a twenty-five-minute walk to Ascot Station. Then two trains. And finally, following the heave of late-morning commuters through Victoria Station, a short shoot on the Circle Line, bound for the coveted pavements of Notting Hill.

The Facebook updates are scored into me like the ink of a tattoo pen pulled across flesh.

Boys' last year at Lakeland House—can you believe it?! Boarding next year. My babies are growing up so fast!!!

Forty-three likes. Ten comments.

Results for Lakeland House pull up several potentials, but adding "London" then "school" to the search terms narrows it down to just one.

It's a ten-minute walk from Notting Hill Gate Station.

Leaving Ascot when I do, I know the children won't be let out of class for a while. But that doesn't matter. For Diana, I always have plenty of time.

12

Then

Our days began to organize themselves into a sort of rhythm. As the mercury rose, guests began to pile into the Villa Medici, and the work was hot, relentless. Snatched spare moments were spent at Sebastian's villa, dipping in the pool or lazing on sunbeds, chatting to whatever public-school waif or stray had emerged.

Sebastian and I hadn't talked about the day after the party since it happened. When he'd finished cleaning up my cut, we'd gone back outside and he'd tipped one of the boys off a sunbed, commanded, "Come on, you lazy fucks, let's get this place sorted," and that was it. But still, I saw him glance at me sometimes, the merest shift of his eyes, checking himself, if he thought he'd said something wrong. There was nothing concrete to suggest a blossoming romance between us—in fact, there was nothing in his comportment toward me to imply he thought of me as anything other than that dreaded word, *mate*—and yet I couldn't help the feeling that it was tantalizingly close; that if we could just find the right moment, or if I could just say the right thing, the scales would fall from his eyes, and he would be mine.

We had an easy friendship. He was interesting and interested, happy to play tour guide in the city he knew so well. Where Diana would be happy to while away hours drinking coffee under the covered umbrellas of Piazza della Repubblica's Caffè Gilli—cappuccinos for me, until Diana told me Italians consider them unspeakably déclassé after noon—he would gamely tour round the Uffizi or see the latest exhibition in Palazzo Strozzi. And he was smart—*so* smart—and *funny*, always ready with a snappy answer or clever quip. Once, we trekked up to hear the monks singing at the basilica of San Miniatio al Monte, Diana moaning all the way about the heat, and he regaled us with the story of the eponymous saint, who was allegedly beheaded in the old city center but fled into the hills, still holding his severed head, where he finally came to rest. Sebastian performed the whole tale with great vigor on the church steps, but then midway through, inspiration struck, and he pulled me up beside him, arms around my neck so that I was peeping through the crook in his elbow, to re-create the severed head. We wobbled through the rest of the story to the great delight and amusement of the crowd of tourists who had stopped to watch, landing in a heap at the foot of the church. As they began to clap he pulled me to my feet and the two of us bowed, victorious.

"You give good head," he whispered, eyes teasing, and then turned to the crowd, waving magnanimously, as I turned pink beside him.

★ ★ ★

Dwindling finances had been an increasing source of anxiety for me as the weeks had gone on, worrying away at me like so many grains of sand inside a shoe. As the others peeled off crisp lire from wads of bank-fresh notes, insisting on sitting tableside at cafés despite the additional *coperto* charge this incurred, I covertly counted centesimi in the palm of my hand, invented "must-see" exhibitions as a reason to down my single espresso at the bar, rushing off before they could see the press of red on my cheeks. No amount of eking out my savings from home, or insisting I really did just want the starter, could match Diana's fiscal abandon, the frivolous joy with which she circled a hand around a table of revelers, bellowed *"Un altro giro"* as soon as the first round of acid-yellow Limoncellos was sucked down. The only thought that sustained me, that gave me secret comfort when the impending bill from a waiter's outstretched palm caused a dry choke to rise in my throat, was of the emergency credit card nestled in the farthest, most untouched corner of my wallet. Not to use; just to know it was there. A talisman against my penury. *Just in case.*

But then, a whole day off together, a trip to the beach—how could I say no? It was Diana's suggestion. Her family had been going to the same place on the Italian Riviera for years; it was the reason they knew Silvia. Sebastian too, and a couple of his nicer friends: a sweet boy called Matthew, a friend from what he referred to—like something out of Forster—as "prep" school, and an Italian, Elio, who always wore a panama hat, and chain-smoked thin white Vogue cigarettes like they were going out of fashion.

It had stormed the day before—one of those brutal, grab-you-with-both-fists storms I had come to learn was typical for Tuscany's undulating terrain. Rain came down like thick sheets, rendering us immobile, the hotel guests relegated to sipping grappa in the living room among Silvia's self-portraits before braving a break for their rooms, spare white bath towels clutched to their heads like members of a pagan cult. Lightning cut jagged lines across the sky, giving only momentary relief before the howl of thunder pierced the air, while Diana and I huddled by one of the French windows, eyes fixed on the dancing sky, supposing our beach plans were over.

But then morning came and, mercurial as a teenager, Florence stretched, unfurled her wrists and rose to meet the dawn as though last night's tantrum had never happened. The only sign of any unrest was the puddles of water we picked past to the station, and the chalky scent of drying concrete in the now-calm air.

The train slunk through the countryside and on to the Italian coastline as a lazy game of Beggar My Neighbor continued among us, the deck of cards nestled between Matthew's and Sebastian's thighs. The open windows pulled into them the rush of breeze, the lingering scent of tree resin then sea salt, neither of which did much to mask the sweet fug of human sweat. It was Sunday; the carriage was full, everyone hellbent on the same intention: to escape the trapped city funk and make straight for the beach. Toddlers wailed next to us, their faces flushed, shoes flung with reckless abandon down the gangway as mothers clucked their tongues and reluctantly retrieved them. Beach sellers crouched between carriages or perched on blue IKEA bags stuffed full of knockoff sunglasses and Burberry print caps, ready to leap off as soon as the train hit Viareggio, the first seaside stop. When we hit Pisa Centrale, Elio jerked the window down fully and leaned out to spark up a cigarette, which he flicked away casually as soon as he spied a guard approaching.

The station at Forte dei Marmi was nondescript: a low-slung building next to a typically Italian row of outlets. I saw no hint of the sea, of the mystical beach town Diana had spoken of with such pleasure—only a pharmacy, pizzeria and motorcycle shop, two out of the three with their shutters down, *chiuso la domenica.*

A short taxi ride—with Diana perched, squealing, across the boys' laps in the back—took us to the destination she'd specified. When I questioned the name, which featured the word *bagno*, Italian for *bath*, she gave Elio a little wink and leaned over the headrest to me. "No one goes to the *spiaggia libera* here—the free beach. You all choose a beach club, a *bagno*, and pay for a spot for the day. It's so much more civilized."

I nodded, pretending I understood, sitting carefully on the edge of my seat to avoid wrinkling the crisp white cotton caftan Diana had lent me that morning, after she'd frowned at the frayed denim shorts and tank top I'd appeared at her door in. Gone too was the magenta patterned beach towel I had folded into a canvas tote bag, which she'd told me indulgently but through decidedly flared lips I wouldn't be needing.

Beaches made me think of Mum, and the infrequent trips we'd made when I was a kid. Blackpool, or Southend. Sandwiches sweating through cling film, the innards compacted. The crinkle of tin foil beneath my fingers, unwrapping a sulphuric, home-boiled egg, the chalky softness of its gray yolk against my teeth. There was Devon for half term once, where it rained for a week, and when I was ten, France, where I was introduced to the mysteries of half board, pilfering breakfast rolls and sliced ham, being reassured they would taste even better at lunch because we were "cheating the system."

So far, this trip felt nothing like those, and I was beginning to think I had no grasp of this sort of place at all. The others had now roamed on from the beach clubs of Forte dei Marmi and were chatting leisurely about other places they had all been to: Saint-Tropez, Courchevel, Mustique. I smiled gamely as even my polite murmurs of inclusion turned to silence, but it made me feel funny inside. Like they could see the discomfort on my face—smell it on me, through the artificial veneer of my borrowed caftan. So I told myself firmly to sharpen up, sucked my stomach in, held my head a little higher as we turned off one of the winding tributaries of side streets and onto what I assumed was the main beach road, and said in a Diana-ish sort of voice, "I'm afraid France has never really done it for me. I'm Italy, through and through." *Civilized*, she'd said. I could be *civilized*.

Stepping out of the taxi, we found ourselves at the entrance of what looked to me like some sort of lounge bar. White wicker sofas and armchairs lined with thickly plumped cushions were draped with limbs tanned a golden bronze, picking at salads or sipping espressos, decked in neatly pressed resort wear and an abundance of sparkling jewelry, or brightly patterned swimming trunks I know my dad would awkwardly label "poufy." Beyond, a vast expanse of fine ocher sand, sucking up the sunshine and reflecting it back into the limpid sky. A man in a clean white polo shirt and navy chino shorts was patterning his way across it, holding a long wooden object, which I soon realized was being used to regiment the sand after last night's churn.

And it wasn't just the sand that was kept in order: the entire seafront expanse was parceled out into cleanly designated plots, each one marked by a navy canopy, held in place by four white wooden poles, beneath which sat a matching set of deck chairs and sunbeds. Not for Diana's *bagno* the odd umbrella pitchforked into the ground, the colorful striped windbreaker Dad had bought in Devon to give us a modicum of privacy; now I began to understand what Diana had meant by a "spot for the day."

Ahead of us, she strutted through the lounge, her cork wedges making an even clip on the white wooden decking.

"Massimiliano!" she called, reaching over to clutch the arm of a tall man in a navy suit.

"Signorina Turner!" Recognizing her instantly, he held her shoulders between his hands and beamed at her like he was greeting a long-lost relative. I watched her kiss him twice, allow him to take the soft apple of her left cheek between his knuckles and squeeze it as though she were a chubby bambino. I watched her, the confident way she turned her head from side to side, the languorous movement of her arms—wrist first, as though they were made of silk—and tried to make my body match the ease of hers. The boys had already wandered off to a cluster of wicker seats and were ordering coffee, so I hovered, alone, clasping my hands in front of me, chorister-like, until at last Diana gave a little nod and beckoned me over.

"It's all sorted," she said as I reached her side. "We've got a tent for the day on the front row. It's a little bit more expensive on the front, but it's worth it for the people-watching, you'll see." I waited expectantly, hoping to be made privy to what exactly this "more expensive" setup amounted to, but she was already calling to the boys and making her way down to the seafront.

Under the so-called tent, more staff members busied themselves around us, laying specially fitted towels and soft navy cushions on the sunbeds and placing another stack of matching navy-and-white towels on the little table at the back of the tent. I thought of my magenta towel, still flecked with pieces of grass from a trip to the park, and had to laugh.

I put my bag on one of the sunbeds and fiddled with the edge of my caftan. The thought of exposing myself in a bikini so quickly didn't exactly thrill me, but the day was already hot, the strength of the sun magnified by the fine sand, and I knew I'd burn the minute I stepped into it if I wasn't careful. With a sigh, I pulled it over my head and reached into the bag for my sun cream, pouring a dollop into my hand and rubbing it as quickly as I could into my legs and arms.

"Here, let me help you."

Before I could answer, Sebastian was behind me, taking the bottle from my hand and upturning it into his palm.

I flinched as his smooth hands rested on my shoulders, rubbing cream liberally over them before working the heels of his hands into the top of my back and down my spine. I felt my nipples stiffen involuntarily, quickly crossed my arms to hide them.

"Sorry," he murmured into my neck, moving a strand of hair from the nape, "cold hands."

I willed myself to stay stock-still, attuning my body to any sign from him that this was more than just a helpful gesture, but before I knew it, he was handing the bottle back to me with a chirpy "All done!" and heading onto the sand with Matthew and a tennis ball they began to toss back and forth.

I put the caftan back on and sat down on the sunbed, deflated.

Beside me, Diana kicked off her wedges and sank herself into a deck chair in the shade, wafting her arms over the seat back behind her.

"Mmm, see—I told you this was nice," she said now, raking a little pile of sand between her toes, stretching out her legs so that the tops of her thighs were visible beneath the hemline of her sundress, which she began to peel off. I caught myself staring. Looking away, I noticed a couple of the male staff members—young and dark haired with deep bronze tans— sneaking a glance. And even Matthew and Sebastian paused. That was just like Diana, conducting herself so coolly over the same act which, only moments before, had caused me such grief. Only Elio seemed unaffected by her. I had noticed it on the journey over: the barely perceptible way his mouth formed a thin line of displeasure when she spoke; how he almost deliberately turned his body away from her when she courted the attention of the rest of the group. Now, with his sunglasses removed from his face for the first time since greeting us, I saw him raise an eyebrow in Diana's direction. Then he drew a deck chair over to the table, dragged the ashtray that rested on it toward him and lit up. Almost instantly, Diana sniffed and wrinkled her nose.

"Do you have to do that here?"

He rose with a loud groan and jerked his head in the direction of the sea. "I'm going for a walk, if anyone wants to join me."

When no one else moved, I saw the opportunity to quiz his apparent dislike further, murmuring something pithy to the others about needing the exercise before heading off in his direction, picking gingerly through the hot sand to keep up with his retreating back.

"Hey," I said when I caught up with him, feeling the cooling relief of the water's edge. "I'll come with you."

He shrugged in a way that didn't tell me if he was pleased or annoyed but turned in the direction of the pier, following the rhythmic stride of the other beachgoers who passed to and fro around us.

We started out in silence, Elio a few steps ahead of me, and so, to fill the time, I observed the beach clubs we passed, taking in their brightly colored tents and wondering what sort of people each one attracted, and why. The seafront, it seemed, allowed for multitudes—young, old, fat, thin, ugly, beautiful. No one seemed to care, strutting purposefully along the water's edge in teeny bikinis and Speedos that didn't leave much to the imagination. Emboldened by this laissez-faire attitude, I peeled Diana's caftan off, resting it over the crook of my elbow and resisting the urge to wrap my arms around my waist. Maybe Diana was right. Maybe, as she'd said before Sebastian's party, I should learn to "own it" more.

"So, you're from Florence, then?" Finally meeting Elio's pace, I decided to break the silence.

"Mmm." It was somewhere between a grunt and an affirmation. "Settignano," he volunteered at last. "It's a neighborhood just to the northeast of the city."

"How do you know Sebastian?" I jumped in quickly, worrying the conversation would lapse.

His shoulders tightened, and he looked up to the sky. "How does anyone know anyone? We met at some party one summer when we were young. Played some tennis together. I spent a semester in London and stayed with his parents. We just... know each other." He inspected his cigarette, throwing it at last into the froth of a wave. My mind hurried to fill the space in time. "And you're English?"

I nodded.

He cocked his head thoughtfully. "I wasn't sure. Your accent...it sounds different from Diana and Sebastian. I thought maybe, I don't know...Australian or American?"

I felt a little twist in the pit of my stomach. Was my difference to them really so obvious, even to an Italian? "I'm from another part of London."

"Oh."

We walked on, until at last Elio came to a stop at a particularly clear part of the coastline, where the crystalline water pooled in shallow waves, giving way to the cement-colored sand underneath.

"Swim?" He was already unbuttoning his linen shirt, but I glanced down at Diana's caftan, so carefully folded.

"We don't have towels..."

"So, we dry off."

He stalked up to a red lifeguard boat—I'd noticed one at the foot of every beach club, the word *salvataggio* painted on in white, along with what I assumed to be the name of the club—and draped his shirt over one of its twin hulls. Gingerly, I did the same with the caftan.

The water was colder than I had anticipated, having been duped by feet acclimatized to the shallows. True to form, Elio didn't wait for me, his smooth body diving under at the first chance, and splashed into the deep with a powerful front crawl.

I waded in up to my waist, holding back a gasp as I finally submerged the rest of my torso, but was surprised at how quickly I grew accustomed to the temperature, doing my best to follow in Elio's wake with my neatest approximation of Guildford Lido drilled breaststroke.

"Rinfrescante?" Elio asked me, with at last something approaching the shadow of a smile.

"Un po!" I conceded. *A little.*

We swam for a bit in awkward silence, occasionally broken by the splash of Elio diving through a wave, surfacing a couple of feet away in a move that seemed designed for me to follow.

Beyond the breaking waves, pedal boats chugged alongside us, and the occasional polished white rowboat, but few swimmers came out this far. The water here was a smooth, dark green, and I could neither see nor feel the bottom. It made me uneasy, and I tried not to think about what could be lurking unseen around my bare legs. Dad was a nervous swimmer, with an unfounded fear of sharks, and Mum never went in the sea because she didn't trust the sewage pipes, so I really had no foundation on which to build my maritime confidence.

"We used to come here very often, when I was a child." At last Elio stopped, spoke. We trod water, facing back toward the beach, to the tents that had become multicolored dots, as if someone had upended a tube of Smarties over the sand. "But then my parents got divorced, and my mother didn't want to come here anymore. She still doesn't like talking about holidays here. Says they seem…" He shook his head. "I don't know the English word. They're not happy memories anymore, they're…colored?"

"Tainted?" I offered quietly, not wanting to break his meditation, not when the cold water seemed to be thawing some of Elio's ice. This was the most I'd heard him say all day.

"*Esatto.*" He gave me a precise nod. "Your parents, they are together?"

"Yes." An image of Mum and Dad flew into my mind. Their dully happy marriage. School sweethearts—Mum only sixteen, Dad just a couple of years her senior. They got married a few years later, Mum barely out of her teens, and then the baby, somewhere, that didn't quite make it, and then me.

"You're lucky, then. Divorce—*tsss,*" he aspirated through clenched teeth. "It really screws you up. My sisters still aren't over it."

"'They fuck you up, your mum and dad,'" I quoted without thinking about it, cursing myself for picking such a trite summation. But Elio nodded sagely.

"I think so, yes."

"No, sorry, it's a poem. Philip Larkin?"

He jutted his bottom lip. "I don't know him."

"It doesn't matter."

I felt as though I was losing him again. Why, exactly, I had such a great need to keep him talking I didn't know, but it seemed important, as though a flowing conversation would be proof to him of my winning personality; that if I could befriend him, I could unlock what it was about Diana that so clearly irked him.

"What were your holidays here like? When you were little?"

But he was already moving back toward the shore, his limbs assuredly dragging through the water. "Shit, if I'm honest. They were always fighting. And I was too scared of the *meduse* to swim in the sea."

"*Meduse?*" I asked tentatively, coming up behind him.

"How do you say?" He spoke louder but didn't turn around. "Jellyfish. I've just seen one now. But don't worry—follow behind me and we should be okay before it stings."

Choking onto dry land, I followed Elio back to the lifeguard boat, watching him throw his shirt over his shoulders. I observed the patches of damp darken the linen as his fingers worked the buttons, and fingered Diana's caftan. The sea breeze licked at my wet limbs, making me shiver involuntarily.

"Why don't you put it on?" Elio jerked his chin at the dress. "You're cold."

He said it so matter-of-factly that I struggled, feeling like a child. "It's Diana's. I don't want to ruin it with the salt."

He rolled his eyes, and I saw it again—that same look of displeasure he was giving her back at the tent.

Emboldened by his modicum of intimacy in the sea, I tried my luck.

"You don't like Diana, do you?"

He ran his fingers through his hair, piecing his wet curls apart so they clung like spikes.

"It's not that I like or dislike her. She's not someone I would choose to spend my time with."

"But everyone likes Diana." It was a fact. I myself had witnessed it: the magnetic way people turned to greet her when she walked into the room, the way space seemed to shift to accommodate her position in the center of it. Even the most difficult guests at the Villa Medici saved a smile for Diana.

But Elio laughed. An acrid laugh that came sharply from the top of his chest.

"I know girls like her. English girls. Italian girls. Girls with money. They think they can get what they want, and so they always get what they want. But their charm is all—" he waved his hand in the air "—*esterno*. Nothing genuine. I don't have any interest in hanging out with girls like that."

Anger flashed in me. He didn't understand her at all.

I shook my head. "You're wrong, Elio. Yes, she has lots of money, but she's generous, and kind. She's not what you say she is. She—"

"You like Sebastian, don't you?" The question came at me like a wave. "You don't have to say anything. I like to watch people. I know it's true." Even with my eyes to the ground I could make out the curl of his lip, could hear the crow in his near-accentless English. "Then if I were you, I would be careful. Because Diana likes him too. And he may not know it, and even she may not know it, but I can bet you that if she decides she wants him, nothing and no one will stand in her way."

A crash of water came toward us, bathing me nearly up to the knees. I hurried to hold the caftan aloft, blushed as I caught myself doing it and forced myself to look at him.

"Diana's my friend, Elio. She wouldn't do that to me." His face remained passive, but there was something in his eyes, a sort of softening pity, that made a hard little bead form in my chest.

"What is it you English always say? *Don't say I didn't warn you.*"

"We should head back," I mumbled, folding the caftan resiliently over my arm. "They'll be wondering where we are."

When we arrived back at the tent, Matthew and Sebastian had moved down to the shoreline, lobbing the tennis ball back and forth with an easy grace. Diana was lounging on a sunbed in the shade listening to her Discman—I could just make out the snake of black wires from her ears, disappearing under the pillow where she was keeping the player cool. Her limbs were wrapped around one another like roots on a tree, but when she saw us, she unfolded herself.

"Finally." She stretched, right arm raised to the sky, wrist curling, righting herself as if from a day's labor. "For God's sake, I'm starving."

We whistled for the boys and began straightening up to head inside to the club's restaurant. As I finally allowed myself to pull Diana's caftan over my now-dry body, I couldn't help but eye her as she handed Sebastian his shirt, observe the way their fingers brushed one another, or the small smile she gave him, the pearlescent peek of white teeth through her lips. Elio had got into my head and I tried to push him out.

The restaurant bore the same rigorous branding as the rest of the beach—white wicker chairs with neat navy-and-white-striped cushions and glass-topped wicker tables—but it was set back in a garden toward the road. The sudden scent of earth and leaves contrasted sharply to the salt and iodine that had blown through my senses at the seafront.

As a menu was set in front of me, my stomach involuntarily rumbled, but when I opened it, I had to refrain from snapping it shut again almost instantly.

Surely those prices had to be wrong.

I looked again, doing quick conversion calculations in my head in case I had somehow got mixed up. But no, there they were, the stream of numbers brazen in their neat, embossed print. I considered the date, counted how many days were left until the end of the month, until we received our next stipend from Silvia, and instantly regretted every coffee, every stick of gum, every unnecessary purchase I had made in the past week when I could have been saving for this.

But now there was nothing I could do, so I scanned the menu, trying to work out the cheapest possible thing I could order that would also be the most unobtrusive.

"Prosciutto e melone," I requested when the waiter was behind me, avoiding sipping from the glass of sparkling water that had already been set in front of me, even though my throat was as dry as the sand.

"And to follow?" I could feel him looking at my neck, but I kept my eyes down, focusing on the cover of the menu I had now closed, the looping gold pattern that bore the club's name.

"Bene così." I'm fine with that.

"You're just having ham and melon?" Diana, having ordered a whole sea bream that I knew she would only pick at, ruffled her nose at me.

"I'm too hot to eat much." Devilishly, I used one of her own familiar phrases, the one she saved for when she couldn't even make a pretense at eating. "You've been in the shade all day, remember?"

"Suit yourself." She handed her menu over to the waiter and pressed her palms together in her lap. "Oh—before you go?" She called the waiter back. "A *bottiglia* of champagne, please? Dom Pérignon." She licked her lips at us as he wrote it down. "It would be rude not to, right?"

Hot, hot. I repeated the mantra in my mind and on my lips as the lunch scene played out around me, a background extra mouthing "rhubarb" for effect. "No, thank you." A hand over my champagne flute, a shake of my head as the bottle was offered to me. "I'm fine." Ignoring the bowls of courgette fries and chips aspirating salty fry into the heavy midday air, placed in the center of the table for sharing.

And I *was* hot, I reasoned with myself, the fridge-cold or-

OUT OF HER DEPTH

ange melon tender on my front teeth, tendrils of white lard from the ham almost sticking to the back of my throat. The train journey, and then the walk in the sun, and the heat of that other thought, of Elio's observation, pulsing through me as I watched Diana grow pink and tipsy, laughing at some joke of Sebastian's, resting her hand on his forearm in a way that seemed familiar, proprietary, so unlike a gesture I would make with such decadent unconsciousness. And him letting it lie there, not a flinch, not a subtle brush away. He liked it there. And leaning over her to take a chip, his shoulder touching hers, sticky, sea-air-baked skin meeting and—

"Shall we just split it?"

The scene shifted, and I was plunged into cold water.

Sebastian rubbed the bill between his fingers, the black ink smudging on the paper.

"Split it?" I didn't realize that I had vocalized the thought, but then Elio caught my eye. I was sure he could see the color drain out of me. "Split it," I repeated, forcing the question into a statement.

"Just easier than working out who had what—it's not even written down here properly. It just says the number of *primi* and *secondi* and whatnot. And then dividing champagne, and the wine and beer, chips, water...it's all a bit of a faff."

"Yeah, can't be bothered." Diana magicked a credit card, landing it casually on the silver dish.

"Fine." Matthew, on her other side, reached into his back pocket and added his.

"I—" I was frozen, inert, the words with which to defend myself stuck in the back of my throat, caught in a web of prosciutto and shame.

"I said I'd buy you lunch." Lightning fast, Elio covered my silence.

"No, no, honestly, I—"

99

"Don't you remember?" He spoke over me, giving me a pointed look. "We made a deal. If you came swimming with me, I said I'd buy you lunch. And look how polite you were, only having your *prosciutto e melone*."

The whole table turned to look at me, waiting for my response, but although I knew what he was doing, and although I knew I should be grateful to him, I couldn't bring myself to succumb to his pity.

"I said I wasn't hungry," I muttered, trying to keep my tone neutral. "Don't be silly. You don't have to buy me lunch—it was a joke," I added quickly, showing him the kindness of keeping up the pretense.

And then I reached into my bag and pulled the emergency credit card from my wallet, so shiny and untouched that not a grain of silver had been worn from the letters. "Split it." I nodded, feeling sick. "Don't forget to add service charge."

Later, much later, when I had washed the salt from my skin and the embarrassment away with it, I knocked on Diana's door.

"Here's your caftan." I held it out to her like an offering, the material folded so thinly it could have fitted in an envelope. "Thank you."

"No problem, my love." She took it from me, kissed my cheek. "Today was fun, wasn't it?"

"Yes." I tried to breathe enthusiasm into my voice. "Di?" I hovered in the doorway, watching her dancing from one foot to another, her fingers playing with the hem of her pyjama shorts.

"Yeah?"

"You don't fancy Sebastian, do you?" The words choked themselves out of me.

"Sebastian? Ha!" Her face morphed into a grin. She reached

out to pinch the rose of my cheek in a way that I was sure was meant to be affectionate but left a residual pain after her fingers had gone. "You funny thing. He's like every boy I've ever met. Far too boring to be my type. What gave you that idea?"

"I...I don't know." And I blushed, hating Elio in that moment, sure he must have read whatever he thought he saw wrong, caused me to see things that weren't there.

"Sebastian." She mulled the word on her lips, her eyes focusing just out of reach, as if saying the name would somehow summon him up. She giggled, squeezed a hand on the side of my shoulder. "Me and Sebastian. To think." I pivoted to go, but as she reached out to close the door I turned back. Just before she shut it, a look crossed her face. A pensive look. A pleased look. A look that told me maybe Elio wasn't quite so wrong after all.

13

Now

The Underground vomits me out into the fresh air, and I can't help the jig of nervous excitement that surges through me as I weave through Notting Hill Gate. It's a gray sort of day, and frosty—but then again, doesn't London always exacerbate both? The clouds are pregnant with pollution, the air thick with the metallic scent of precipitation and car fumes. I had half thought—having managed to circumnavigate rush hour—that the streets would be quiet, but then I had underestimated Notting Hill, underestimated the whack of scurrying bodies, heads down, eyes on phones, who scuff at my sides and at one point send me spinning in an ungainly pirouette. "Wotchit," the offender grunts, barely pausing to remove an earbud.

Just a road back and the streets thin out, the busy thoroughfare replaced by narrow whitewashed town houses; cluttered antique shops I would barely be able to afford the air in; million-pound private properties with a name or door number etched on in calligraphed black paint, the owners of which have at least a fifty percent chance of possessing either a made-to-measure suit or a double-barreled surname. The smell of baking stops me, pulls at my stomach, empty but for the lingering ghost of last night's vodka and this morning's caffeine hit, and I practically press my nose against the glass of a sugar-pink-painted café with a complicated French name scrawled above the door in looping white letters.

Inside, a sea of that well-worn archetype known as the yummy mummy: fresh from the gym, tight athleisure wear expensive enough to wick away any hint of exertion; tiny forks pushing around tiny cakes in competition to see who can make a pretense of eating the most; expensive babies in expensive strollers who will grow up to begin the cycle anew. What collective noun would one give to these women? A sneer of yummy mummies? A snub? I have half a fear that one of them might be her, but when I look around, they are all the same shade of salon blond, not a streak of her signature red in sight, and I proceed to the counter.

I order loudly, defiantly, selecting the most alarming pastry I can see—a voluminous French horn crammed with white clouds of whipped cream. And a latte—no, not skinny, full fat, please—and sit among them all, letting the cream settle on my lips for a second too long before licking it off. *I am not one of you,* I want to crow, *but look at me, sitting among you, every right to be here.* Even though I'd balked when the cashier told me the cost of the pastry—how can cream and sugar cost that much?

The mummy chatter reverberates around me as I eat, and I allow myself to surreptitiously take out my phone, navigate to Facebook, to her page, and look, shielding the screen with my hand in case one of them knows her. There's an update, I see. She and the husband, and another couple, squashing into a selfie, holding martini glasses full of brown liquid up to the camera. Behind them, you can just make out a perfect view over the Thames, the twinkling pinpoints of city lights like a star cloth behind them. She's wearing an emerald green dress, slashed at the neck to show off the points of her shoulder blades. I always thought that color suited her.

What else but espresso martinis on the Vertige rooftop to celebrate Jonny and Jim's deal finally going through? Congrats, boys—you're finally free!!

The picture was uploaded last night, at ten o'clock. I think of myself at that same moment, the news no longer playing but still unable to get the sight of Sebastian out of my head. Does she know? Does she think about him at all? About me? I look at her wrinkle-free face, at her wrinkle-free life, and a wave of satisfaction washes over me. If she doesn't, I'll have to remind her.

I feel giddy, high on caffeine and sugar, delighted at the thought of finally getting one over on Diana. *You thought you could keep me away but look, here I am.* A cackle I thought would be silent escapes my lips, and the woman on the table next to me gives me a disturbed look. I cram the rest of the pastry in my mouth, smearing the excess off with the back of my hand, and give her a creamy smile. She wrinkles her nose, turns away.

But then when I leave, when I catch sight of my reflection in the highly polished glass windows, reality sets in, and I find my shoulders dropping an inch. I'd thought I'd planned my outfit so carefully that morning, the long black wool cardigan, white shirt, black jeans. I thought black would make me look chic. Now I see myself reflected not only in the glass, but in the manicured nails of the women in the café: not chic—cheap. The cardigan is bobbled at the elbows; the jeans are faded from the wash, more gray than black, and displaying the stubborn little pouch of flesh above the waistband that nothing gets rid of, and drinking and ready meals only help along. I'm sure I can see a sheen of saturated fat around my mouth, the horror of which would send any of the women in there running for the nearest outpatient procedure. Bile catches in my throat, and I momentarily consider going back inside, sticking my head down the toilet and allowing the stench of disinfectant to absolve me of my sin. That's what they always do to you, women like that: make you think you're above them, until you see yourself in their relief.

Instead I storm off, nails digging pinpricks of pain into my palms, find myself coming to a halt a few doors down. It's a posh women's clothing boutique, all high shine and minimal white interiors; I can already hear the clack of the sales assistant's stilettos as I walk through the door. When she approaches me—leopard-print heels, red lipstick, pearls—I point to the item in the window that caught my eye.

"Can I try that one, please?"

Leopard Print casts her eyes over me, and I see her eyebrows rise, not ever so subtly.

"The camel? It comes up quite long. We normally recommend it for taller ladies." Her accent may be neutral, but I can tell instantly that it's not the rounded plumminess of a native. I wonder how many years and pounds she's spent wiping it clean.

"Size twelve or fourteen," I enunciate.

Her mouth follows her eyebrows upward, and she clicks over to the counter. "Bear with me. I don't know what a fourteen is in French sizing."

As soon as I touch the coat, I know I must have it. It *is* long, skimming my ankle bones, but made of the softest material I've ever felt—

"One hundred percent cashmere," Leopard Print remarks, seeing my hand stroking the lapel. I turn in the mirror, admiring my toffee-clad frame, and find myself standing taller, raising my chin higher. I picture myself going back into the café with some excuse—*Sorry, I didn't happen to leave my phone...?*—and seeing them notice me, wonder who I am. It doesn't matter what I am wearing underneath; in this coat, I am elegance personified.

"I'll take it." I beam at her, my wonder coat blanketing over any ill will I have toward her. "I'll wear it now."

If she looks a little surprised, she tries hard to hide it, bending instead to retrieve the tag from the left sleeve and ushering me over to the counter.

As she pushes buttons on the register, I fiddle with my wallet, ready my card in my hand. She reaches out for it. "That'll be eight hundred and ninety-five pounds, please."

All the entrails in my body seem to judder to a halt. My lungs feel as though they've been squeezed to nothing.

"Sorry?"

She blinks sharply, repeats it again, but I heard right the first time. Idiot, *idiot* that I am, I fleetingly saw an eight on the label, and assumed it was the beginning of an eighty. What kind of a moron thinks a pure cashmere coat would cost eighty quid?

"Would you like to think about it?" She fills the silence, and I can hear in her tone the patronizing quotation marks she puts around "think about it," that common form of English politesse that means you've changed your mind but don't want to say it.

But I know I can't give it back, not now.

I try to picture my bank balance, the date my salary hits, the bills that have gone out.

There is the stipend, of course: the monthly "gift." I know I should be sensible, save it for something more necessary, but wouldn't there be some delicious irony in using it for this?

I dutifully hand over the card, flinching momentarily until the assistant offers me the receipt and something approaching a smile.

Released, I step out onto the street in my new purchase, zeal renewed. I am ready for her. Ready for Diana. A sheep in wolf's disguise, ready to seek out a creature of the opposite persuasion.

14

Then

The credit card charge weighed heavily on me, as thick and bilious as a too-large slab of Carla's homemade tiramisu. When a letter arrived for me addressed in Dad's uncomplicated grammar-school cursive, I was convinced it would be a missive from him, wanting to know exactly what sort of "emergency" warranted nearly a two-hundred-pound charge and when I planned to pay it back.

Instead, his usual cheerful burble burst forth from the pages, as though the envelope could only restrict his excitement for so long.

—new roses from the garden center, to go along the back wall of the garden, although Mum thinks I'll kill them in a month, you know what Mum's like. And Auntie

Maureen sends her love and wants to know what to get you for your birthday, but I said money was probably best, get you a few rounds in Freshers' Week, ha ha. And the good news is, I think I've finally talked Mum round about getting on a plane! It took some persuading, but I convinced her that if she didn't do it now, when would she ever. So, what do you think, pal? Fancy giving two old bags the grand tour of Florence?

There was a second's delay in me processing this. But when I did, it was as though I had swallowed lead. Mum and Dad. Coming to visit. *Here?*

I looked around the plush furnishings of Silvia's drawing room—the gilt-edged chair I was sitting on, the delicate scroll-leg writing desk by the window—and tried to imagine my parents imposing themselves upon it. Dad's Labrador-puppy enthusiasm, asking a dozen questions about everything, a jabbing finger in danger of knocking or breaking anything at waist height. Mum's jealousy thinly disguised as disdain. I couldn't let it happen.

The letter still clutched in my hand, I knocked nervously on Silvia's closed study door.

"*Pronto,*" her voice commanded from inside.

"*Salve,* Silvia." I used the formal "hello" instantly on my most courteous form. "You mentioned once, that if I ever need to use the telephone to call home…?" I twisted the paper back and forth along my fingers, forcing myself to make eye contact with her, to look pointedly at the old-fashioned rotary dial phone on her desk.

"Ah." It took her a moment to gauge the meaning behind my too-subtle request, but then she placed her bejeweled hands on the desk, surveyed the papers in between them. "Ah, yes.

Certo, of course you can. Give me just half an hour to finish this paperwork and then the room is yours."

I felt my heart flap against my chest as the international dial tone sounded, half praying for voice mail, but then there was a click, followed by Mum's heightened telephone voice: "Good afternoon. Bailey residence."

"Hi, Mum, it's me."

There was a pause as the penny dropped.

"Rachel? This is a nice surprise." I was taken aback by her pleasantness. "We thought that you'd forgotten us."

That was more like it.

"Sorry, Mum. It's been really busy here." The excuses flooded out of me. "I've barely stopped working, and it's been hard to get to the phone, and I…" I paused, breathed. It was pointless trying to appease her. "Anyway, how are you? I got Dad's letter. You saw Auntie Maureen? How was that?"

I was baiting her, knowing that nothing got Mum going like Dad's older sister.

"That busybody. You know what she's like. Didn't stop talking the entire time she was here. Poking her nose around the place trying to find fault with everything…"

"Mmm-hmm, mmm-hmm…" I made appropriate-sounding interjections, allowing Mum to get out the steam she had evidently been bottling up. "And how's Dad?" I finally asked, assuming she would understand what I was insinuating.

"Dad's fine. In the garden with his blooming roses… I'll get him for you, shall I?"

"It would be nice to say hello."

"Hang on." The line fell silent, and I thought she'd gone, but then I heard her breath on the line. "Everything all right there, by the way? You're enjoying yourself? Having a good time?"

"Yes, Mum." My mind explodes with a thousand different stories I could tell her, none of which she'd understand. "It's been...great."

There was a pause, and I thought for a moment she was going to press me further, but she must have thought better of it, because the next thing she said was, "I'll get him for you."

"Rachel!" What Mum lacked in enthusiasm, Dad made up for in spades, asking me a myriad of questions—how was the hotel, the weather, my Italian, the people? I let his familiar chatter wash over me with a surprising pang of homesickness, but when his questions began to thin, I knew I couldn't spool him out much longer.

"Dad...your letter...about coming to visit?" I pressed my lips together, knowing I just had to get it done. "I'm just not sure it's going to be feasible."

"Oh?" Across the distance, I pictured the pinch of his mouth, the way his beard twitched to the side when he encountered something unexpected.

"It's just that it's so busy here. I don't think I'd get any time to show you around. It seems so silly for you to come all this way and not see me. And you know how Mum hates the heat..."

"Oh. Oh yes, of course. It was just an idea. I was getting carried away with myself."

I'd disappointed him. I hated disappointing him. "No, no, it was a great idea! And I can't believe you managed to get Mum to agree to a flight! But look, Florence will always be here. Maybe we can do another trip, during one of the holidays? I can be your official guide, give you the full insider treatment."

"Sure, pal. Whatever you think's best."

"Great. Let's plan it." I bit my bottom lip. "I...I've got to go, but I'll write back soon? It was honestly so nice to hear from you!"

"Sure, kiddo. Look after yourself."

"Thanks, Dad. You too." I swallow loudly. "Love you."

"You too."

I was grateful when I heard Silvia's soft knock on the door, pulled my fingers away from where they had been keeping the phone handle warm.

"*Tutto bene*, Rachel?" she asked cautiously, jarring my name with hard consonants as always—she never would master the English *ch*.

"Yes." I smoothed my palms over the waistband of my skirt. "Yes, Silvia. Everything is fine. Only…" I faltered, the idea that had been percolating in my mind forcing me to seize the opportunity, no matter how awkward I felt. "I was wondering if there would possibly be any more work for me to take on…" I looked down at my feet. "Paid work…?"

I glanced up at her from beneath the protective curtain my hair had formed, saw the shade of displeasure cloud her features. Silvia hated talking about money.

"I apologize, do you not feel your position here is very fair?"

"No, no, that's not it at all." I was mortified; I wished at that very moment one of Silvia's antique chandeliers would fall from the ceiling, struck me clean on the head. "You have been so, so generous, with the room and all the food I could eat…it's just that there are other expenses that seem to be adding up, and if there is a way that I could meet those while providing you with some extra help, that would be wonderful."

A playful smile blossomed across Silvia's features. "Ah. Being friends with Diana is an expensive habit."

I blushed, nodded.

"Well, I admire your entrepreneurial spirit." She walked

across the room, set the papers she had been holding down on the desk and leafed through them. "And there is one thing you can do." She held out one of the sheets of paper. It was a bill. The name across the top said Lavanderia Vardi. "This is what I am currently paying Signor Vardi each week to clean all the hotel bedding. If you can do that yourself, here, for half the cost, you have yourself a deal."

I did the maths: for half of what Vardi was charging Silvia, it would take me just over three weeks to pay back my credit card. But after that, everything else I earned would be mine.

I gave Silvia a smile and held out a hand, something of her businesslike manner rubbing off on me.

"Va bene," I said, as she shook it. "It's a deal."

And so it began: each morning, before Diana or anyone else was up, I would go down to the laundry room, collect yesterday's dirty linen and set it to wash. When the cycle was finished, I would take the armloads of wet cotton to the small courtyard around the back of the main house and pin it carefully to the washing line, letting it dry in the thick summer heat. Before bed, no matter how late it was, how long my shift had been or how much I had been drinking with Diana, I would round up the dried sheets, fold them carefully and place them back in the laundry room, ready to use.

I thought Diana was none the wiser. It wasn't that I lied to her, exactly, more that I omitted to mention my new "job promotion." But of course, being Diana, she noticed everything.

We were perched on the buttress of the Ponte Santa Trìnita, idly watching the slither of tourists as they processed over the Ponte Vecchio in their predictable ouroboros loop: just a hiss over the bridge to admire the Palazzo Pitti before slinking back to the safety of the historic center, never daring to venture into the wild, untamed Oltrarno. Beneath us, the languid smoke-green waters of the Arno barely moved, and its stillness brought us a sense of calm as I tried desperately to wrap my head around the *futuro anteriore* tense in my thick Italian grammar book. Diana lay beside me, reading the imported *Vogue* she'd procured at vast expense from the English bookshop on Via delle Oche. Silvia had warned us that morning that these days of enjoying each other's company freely were limited— as the villa swelled with summer visitors, it would mean all hands on deck, breaks taken alone and in strict shifts—and so for now, we were making the most of our companionship.

Diana lay on her stomach, expensively faded jeans shielding the backs of her legs from sprouting any more of what she referred to as her "hideous freckles," her hair falling over her back like a cocker spaniel's mane. Absentmindedly, I found my fingers reaching to pluck a curl of it, stroking its softness, when I felt her grasp hold of me, pull my arm toward her eyeline.

"What's up with your hands?"

"Nothing. What do you mean?" Reflexively, I grabbed my hand back, shielding it from her, but she pushed herself up on her forearms, wriggled into a seated position and held out her palm impatiently.

"Let me see." I reluctantly held the offending hands out, not quite meeting her eye. "Ugh, Rachel, they're *gross*."

I peered down at them and had to admit that she was right. It had hardly been that long, but the constant exposure to industrial bleach and water had turned the skin dry and pink, the nails chipped from wringing out ten bedrooms' worth of sheets, pillows and towels by hand. Held in Diana's faultless French-manicured fingers, they looked like an ogre's.

"They're just a bit dry," I mumbled, letting them go limp against her. "I'll buy some hand cream."

"But from what?" she pressed. "Hands don't suddenly go all dry and cracked like that. What have you been doing?"

"Nothing." I tried to snatch my hands back, defensiveness creeping into me, but she held firm.

"You're lying to me." She leaned into me, forcing me to look at her. I couldn't help but notice the instant coldness that colored her tone. "Friends don't lie to each other."

She knew just how to get me, phrasing it like that. "I've been doing the laundry for Silvia." Embarrassment constricted my throat, made my voice small, tight. "In the mornings, before our shift."

Diana's nose wrinkled like it did whenever one of the *zingari* women came too close. *"Why?"*

I sighed. Despite my subtle hints, despite the painfully obvious disparity between Diana's wealth and mine, the subject of money had never been discussed openly between us. How could Diana ever understand the need for an extra thirty-five pounds a week when for her it was the equivalent of finding loose change down the back of the sofa? "Di." I took my hands from her, pressed the palms together, feeling the rough skin more keenly now that she had cast her eyes over it. "I'm not like you."

"How do you mean?" She said it sweetly, but I couldn't help but wonder if she was really that obtuse, or whether there was something lurking playfully in the corners of her eyes that suggested she just wanted me to say it.

"I...I need the money." My skin prickled in the still air. The buttress seemed smaller than it had when we first sat down, and I had a dizzying sensation of overbalancing, my body falling into the brackish waters below. "The dinners, the trips... I love them all, but I can't afford it like you can. My parents are... It's not like with you—I can't just be nice to them and hope they send me a check. I'm on my own."

Diana rolled onto her back, hair fanning onto the rock beneath her, every inch the siren.

"I can't *bear* talking about money." She groaned, mussing fingers through the tendrils at her temples. "It's the stupidest thing in the world."

"That's easy for you to say, when you have loads of it."

If Diana noticed the snub, she gave me the benefit of ignoring it.

"It seems so ludicrous, me sitting here doing what I like when I like, and you having to scrimp and save for every morsel of food you put in your mouth."

"Well, I wouldn't say it's quite—"

"No, listen." Diana reached out for my arm, pulled me to her so that we were lying beside one another, gazing up at the limpid blue sky. "You're my friend. I want you to be happy, because it makes me happy. I want to be able to enjoy this summer, and I'll be miserable if I think I'm forcing you to do things you don't want to do. So, whatever you want, just ask."

"Di, you can't be serious…" I tried to sit up, but she wrapped herself around me, holding me close so that my head rested in the crook of her narrow shoulder.

"Honestly. Think of it as yours. It's only money. Silly, silly money. Fun is much more important."

"Diana…"

"Shush. I won't hear another word about it. I'm not joking— if you mention it again, I'll be very angry."

Chastened, I obeyed.

I didn't like taking money from Diana. And I couldn't bring myself to outright ask for it. But somehow all the same I found myself the recipient of her gifts. A round of drinks on her. A dress she saw me fingering in a shop that wound up boxed and wrapped in tissue paper on my bed the next day. Reaching in my pocket to pay for a cappuccino, I'd feel the rough edge of a banknote tickling my fingers, hear Diana's tinkling voice telling me not to worry about the change. I kept doing the laundry for Silvia until I had paid my credit card off in full, but then told her as obscurely as I could muster that it was becoming too much work, offering to go to Signor Vardi myself to repair their relationship.

And although I didn't like to admit it, there was something so nice about not having to worry over money. To see a bill arrive at the table and not involuntarily hold my breath. So, if Diana asked me to do the odd little thing for her—take on her early shift, pick up her dry cleaning, walk a package into town to be posted—how could I possibly say no?

Diana already had me by the heart. Now, she had me by the purse strings. And I was too grateful—or, perhaps, too blind—to think that there was anything wrong.

15

Now

The noise of the school is distinct even before I round the corner. A swell of small, shouting voices; the soft clock of balls ricocheting off a surface; the occasional shout or tinny whistle of a teacher. As I approach, the voices take on form, spill out of the school—a handsome Victorian town house suffocated by ivy—and fall into the waiting arms of their designated adults, smelling of waxy crayons and craft glue and that sticky, milky residue that seems to emanate from all children.

My heart beats a little faster as I scan the crowd for her, and I cocoon myself tighter in my camel coat, stroking its softness for reassurance. I spot the boys soon, their features familiar from Diana's profile picture even if her unmistakable genes hadn't given them away. I watch them, skinny limbs stuffed into puffer jackets, faces just visible beneath matching knitted beanies, the same pale tone as hers, and try to blend into the flurry as I follow their path.

"I'm not sure we've met?" A woman in patterned running leggings and a tailored black gilet nudges me. "Which one's yours?"

"Oh." I'm caught off-balance, trying not to look directly into her black-lacquer-rimmed eyes. "I'm just helping out a friend."

"How nice!" She gives me a smile while simultaneously waving into the crowd and collecting a girl with long brown plaits by the wrist. "Which one?"

"Ah...there she is." I point abstractly into the distance and for some reason give her a salute. "Sorry, got to run."

I lose myself deeper in the scrum, look back with relief when I see that the woman is distracted enough by the painting her child is holding aloft to forget all about me, and then home in once more on the boys. The older one waves, grabs his younger brother and makes off down the wide stone steps toward the pavement. I whip around, saliva drying in my cheeks at the very thought of her being so suddenly in such proximity. But when they reach their descent, I see it's not her they're greeting at all but a small Asian woman, clutching the handle of a pram whose insides just betray the pink T-bar shoes of a snoozing toddler. She silently doles out juice cartons and apples from the underbelly of the pram as the boys gyrate around her, replaying their day in animated mime.

The nanny. Of course it's the nanny.

I find myself compelled to move as they do, hugging the inside of the pavement and keeping enough people between them and me that no one could possibly notice anything untoward. They make their way to the main road and onto a bus where I stand near the front, keeping the corner of the pram in my peripheral vision, and when they're off, I follow a few steps behind, finding myself compelled to pick up my phone and make a pretense of tapping at the locked screen and then holding it to my ear.

"Yes, I'm just off the bus," I say to the silence. "I'll be a few minutes."

The streets widen here, explode with cherry trees that in spring will burst into blossoms but are now mere carcasses, dark limbs twisting over me as I follow the nanny around the corner and onto an avenue of grand pastel-painted town houses. She stops outside one, a wide semidetached painted a pristine duck-egg blue—*Only a semi, Diana darling? How very non-U*—pulls a plastic packet of wet wipes out from underneath the pram and proceeds to wipe down all three children. A tank of a black Range Rover sits in the drive—"Chelsea tractors," Dad calls them—and I try to picture Diana's slender arms resting on the steering wheel. I dawdle for a moment too long, watching the child-washing spectacle play out, and suddenly feel the nanny's eyes on me, her wipe poised over sticky fingers.

"Hello?" I speak very deliberately into my phone. "Yes, I'm a couple of streets away. Sorry, Google Maps is playing up."

Satisfied, she continues, eyes back down, and I scuttle away, cross the street, but not before a chorus of mewls pipe up—"Muuummmyyy!"—and I grind to a halt, dart toward a tree trunk and watch, unobserved.

The front door opens and there she is, Diana in the flesh, somehow more lovely and more perfect than I anticipated. She's dressed entirely in black—sheer polo neck, tight jeans—and the effect is stark against her skin, the auburn hair pulled into a neat ponytail. On anyone else it would look harsh, goth, but on her it serves to enhance her elfin features more.

My moment has arrived. The whole purpose of this day,

the whole reason I've crossed cities, sacked off my day's plans, is just a few feet away.

I clench my fist, ready my body to step forth. And... And I can't move.

I want so badly to go over there. I want so badly to storm over to her, rip that pretty ponytail loose and thrust Sebastian's letter into her face, demand of her the answers to the questions I've been forming in my mind since I left Ascot this morning.

And yet.

I also want to soften into her embrace, like the children who now cling to her limbs, tell her how I have missed her, stroke her hair and see her smile at me like she used to.

And I know I can't do either. Because I look at her—really, really look at her. Framed by the doorway of her perfect house, her perfect life. And then I look down at myself. And a little well of sick starts to form in my gut. The coat, which had seemed so impossibly glamorous, now looks tawdry, highlights the inadequacies of the clothes—the person underneath. Whether I am here to tell her I love her or hate her, the reality is she doesn't need me, want me or fear me. Whatever I have to say to her will be less significant than a fly buzzing in her ear. I can't do this. Not yet.

And I feel myself backing away. Not breathing fully until the door clicks shut and Diana's face disappears from view, any chance encounter wiped fully from my mind. I dolefully retrace my steps, ignore the smirk of the sales assistant as I return the coat.

We can both hear the tremble in my voice when I tell her I've decided it's not quite my coloring.

On the train home, I hurl abuse at myself, using words to cut into my core, because I am too much of a coward to actually take knife to flesh. A seat becomes free at Twickenham, and I pick up the discarded *Metro* to distract myself. The pages are a blur of light political scandals and celebrity gossip, but then I catch sight of a picture, *his* picture, and I stop myself.

Freed Florence Killer to Give First Interview

In the photograph he looks weary, trying and failing to hide his face from the zoom of a lens. Stubble dots his cheeks and chin, and he looks grayer, somehow, in skin and hair. But there's something in his eyes too, something discernible even through the distance and the cheap ink of the paper. Something only someone who has stared into that face as many times as I have over the past twenty years would notice. A conviction. A determination. And somehow, even though I know it's not possible, I feel as though he's staring directly at me.

It's an expression that tells me I haven't heard the last of Sebastian Hale.

Which means Diana hasn't heard the last of me.

16

Then

Our two was becoming a three: Diana, Sebastian and me. Sebastian began to spend more of his time over at the Villa Medici, lounging in the kitchen with Silvia, reading under the shade of a tree or swimming languid laps of the pool as Diana and I bustled about, resetting sunbeds or taking orders for cold drinks. I like to think that he sought out our company—my company specifically—but I also think he was lonely. Friends petered out, and there was no sign of his family—in fact, he barely mentioned them. The two of us were still nothing more than platonic, but I couldn't help holding on to the conviction that all he needed to do was see me in the right light, and then he would realize what he had been missing.

Under Diana's tutelage, I tried with renewed zeal to evolve myself into the type of girl Sebastian would admire. I was a quick study, and her sharp tongue—"It's ba*th*room, not ba*f*-room, and don't call it that anyway. It's the loo or the ladies' room"—soon honed my speech. A combination of penury and observing Diana's birdlike eating habits saw the fat melt off me like a hot knife through butter, and I was soon following her to the local tailor to have my uniform nipped in, so that it moulded to my newly lean, tanned body like a second skin. I would sometimes catch myself in the midst of a mannerism—a particular shake of the head or flick of a wrist—and find myself hard pushed to tell if it was something I had always done or if it was a new, affected Diana-ism. Like the well-worn mouth of the bronze *Porcellino* statue, my old self was being buffed away, and I wasn't sorry to see it go.

If Silvia noticed, it was with approval. Not long after I had had my uniform taken in, she stopped me in the corridor—I was pushing a trolley full of towels, and those little bottles of shower gel and shampoo our affluent guests always stole—took my chin in her hands and tilted it to the light streaming through one of the French windows, noticing, I am sure, the new lipstick I was sporting, a dusky rose shade called Kiss Me Quick that Diana said would bring out my coloring.

"Italy suits you, Rachel."

"Thank you, Silvia." As much as I sought her approval, I wasn't sure I liked this level of scrutiny. Could she tell that it was all Diana's doing, that underneath I was still the plain old Rachel I had always been? Or, worse, could she see through to my innermost core, know that my ultimate desire was the heart of her beloved godson?

Carla, queen of the acid retorts, took to calling me *l'ombra*—but whether she meant that I was Diana's shadow or merely the shadow of my former self, I couldn't say. And in any case, I didn't feel like a shadow. If anything, I felt more alive than ever before, burning brightly with my own possibility.

And with Sebastian, it was maybe, possibly, beginning to have an effect.

"You look nice," he'd started to say, when we met at one of the bars that lined the Oltrarno, or popped over to Villa Allegria during a break, a quick respite from the madness of Silvia's. "Have you worn that before?" He'd incline his head, looking at something which, mere weeks ago, would have been manhandled into a drawer, but was now washed and folded neatly, hung differently on me, better.

He treated me differently too—pulled out chairs for me, raced ahead to open doors. And I responded to it—much as it shames me now to admit it—allowed myself to be reshaped into the manifestation of the weaker sex because I saw how it flattered his ego. Without hesitation, I handed him jars to open I knew a flick of my wrist would undo. Listened patiently as he explained the notes of a particular bottle of wine—"Cherries, yes, you're right, I get that too"—when I'd seen it said it on the back of the bottle. When looking down a menu, I'd allow a little frown to creep across my face, bat my eyelashes at him demurely—"What do *you* think, Sebastian? The gnocchi, or the penne?"—although whichever one I chose, I "couldn't possibly" finish it all, and would offer him my half-empty plate, hand on my vanishing stomach, simpering smile on my face. I was learning a valuable life lesson that would carry me long into adulthood: to grow a man's heart, a woman must often shrink her brain.

Toward the end of June, Silvia closed the Villa Medici to go back to Milan. The trip coincided with the Feast of St. John, a public holiday celebrating Florence's patron saint that involved parades, fireworks and the final match of a traditional Florentine sport, *calcio storico*, that I learned was like a particularly aggressive mixture of rugby and football, with the historic center's four major neighborhoods—Santa Croce, Santo

Spirito, Santa Maria Novella and San Giovanni—competing for victory.

"I hate it." Silvia gave a shudder of displeasure when she announced the closing dates to us before the breakfast service. "Everyone gets drunk. The city is full of tourists. It's a mess."

How exactly all this would cause her disruption up in the hills I wasn't sure, but I got the impression that it simply affected her sensibilities, or rather, that she was getting quite restless in Florence, and found it the convenient excuse she needed to retreat to her fashionable urban home. I was glad for her that the *pensione* was merely a passion project, because I was sure any sound business owner would be hiking up prices, cashing in on the key occasion, rather than shutting up shop. But that was Silvia for you.

The Feast of St. John fell on a Thursday, and Silvia planned to be gone from early on Thursday morning until Friday night, leaving Diana and me at a loose end for nearly two full days. Diana, who was growing frequently more jaded with the minutiae of service life, was delighted.

"As soon as she's gone, I'm taking a sunbed into the shade and I'm not getting up again until Saturday." She stretched languorously, her body slinking in the air. "You can bring me breakfast on a tray, and I'll pretend I'm a guest."

I laughed nervously, not entirely sure she was joking. "Don't you want to see everything that's going on in the center?"

"Ugh, *no.*" She wrinkled her little nose, and for a second she reminded me of Silvia. "All those people? It sounds hideous. Nope, I'm staying here. You can go if you like." A conspiratorial smirk crossed her face. "Why don't you ask Sebastian?"

We met in the afternoon, to give enough time for the initial wave of crowds to disperse. The *calcio storico* had already been canceled—as apparently it often was—broken up by riot police after one of the players punched the referee and the whole thing descended into a forty-man brawl. We walked past the abandoned pitch in the shadow of Santa Croce where the ghosts of barriers and ranked seating remained, and scoured the ground, Sebastian convinced he could see flecks of blood on the concrete. After, we wandered to a little gelateria on Via dei Neri that Sebastian said had always been his favorite, animatedly convincing me that the pistachio *cremino*, a ricotta ice cream with swirls of pistachio butter running through it, was "out of this world." He insisted on paying, and then the two of us strolled in near silence toward the river, and I allowed myself to romanticize that we were on a date. It was so rare for us to be alone together like that.

The ice cream melted quickly in the heat, dribbling white liquid down the cone and over my fingertips, which the old me would have sucked off but the new me dabbed at delicately with a napkin, until I heard an indignant "Oh *crap*," and turned to see the ball of Sebastian's ice cream on the pavement beside him, a thick line of cream snaking its way down his blue polo shirt. He was holding his hands and the now-empty cone aloft, looking almost pitifully at the ball melting into a puddle on the hot concrete, his shoulders frozen as if not quite sure what his next move should be.

I laughed involuntarily and he pouted, his lower lip jutting out in a way that was both comical and adorably childlike.

"Not fair," he whined, craning his chin toward my cone. "Give us some of yours, then."

I slung my body away from him, playing along, swerving his sticky hands reaching for me.

"No chance, mister. It's not my fault you can't eat your ice cream like a grown-up."

His hand came out of nowhere, batting the skin just above the crook of my thumb and forefinger, and suddenly my cone wasn't in my grasp at all, but on the ground beside me.

"If I'm not having any, you can't either."

"Hey!" Laughter still circled the edges of my voice but petered out quickly, and I couldn't help a slight feeling of alarm. Something in his manner was reminiscent of a spoiled child used to getting things his own way, the same child who knew the maids would always be there to clean up after him.

We both stared in silence at the ice cream puddling at our feet. I was vaguely aware of the tourists battling past us, but more so my body started to attune itself to our proximity on the narrow path; to his hands resting just inches away from my shoulders, the smell of sticky sugar milkiness on his breath, even the slight film of cream that clung to the fine hairs on his upper lip. And there was something else too. A shift in atmosphere. A subtle change in the air between us that made the blood rush to my ears. And then somehow, without my conscious mind being party to the decision, I reached up on tiptoes and kissed him clean on the mouth.

His fingers latticed through my hair, holding me softly by the back of my neck as he held me close, kissed me back. But almost as quickly as he was touching me, he pulled himself away from me, gasping for air as our lips broke apart.

"Rachel, stop." He ran a hand through his hair, shuffled awkwardly on his feet.

Shame instantly flooded through me in a surge of heat and I turned away, trembling.

"Sorry. I shouldn't have… It was stupid of me."

My napkin was still clutched in my hand and I wiped my fingers zealously, although, like my humiliation, the residue of ice cream remained.

Unable to look at him, I heard Sebastian blowing air through his cheeks. I waited.

"No. Don't. Don't be silly. Don't apologize. I really like you, Rach. I just don't want to ruin our friendship, y'know?"

He tried to touch my shoulder, but I stiffened up. His tone may have been intended as a tonic, but his words were not.

We walked on in silence, the ice cream forgotten.

The afternoon passed as a distraction. We joined the crowds in Piazza della Signoria to watch the parade weave through the center, a steady thrum of drumbeats accompanying the procession of Renaissance costumes, tights and pantaloons in ruby red and emerald, and faux Ye Olde Times banners with gold crenellated edges hoisted into the air. We ate dinner in a trattoria just around the corner from the Uffizi—an unassuming local place hidden in plain tourist sight, heavy wooden tables pushed too close together, menu hand-scrawled on grainy yellow paper, a bottle of rough, stringent Chianti held in a straw flagon. We didn't talk about the kiss.

After, we watched the fireworks erupting over the Arno, illuminating the precarious buildings on the Ponte Vecchio and causing shimmers of colored lights to dance on the water's surface. Sebastian stood next to me but not touching, his head tipped skyward, joining in enthusiastically with the buoyant crowd, their claps and shouts of *"Forza! Forza! Brava!"* mingling with the staccato rhythm of the explosions. The memory of earlier rose inside me, compressing my chest, making my tongue feel thick and heavy in my mouth. I squashed it down, but a single tear escaped from the corner of my right eye and I turned into the crowd to smudge it fiercely away with the heel of my hand.

It was late when we returned to the Villa Medici. All the lights were off inside, but when we walked through to the garden, Diana was curled up on a wicker chair on the terrace, a single porch light casting a creamy glow over the book on her lap. On the table, a pair of portable speakers gave a tinny whine to Jewel's acoustic guitar. By her feet, a citronella coil was nearly burned through, a pile of soft gray ash forming underneath it. Next to it, a bottle of vodka was propped in a nearly melted bucket of ice. Diana liked her spirits neat, cold, low in calories.

She stretched when she heard us, craned her neck without fully committing to turning around. "I thought you two had skipped town and left me."

We tittered, but I thought it sounded forced, flat. I don't know whether Sebastian felt it too, but the sudden inclusion of Diana seemed to highlight the solitude of our day.

"Well, I've had a lovely time," she carried on into the silence, not noticing or not caring if the atmosphere seemed askew. "I stayed in bed till midday, then I read all my magazines, went for a swim, called some friends on Silvia's landline and had a nap. And now I'm quite pissed." She raised a glass in evidence. "I wish Silvia would go away every week."

"You'd be happy if Silvia was away every day, Di." Sebastian pulled out another seat around the table and took the neck of the bottle, releasing it from the bucket. Ice water dripped across the tabletop as he brought it to his lap. "Then you'd be able to justify the fact that you never actually do any work." He seemed buoyed, somehow, grateful to have Diana to direct his energies toward.

"That's so untrue!" From her fetal position, she tucked her leg into her chest and then jabbed it toward him. Her bare foot landed on his shoulder, toes ruby red and shiny. "Rachel, tell him how hard I work."

"She works really hard," I parroted, distracted. They both laughed, but I felt as though I had swallowed a heavy weight that now sat in the depths of my bowels, dragging me down. "I think I'm going to go to bed." The smell of vodka teased my nostrils, nauseated me. "I didn't realize how tired I was from walking around all day."

"Boring." Diana tutted. "Don't you want to stay and get drunk with me?"

"Not tonight." I squeezed her shoulder. "Sorry."

She shrugged. "Suit yourself."

Sebastian fiddled with the bottle, rolling it over in his hands. "I might stay for one." He didn't look at me.

Diana snatched the bottle back from him, uncapped it. "Great. Company. Grab a glass from the kitchen." If she sensed a current underpinning the medicinal scent of citronella, she said nothing.

"Well…good night." I shifted my weight but made no move to go. I craved some sign, some indication from Sebastian that all would be well. And at last, there it was. He touched me lightly on the upper arm—barely a whisper of a caress— looked up at me, smiled.

"Good night, Rachel. Thank you for a lovely day."

I woke, dragged from the pit of heavy sleep, and thought it must be morning. But when I groped for the watch on my nightstand, the glow of numbers in the half light from the window told me I'd only been asleep for an hour, two at most. Thirst pounded a pain in my temples. I'd eaten too much, more than I'd meant to—tearing salty, viscous hunks from the bloody *bistecca fiorentina* and swallowing without chewing to better fill the emptiness inside me—and drunk too much red wine, the remnants of bitter tannins sucking the moisture from my gums. I reached for the glass on my nightstand and, finding it empty, stumbled out of bed in search of the bathroom, sleep still weighing on my legs like sandbags.

I resisted touching the light switch in the corridor, mindful of both the flood of electric light to my darkness-dulled senses and the risk of waking Diana from what was no doubt now a turbulent, drunken slumber. But when I tiptoed past her door, I saw that it was open, was surprised to hear a muf-fled groan coming from inside. I froze, blushed, recognizing almost instantly the nature of those fecund, low moans, not wanting to be privy to whatever carnal pleasures she was en-acting inside. My body, however, had other ideas, and in my sick, twisted fascination—with Diana, with the most intimate parts of her I could not, could never reach—I looked.

Movement under the bedclothes. A corporeal writhing within the sheets, whose twists and turns elicited more cow-like lowing, heady farmyard grunts. My skin tingled, my nip-ples involuntarily peaking against the soft cotton of my T-shirt, and I knew that if I were to reach a hand down to touch the soft center where my thighs met, the flesh there would be hot, damp. A ragged breath caught in my throat, stale with my own self-loathing, and I forced myself to turn away, bathroom forgotten, as a limb emerged from under the covers, soft skin pale and sweet with the smell of exertion. And then another limb joined it—an arm—clutching blindly at the white sheets as a cry ripped from the body in unfettered ecstasy.

And then.

Then the corridor lurched around me.

I pressed my body against the coolness of the wall at my back, trying to breathe through the pain and horror as the re-alization battered me, waves rolling over a sinking ship.

Because there was not one body inside that bed, but two.

Two bodies.

Hers.

And Sebastian's.

17

Now

I have fallen into a doze, but the train pitches into a tunnel, jolting me awake, sending the newspaper flying to the floor. Sebastian's face lands upright on the industrial gray carpet.

"Nasty one, isn't he?"

It takes me a second to realize that the woman two seats down is talking to me.

"Sorry?"

She bends over and picks up the paper, holds it out to me. "That Sebastian Hale. Don't trust him as far as I can throw him. Eyes are too close together." She has lipstick on her teeth, vampiric smudges that glisten when she talks. "Can you believe he's never admitted he did it? And you know his family arc loaded? Rich people like that, they're always trying to get away with things, never take responsibility for their actions.

I'm glad, at least, that it hasn't been something he could buy his way out of, even with that fancy-pants lawyer."

I nod noncommittally, hoping to extract myself from the conversation, but she settles back in her chair and I can see she's just getting warmed up. She circles her arms around a pair of enormous breasts, hands not quite reaching to the opposite elbow, and nods triumphantly. "Saying that... Imagine if he was innocent? All those wasted years. I hope they make a documentary about it—Netflix or something—like that one... What was it called? *The Making of a Murderer.* Did you watch it?"

"You have lipstick on your teeth."

"Oh." She hovers an embarrassed hand over her mouth, searches in her bag for a compact and goes through the charade of grinning into it, chimp-like, rubbing at the red with the tip of her finger. "Thank you for telling me. My kids are always having a go at me about that. I really ought to get a lip liner."

"Pleasure." I unfold the newspaper definitively, blanking out Sebastian's features with a different tawdry sheet of black-and-white gossip. I feel the woman's eyes on me, searching for another line of entry, but eventually she gives up, pulls out her phone and speaks loudly into it.

"Hi, darling, are you home already? Yes, good girl. Can you do me a favor? Can you put the oven on to one-eighty? There's a chicken Kiev in the fridge. I'll grab some veg on the way home. I should be home in twenty..."

It's dark when I get home. I stand in the doorway and wash the flat with fluorescent white light. For ages I resisted switching to LEDs—I know they last longer, but I've always found the light so much more artificial than good old-fashioned halogen—but the living room ceiling has far too many bulbs in it for the electrics, so they were always blowing, and, well, when you don't have a man in your life…

LEDs it is.

I power up my laptop as a decanted tin of Heinz tomato soup whirs in the microwave. I'm not really hungry, but I know I will be later, and something about the routine energizes me.

I check my work emails as I eat the soup and am surprised to find barely anything of interest. Once I've deleted the junk mail and the chains I won't bother replying to—"Suggestions for the teachers' Christmas charity performance?"; You won't believe what one of the girls asked today"; "Whip round for Jennie's maternity leave gift"—I clear everything else before my spoon scrapes the bottom of the bowl. I don't really know what I was expecting; I'm hardly Scarlett Johansson.

I'm about to hit the *X* in the corner when the page automatically refreshes, and a new message blinks into my inbox.

When I see the sender's name, the blood freezes in my veins.

"Hale, Sebastian."

I don't want to, I don't want to, I don't want to. Even as I am thinking it, I am moving the cursor over the email, clicking it open.

Dear Rachel,

The face from the newspaper hovers into vision. I imagine him sitting at a desk in his parents' house, where they say he has retreated to, cracking his knuckles as he lays his fingers on the keys, begins to type.

Did you know that this is the first email I have written without supervision?

Imagine that: every letter you press, every word you form, watched over and approved.

I suppose, at least, it makes one learn to be more considerate about what one is going to say.

My internet skills are rudimentary, to say the least. The World Wide Web has come a long way since the AOL dial-up tone. But even a Luddite like myself can find a person's email address with a few clicks on Google and the wherewithal to work out the format of the Graybridge Hall email template.

Which is all a very roundabout way of saying, "Hello, Rachel."

Rachel, you haven't responded to my letter. To any of my letters, in fact.

Not that I expected you to: I know what was agreed during the first trial, I know what I—what my lawyers—promised. And I truly am sorry if I caused you undue stress or anxiety, but I am also sure you can appreciate the situation I was in. Have been in, until now.

But there are no lawyers anymore, Rachel. No trials. It's just me.

You may be wondering why it even matters anymore. I'm out, I'm free—why can't I just move on?

But I've lost twenty-one years of my life. Fuck it, not just those twenty-one years—do you think I can ever live a normal life again? Do you think I'll ever be able to walk down the road—despite the verdict, despite the fact that there was nothing concrete to even send me down in the first place—without the eyes of judgment upon me?

Don't you want to help me put things right?

I've always believed that you know something about that night, more than you've let on. I've always hoped that it was an accident—whatever it was, whoever (if anybody) was involved—but your silence makes me wonder toward the contrary. If there's anything you remember, anything that would just help me in any small way, don't you want the chance to do it?

You were my friend, once. Can't you find it in you to be so once again?

Yours,

Sebastian

My phone vibrates, sending shock waves across the countertop and making me jump.

A message from Alex:

Are you in tonight?

I look back at the laptop screen, the black letters of Sebastian's email almost three-dimensional against the blue light. Then I hover the cursor over the rubbish bin icon, and in a whoosh he disappears.

Yes, I type back before I change my mind. Come over? I move around the flat to clear up three days of debris: lasagna dish and empty bottles in the bin, wineglasses and plates in the dishwasher. The smell of old food still clings to the air, though, fetid and dank, and I hastily light a giant red Yankee candle—unused since my students cheerlessly presented it to me last Christmas—hoping the smell of synthetic cinnamon will disguise my pathetic solitude. The buzzer goes, and Alex breezes into the room, a bottle of wine under her arm.

"Leftovers, from the other night," she says, opening cupboards and helping herself to glasses and a bottle opener, probably more comfortable in this space than I am myself. "One of the advantages of having people over. Shame you didn't stay longer." The wine glugs merrily into the glasses. "Guy had the best gossip. A history teacher at Fairfax College is sleeping with one of her sixth-form students, and now she's *pregnant*." She hands me a glass and eases herself onto one of the stools by the counter—an area that was referred to with false charm by the estate agent as "the breakfast bar."

"No!" I play along, hitting just the right tone of scandal to fuel her on. Fairfax College is the boys' boarding school not too far from Graybridge, almost its equivalent in terms of exclusivity and fees. I realize I have barely spoken to anyone all day—the brief conversations I have had have been transactional at best. It makes me think of Sebastian, always so sociable, never enjoying being left with his own company; did he ever have friends in there, people he could talk to? What does a convicted murderer find to chat about, day to day? The weather? I take a large gulp of wine, tune back into Alex's monologue.

"…so, I get Guy's point—the kid's eighteen, so at the end of the day they're both adults—but I still think it's unethical. I mean, if the genders were the other way around, and it was a male teacher and a female student, can you *imagine* the fuss that would be made…? Rachel? Don't you think?"

She's looking at me, eyes fiery with the delicious horror of it, and I realize that the interjections I have been making to what I assumed were hypothetical questions weren't good enough. Social cues—not always my strong suit.

"Sorry. Totally." I reach into my mind, try and find something she'll snatch hold of. "It's abusing a position of power."

"Right?" And I know I've got her. Alex hates any sort of miscarriage of justice. She works for a bathroom company, designing luxury bathrooms for all the big houses in Sunningdale, South Ascot and the like; one sob story about a messy divorce or planning permission gone wrong and she's handing out discounts and free services like sweets. "Not to mention all the additional time and attention the student will have been getting compared to his classmates." She takes a swig of wine, babbles on. "Picture the pillow talk. 'Oh baby, that was the best I've ever had. Yes, of course I'll read over your essay another time.' Got anything to nibble on? I'm really peckish."

It takes me a split second to realize this last bit isn't part of her bedroom fantasy.

"I think there are some Doritos in the cupboard, and there

might be some salsa in the fridge unless it's gone bad... I'll check."

I rummage around the back of the pantry and unearth the Doritos, previously opened but sealed with a plastic clip so probably not stale, and deposit them in a bowl. The salsa, I see upon opening it, has a bloom of green mold on the top, just a couple of green spots forming there like a scabbed knee. I chuck the whole jar, lid on, into the bin under the sink.

"Who's that?" Alex asks, as I replace the laptop with the bowl of crisps, unwittingly jogging the screen saver off and jolting the computer into life.

For a horrific instant I think I haven't deleted Sebastian's email after all, but then I realize it's switched back to the internet, to Diana's Facebook page.

"Oh, just an old friend, from the summer before uni."

"She's gorgeous."

I swallow. "Mmm."

"Is she our age? How the fuck does she look like that?"

"Yup. Older, actually. Just a year, though." I rub my fingertips at the top of my temples, where hair and skin meet. I can feel the throb of a headache forming. Sebastian's email made me momentarily forget her, but now Alex's attention refocuses her, makes me uncomfortable. "Sorry...are you not friendly with her anymore? Doesn't sound like you like her much."

Alex takes a crisp from the bowl. I hear the crunch of it in her back teeth, watch the fine spray of orange additives deposit themselves in the corner of her mouth until they are transferred to the back of her hand with an unselfconscious wipe. And I can't bear the idea of her feeling sorry for me. Because, of course, if she knew that Diana and I weren't friendly anymore, Alex would guess instantly that it would have been *she* who ghosted *me*. How on earth could it be the other way around? So I find myself saying, "Oh yeah, we're still really close—we see each other all the time."

I am sure Alex can hear the lie—there's something in my voice, too high-pitched, too stilted, that rings untrue. I sense the mental eyebrow raise, even if there's not one there to witness. And yet I carry on.

"I was with her today actually. Popped down to London to see her. She lives in Notting Hill. Met her at the kids' school—she's got three. They're adorable—look." My fingers find the laptop keys, scroll distractedly down to the picture I found before. "They love me—call me Auntie Rach." An alternative vision of the day forms in my mouth faster than I can think it. "We took them to this patisserie Di and I love, got them jacked up on sugar. I think that's why I'm so tired." I bleat a laugh. "Had those little monsters crawling over me all day. Actually—" I rise from where I've been bent over, elbows resting on the counter "—you know, I think I'm more knackered than I realized, and I have a ton of emails to get through. I sort of bunked off for the day. Don't tell anyone! Would you mind if we called it a night?"

I watch the lines on Alex's forehead pinch together, her fingers tighten around the stem of her half-drunk wineglass.

"Oh…yeah, sorry." She takes a large gulp of her drink and gathers herself to stand. I hear the pulse of her throat, swallowing. "Didn't mean to keep you late."

"It's nice that you're still so close with your old friend," she says from the doorway, as I wait with one hand on the frame. "You should invite her down from London sometime. You could have a dinner party—you know you always say you'd like to…" In a flash I see her assessing the room, which, although now tidy, is not set up for guests. "I could lend you my table and chairs."

"You know, that's a really good idea. Thank you." I give her shoulder a squeeze, hoping the gesture of complicity will dissipate the weird atmosphere that has now descended. "And her husband, James, although he's normally working late, proper City boy. I'll give her a ring tomorrow and find some dates that work. Of course, you should come too—I'd love you to meet them."

"Great!" Alex smiles at me warmly, gives me a little wave. "Let me know if you're at a loose end this weekend. There's a play I fancy seeing in Windsor."

"Sounds good—definitely—text me the details."

With the door shut safely behind me, I finish my glass of wine, Alex's too.

I can almost picture it, the alternative day I conjured so vividly, like fragments of a ghostly dream. I'd met her at the school gates, the informal hug of a short reunion. *There they are!* I'd spotted the boys before her, given them a wave as they'd clambered down the stone steps. *It's Auntie Rachel!* And then we'd wended our way down the back streets, Diana taking the stroller, me with one of each of the boys' hands in mine, reminding them to look both ways as we crossed the road. We'd walked past the boutique and Diana had nodded toward the coat in the window—*That would look great on you, Rach*—and I'd responded with a shrug: *I've been in there before, the sales assistant is a complete bitch (sorry, boys). Wouldn't buy anything from her if you paid me.* In the café, the boys had jostled for seats in the corner, elbowing their way out of their puffer jackets, and I'd held both hands out in reassurance—*No, no, let me*—returning with a tray of sticky buns for the kids and strong skinny macchiatos for me and Di, which one of the boys nearly knocked over the instant I set it down, but which I quickly saved and righted. *It's always so nice to see you*, Diana had said to me, after a stern but loving word to the perpetrator. *I wish you'd move to London, so we could do this more often.* And I'd ruffled a mop of red hair, given its little freckled owner a kiss on the top of his head. *I'd love to, especially if it meant seeing more of my godsons, but you know how much my career means to me...*

It takes me a moment to come down from this high, so warm, so cosy am I in this portrait of friendly conviviality. When I do, the lights of the flat feel more sterile than ever, as though mocking my solitude, and I flick them off, plunging the room and the fantasy into darkness.

I can't help taking a final look at her, though, before I go to bed. Five new comments.

"You see, Diana, how nice it could be?" I stroke the screen, picturing the silky feel of that red hair, the musky smell of the rose perfume she always wore. "Even Sebastian said it—we were friends, all of us. We could still be friends, you and I. Just like the old days."

The laptop is warm on my upper thighs, the engine fan whirring from where it rests on top of my duvet cover, making me feel drowsy.

"It was all I ever wanted, to be friends with you." My eyelids grow heavy and I know I should move the laptop to the side, go to sleep, but before I do, the thought enters my head: *Would it do any harm?*

I think of Sebastian's email, extinguished but unforgotten.

Why should she be allowed to carry on in this blissful ignorance, when I'm not?

I reach a finger to the mouse pad, move the cursor across the screen to the silhouetted head and shoulders, the two simple words next to it: "Add Friend."

Click.

18

Then

I was paralyzed against the wall of the corridor. Inertia trapped me between slamming open the bedroom door, flooding the overhead light upon their seedy indiscretions, or running back to my room, pressing the cool pillow over my head, trying to rub the vision out of my eyes, the crude sounds of their love-making from my ears.

My trip to the loo had been forgotten, but now I was scorched with thirst, desperate to drown the emotions that swirled around my body. I continued on, half hoping the sound of my footsteps would disturb the lovers, but made it to the bathroom door unhindered. Inside, I resisted the urge to turn on the light switch, preferring instead the chalky blue half-light that washed over the tiles from the unshaded window.

I was still holding the glass in my right hand, my fingers

wrapped limply around it, and I filled it—once, twice—letting the metallic tang snake down my gullet as the beginnings of a headache clenched dully at my temples.

I wanted to cry.

I looked at myself in the bathroom mirror, head and shoulders framed like a pitiful rendition of a Renaissance portrait, willed the tears to come, but despite the excess liquid that now filled my body, my eyes were dry.

I considered berating myself. My dullness. My unattractiveness. My charmless behavior earlier that day, the thought of Sebastian's rejection coming to me, fresh as a paper cut. But what would be the point?

Sebastian and Diana. It was inevitable, wasn't it? Whatever I did, whoever I tried to be. Even before Elio's warning that day at the beach, a part of me had always known it to be true.

Young and rich and attractive, falling in love under the Tuscan sun—the story wrote itself. The universe had plucked their stars in the sky and played them together in perfect harmony; there was no place for my discordant note in their love story.

I stumbled back to bed and collapsed numbly into a tuneless sleep.

I woke with a start, air surging into my lungs as I gasped for life, convinced I had slept hours into the day, but when I looked at the clock, it was only seven. I dressed, tried my best to avoid looking at Diana's room as I went past it to the bathroom, but noticed the door was now closed, silence from inside.

In the lemony morning light, I breathed in the quiet of the empty villa, the gossamer-thin scent of pines and citrus trees that cleansed the air. Silvia wouldn't be back until the early evening, the first guests not due to arrive until the following morning. I had hours alone with my thoughts. With Diana and Sebastian. I padded into the kitchen and made a coffee, tried to leaf through one of Silvia's Italian romance novels in the guise of improving my Italian, but the words convulsed on the page, my eyes unable to still them. The coffee hit me in my core, creating a bubbling sourness that made my nose wrinkle, my lips pucker together. I pushed it aside. Waited.

Through the kitchen window, I watched her emerge from our building, step barefoot onto the lawn, the pads of her feet curling and uncurling over the blades of grass. She stretched, pulled at her dressing gown—a white cotton kimono patterned with hand-stitched green palms—and smoothed her fingers through her mussed hair. Did she smell of sex? Did she smell of him? I looked, my ears straining for the sound of him, wondering what the two would do when they found me here to confront them. But she was alone.

She came closer and my heart beat faster, waiting, watching, planning. She spied me through the window, waved with a trill of her fingertips, smiled, and in that moment, I hated her. Hated the kind way she looked at me, her tranquil movements as she minced toward the kitchen, oblivious to my knowledge. Knowing, from her gait, the ease of her features, that she thought she had escaped undetected.

"Morning." She stepped through the French windows, the epitome of bright and breezy. "How did you sleep?"

I swallowed, the saliva gummy in my throat, thoughts trapped in it like in a spider's web.

"Fine. You?" I managed.

"Hanging a bit." She mimed a guilty grimace, and I sought in her features some sign that this went below the surface, below merely the regret of alcoholic overindulgence. Her eyes were clear, passive. "Are you not drinking this?" She pointed to my espresso cup, cooling at the edge of the counter. I shook my head. "Great." She downed it with a hearty gulp. "What shall we do today, before Silvia gets back and ruins everything?"

★ ★ ★

I could have said something. Confronted her then and there. But to do so, I would have to have been a different sort of girl. We both would. And I was far too in awe of her, too pulled by the swell of her tide, to find the words I needed. So instead, I followed her, a child trying to catch a butterfly in their hands. Let her lead me like the dumb little sister I had allowed myself to become.

I remember once, when I must have been about six, playing in the attic when I stumbled across a box of some old baby clothes. I took them down to my room and dressed my doll in them—I had one I really loved, despite, or perhaps because of, the fact that her black hair was always matted, and she had one eyelid that was always stuck in a permanent stare. When Mum came to fetch me for dinner and saw the clothes, she went white, and then sort of purple, hauling me up by the wrist so the doll clattered to the ground beside me, shouting at me to put them back where I found them. I cried—I thought they were mine, didn't understand why she was being so mean. But they weren't mine; they were my brother's—Jason—the baby that didn't quite make it.

"Jason died when he was a baby. Before you were born. Now put them back where you found them and wash your hands for dinner."

It was the only thing she ever said about him, unsentimental creature that she is, and there's been little more that I've been able to prize from anyone else in the family, so he's always existed for me as this half-formed thing—my almost big brother—and I as a not quite little sister. Which I'm sure some therapist would unpack and say explains why I have gone through life seeking out an ersatz older sibling, why I was so happy to let Diana adopt that role.

It turns out that we did very little that was actually constructive for the rest of the day. And then Silvia came back and there was the villa to tidy, rooms to get ready, brass to be polished. But the evening eventually stilled, and as we walked back across the gardens to our rooms, the thought of going back in there with her—stepping into the same corridor where less than twenty-four hours before I had listened to the sounds of her betrayal—choked me, so that as I touched the cool metal door handle and felt its release in my hand, one word, one name, broke free from me.

"Sebastian."

"What was that?" Diana, oblivious behind me, touched my shoulder. It burned. I pulled away. All the hurt, all the anger that had been slowly building inside me all day, was threatening to erupt. And despite myself, a part of me was still too scared of losing her to let it free.

Tears scored my cheeks. I blinked them away, pressing my lips together so tightly I was sure I would cut the skin.

"I saw you last night."

Once the words were out, I felt a tremendous wave of release. It was no longer just mine now, this pain. She knew. She had to know.

Her face, as she processed this news, was like watching time-lapse photography on one of those nature documentaries—seasons passing, landscapes changing. And having spent as much time as I had reading those features, I could tell exactly what thoughts were running through her mind. There was indignation, lips puckered together; and embarrassment, the slightest pink blush overcoming her pale skin; and even an attempt at that haughty Diana pride, chin tilted, eyes narrowed, her birdlike shoulders tensed. But then she deflated, each twitch, each muscle on her face softening. And I felt a hand on my wrist.

"Rachel, I'm sorry."

Of all the reactions I had expected, this remorse, this gentleness, cut through me. And despite myself, I couldn't help feeling a tinge of regret. Despite what she had done, *I* somehow felt like the bad guy for exposing her.

"It's okay, Di." Wanting to comfort her. Wanting to take it back, to reverse time and pour the words back into my mouth.

"No, Rach. It's not." Tears pooled in her eyes and she brought a hand to her cheek. "I'm an awful person. The worst friend. How can you ever forgive me?"

"I…I do. I—" Her face crumpled into a mass of messy sobs, and I found myself stroking her shoulder, a calming susurration blowing from my lips. "Please, Diana, don't cry."

"I'm a terrible friend," she wailed, shaking her head. "I don't know why I do this. I self-sabotage. I drink too much and do stupid things. I think it's because of my relationship with my father. My therapist says I have issues with men and control. And now I've ruined our friendship, *and I don't even like him, Rach.*" She looked up at me mournfully, brown eyes surprisingly clear through her tears. "It was all such a terrible mistake."

"It's okay, Diana, it's okay." I was torn in two. Even as I took her in my arms, rubbing her back with the palm of my hands, some part of me—the part that sat telescopically watching from on high—was crying out at me to stop being so stupid. But I reveled in being the source of her comfort. I delighted in the way that, in my arms, her body quieted, and then stilled, resting her forehead against the crook of my shoulder. I felt the dampness of tears on my T-shirt, and when she pulled away, she left behind two black crescents where her mascara had smudged.

"And now I've ruined your top." She pouted pitifully, tears threatening to fall again.

I took a thumb to her cheek, wiped the remnants of the makeup from under her lids, feeling the soft smoothness of her skin.

"It'll come off. It's just a T-shirt." She gave me a weak smile. "We all do stupid things, Di. We all make mistakes. Besides, we're only young once—we should be experimenting, right?" I said this for her benefit but tried to believe it myself. "I know it wasn't malicious. I know it wasn't intentional. I promise I forgive you."

"Oh, Rachel." Diana sighed deeply, rested her back against the wall. "I promise you, I'll make it up to you. You're such a good friend. The best." As her fingers reached for the door handle, my stupid heart fluttered, felt light. "I honestly never meant it to happen. But Sebastian and I just get each other. We come from the same world. I'm sure you understand."

She closed the door without looking back. I was left in the corridor. Alone.

19

Now

It doesn't take me long to regret my trigger-happy actions. Once the glow of Diana's proximity has worn off, and my hopes for an eighties-movie montage-style reunion give way to the understanding that my foolish Facebook friend request has either gone unnoticed or been disregarded, I am cycling between embarrassment and horror before I've brushed my teeth.

I am consumed by her, though. And the fact that my attempt to see her was such a miserable failure only makes my need more palpable; a demon living inside me, demanding to be fed.

Instead, I fuel myself with whatever I can find of her online, memorize every picture she has uploaded, every update, every story. Christmas, birthdays, holidays—I salivate over each one, and it's as though I'm there for them all. Aperitifs in Cap Ferrat—I can feel the cool glass of Whispering Angel rosé in my hand, the bright ring as it clinks with hers. Christmas at her in-laws' Scottish pile, all of us in matching Archie Foal knitwear, surrounded by a pile of gift store–wrapped presents. Picnics in Holland Park, the edge of a Fortnum & Mason hamper just out of shot, me unfolding the tartan blanket, letting it float on the breeze before it flutters to a gentle rest on the grass.

Her life burns so brightly it gives me blisters, but I know I can't possibly go to her, the Rachel I am now. My visit to London made that clear. Just the thought of stepping over the threshold of her speckless home—me in my dowdy jeans, me a nothing teacher with split ends and a doughy midriff— triggers that same teenage desperation I felt so palpably that summer, that need to hone and tuck and tease and *Dianafy* myself.

I make a cup of coffee and drag myself back to bed, curtains still drawn, and scroll her pictures for inspiration, wincing into the lurid blue light of my laptop screen:

Another great sesh @FlashCycle Mayfair. Thank you, Donnie, for helping me keep it TIGHT!

Three hundred likes accompany a picture of a beaming Diana in patterned leggings and a figure-hugging racer back, not a single red hair out of place. I prod the white flesh peeking over the top of my pyjamas, google FlashCycle and learn it's some sort of cycling class, but from the thumping dance music emanating from the pulsating black home page, it looks more like a nightclub.

I haven't exercised in years, but the next morning I manage to dig out a pair of grotty old trainers from the depths of my closet, pull on a pair of leggings and an old T-shirt and stagger to Windsor Great Park. I'm out of breath in minutes, a stitch biting underneath my left ribs, and when I finally make it back to the flat, I crawl under the bedsheets and pass out fully clothed. The next day, barely able to walk, I sign up to the gym, where a tiny brunette with a T-shirt that says No Pain, No Champagne offers to give me a complimentary "PT session." It takes me a moment to realize that PT means Personal Training, and the thought of this tiny terror watching me red-faced and sweating all over the gym equipment makes me pause, until the thought of Diana's photo, only the merest blush on her cheeks signaling it was taken *after* a class, spurs me on.

"What do you want to work on?" the girl asks on the gym floor, hand resting on a perfectly toned hip.

I look down at my gray sweats. "Everything."

I wobble through the next hour, trying to keep up with the brunette and remember the difference between my lats and quads as she gives me a smile as perky as her tits and encourages me—"Come on, Rach…! Just *ten more*…! I know you've got it in you!"—each sentence punctuated with an exclamation mark. Afterward I vow never to return, but the next morning I step on the bathroom scales and see that I've lost half a pound; I find myself calling up the gym to book in ten more sessions. The alcohol goes next. I pour half-empty bottles of wine and gin and whiskey down the sink, their fumes intermixing like that awful forfeit from the drinking game I played as an undergrad, King's Cup, where everyone added a slug of whatever they were drinking to a communal glass, and the loser would end up having to drink it all to the tune of "Down it, Fresher!" I don't quite manage the vodka, though. I sneak the bottle into the back of the topmost shelf of the pantry, behind the tins of sweet corn and packets of microwave rice, and tell myself it's just for emergencies.

And then it's the diet. Out goes the lasagna, the late-night, essay-marking, takeaway-pizza "treats." I can't quite face the prospect of cooking everything from scratch, but I stock up on *Weight Watchers* magazines and calorie-counting books and start making what the cheery women holding up oversize jeans against their newly trim figures call "healthy choices."

Alex notices. We're in the pub where I'm nursing a vodka soda lime— the dieter's drink of choice—when she narrows her eyes at me.

"There's something different about you."

"How do you mean?" I bait, secretly pleased.

"I don't know. I can't put my finger on it, but you look… good." She cocks her head to the side, gives my face a long once-over. "Have you lost weight?"

I take a sip of my drink and hold the liquid in my mouth, enjoying the bubbles snapping against my tongue and cheeks as I let her assess me.

"Maybe a little," I say finally. "I thought it was time I took care of myself."

Alex perks up at that, pats me decisively on the wrist. "Good for you."

Each night in bed I enact the same ritual. First, I scan the news for updates on Sebastian, now officially sequestered at his parents' home, which I know from the *Daily Mail* is a 15.8-million-pound mansion in rural Sussex. When I am re-assured that there is no mention of me, I turn to Diana.

I soon exhaust the back catalog of her Facebook profile; it turns out she's not as frequent a poster as I had first thought. Instagram proves more fruitful, once I reinstall the app on my phone. I deleted it almost as soon as I downloaded it a few years ago, when I discovered that all people seemed to care about was posting pictures of food accompanied by a list of innocuous hashtags… I have no great craving in my life to know that Brian Johnson found his avocado toast "hashtagyum."

After a quick tap around the app, where I am spooked to discover that people will know if you've viewed their daily "stories," I set myself up with a completely new profile: bland, homogeneous, non-self-identifying. And from there, I lurk happily on Diana's page, the convenience of moving from laptop to mobile an added bliss, scrolling in a mesmeric cycle across the screen.

I map a rich picture of her life, like one of those spider diagrams they taught us to use for essay planning at school, branching out from her profile to that of her friends, the things they do, the places they visit, what they eat, what they wear, how they think, talk, feel. I know that Betsy has twin daughters and had long dark hair until she got "the mummy chop," and that it's just forty-one days until Cynthia goes to Barbados, "hashtagweightlossjourney," "hashtagleanandmean." I know that the first Wednesday of the month is girls' night out at the Electric Cinema, which a deeper dive tells me is one of those fancy cinemas with the leather seats and bars at the back, but that she's also into book group (love-love-LOVED *Eleanor Oliphant*, not so big a fan of the latest Scandi thriller), hot yoga and volunteering once a month at a nearby dogs' charity. She likes kale salads and green tea but isn't a fan of matcha lattes, and lives for date night but also loves her Sunday snuggles with the whole fam. She wears a lot of blue and green, which is reassuringly how I remember her, sports big tortoiseshell sunglasses at any hint of the sun, always has her hair perfectly blow-dried and always has her nails done, almost always wears heels and *always*, always smiles.

That's what I notice the most about her. How much she smiles. How free she is. How happy.

I try one myself, a Diana smile. I open my wardrobe door,

where my only full-length mirror lurks, and imagine I'm posing for the camera.

But it seems stale, my smile. Nothing like hers.

I try again, head tilted slightly back, pretend I'm laughing at some blue joke Diana's just told.

It doesn't work.

And so I try harder: to think like her, to be like her. The memory of the camel coat lingers on me like a bad smell, but I browse the shops at the Lexicon and splash out on some new clothes—navy blue and emerald green, more fitted than my normal attire, but they look much better, especially as my body begins to shrink and harden. I fish out a pair of black heels and totter about the flat in them, practicing walking heel to toe and leaning back slightly, like the internet forums advise, until I feel confident enough to try them down the street, around the block, to the pub. I get my nails done. Just plain pink the first time, but then bolder, a deep ruby red. And at the end of the month, as soon as my paycheck hits, I treat myself to the largest pair of sunglasses I can find.

Something still isn't quite right, though. It's as if the closer I get to being like her, the more pronounced our difference is. I frown at my leaner, more elegant self in the mirror, turning myself this way and that, trying to ascertain exactly what it is that's upsetting the balance. I twirl a lock of hair around my finger and then freeze as I catch sight of it in my reflection. That's it.

I search my phone for the number I'm sure I have saved somewhere, make an appointment for the next available slot they have, so I can't possibly chicken out.

And emerge from the salon several hours later with a shock of beautiful, shining red hair.

20

Then

In the days following Diana's conquest and my own failure, I tried my best to put any romantic thoughts of Sebastian out of my mind. I couldn't help observing them, though, searching for some sign of a blossoming relationship: tiptoeing past Diana's room in the dead of night, in the hope of spotting them in the act of some coital liaison.

It was an odd sort of feeling—not disappointment, but something akin to that—to see nothing come of it. For my emotions to have been pushed aside so abruptly for the sake of a drunken fuck seemed, in its own way, worse than the alternative. But the next time they saw each other—and I made sure I was there the next time they saw each other—it was as though it had never happened. Toward Diana, Sebastian appeared his normal self: charming, courteous, but decidedly platonic. Diana, for her part, seemed entirely unaffected by his lack of interest, with little more than a cool eyebrow raise to indicate there was anything amiss. Toward *me*, Sebastian seemed as kind as he had always been—no hint that he even remembered my embarrassing amorous pratfall. And, naive as it may sound, I took comfort in this, considered the playing field leveled. He said he didn't want to ruin our friendship, so I just had to prove to him that what we could have was *better* than that.

The days, however, picked up into an endless, fast-paced rhythm, and although there were the inevitable late-night drinking sessions, the occasional champagne-soaked party at Sebastian's and one crazy midnight race around the outskirts of Florence in rented golf carts, the dolce vita became a great deal less *dolce* as Villa Medici was hit by the full force of peak season. I felt as though I were in the eye of a tornado, pulled into the orbit of the villa, with no choice but to allow the whirl to take me in the direction it needed me to go.

Every room was fully booked. Back to back. We even had to turn away the occasional chancer who blew in on the gust of a recommendation, begging for a last minute cancellation. Silvia morphed from our louche, unfazed hostess to a tight-shouldered, frantic controller, snarling catlike at the slightest provocation. No matter how much deodorant I applied each morning, I would finish the day drenched in my own sweat, rotating uniforms on an almost daily basis. My feet ached from almost constant frenetic motion, grew indignant blisters on the heels and big toes that seemed to perpetually cycle through bursting, weeping and re-forming. Carla was permanently puce, screaming heavenward to Madonna as her coils of tagliatelle wilted and grew sticky in the heady kitchen air, coming inches closer to striking poor little Marta on a daily basis.

A few days into this hell, I was crossing the terrace into the kitchen when I heard an almighty crash from the pantry, accompanied by a primal shriek. I quickened my steps to find Marta lying on the cool marble tiles at the base of a ladder, a wooden shelf and the jars it must have been holding scattered around her.

"Marta!" I knelt beside her, clumsily righting the jars and moving the debris aside.

"Mia caviglia! Mia caviglia!" she wept childishly, clutching at her right leg, which was twisted at an awkward angle beneath her.

"What happened?" I asked compulsively, although the answer was obvious. *"Cos'è successo?"*

"I fagioli," she attempted through ragged breaths, pointing miserably to a supersized jar of soaked borlotti beans that had rolled, unharmed, to the edge of the kitchen. *"Per cena stasera."* And then, the pain revisiting anew, *"Ai, ai, ai!"* She balled into herself, collapsing into sobs.

"I'll get help." I stood, awkwardly, embarrassed by this visceral show of emotion from a girl I had barely said more than good-morning to, then called into the open corridor, *"Aiuto!"*

The ankle was broken in two places. She'd need surgery. The report came later that afternoon, after we'd bundled her, alone, into an ambulance to the Santa Maria Nuova hospital, all of us too busy to accompany her. We watched her miserable, tear-streaked face disappear through the ambulance's double doors and then turned silently to assess Silvia, mouth tighter than a hairline fracture.

"Well," she sighed brusquely, pressing her palms to the sides of her sharply pressed cream chinos. "Someone had better go and fix that shelf."

It was Carla who cracked, predictably. My acute sense of knowing my place meant that I would never have questioned Silvia's authority however hard she made us work, while Diana somehow continued to breeze through the busy days as though we were a staff of twelve…which on reflection, may have been something to do with the fact that she continued to work with the same vigor as she had in the quieter period, with me picking up the additional slack. But Carla, once she realized that Silvia was not even entertaining the possibility of a replacement, reached her limit.

She was clever; I'll give her that. She waited until Sunday afternoon, after they had both returned from their respective churches and were feeling penitent. Then she quietly but firmly asked Silvia if she could have a word with her in her office. They shut the door, but it made little difference as we could still hear the rising crescendo of Carla's protests. Diana alerted me to it—I was folding towels in the laundry room—grabbed me by the wrist and demanded I translate the throaty Florentine tarantella that was now dancing between them.

"'If you expect me to work like a slave for the next month… Not exactly'—*manovalanza?* Oh, I think that must be manual labour, she said something about carrying bricks… 'Pack my *valigie*'—that means bags—'first thing tomorrow…'"

"'You can't do that—we have a full hotel!'" I hissed the rapid translation, thinking and speaking almost simultaneously.

We clutched at each other, backed against the corridor wall, and in that moment, I looked into Diana's wide eyes, the conspiratorial glee in those flecked irises, and felt once more the thrill of our united friendship, how close I had come to losing it.

The voices stilled, and our glee turned to panic as we heard the unmistakable whine of a chair against Silvia's highly polished oak floor, the clack of footsteps moving toward the door. We were safely around the corner by the time they emerged, just close enough to see them squaring up to one another solemnly: two generals agreeing to the terms of battle.

"*Domani.*" Carla folded her arms, meeting her employer's gaze dead-on.

"*Domani. Va bene.*" Silvia, wearisome, resigned, held out a hand.

Carla shook it. Nodded.

And that's how they hired Valentina.

21

Now

A marathon of change begins with taking the first small steps.

At least, that's what it says in the book that catches my eye in the window of Waterstones:

A Brand-New You: Fifty Small Changes to Shake off the Shackles of the Past and Be the You That You Deserve

I skim the pages in-store, making a note to buy the book cheaper on Amazon later, and realize that many of their words of wisdom are already part of my new regime. And it's true; I do feel like a brand-new me. I have a renewed zeal for life. I am sleeping better. My skin is clear, my eyes free from bags. Hell, I swear even my teeth look whiter.

People start to give me compliments. Nothing major: a

maths teacher admires my haircut; someone wonders if I'd refer them to my gym; one of my students, with full-blown precociousness, asks if I've got a boyfriend. But together they add up to make me stand a little straighter, and like those early days of my friendship with Diana, a little bit of sunshine goes a long way.

And yes, I do realize the irony that what I'm doing is not "shaking off the shackles of my past" so much as clinging on to them tighter.

I know that I can only hold Sebastian at bay for so long—that knowledge makes me triple-check my locks, glance behind me as I enter the school gates, a prickle of cool air on my neck causing me to search the distance for his blue-eyed stare—but for now, it is Diana who gets my full attention.

For her, life goes on as obliviously as before, one skinny double-shot latte at a time.

She doesn't know I'm one step behind her.

One Monday morning, I find myself in London once more.

This time a dentist appointment—"Gosh, I'm so sorry, I thought I'd mentioned it months ago"—aids and abets me. The renewed Rachel doesn't even flinch when Ms. Graybridge narrows her eyes at her, says she certainly hopes this isn't becoming a habit.

It would be a lie to say that I have thought deeply about where I am going, but when I emerge at Monument Station, something about it feels right.

It is a dry day, the sky high and limpid overhead, making the glass-fronted skyscrapers feel even grander, more imposing.

I get lost in the modern maze of it all, following the moving dot on my phone in and out of Leadenhall Market, darting through shaded passageways filled with coffee shops and food outlets, all takeaway only, all emphasizing their speed, because businesspeople don't have time to sit or wait. But eventually I find it: the vast, Lego-like structure of 30 Fenchurch Street.

The information I've managed to garner about James "Jim" Hogg is thin on the ground—unlike his digitally verbose wife, his social profiles are nonexistent. But a page on the Spirex Capital website—the company name I have recalled and logged from Diana's posts—reveals an Oxford degree, a background in consulting, an MBA from INSEAD business school. Yeah, don't we all? A small square picture of the man in question verifies he is indeed Diana's Hogg.

Standing outside the revolving doors of 30 Fenchurch Street, I feel good. I woke up an hour early this morning to follow an online tutorial on how to style my hair into what they call a Big Bouncing Blow-Dry. My dress, a ribbed woollen mini in deep navy, shows off my newly forming quad muscles. I feel giddy, light-headed. Although that may be down to the fact that I have consumed fewer than six hundred calories in twenty-four hours, part of a new intermittent-fasting diet I am attempting.

The interior alarms me somewhat—an internal courtyard surrounded by floor-to-ceiling windows, stacked on top of each other and reaching high into the ether—but I shake it off, march purposefully to the front desk and wait for one of the women behind it to stop typing long enough to look up at me and ask, in a bored sort of voice, "Can I help you?"

"James Hogg, please, Spirex Capital."

"Is he expecting you?"

The woman has already taken her eyes off me, resuming a steady rhythm on the keyboard in front of her.

"No," I say, stumbling over what, on reflection, is quite an obvious plot hurdle. "Not exactly, but—"

"I'm afraid if you don't have an appointment, we're unable to let you up." She is already picking up a ringing phone, using the cap of her shoulder to prop it against her ear. "Thirty Fenchurch Street."

"Could you at least tell me what floor...?"

She holds a finger up toward my face—"One moment, please, I'll connect you"—taps some numbers before placing the phone back on its hook. "Would you like me to buzz him for you?"

"No." I try to keep my voice as measured as I can. "No, thank you. I'll wait."

My shoes clip on the highly shone marble floor as I head over to one of the leather-covered sofas in the lobby. There are newspapers arranged in a contrived fan on the coffee table in front of me and I pick one up, scan it idly. No mention of Sebastian today. Every time a lift door opens, I scrutinize its besuited riders, search for James's face. There's a coffee shop in the building and I order one to take away: black, strong; that's how I drink it now. I keep my eyes trained on the lobby, have to be called three times to take the cup: "Excuse me, ma'am?" Reclaim my seat. Watch.

Finally, I see him. The lift door opens and there he is. Deep blue suit, clearly tailored to fit his lean frame, white shirt, yellow tie, slicked-back hair evoking Christian Bale in *American Psycho*. As he strides toward the door, he unfolds an overcoat from the crook of his arm, swings it over his shoulders, and I find my feet, feel myself rising, walking over to him, and, "Excuse me, James?"

He stops, swivels on his heels, scanning the lobby for the source of the request. His eyes rest on me, and I can tell he is trying to place me.

"Sorry, was it me you were looking for?"

I summon all the wisdom of *A Brand-New You*, picture breathing in confidence and breathing out negative thoughts as it recommends in chapter three.

"Yes, I'm—" I swallow, soften my estuary accent. "I'm a friend of Diana's."

"Oh." He blinks and his eyes flick over me, take in my blow-dry, the curve of my décolleté. It's not that inconceivable, is it? And then his features soften, and he holds out a hand to shake. "My apologies—we haven't met, have we? Did we have an appointment? I have a new PA and she's been struggling with my diary somewhat."

I smile internally: we haven't met, not exactly. Although I saw him once, exiting the church on Sydney Street, top hat aloft, holding Diana's hand as they danced through a haze of confetti. That was roughly around the time she stopped returning my calls.

"No, no, we don't have an appointment." I resist the urge to dance from foot to foot, ground myself on both legs, aware now of all the people walking past us, rushing to get to meetings, or out of them. "I'm Diana's friend from Florence." I wait, search his face for some sign of recognition. When I see nothing, I add, "Rachel?"

And then I see it. His eyes widening, features morphing, cycling through surprise then annoyance then anger. He knows about me, then. I thought he might, to some extent.

"Outside." The word is a hiss, fricatives expelled through gritted teeth.

He pushes past me, out of the revolving doors. I follow.

A gust of freezing air hits me upon exit, making my breath catch in my throat. I quicken my stride, trying to match his pace, one hand attempting to keep my blow-dry intact.

"What are you doing here?" He keeps his eyes forward, rhythmically weaving through pedestrians with barely a change of trajectory.

"I need to talk to you." I sidestep, narrowly avoiding a woman with a tray of coffees.

"We have nothing to talk about."

"If you would just listen to me for one moment—"

"I am a busy man. I don't give out moments to whoever wants them."

I am striving to keep my cool, but I am at the existential dread stage of drinking too much caffeine, and this and the cold air are filling me with jitters.

"Please." I hear the ugly desperation in my voice. The cold makes my nose run and I smear it away with the back of my hand.

"Look." He grabs hold of me by the shoulder, pulls me into a narrow side street. I can still feel the pinch of his hand through my coat when he lets go. "I don't know why you've shown up here out of the blue like this, after all this time, but I know all about what you put Diana through in the past and I don't want anything to do with you."

He speaks quickly, his eyes darting around as though expecting to be discovered.

I try to make sense of what he's saying, gauge how much he knows about that time, about Sebastian. A dull buzzing in my pocket distracts me—my phone. I ignore it.

"What I put her through?"

I see him roll his eyes. "The constant calling the house, the showing up unannounced. Gosh, when I met her, she was a wreck about it." I think of strong, proud Diana as a wreck and can't quite picture it, not with any veracity. "She was so desperate to help you, poor thing. She told me that you had a lot of issues. We thought, when it all seemed to go away, you had finally got the help you needed. Diana may seem like she is invincible, but she's actually very fragile, and I will not, *I will not*, have you dragging her through all this again. Do you hear me?"

I think back to the time she first met him. We were still

speaking then, here and there. Mainly me ringing her, per-
functory catch-ups which always ended with her saying, "Well,
gotta go…" But then I felt her slipping away from me, and the
old fear started to rise up again. It was shortly after that that she
got me the job at Graybridge Hall, severed whatever she could
of our last remaining ties. But it was never like how he was
depicting, what he was saying…it sounds deranged, stalkerish.
But I wasn't stalking her; I just didn't want her to cut me out
of her life. I feel a tear threatening to fall. The phone starts
up again, an incessant vibration. It stops, then starts afresh.

"Could you not just talk to her for me?" It comes out like
a whimper, and I hate myself. "I know she won't talk to me
directly, but I really need her right now, and if you could just
explain… I don't mean her any harm."

He looks down his nose at me, and I see a sneer creep over
his features that wouldn't be out of place on Diana. "I shall do
nothing of the sort." My phone rings again and I think about
removing it from my pocket and throwing it into the street.
"You have turned up today out of nowhere, ambushed me at
my place of work. If you think these are the actions of a sane
person, you need to take a long, hard look in the mirror."

He draws himself up and brushes off his coat, and I can see
he is about to turn to go.

"Please." One last roll of the dice. One last summoning of
my newfound lease of life. I grab him by the wrist, reach into
my pocket—the other pocket, not the one that won't leave me
alone—and hand him the envelope, the letter from Sebastian.
If nothing else, maybe that will make her see. "Could you…
could you at least give her this?"

He looks down at my fingers, gripped around his wrist,
and I instantly remove them. Then he takes the letter between his fingertips, and for a moment, I let myself feel a little burst of hope.

He tears the letter in half, quarters. Gives the pieces back to me.

"I won't tell Diana about your visit. But don't think I won't hesitate to get the police involved at the first sign of trouble from you. Do I make myself clear?"

I look down at the torn bits of paper in my hand. "Yes."

When he is gone, I press my back against the wall behind me. Take out my phone, which has finally gone quiet.

Eight missed calls from a number I don't recognize.

One voice mail.

I press the phone to my ear, already anticipating the voice on the other end.

"Rachel," Sebastian says, his voice low, calm. "Check the news."

22

Then

The first thing I heard of Valentina was a splutter.

The phlegmy choke of the car engine broke through the morning birdsong and clatter of coffee cups before revving off and away, and a few seconds later there was the distant squeak of the iron gates, followed by a figure carrying an elephant-gray leather suitcase by the handle—the sort you see in period dramas starring Helena Bonham Carter as a wide-eyed ingenue. Stooping to set down Mrs. Collins's fourth pot of tea that morning, I squinted across the garden to try and make out who this intruder could be. A guest? Where would we fit them? And with *that* suitcase? Surely not.

I smiled inwardly at that last thought—at how seamlessly Diana's voice now formed opinions in my head. I continued with service, keeping one eye on the figure as it moved hesitantly toward the terrace, finally coming to rest at the edge of the flagstones, suitcase now a shield held warily in two hands. I saw her looking round, her dark eyes taking in the scene in front of her, and I waited, wondering how or when she would make her presence known, but she just stood there, sucking in her bottom lip, her left ankle quivering with indecision.

I continued to ignore her, but when I reached the Jamesons' table, the one closest to where she stood, curiosity got the better of me and I gave her a small, dismissive nod.

"Posso aiutarla?" Can I help you? I asked in formal Italian.

"Sì!" She gave me a grateful smile. "I am the new girl, Valentina Carrozzo. I'm starting work today... I'm looking for Contessa Daniele?"

I was surprised—and a little annoyed—to hear her switch so fluidly to English, casting aspersions on my linguistic abilities, or at the very least unmasking me as a non-native.

"Oh—yes, of course. Give me two seconds." My tone was neutral, but my mind was whirring, eager to report back to Diana. A new girl...so Carla had won. I put the Jamesons' empty plates on the tray I was holding, and then beckoned her with a jerk of my head toward the house. *"Vieni."* I switched stubbornly back to Italian. "I'll show you where to go."

I carried on a rolling chitchat as we paced down the corridor to Silvia's office, hoping that my prudent questions managed to disguise the fact that my eyes were roving over her from head to toe. I don't know why she raised my hackles so—I had cared little for whether Marta was coming or going—but something about her presence seemed like an invasion on my peaceful morning, and instantly I felt the need to "other" her, to mark Diana and me out as a circle of two, with Valentina very definitely remaining on the boundary line.

Perhaps it was her timidity—that attribute I had seen employed so many times by the girls back home to demonstrate their femininity, and which therefore immediately struck me as false—an apparent wholesomeness which I was sure was too good to be true. She smelled of soap, which seems a rudimentary description but is exactly what it was: just soap, clean and fresh and uncomplicated. Her hair was neat and long, tied in a rope of a plait that sat firmly down the center of her back, and had that glossy shine which can only be achieved by doing absolutely nothing to it. She wore a simple, well-fitting black dress, capped sleeves with a scooped neck and large wooden buttons down the front, both prudish and sensual at the same time, and the pièce de résistance: what my mother would call "sensible shoes," well-made black brogues of such a dainty size that they made me want to hide my own garishly high-heeled clodhoppers.

I left her at Silvia's door with a knock of introduction, parting with a smile and the game promise to "give her the tour" later, my ill will manifesting in overt cheerfulness. When I found Diana, buttoning her uniform to begin her shift, I was brimming over, breathless with the need to share my discovery, and was therefore irked to find that she had little to no interest in hearing about it. "I did think it was bullish of Silvia to imagine Carla could manage," she said distantly into the mirror, pulling at the circular pearl on her left earlobe before deciding against it, removing both earrings and opting instead for a choker with a gold disk that I had picked up in a flea market in Sant'Ambrogio, and she had instantly fallen in love with. "Glad Carla wasn't a pushover about it."

"Well, hopefully Carla'll put her through her paces."

Out of habit, I went over to her desk, picked up the pearl studs and tidied them away in her leather jewelry roll.

Diana shrugged, shuffling first one foot and then another into her shoes. "I doubt we'll have much to do with her. We never did with Marta." The image of Valentina's doll-like brogues struck me. What if she and Diana became friends, united by their petite feet, and suddenly I was the one out of the circle, me of the giant clown feet? "And if she's local like Marta, she'll probably come from home. We'll only see her when she's on shift."

"I don't know about that—she had a suitcase."

"Hmm." At this, Diana perked up, one artfully tweezed eyebrow rising. "Well, in that case, I hope she's up for a martini or two."

I was curiously surprised to see that Diana's indifference to Valentina survived their first meeting. We lay on her bed postservice that evening, no plans for the night but listening to *The Miseducation of Lauryn Hill* on repeat, Diana's head in my lap as I attempted to re-create an intricate plaited hairdo she'd seen in that month's *Tatler*, while trying my best to incite in her the same level of irritation toward the girl that I had felt so instantaneously.

"She obviously knows she's pretty. Did you see the way she was playing with her hair at dinner? Running her fingers through it and tousling it to the side like that? Only someone who's aware of how they look does that. She was doing it the whole time she was talking to Mr. Jameson—it was so obvious she knew he was trying to flirt with her."

"I suppose she is pretty, to a certain kind of person." Diana squirmed away from me to reach onto her nightstand and pluck a cigarette out of the white packet resting on it. Like clockwork, I stretched behind me and pulled up her bedroom window, letting what little breeze there was whip up the curlicues of smoke. "Bit too country bumpkin for my liking. She needs to sort those brows out."

"Yeah, I bet she has a massive bush," I baited.

Diana loved to discuss the size and shape of people's pubic hair, citing her own tidy triangle as the pinnacle of taste. Her latest hobby was a game she'd nicknamed Smelly Fanny: picking a woman we'd come into contact with and starting a lazy debate about how smelly we thought their bits were. Carla "stank to high heaven." Silvia was "clean as a whistle." Cecily, the girl from Sebastian's house party, had "notes of yeast."

The game had caused me such anxiety when she'd first introduced it that I'd swiftly made an appointment at Diana's own smart beauty salon on Via Tornabuoni, hobbling back to the villa an hour and a half later looking like a raw plucked chicken down there, and had started a twitchy habit of subtly turning my nose downward to have a furtive sniff, in case she found cause to label me unfavorably.

Now, I saw the left corner of her mouth twitch into a smirk, waited hopefully for the game to begin.

"Probably." She stretched her cigarette hand out blindly behind her and flicked ash into the air. And then she gave an aristocratic wave of her wrist toward her desk, upon which sat a pile of magazines. "I need a new handbag. Help me pick one."

So, it seemed, cunning as I tried to be, there was nothing I could do to move Diana to feel anything more than indifference toward Valentina. As she had predicted, we saw rather less of her than I'd thought, tethered as she was to Carla and the kitchen. But I couldn't fight my initial feelings of irritation toward her, and the more polite and congenial she appeared toward me—always ready with a pleasant "Good morning, how did you sleep?" (always in English)—the more her saccharine gentility seemed to rub away at me, like an overstarched collar scratching at a particular spot on your neck until you rip the whole damned shirt off and vow never to wear it again. Resigned, I readied myself to bear the burden of this irritation alone, telling myself sharply to *get over it*, to be thankful to have Diana, with no rival for her affections.

And that, indeed, was the way it looked like the cards were being dealt.

Until Valentina met Sebastian.

23

Now

My fingers are already dancing across the screen as I walk out of the passageway and toward the station.

Rachel, check the news.

I fight the underground Wi-Fi blackout and patchy train signal as I make my way across the city and back home. There he is on every news site, the top story, the angel-faced criminal. If I thought he was opting for a quiet slipping away, I would be sorely disappointed. On the first page I click to, a picture of his mother, poised on the edge of a sofa, a classically cut Chanel tweed suit perfectly balanced with the backdrop of antique furniture behind her. I can almost hear her cut-glass accent as she talks soberly about justice and new beginnings and moving on. I wonder if her loyalty to him is as impeccable as she makes it out to be, if she believes wholeheartedly in the "great miscarriage of justice" she cites the past twenty-one years to have been, or if she wakes in the night, heart racing, blow-dry matted to the back of her sweaty neck, and wonders if she is the mother of a murderer. His father, until he died a few years back—heart attack—did he reassure her, hold her clammy palm during those midnight hours and tell her there was *no way, not our boy, not Sebastian*, only to lie back once he had settled her, staring at the blankness of their ceiling, and wonder where they could have gone wrong?

Sebastian himself, looming large in a video interview once I switch pages to rid myself of his mother's pinched face, has changed dramatically in just a matter of days. Gone is the haunted look of nights spent in a single cell, the grayness under his eyes faded to nothing and his skin pink and scrubbed. He is clean-shaven, making his face appear fuller, his hair clipped close and neatly styled, and he is dressed in an expensively tailored shirt in the perfect shade of dusky blue to complement his complexion, picked out, no doubt, by a stylist with the sole purpose of making any daytime-TV-watching housewife swoon. If the sound were off, devoid of any context, he could be a Tory politician, an actor discussing his latest role…until you see the digital bar scrolling the bottom of the screen, that six-letter word he will forever be tied to, no matter his present: "Murder."

I try to watch it on the train, but my lack of headphones gets tuts of disapproval from the other passengers, and the video keeps freezing or cutting out, so instead I hide the phone in the depths of my pocket, force myself to stare at the blurring gray-and-green landscape out the window, until the train doors release me.

At home, I barely stop to remove my coat before I swipe open my laptop, hungry to make up for the lost hours.

I sink into a chair, the laptop on my knees, and navigate to the page I had been frozen on before: the interview.

As he speaks, I breathe, a sense of calm washing over me as he begins to cover the same familiar ground: he was drunk; he'd been drinking all day; he was angry, that's true, but that doesn't make him a murderer. *There's nothing about me*, I reassure myself. *It was just an idle threat.*

As his melodic voice fills the room, I am aware of the adrenaline pumping through me, the inertia of the train journey and my now-sedentary state sitting at odds with my need to move, to "do."

I get up from my chair and reach for the laundry basket, begin robotically folding T-shirts on the kitchen counter as I listen to him retelling the story we both lived. The repetitive movement works and I feel the last of my anxiety escaping.

But then the interviewer's voice stops me dead, a scrumple of still-damp gray cotton clenched in my fist.

"But the big news you wanted to reveal today is that you're writing a book?"

"Yes."

The T-shirt falls from my hand.

I fumble for the remote, blast the volume on full. The interviewer smiles, pleased to have got the scoop. *"That's very exciting. And it will be about that night, and your experiences since?"*

"Mmm-hmm, that's correct."

"Fascinating. And what do you hope you will gain from writing it?"

He pauses, and I can see he is constructing his words carefully, picking each one out as cautiously as choosing a block from a tower of Jenga.

"I want a chance to tell my story." He presses his fingertips to his lips as if in prayer. *"I think it will give me some closure..."* He swallows; I hear the saliva pulsing down his throat, picked up

176

by the lapel mic that nestles next to his right jawbone. *"And some answers. I have always maintained my innocence. I have always believed it was an accident, one I had nothing to do with, and that if I could find a way of uncovering what really did happen that night, I would at least be able to prove it to myself, if not to all of you."* And then he turns to face the camera, giving a full view of those arresting blue-gray eyes I used to wish would look back into mine, and now want to look anywhere but. *"I think someone out there might know what happened that night. But if not, maybe writing this book will help me—or them—remember."*

24

Then

It was nearly a week before Sebastian and Valentina crossed paths. He had flown back home, lured by various social engagements and somewhere called the Met Bar, where apparently he had once kissed a Spice Girl, although he refused to say which one.

I missed him, but for Diana and me, there were still parties. We fell in with a group of English students doing a history of art course at the British Institute, who were renting an apartment with a roof garden in San Lorenzo. They introduced us to Florence's megaclubs, a strip of them out by Cascine Park, where prostitutes in thigh-high white PVC boots lingered amid the trees and the sweet smell of weed clung to your clothes if you stood in one place for too long. At Tenax, under the pulsating strobe lights, they ordered bottles of vodka which arrived in ice buckets, stuffed with sparklers in the neck, fizzing and crackling over our reserved table. Diana, fizzing with energy herself, eyes like tiny pinpricks, grabbed me by the wrist and dragged me into one of the club's matte-black toilet stalls, unfurling the fingers of her right hand to reveal a tiny, clear plastic bag. It smelled, when I conceded, dipped my nose toward one of the studiously carved white powder lines, like horseradish, and it felt, as Diana paraded me back onto the dance floor, like one of those sparklers had gone off inside me, bursting me into life. There, we tangled into one another, shooing away the swaying Eurotrash boys who sidled up behind us and gyrated their hips into our bums. We interlocked our fingers and raised our sweaty hands skyward, belting along to Jamiroquai and Ultra Naté until the taste of vodka grew stale in our mouths and we stumbled, blinking, into the cream-colored dawn and passed out together, finally, on Diana's bed, surviving on the barest whisper of sleep before the working day started anew.

Valentina was nothing but an inoffensive shadow, the briefest flicker of a flame in the dark, to smile at, to nod to in the corridor before I recalled some special, private joke of Diana's from the night before and, laughing secretly to myself, slipped away. And I was happy, with just the two of us. And I didn't need Sebastian or any other boy, because I had the best thing in the world, the best *friend* in the world. And I thought, *This, this, this is nothing like I thought my summer would be, because how could I imagine it…how could I picture it…how could I ever envisage that I would ever feel so, so, so, so much?*

And then, just like that, he was there. In the kitchen, just like the morning I had met him. I heard his laugh first—the low timbre of a chuckle I had come to know so well—and, despite myself, followed it down the corridor as keenly as if it were Ariadne's thread. Because despite myself, despite all my best intentions, the thought of seeing him again stirred up all that initial hope, all those old feelings of excitement and longing and desire. Absence makes the heart grow fonder, I guess, or some other Hallmark bollocks.

He was sitting on one of the kitchen counters when I came in, tan a little bit faded, hair a little less floppy, thanks to some expensive Jermyn Street barber. He leaped off the counter when he saw me, swinging his legs to put himself in motion and landing with a thud on the stone floor before coming to meet me at the door frame. "Cambridge! I was hoping I'd see you." He grinned that grin of his, pulling me in to kiss me on both cheeks, smelling so familiarly of the clean lavender-and-citrus cologne I knew was Calvin Klein CK One because I'd asked him once, offhand, only to stop into a pharmacy every time I passed one, hoping to find a tester bottle, get a cheeky spritz of him.

Childishly, cheek pressed against the soft linen collar of his shirt, I couldn't help a little leap of my heart at that—he was *hoping* to see me, he *wanted* to see me—and I heard myself answering back, "I was hoping to see you too."

"Oh, you know each other?" A third voice cut through my reverie, and I looked around Sebastian's back to see Valentina, a soft gray apron tied at her waist, cutting strips of pasta from a folded-over sheet of dough and twirling them into flour-sprinkled nests, ready for tonight's *tagliatelle ai funghi*.

"*Ciao*, Valentina." I tried to suppress it, but I was instantly annoyed by her intrusion on our reunion, looking every bit the bucolic Italian fantasy: hair swept into a messy bun, tendrils escaping across her temples, a dusting of flour on her left cheek and just the slightest glow of sweat glistening on her exposed décolleté.

"Yes, we're friends," I said boldly, stepping fully into the room as if staking my claim to it.

"*Good* friends." Sebastian bumped my hip with his and I felt a little giddy. "In fact, I brought you a present."

"Oh?"

The pleasure and surprise must have been obvious on my face, because he laughed. "Don't get too excited—it's only small." But I was excited, whatever it was, because it meant—and there was no denying it—that he had been thinking of me while he was gone.

He reached into a canvas tote bag he'd slung on the kitchen counter, and I heard the rustle of plastic, my excitement turning to confusion when I noticed the familiar blue and white of a WHSmith carrier bag. He offered it to me, arms outstretched, the bag placed gently in the palm of his hands as if he were holding a baby bird.

I hesitated. He nodded encouragingly, a cheeky smile playing about his lips. I took it from him, surprised by its lightness, and began to unfurl the bag which he had wrapped over and around itself.

Inside: an orange packet, bold white block caps bearing the unmistakable name.

"Nik Naks?" I held the crisp packet up, the foil crinkling at my touch.

"Nice 'n' Spicy flavor!" He seemed pleased with himself, the smile blooming into a wide grin that made him look for all the world like a little boy.

"Um, thank you?" I turned the packet over in my hands, trying to act pleased. The air had been let out from the cabin pressure, giving the packet a sunken feel, through which I could make out the individual nodules of the chip sticks, imagine their neon-orange glow and the crunch of them between my back teeth. I like crisps as much as the next person, but they were hardly romantic.

He pouted, obviously registering my underwhelmed expression. "Don't you remember? We were talking about what we couldn't live without from home, if we lived here forever, and I said Nik Naks, and you said they were your favorite crisps too."

I scrabbled to recall this particular conversation, and in the dim twilight of some cast-off memory, I did recall some menial late-night chat around Sebastian's dining room table, a few glasses of Chianti deep. But the fact is, whatever Sebastian said, I would have agreed with him. If he had said he thought Mussolini was actually quite a good leader, I would have agreed that, yes, he did do a lot for Italian industry after all. The content was immaterial, as long as it was he who said it.

"Yes, of course I remember." I quickly tried to right myself, to appear pleased and grateful. Surely it was good enough that he had thought of me? "God, I've missed them. It was so sweet of you to think of me." I leaned over to kiss him, lips touching the warm dampness of a freshly shaven cheek.

"What are they?" Valentina's voice intruded, and I felt my shoulder blades tightening even as I turned to smile politely at her.

"The *best* crisps." I held the packet out to her, hoping Sebastian would note my enthusiasm. "You can't get them here."

"Hmm." She leaned across the floury work surface, knife poised to slice through another coil of dough, and read the packet. "Nik Naks Nice 'n' Spicy." She pronounced the *n* like the letter instead of the abbreviation. "I've never heard of them."

"You've got to try them!" Sebastian motioned toward the packet, and I felt my fingers clench involuntarily around it. "Go on, Rach, open them."

"Oh." The leaden weight of disappointment sank into me. It hardly seemed like a present for me, if I was sharing them with her, but if I refused, I risked coming across as awkward and mean in front of Sebastian. Reluctantly, I pinched both sides of the foil and pulled them apart, releasing a burst of flavorants into the room. "Go on, Valentina, you can have the first one." I offered it up to her, putting on what I hoped was a pleasant expression.

She downed the knife and stepped toward me, reached into the packet and plucked out an orange finger. And it was at this moment, this exact, finite moment, that I saw everything change.

She crunched. She breathed in deeply as if tasting a fine wine. And then I swear, I swear, she batted her eyelashes at Sebastian as she looked directly into his eyes and said, "I don't care for them."

Sebastian, instantly tickled, let out a loud guffaw. "Well, you're obviously a hard one to please."

He instinctively moved closer toward her—I saw her watching him as he did, saw her take a lock of escaped hair from the nape of her neck and wrap it around her finger as she said, shyly, "Not really."

He reached over and brushed his fingers softly across the side of her face. "You have flour on your cheek."

She blushed.

I was still holding the crisp packet.

From that first moment, it felt as if there was something almost fated about it all. That Marta should have been injured. That Valentina should have been picked as her replacement. That Sebastian should have met her and fallen so deep, so fast. Because after that moment in the kitchen, it was as though they were planets moving in the same orbit, pulled by some magnetic force that made it impossible for them to stay apart.

He was there, suddenly, all the time, his gentle laughter greeting me every morning, reverberating around the kitchen walls as soon as I crossed the threshold. Although, of course, it wasn't me he was there to greet. The place on the kitchen counter soon became his, and he would sit there, legs swinging freely, a cappuccino growing cool beside him, the white froth dissipating and sticking to the side of the cup. He was "keeping her company," he told Silvia after her initial grumble of disapproval, not distracting her from her work. And Silvia, desperate to please her godson, had pinched his cheeks as if he were little more than a toddler and patted him indulgently.

"Whatever makes you happy."

And under Valentina's spell—Valentina who rarely drank more than a carefully meted out glass of wine—Sebastian became less interested in our petty evening frolics. Sitting on the terrace of the Villa Medici long after hours, he was content simply to sit beside her, her hand in his, slowly tracing circles on her palm. And when she declared, olive limbs stretching gracefully, that it was time she was in bed, up he would get, a puppy with his master, holding her hand patiently as they walked across the grass and saying his goodbyes with no more than a chaste kiss on the lips. He would pass us again, on his way back through the villa, hands in his pockets and a dreamy smile playing about his face.

"Stay for one more?" Diana would always call, the tantalizing neck of a full bottle in her hands.

"No, thanks," would come the reply, a sheepish shrug of his shoulders. "I should get to bed." And then he'd nod to us politely, glancing once more toward Valentina's room as if hoping for that final, fleeting glimpse of her, before turning to go. "Good night, ladies." He'd give a little wave, and then disappear into the night.

25

Now

The news of Sebastian's book sends ripples through the media. There are talks of a multimillion-pound contract, a top publishing house, international rights...

And the closer he gets to me, the more I find myself thinking about her.

Does she know? How could she have missed it? Does she care? Does she dismiss it, switch off the news with the pointed tip of a well-manicured finger? Or has he written to her too, sent a cool white envelope slicing through her polished brass letterbox and landing on her peaceful life with a thud?

I know now that the phone calls will keep coming. Innocent enough in tone, at first—"Please, Rachel, why won't you call me back?"—but soon, the bite in his voice becoming stronger: *"Come on, Rachel, you must know something...*

Rachel, who are you trying to protect…? ANSWER ME, GOD-DAMMIT!"

I consider blocking his number, but I know it won't do any good; any barriers I place on him will only fuel him to find new ways of entry.

The morning after his first call, I find myself hesitating before checking my emails, jumping at every ping of my phone. When I see with relief that there's nothing, I head into school early, seeking distraction. I have a class first thing—my small group of A-level Italian students, who I know won't have worked on the translation I've set, a particularly easy section from an Italo Calvino short story I know they could do with their eyes shut. Graybridge girls are all whip smart but bone lazy; most of them will waltz into places at Oxbridge with barely a sleepless night between them, such is the power of a good education and the self-belief that comes with privilege. Which makes my own pathetic grind, my own miserable failure, an even more bitter pill to swallow.

I still remember the first day I arrived at Cambridge as an undergrad, trying to put the events of Italy behind me. Carrying my cardboard boxes across the quad, hauled from Dad's ill-parked position at the very top of Trumpington Street, I couldn't help noticing how like my beloved Florence it was—the way those majestic buildings sprang up as if out of nowhere, hugger-mugger with mundane modernity—and how very unlike it. Because here, there was space; here there was a freshness in the air, which instilled in me a sense of hope that I would be able to start anew.

I loved it, at first. Finally I would be surrounded by people like me. People who wanted to learn, who didn't think that doing one's work or putting a hand up in class necessitated the title of swot, as my school days had largely determined. I ignored the distractions of Freshers' Week: the midnight chorus of vomiting in—and often outside—the shared bathroom after a night at Cindies; the boys who got sent to the dean for stuffing the porters' lodge pigeonholes with urine-filled condoms as part of a drinking society initiation; the endless, endless chats about shagging. Instead, I found a small group of friends who were quiet and unassuming, to whom Dad, meeting them all in Auntie's Tea Room during an infrequent midterm visit, would refer as bluestockings, and I finally began to relax.

I even found romance: a geography student called Ben, whose mother visited bimonthly with baked goods and sometimes a whole roast chicken. He wore socks during sex and had an irritating habit of squeezing his spots in my sink, but he was sweet and well-meaning and pretended he liked football so that he'd have something to talk to Dad about when he came to visit, and took me to see the fireworks on Parker's Piece and told me he loved me as they exploded overhead, which was a lovely idea once I got him to repeat it louder.

But it wasn't enough. Not enough to stop the letters coming. The calls from Sebastian's lawyers. It wasn't enough to stop the memories surfacing, the smell of seawater and polished wood as fresh as if I was there, right there, or to stop the dreams that would wake me in the cold, sweat-drenched night, make me avoid going to sleep altogether. And Ben eventually got bored of me staring listlessly into space over pints at the Eagle, or kicking him as I stumbled out of bed in the early hours to cry alone in the corridor. He seemed to prefer instead the uncomplicated laughter of Susie or Sally, the blond-haired mathematician who began to show up to our weekly pub quiz until I finally got the hint and stopped showing up myself. Stopped showing up to everything, actually: lectures, meetings with my director of studies, the shower.

In a way, I suppose it was flattering that anyone noticed. I thought that, in the brevity of the Michaelmas term, I had managed to create for myself a warm comfort blanket of anonymity where my peers jostled to be noticed for their interesting achievements. But the college knew, of course, that I was involved to some extent with the case. We were advised as such, should it come to a point where I was actually forced to testify. And I had told a couple of trusted people right at the beginning, made myself a hot piece of gossip for about a week, until a girl in the year above's boyfriend accidentally killed himself by doing something with the unpalatable name of "asphyxi-wank" and I became yesterday's news, today's fish-and-chip paper. So, when it became clear that no one had seen my door opened in the past week, the pastoral care wheels were put in motion pretty fast. As you can imagine, in an environment full of highly strung, type A teenagers, the college had its rescue protocol down pat.

I think of that morning, the morning I officially left, as I approach Graybridge's ivy-clad gates, the memory still as sharp as an intake of breath on the first morning of frost. The girls here will probably never realize how lucky they have it. They'll never need to. They'll all emerge from the cocoon of the school's Victorian redbrick and slide into coveted positions as perfectly fitting for them as a custom-made suit, never having to worry about doing the wrong thing or speaking a certain way. They'll never know how it feels to have one chance, one golden opportunity, and see it recede from view out of the back of a secondhand Toyota.

The girls are still in chapel when I walk through the great gates, the hallways quiet but for the odd muted clop of a teacher's sensible heel on the patterned carpet. I take the opportunity to head to my classroom—like all the senior rooms, decked out like a small study, with a working fireplace and sofas in place of desks "to encourage the collegiate feel"—and turn the radiator on full, shuffling papers and setting out books to prepare myself for the girls' arrival. I am distracting myself, keeping my hands busy to stop them reaching for my laptop, checking again for him, but the monotony of it works, lulls me into a steady rhythm so that I am surprised when I hear a knock at the door, glance at the clock on the wall to see it's already eight thirty. It'll be Claire, a stocky girl from Edinburgh who I actually quite like: impeccable timing, ardent feminist. Even so, I wait another ten minutes until I open the door, enjoying the thought of them sitting on the floor outside, debating whether they would have had time to grab that oat-milk single-shot cappuccino from the common room after all. But when I do eventually open up to let them in, I'm disappointed to find they're not sitting expectantly at all, but glued to their phones, pupils mesmerized by the artificial light. I'm about to call them in when I happen to look down at one of the screens and recoil when I see Sebastian's face staring back at me. A quick glance and I can see they're all looking at it.

"What…what are you all watching?" I lick my lips, try to keep my voice steady, try not to alert them to the fact that I am anything other than indifferent.

"The Sebastian Hale interview." Kate, oversize jumper and bouncing blow-dry working overtime to hide her perpetual eating disorder, taps a bony pink fingernail on the screen. "It was on Sky News last night. It's trending on Twitter." She touches the white play button under his chin and Sebastian is animated, speaking passionately into the camera, at ease in front of it as if he's been doing it his whole life. It's too quiet to hear properly, but Kate shifts her fingers to the side of the phone and suddenly Sebastian's voice fills the air, at once so familiar and long forgotten.

"...and so, I just knew from the start that they had it in for me. Believe me, I wasn't so naive that I couldn't see the picture that was being painted for the court. It was obvious that the prosecutors were going to build a case for me being some foreign party boy, corrupting one of their own. Whatever I said or did, they had made their mind up about me before I even stepped into the dock."

"Come on, we've got a lot to get through." I turn back inside, unable to watch any more. My throat burns with fresh bile.

"So-rry." I hear the eye roll in her voice as Kate extinguishes his monologue with a single click, and the group haul themselves to their feet. Boring Bailey rears her head again.

There's four of them: Claire and Kate, plus Sasha, a leggy Russian who speaks six languages and is rumored to be a distant relation of Czar Nicholas, and Alicia, whose mother was one of the original It Girls, and who last term took three weeks off to be the face of a Gucci campaign.

They shuffle into the room and take their places obediently—Kate squeezing in between Sasha and Alicia on the sofa, Claire on the chair; the same order every week—but the chatter continues.

"I just don't think he did it." Kate shakes her head and her blow-dry swirls around her shoulders, masking a glimpse of her fragile clavicle as her sweatshirt slips off her shoulder. "He doesn't look like the murdery type."

"But what is the murdery type?" Sasha opens an oversize croc-skin handbag and pulls out a pair of large gold-rimmed glasses, which on anyone else would look comical but on her look impossibly chic. "You're just saying that because he's fit.

Ted Bundy was hot. Even Charles Manson was a looker back in the day."

"*No*, it's not 'cause he's *fit*. He's old, anyway. I can't explain it, but there's something gentle in his eyes. It says innocent to me."

"Well, maybe he didn't do it on purpose. It could easily have been manslaughter. An accident. I read that that was what his lawyer was trying to get him to go with, to get a plea bargain, but he refused to say he had any part of it." Kate takes a swig of water from one of those clinking metal bottles they all carry these days, pseudoenvironmentalists that they are, re-caps the lid with a tinny whirl. I can see Claire readying herself for a fight, as she's prone to do at the slightest provocation.

"Bull*shit*." Her face reddens, proving me right. "Sorry, but I refuse to be taken in by his white-male-privilege mind games. The guy's guilty as sin and he's served the time he deserved. Tried to clear up a problem he didn't want to deal with and thought he'd get away with it because of his pretty-boy features and his father's bank balance. Not buying it."

"That's rich, coming from someone who arrived for term by helicopter," Kate spits, riled as I knew she would be. She crosses her arms. "Just because you have money doesn't automatically make you a bad person. That's its own form of prejudice."

"I'm not saying it does," Claire responds, "but we all know that type. Most of your ex-boyfriends, for example…"

The conversation spirals; they're not talking about Sebastian anymore at all but getting into a heated debate about privilege and nature versus nurture and cultural appropriation, puffed up with their youth and their conviction that if they shout the loudest, they're making the most prudent point.

"*Guys, guys,*" I shout over Claire, who I am pretty sure is reaching the end of what she remembers about communism from her GCSE politics syllabus. I wave the book on my desk at them. "Italo Calvino. The translation. How did you get on? You can talk about whatever you want if you can prove to me that at least one of you has done it."

Their voices quieten, but my mind doesn't. I stumble through the class, hesitant, clumsy. I mix up Umberto Eco and Roberto Saviano, and Sasha corrects me instantly, seizing on it like a little bulldog. When they finally leave, my armpits are soaked; I press my fingers into them and inhale the sweet funk of cucumber-scented deodorant and lingering sweat, then wrench the radiator knob back down, heaving a window open to let some air into the now-suffocating space.

I play the video, once, twice. The second time, I listen with my eyes closed, take in his words with the picture of him as I remember him best in my mind's eye. *He is so eloquent.* Not that speaking was ever a problem for him, but now there seems to be a grace to his words that I recognize from the cadence of his last few missives, which I can only imagine must come from his years of incarceration, going over and over it all in painful, minute detail. Each word is measured. Each sentence constructed like a piece of music, with a rhythm and flow, rather than the senseless verbosity of youth that my students demonstrated earlier. But is this something I should be admiring, or is it simply good media training—the privilege of having the best, most expensive lawyer, even if not the lawyer who could have set him free? How much does he truly remember about that night, and how much responsibility, if any, does he take for it—or at the very least, the events leading up to it?

I finally take Alex up on her offer of the theater. I have been so busy lately that I haven't had much time for her. And although she seems pleased about what she sees as my new joie de vivre, I can tell she's starting to get pissed off at me constantly deflecting her invitations.

She's at work late, finishing off designs for a project that has been brought forward, and so we meet in the foyer, take our seats moments before the curtains open. It's a touring production: a millennial-produced reworking of Sarah Kane's *Blasted*, set in Trump's America, a far cry from the theater's usual comfort food of Noël Coward and fifties musicals.

The actor playing the journalist, Ian, is just out of drama school, and from the whoops in the stalls, I imagine so are most of the audience. He struts and swaggers about the stage, pausing for cheers on his first entrance, taking particular gusto in the scene where his character scoops out and eats a dead baby's eyes. Perversely, I think Kane would have got a kick out of seeing her seminal work played for laughs.

The wind blasts through us as we leave the theater. We pass on the overpriced gin and tonics in the theater bar in favor of the pub near our block of flats—far enough from school that I won't risk running into students—and I buy us a bottle of wine, second best on the list, because Alex paid for the tickets, and a packet of Quavers that I open up flat and place between us. I shouldn't really—I've been so good of late—but I haven't eaten all day and I can't deal with Alex asking any more poking questions.

"Rach." Alex's voice is tentative, and I pause halfway through a cheese-flavouring-fuelled crunch. "Don't take this the wrong way...but is everything okay?"

I lick my fingers, savor the sizzle of Quaver dust evaporating on the tip of my tongue.

"What d'you mean?"

"I don't know, I just feel like the last few weeks or so, you've seemed a bit...off?" She takes her wineglass between her two hands and swirls the liquid around without drinking.

I feel myself prickle.

"Really?" I respond coolly. "I don't feel like I've been any different."

"You know that you can talk to me about anything, right? We're pals." This time she does drink, and I watch the clutch of her throat as she swallows the onomatopoeic "quench" of her gullet squeezing and opening.

"I'm fine, honestly."

She nods. "Can I ask you something?"

I don't know how I sense it, but I already know what she's going to say. Adrenaline involuntarily floods my body and I feel the whoosh of blood in my ears.

"Mmm-hmm." I reach across for the bottle and fill my glass, cultivating nonchalance.

"Did you know that guy? Sebastian Hale?"

At the sound of his name, my chest tightens. I think of my phone, buried deep in my handbag, the potential missed calls waiting for me.

When I don't answer, she whistles. "So it's true."

"How did you know?"

In my peripheral vision, I see her shrug.

"You mentioned, once, that you spent the summer in Florence before university. And you've started acting funny almost since the day he was released—it was all over the papers. I did the maths and—okay…" She takes an awkward slurp of her wine. "I googled you. That article…?"

I swallow. That fucking article.

I'd barely started at Graybridge. It had been so long that I was lulled into a false sense of security that no one would be bothered anymore, but I hadn't reckoned on the ten-year anniversary, the papers dredging it all up again for an easy win. In most of the articles, I was barely more than a sneeze of a first name—who cares about a nothing bystander with no juicy backstory to go after?—but one of the papers managed to track me down, connected me to both the school and Sebastian, and the next day, my silhouette against the Graybridge gates was published alongside the charming headline:

Top Girls' School Employee Is Murder Mate

Ms. Graybridge was furious, wanted me to leave at once. I begged her to stay, promised that would be the first and last time it happened, and that night I rang Diana up in hysterics—back then she would still answer when I called—trying to understand how they could have reached me, when her name seemed to be entirely absent from all the reports.

Miraculously, the next day, Ms. Graybridge apologized, offered me my job back. And after that, there were no more articles, although the powers of the internet still render that one discoverable. And now I realize that that must have been how Sebastian first tracked me down too.

"So, it's true, then? You really knew him? You were there?"

I blink up.

Alex has shifted in her chair so that she is leaning right into me, her eyes brightening with the thrill of scandal. There is a tinge of deep red above her mouth from the wine, and it highlights the dark hairs on her upper lip. I give an internal, involuntary shiver of revulsion; I want to point them out, tell Alex she really should get them sorted. But then I hear Diana's voice in my head, remember one of the first things she said about Valentina, one of the first indications that she was riled by Sebastian's obvious interest in her: "That's the problem with Italians. Hairy. Hope he enjoys snogging someone with a mustache."

I know Alex is my friend, but suddenly I don't want to be here right now. I don't want to talk about him. I just wanted to have a nice evening with a friend, sitting in the pub and drinking wine, and pretend for just one second that I have never heard the name Sebastian Hale. "You know, I need to get up early tomorrow. I have to fit in a run before work. Do you mind…sorry… I should get going." I stumble to stand. Wipe my hands free from crisp crumbs on the back of my jeans.

"What? Rachel, seriously?" Alex hovers above her seat, tries to place a hand on my arm, but I take my coat from the back of the chair, free my arm to put it on. "We've just sat down. If you don't want to talk about it…"

I pick up my handbag from the spare chair next to me. "No, honestly, it's nothing to do with that. I just really need to go."

"Well, let me come with you." She stands up fully. "We're going back to the same place, it's ridiculous."

"No, really, you stay. Finish the wine." I am already backing away from her, looking toward the pub doors. "I'll see you soon."

When I get outside I gulp in the fresh air, walk in the direction of home until it starts spitting and I find a cab.

An hour later I hear my doorbell ring, followed by a knock on the door.

"Rachel, are you in?"

I ignore her until she goes away.

I can't sleep that night, flicking between checking my phone and scrolling through Diana's pictures.

When my phone beeps at just past three, I am ready for it.

Rachel, he says, in a text this time.

I am sorry if my earlier messages have sounded like a threat. I don't want to do you any harm. This is the last time I am going to contact you, but I want you to know that I am here, waiting for you, when you are ready. Do the right thing. I know you want to.

An hour later, I fall into a fitful sleep, specters of Diana, Valentina and Sebastian dancing before my eyes.

I want to do the right thing. But I'm not sure I know what that is anymore.

26

Then

"I hate her." Diana bounced into my room, reaching a hand to the back of her head to unleash the bun that had been keeping her curls at bay and shaking her head so that they tumbled down her back.

"Who, Silvia?" I looked up from the copy of *Il nome della rosa* I was struggling my way through, the first full-length Italian novel I had tasked myself with reading.

"*No!* Valentina." She flopped dramatically onto the bed, hand on temple, the base of her skull narrowly missing my feet, and picked up the pocket Italian dictionary beside me. "She's so…" She flicked through the pages, pausing to press a newly French-manicured finger against the top right-hand corner of the page. *"Muto."*

I was silent for a minute, confused as to where she was going with this particular insult, before realization hit me. "No, that means *dumb* as in *deaf and dumb*." I laughed affectionately, reaching to rake a hand through the nest of hair which fanned out above her, freshly washed and smelling powerfully of the rosehip-and-hibiscus shampoo she'd had sent over from her hairdresser's in London.

She moaned softly as my pulling fingers caught all the little nerve endings in her scalp, pressing her shoulders into the sheets like a cat having its belly rubbed.

"Well, that's even more appropriate for her, then," she meowed. "Meek little thing. She may as well be mute."

"Di!" I batted her shoulder as if shocked, but I couldn't help the ripple of pleasure that pulsed through me. Diana had been so unaffected, so unbothered by Valentina. Hopefully now she would see things my way.

"It's true." She pulled herself up into a sitting position, resting her back against my wall and hugging her reedy arms around her knees. "She's fucking pathetic, Rach. You called it right from the start."

I marked the page in my book and set it down beside me, eager to goad her more. "That seems a bit harsh. Has she done something in particular to antagonize you?"

"Fuck off with your big words. Not everyone's going to Cambridge, you know."

Her tone was sharp, the words tiny razor blades cutting at my skin, and my whole body tensed in reaction, half-afraid she might actually strike me.

"Sorry," I murmured sotto voce, looking down at the bedsheets.

This was typical Diana: when something hacked her off, she took affront with the whole world.

We remained in silence, me not daring to speak and her not deigning to. I could practically feel the heat coming off her, could see from the flicker of her eyes, the intermittent flaring of her nostrils with each breath, that she was playing something through in her mind.

"I don't know what Sebastian sees in her." The sentence punctured the still air. I blinked but said nothing, hoping my reticence would encourage her to speak what was on her mind. "This whole 'good Catholic schoolgirl' thing isn't fooling me. I'm convinced it's an act. Deep down, she's just like the rest of us." I watched her relax, her limbs loosening as I saw her thoughts taking hold of her. "Deep down—" she slung her legs underneath her, continued "—she's no better than us. She pretends she's all holier-than-thou, all butter-wouldn't-melt, but I've seen the way she acts when she thinks no one's watching. I've seen the way she looks at Sebastian, the way she moves her body so her tits and arse stick out for everyone to take notice. She may be a virgin, but deep down, she's a whore like the rest of us."

She fumbled for a cigarette, pressed the butt against her lips and sucked hard.

"How do you know she's a virgin?" I swallowed dryness, spluttering as an inhalation of smoke hit the back of my throat.

It was such a loaded phrase: virgin. One that sent me chillingly back inside the school gates. An insult casually slung about from boy to boy, to indicate the height of ineptitude: "Come on, Dave, you big virgin." The biggest source of gossip in the girls' bathroom on a Monday morning: "Did you hear Emily and Steve did it on the weekend?" Some of the boys had a list, adding girls in order as one by one they "lost their V-plates." Nobody wanted to be Maria Jones, first on the list and already on to her third sexual partner, or Becky Freeland, a doe-eyed girl who had held out a year before doing it with her long-term boyfriend, only to be rumoured to have got—whisper it—an STD. But neither did you want to be one of the weird Christian girls who were "no sex before marriage," or cross-eyed Caroline Baker, or Frankie Charlton, labelled "too fat to fuck." Or me.

At school, I wore my virginity with patience. It wasn't that there was something abhorrent about me, more that I was rather too uninteresting to bother with. I figured it was only a matter of time before the better catches got ticked off, and my number got called out, like one of those triangular pieces of paper you get at the butcher's: "Fifty-five? Do we have a number fifty-five here? Take off your knickers and go lie down over there." When it didn't happen before graduation, I still wasn't bothered, figured I had bags of time, three years at university at the very least, before it became a problem. But that was before I met Diana. Diana, who spoke of sex so frivolously, so matter-of-factly from the get-go, that she could have been talking about changing the bedsheets, not rolling around in them. At first, I had simply murmured in vague agreement when she'd started up about it, to the point that I guessed she'd just *assumed*. So, when she did actually come right out and ask me, "So what *was* your first time like?" I'd been too embarrassed to correct her, instead made up some shaky fabrication about my parents going away for the weekend, a generic boyfriend who was "patient and kind." The rest I'd filled in from *Just Seventeen* magazine.

I thought she had bought it—at least she didn't question it at the time—but if she was raising suspicions about Valentina, how did I know she didn't have some sort of sixth sense, some ability to sniff out the virgin in you; that she knew all along I was just making it up?

"Well, first of all, it's obvious." She tucked her legs tighter underneath her, and I felt myself stiffen. "She's Catholic. And went to a convent school. Even if she didn't think sex before marriage was going to send her straight to hell in a handbasket, where was she going to find anyone to do it with?" I relaxed. I was safe. "And second of all, she told me."

"She *told* you?" At this I sat up. The idea of Valentina and Diana involved in some sort of heart-to-heart would have been laughable were it not irksome.

"Ugh, *yes*, Rachel. Pay attention. That's what's pissed me off." She swiveled herself round to face me. "Sebastian had stopped by to give her some flowers—the goon—and she was putting them in water in the kitchen when I was finishing breakfast service. I haven't really had the chance to talk to her alone about the whole Sebastian thing, and I thought it was only fair to her for me to tell her…you know…about me and him." She did me the courtesy of looking awkward, but I flinched at the memory nonetheless. Their bodies writhing beneath the bedclothes, the smell of sex I had been convinced was potent, even though it couldn't be possible, could it, for me to smell it out there in the corridor? How much had Diana's need for confession really been out of fairness, and how much had she just wanted it known?

"I told her what I told you," she continued, "that it was only one time, that it didn't mean anything. I said I was sure that the number of times they'd done it would have wiped well clean any memory of me. And that was when she said that she was a virgin. But she didn't just say that." She resettled herself, and I could hear the irritation beginning to creep into her voice, the telltale rise in pitch and volume. "She told me that she was 'saving herself until marriage,' with this supercilious little smile like she was so damned pleased with herself, not just for the act itself, but for knowing the English phrase. And she didn't stop there. She started going on at me about waiting. How 'special' it was going to be, how 'true,' how it was the 'proper way.' Just on and on, like some bloody living embodiment of the Virgin Mary. And even though she didn't say it, I knew the implication was that she was judging me for the contrary, like what she really wanted, if it wasn't for the perfect-little-angel act, was to call me a slut and get on with it. And *then* she said—and this is what really made me want to laugh—that Sebastian 'understood,' that he 'respected' her for it, that he was 'happy' to wait too, *'because he loved her.' Love*, Rach." She looked up from where she had been uncharacteristically picking the edges of her manicure, flecks of baby-pink nail showing beneath the varnish. "How fucking deluded."

Somehow, the insult didn't seem to land. As though she'd run out of energy before she managed to finish the phrase. And she suddenly looked small, sitting there, and young. Could it be that I had been fooling myself, thinking that her sleeping with Sebastian had purely been for the conquest? Was she just as enamored with him as I was, her proclaimed lack of interest nothing more than a hard shell forming around her, to protect herself from the soft humiliation of rejection? I couldn't let myself think it.

"There must be a way to show him, Di." I took her hand, squeezed it. "Prove to him that that little goodie two-shoes is nothing but a fraud."

As her fingers squeezed back, a slow smile began to spread across her face.

"You're right."

"I am?" Tingles of doubt began to creep across my spine as I watched the germ of an idea begin to form. It was nothing, a throwaway comment, a vision of Diana and me as spurned women, played with and spit out, banding together against a common enemy, but now I worried what I might have unleashed.

"That's what we'll do, Rachel—we'll show him. We'll topple Valentina's halo, prove to Sebastian it's nothing but tacky gold plating." The energy bouncing off her was palpable, crackling in the air as she clutched me tighter. "But it's never going to work if she thinks we don't like her." Her features lit up with a lurid brightness, and I knew in that moment that there was no going back, that whatever Diana had decided had taken root in her mind, shooting upward like the bright yellow sunflowers blanketing the Tuscan fields. She dragged on her cigarette, tilted her chin and let a perfect smoke ring escape her lips. "We have to befriend Valentina, make her earn our trust." Then, in one smooth motion, she dragged her index finger through the ring, made it disappear. "We'll build her up. And then we'll fucking destroy her."

27

Now

The weeks after the trip to the theater, I bury myself in my new regime, trying to forge a new life, a new way of being, even though my hunger for Diana's updates grows more gnawing by the day. One Friday night, I leave the intoxicating light of Diana's profile picture long enough to go to Alex's for dinner. I wouldn't say I have been avoiding her exactly since the theater, but I've been distracted, and she has now asked me three times about this dinner and I can't think of another excuse to say no. I wear a new leopard-print wrap dress I saw on Diana two weeks ago and then spotted in the sale at Whistles, and an old pair of suede knee-high boots which I once promised myself my calves would one day slim into, and now they finally do. I have to say that I am feeling rather good about myself. If I do say so myself.

When Alex opens the door, it makes me realize what my place would look like if I made a concerted effort to tidy it—the layout is nearly an exact replica of mine, only hers is spotless, whereas mine is an explosion of books and paper and clothes. The sofa has been pushed back against the wall, coordinating cushions neatly plumped, and its positioning makes way for the foldout dining table she previously offered to me, now covered with a white linen tablecloth and set with candlesticks, a tall vase of deep red flowers in the center. On the breakfast bar I spy a black slate rectangle balancing circular blinis, cautiously dressed with little mounds of smoked salmon and cream cheese. Just beyond them, champagne flutes are laid out in precise lines, a couple of bottles waiting next to them in a clear plastic ice bucket.

"This is all very nice." I nod to the bar, impressed, as I cross the threshold.

I see something flicker across her face that looks oddly like disappointment, but then she busies herself with pouring me a glass. "Well, it's nice to make an effort."

The end of the sentence is overridden as a couple walk through the door I've left ajar: a short man with a bushy gray beard who is undoubtedly an academic, and a slender brunette carrying a bunch of supermarket flowers.

"Alex! Happy birthday, dear!" he booms, stalking over to her and placing three enthusiastic kisses on her cheeks.

"Birthday?" I feel all the blood leaving my chest, rising to my cheeks and the tips of my ears, where it thuds hotly.

Alex hands me the glass without looking at me. "Yesterday."

I take it, my hand already clammy as condensation forms against the pads of my fingers. "Oh God, yes, of course. I did know, I just—"

"It's okay." She turns purposefully to address the flutes. "You've been preoccupied. Rachel, I don't think you've met

Guy before. He's a teacher at Fairfax College—I'm sure you'll have loads to talk about. And this is Guy's wife, Emily, a dentist. Guy, Emily—Rachel lives down the hall. She's an Italian teacher at Graybridge Hall."

I notice the word *friend* is absent from my introduction.

"Well, jolly nice to meet you, Rachel." Guy pumps my hand, and I notice he has one of those faux anglicized American accents, and a thick, nasally voice that sounds almost as though it's being muffled by the beard. If he notices the awkwardness of our exchange, he does nothing to allude to it, gulping noisily from the flute as he takes in Alex's open-plan living room and kitchen. "I spent some time studying in Italy myself, back in the day. '*Nel mezzo del cammin di nostra vita*, something, something, *ché la diritta via era smaritta*.'" He pronounces it heartily and flatly, no smattering of an accent, and gives me a pleased wink. "Dante."

"Yes."

The four of us rattle in that open space, me, Guy and Emily obviously the only ones who have finally accepted we're too old to care about being "fashionably late." The edges of the salmon curl, take on a waxy sheen. We seem to enter into an awkward rotation of one person taking a blini every five minutes, thereby leaving enough for the remaining guests while gesturing that the party is in motion. Assuming his predetermined role as Only Man, Guy takes on glass-filling duties. The first time he does this, he accompanies it with a singsong "An empty glass is a full glass!" and I get the worrying premonition that he will try to induce drinking games by the end of the night.

Alex wears a pained expression as we run through the gamut of small talk and keeps looking hopefully toward the door. The smell of meat juices fills the room and she lowers the temperature on the oven.

Emily looks at the open recipe book on the counter and gives her a reassuring smile. "Don't worry—it says the lamb needs time to rest before serving anyway."

When the buzzer rings, Alex practically sprints to answer it, holding the door open long before necessary as she waits for them to make their way up the stairs. Three people arrive—two I know, one I don't—and instantly the atmosphere changes, gets more relaxed. Three more guests straggle in one after the other, and when I count the hodgepodge seats crammed around the dining table, I realize our party is complete.

The room gets warm—someone opens a window—and Guy finds the speakers in the corner and plugs in his iPhone, allowing the deep chords of a Spotify jazz playlist to underscore the conversation. Finding myself with no one to talk to, I wander over to Alex, hovering by the oven, and ask if I can help.

"You can get the plates down, and do cutlery."

I spy the shine of sweat on her forehead and put a steadying hand on her shoulder. "It's going really well. People seem to be having a good time."

She gives me a grateful smile. "I know, but it's the first time Jasper's met any of my friends, and I've spent all my time over here sorting the food. Have you had a chance to talk to him yet?"

My mind blanks as I Rolodex through the people at the party. In typical Alex fashion, there are equal numbers of men and women. Apart from Guy, there are two more men I have met before, and two I haven't. One, a Japanese guy with slicked-back hair and a slim-fitting navy cardigan, is rubbing the shoulder of the man next to him, which only leaves the tall man drinking champagne and checking his phone. Olive complexion, brown curly hair. From what I remember from Alex's past love affairs, he seems spot-on her type.

"Yes, a little. He seems…lovely."

I know this is what she wants to hear and am rewarded almost instantly with a beaming smile that makes her whole face relax.

"He is, isn't he? I was really hoping you'd like him—I have a really good feeling about this one."

"It's been…a while now, hasn't it?" I am deliberately vague, trying to trace back past conversations to any mentions of him.

"A couple of months. I'm meeting his mum over the holidays. Staying for Christmas."

Jesus, Alex is right: I have been preoccupied.

By the time we sit down for dinner, I have a slight sway on, a combination of being the first to arrive and my recent reduction in alcohol consumption having lowered my tolerance.

For the ultimate *Abigail's Party* effect, Alex has drawn up a seating plan, so I find myself plopping down with a little more gusto than I had anticipated next to Jasper. "Jasper." I give him a warm grin and hold out a hand, determined to make amends to Alex by paying him the utmost attention.

"That's me." He holds up a bottle of wine of each color and I point to the red. "Sorry, remind me…you are…?"

"Rachel."

"Oh yes, that name sounds familiar. Sorry, Alex has mentioned quite a few of her friends. It's tricky trying to remember who's from where."

"I live down the hall, if that helps?"

He screws up his forehead. "Hmm, I'm sure that rings—"

Whatever recollection he is about to have is cut off by Alex clearing her throat as she sets down a platter of roast lamb and commands everyone to "dig in."

The conversation starts off as inclusively polite, taking in such uncomplicated topics as the best new shows on various streaming platforms, and which Ottolenghi cookbook everyone likes the best, until people retreat to the safety of smaller, more intimate discussions. I try to keep up with Jasper and June, a friend from Alex's netball team, talking about books, but once they hit on a thriller they've both read and loved, I can't help but drift away, pretending to be deeply engrossed in the food in front of me.

"So, Italy." Guy, next to me, nudges the soft tissue of my upper arm with his. He chews with his mouth open. The sound of masticated lamb fat gnaws at my eardrums.

"Mmm-hmm."

"You must travel there a lot?"

I know he is being friendly; I know nothing about this phrase is offensive in any way, but something about his presence alone irritates me. I try my best to master it, swallow down a mouthful of couscous salad and carve a smile onto my face. "Not as much as I would like."

"Do you have a favorite city?"

I give this some genuine thought. "Rome for the buzz. Venice for the beauty. Naples for the people."

"How about Florence? Ever been there?"

I prickle.

"I lived there, actually," I say carefully.

"Aw, really?" He sets down his fork and looks at me with such frank interest that I feel slightly bad for dismissing him. "How cool is that. Where did you live? I've been a couple of times. Love it there."

"Just up in the hills." I concentrate on cutting a piece of meat. I've never really liked lamb—it's always tasted a bit like soil to me. "I was working there, at a hotel. It was years ago, though—in the summer before uni."

Guy rests his elbow on the back of the chair, pivoting himself to face me with the full force of his American enthusiasm.

"Aw, wow. If it was back then, you might even have crossed paths with that murderer guy. The one that just got out. Do you think you did?"

The smell of the lamb is now making me feel ill. I put my knife down. "Well, I—"

"Sebastian Hale!" Guy cuts across me, snapping his fingers. "That's his name. I was just reading about him this morning. Did you? Did you ever meet him? What a creep."

"I—"

"Sebastian Hale!" On my other side, Jasper suddenly springs to attention and turns around. I feel like I'm trapped in one of those Indiana Jones–style temples, the walls on both sides closing in on me. "Sorry to interrupt, but I've just remembered why I know your name. You're the one who was friends with Sebastian Hale."

Guy's eyes get so wide I fear they might actually fall out of his head.

"You *knew* Sebastian Hale?"

I swear, if I have to hear his name one more time I will scream. I can feel my face getting red and hot, and even worse, the rest of the dinner party starts to quiet down, and one by one they all look at me. Staring past the blur of their intrigued expressions, I turn to face the head of the table, where our hostess looks back at me with a mixture of embarrassment and apology.

"You told him?" I try very hard not to raise my voice, sucking in my diaphragm to keep the anger from bursting out at me.

"I didn't know it was a secret." An awkward smile falters on her lips and she inclines her head to the rest of the guests, as if asking for their help or backup.

"You knew it was something that made me uncomfortable." I can feel the silence in the air, the stillness of knives and forks paused against plates.

"I honestly didn't think it was that big a deal." There is a pleading undertone to her voice, and I know I should drop it, that I'm spoiling the nicety of her birthday dinner, but I can't.

"You knew I didn't want to talk about it when you asked. You must have guessed it wasn't something I wanted to make common knowledge. Besides—" the anger is sparking now, and I know I won't be able to contain its fire for long "—it's not your information to tell. I never said it was okay for you to just go telling people left, right and center, like it's a piece of gossip. I'm not some pawn for you to make a move with as yet another desperate attempt to catch a man."

I know as soon as I've said it that I've gone too far. I see the emotions fly through her—hurt, anger, humiliation— and wish I could reach into the air and stuff the words back into my mouth.

I look down at the glistening pile of uneaten lamb on my plate. "Alex, I'm sorry. I didn't mean that."

Jasper coughs next to me, and I can hear Guy clearing his throat as if he's about to dive in and rectify things.

"I was worried about you." Alex's words hit me unexpectedly. "That's why I told him. I was worried about you."

"Worried how?"

Alex sighs, places her knife and fork together on her plate. "Look at yourself, Rachel. The clothes, the makeup, the hair. I know you said you were getting yourself together but it's just…not…you." Instinctively, I touch a hand to my freshly washed hair, soft and sleek due to the armload of products I left the hairdresser's with and now use religiously. "And it's not just the way you look. You're always distracted. Sometimes, lately, we'll be having a conversation and it's like you're not in

the room. You may as well not be there. You're always looking at your phone. You're always scrolling through Instagram
or Facebook, and you've never taken the slightest bit of interest in any of that before. Always looking at that girl—the one
you said you were such good friends with, but you've never
even mentioned her before. It's like it all seemed to start around
the time Sebastian Hale got released. It's like you've become
a completely different person and I don't know who you are
anymore. To be frank, I—" She huffs, purses her lips together
like she's thinking twice about whether to let whatever words
are lingering there loose. "To be frank, I'm surprised you even
showed up tonight. I thought you'd forget."

I feel like a child being told off in front of the whole class.
"Of course I didn't forget," I mumble pathetically.

"Did you even know it was my birthday?"

"I—" I can feel the lamb sitting heavy in my stomach, mixing about with the too-much red wine I've drunk and causing my stomach acid to bubble around it.

"Did you even know it was my birthday, Rachel?"

"I…" My stomach clenches involuntarily, and I swallow
down a dry heave. I can feel everyone's eyes on me, hear their
silence, and suddenly have the overwhelming realization that
I am going to be sick. "I need to leave."

I push the balls of my feet into the floor, knocking my chair
backward as I rise. I hesitate, reaching a hand toward it as if
to pick it up, but then another wave of nausea overcomes me,
and I propel myself toward the door.

"I'm sorry, Alex. I really am, I—" I just about manage
to force the words out before my stomach contracts, and I
clamp a hot palm against my mouth as I stumble out of the
flat, knocking shoulder-first into the corridor as I force my
legs to carry me home.

I don't make it to the toilet in time.

My stomach upends itself onto the gray linoleum floor as the front door swings shut behind me. Orange liquid splashes the side of the kitchen counter and streaks my tights. I wipe a string of saliva from my chin with the back of my hand, taste bits of undigested food in the corners of my mouth.

Weirdly, I feel better.

When I've cleaned up the mess, I turn the shower on, full and hot, stand underneath it for a long time, letting the water slacken my blow-dry and drip into the crevices of my naked, not slim but slimmer body.

Alex is right, I realize, sitting on my bed, my skin dry and my hair turbaned in a soft, fresh towel. I'm not myself. I have been distracted. I sit back against the pillows, take my phone from the bedside table and flick to her profile.

She's at the opening of some restaurant in Mayfair. There's a little video, her and some friends in a bubblegum-pink-and-gray marble bathroom, giggling and blowing kisses at the camera. The video loops and reloops, the same three-second clip over and over: the jut of her shoulder, the tip of her head, her fingertips touching the pout of her lips for just a second before releasing them. The caption reads, "These girls are THE BEST!" next to the emoji of two blonde girls in black leotards dancing side by side. It was posted less than an hour ago, and already, there are over four hundred likes.

I wait for the same rush I've had before—the tickle of endorphins that usually accompanies my daily screenings, but it's gone. I try a previous picture, an old favorite—her posing under a blooming cherry tree, her fists aimed at the camera, full of petals that are already spilling out of the sides. The caption, "Cherry Bomb!" is accompanied by the cherry, bomb and crying-with-laughter emoji. The ingenious witticism has received fifteen hundred likes and sixty-three comments.

A giggle tries to escape me, gets caught in a snort. Beautiful fool.

Sebastian isn't going to leave me alone; that much is clear. For too long I have been avoiding him, the truth. Now that he's out, it's only a matter of time before they both catch up with me.

But before they do, it's time I did a little catching up of my own...

28

Then

In uniting against Valentina, Diana and I rediscovered each other. I hadn't realized until that point that anything had changed, but somehow, in coming together against a common enemy, it felt like those first, blissful days, before Elio had planted the seeds of doubt in my head, before Diana had let them flower.

I don't think either of us contemplated what the endgame was. I don't think either of us thought about *how* bringing Valentina down would help our individual causes, or who the victor would be if we managed it. We were both too caught up in our own folly, too pleased with our own cleverness, to concern ourselves with what would happen afterward.

To destroy Valentina, we had to befriend her first.

That part seemed simple enough—we saw her every day—except that when we weren't all working, Valentina was always with Sebastian. We'd invite her to hang out with us, to grab coffee on a break, to have lunch with one of us on a day off, drinks after the last guest had gone to bed, but at every opportunity she demurred. Our opportunity came, unexpectedly, from Sebastian's mother.

Mrs. Hale was a woman of formidable mental character, who knew exactly what she wanted and how she would go about achieving it. Sebastian both adored and feared her, in perfect oedipal balance, and so when he told us she was coming to Italy, Diana and I both knew immediately that it would be a case of jumping and how high.

"I have to go to Rome for a few days," he told us mournfully, the afternoon after her arrival. He squeezed Valentina's hand, and from her raw, red-rimmed eyes, it was clear she had already heard the news. "My mum wants to go sightseeing, and she wants me to go with her and keep her company. I have some mates I wanted to visit anyway, so it seemed like a good plan. Will you keep an eye on this one for me?"

I couldn't help an internal sneer at how ridiculous this sounded. Excuse them as I could—I knew full well the Technicolor quality the days seemed to take on out there, when a day in someone's company felt like a week—the song and dance they were making over a few days' separation seemed more than a little extreme.

I saw Diana's lip curl. Her hand found mine and she gave it a secret squeeze, a squeeze that told me our feelings were entirely aligned. And then she rearranged her face, gave Sebastian her sweetest smile.

"Don't worry." She patted both their arms. "We'll look after your little Valentine." And then she turned to me, and very subtly raised an eyebrow. "We'll have girl time. It'll be fun!"

★ ★ ★

It took less than twenty-four hours for Valentina to break.

It was late afternoon. Lunch service was finished and most of the guests were either out sightseeing or snoozing in their rooms to escape the heat. Diana was in town at an internet café, conducting her weekly catch-up with the home friends I didn't like to remember existed, and so I was feeling restless and bored, which always made me hungry.

I padded into the kitchen in search of a snack, hoping to find some of Carla's homemade focaccia left out, planning an afternoon with a sandwich and a book of Italian short stories I was plodding my way through. Carla had gone for the day, leaving Valentina in charge of the few guests who'd booked in for dinner, but there was no sign of her when I walked through the door, so I pulled a plate down from the cupboard and began rifling through the contents of the fridge. Before long, I noticed a strange snuffling sound coming from the storeroom—the same one where Marta had fallen from the stepladder only a couple of weeks before—and began a mild panic that it might be mice, which weren't uncommon in the Tuscan countryside and which I was absolutely terrified of. I tried to ignore it, but the sound grew louder and strangely more human, and so, armed with a broom and my duty as a good employee, I tiptoed over to the storeroom door and squeamishly yanked it open.

Relief mingled with confusion when I realized that it wasn't a mouse, but Valentina. Crying.

"Valentina? Is everything all right?" As much as I disliked her, I couldn't help feeling sorry for the girl, crumpled up on the stone floor, with her long arms tangled protectively around her knees.

"I'm fine." She sniffed, looking balefully up at me. "Please leave me alone. I didn't think anyone would find me."

"I'm not just going to leave you here like this." I crouched on the floor beside her, pressing my back against the shelves stuffed with flour and dried pasta and beans. The room was cold, never receiving so much as a flicker of natural light to warm it, and I tugged my skirt around me, protecting my naked legs from the bite of bare marble as I settled. "Tell me what's happened."

"Why do you even care?"

I fought the urge to say something catty, opting instead, simply, for "Try me."

"He hasn't called," she said eventually.

"Sebastian?"

She nodded. "He said he would call as soon as he arrived. That was yesterday lunchtime. I've picked up every phone call to the house and none of them have been from him. He's forgotten about me already."

"I'm sure that's not true." I reached an arm out awkwardly and patted her shoulder. "I'm sure he's just…busy."

Valentina pressed her head into her hands and exhaled raggedly. "That's the problem. I know he will have been busy. I know what those friends of his are like, and I know the kind of girls they are friends with—beautiful, rich, English girls. I know they're the type of girl he normally dates, and I am nothing like that. And he's been so—what's the word in English—*frustrato*…?"

"Frustrated?"

"Frustrated, yes. I know he's been getting frustrated with me lately because I won't…I won't… You know…"

"Sleep with him?"

She nodded. "*Esatto.* I know he said it didn't matter, at the beginning. But now it's like anytime we're on our own, he keeps trying, like he thinks I might change my mind. I'm sure that in Rome he'll get a taste of what he's missing, and by the time he comes back, he'll have forgotten all about me."

"I'm sure he won't have forgotten you, Valentina." I was speaking, but I was only half listening to the words as they left my mouth, because already I was seeing the opportunity that we needed presenting itself. "But why don't you let me and Diana take you out tonight, and forget that silly boy? You shouldn't be sitting around waiting for him. Let's go out and have a good time."

That night, after the evening shift, Diana and I stole Valentina away to our favorite spot in the center of town, a tiny, sweaty club just around the corner from San Lorenzo market.

"Drinks are on me tonight, girls," Diana shouted above the pulsating Euro dance music, whipping a credit card out between two fingers. "I told Daddy I missed him. He sent me a check."

"Di, are you sure?" I asked out of politeness, although of course I knew, and so did she, that this was always the arrangement.

"Absolutely." Diana pressed the credit card to her lips and used it to blow me a kiss. "What else is this for? What can I get you?"

"I'll just have a glass of wine, thank you, Diana." Valentina clutched a hand to the denim jacket Diana had urged her into borrowing. She had warmed fairly easily to the prospect of going out with us, but now that she was there, I could see she was wondering if she'd made the right decision.

Diana tutted. "This isn't a restaurant, Valentina. It's a club. You can't drink wine here."

"Oh." Valentina looked genuinely embarrassed. "What about a beer, then?"

I could feel Diana internally rolling her eyes, but instead

she chucked Valentina affectionately under the chin. "You are a silly one. Vodka sodas all around it is. Rachel, you and Val go find us a good space to dance."

It was clear that what Diana brought back was not just a double measure, but a triple: even I couldn't help a slight splutter as the alcohol hit the back of my throat, but poor Valentina grimaced with horror as soon as the rim of the glass touched her lips.

"I can't drink this." She shook her head. "It tastes like medicine."

"Oh, come on, Valentina." Diana had already thrown her hair into a bun to ventilate her neck against the heat, swaying her hips in time to the monotone thudding beat. "Think of Sebastian off in some club in Rome, doing goodness knows what."

At the sound of his name, Valentina's eyes rounded like a smacked puppy's. She looked at both of us in turn, and then back down at the glass.

"Why should he have all the fun?" I leaned in, the devil on her shoulder.

She closed her eyes, took a breath so deep her shoulders rose. When she exhaled, she raised her glass. "You know, you're right. Why *should* he have all the fun?" And in one swift motion, she brought the glass to her lips, drained it and smiled back at us. *"Salute!"*

"Salute!" Diana and I chorused, downing our drinks in unison.

When we returned to Villa Medici, voices hoarse, tendrils of hair plastered to our necks, the first flush of dawn was peeking through the clouds. We sneaked on tiptoe through the house, sandals held aloft, only permitting speech when the door of the staff accommodation clicked shut behind us, engulfing us in silence.

"Have fun?" Diana pressed a hand to Valentina's shoulder, and Valentina, sweat still beaded on her forehead, eyes wide and bright, nodded back.

"*Sì. Veramente.* So much fun."

And she had. Because if there was one thing Diana knew best, it was how to have a good time. She had thrown at Valentina the full hit of Diana fairy dust, all the magic and tricks I had come to know so well: the ones that made you feel like you were the center of the universe, a sun around which Diana's world turned. Ordinarily this shift of attention would have upset me, but I knew that she was doing it in the fight for our common goal—it only took a subtle look exchanged over Valentina's sweaty, dancing head, the glimpse of a shared laugh hidden behind palms when her drunken limbs nearly clattered to the floor, to reassure me of that. And so I had followed in Diana's wake: flattering Valentina, her slinking hips, her bouncing breasts; flaunting her to the men who sidled up to our gyrating trio and mashed their hips into ours; cheering her on—"*Dai, dai, dai!*"—as we encouraged her to knock back the free tequila slammers offered to us, the ones that Diana and I subtly chose to pour out onto the floor.

"Don't go to bed just yet." Diana smiled softly at Valentina, who was turning to make her way down the corridor. She tugged her hand, nodding her head toward her own room. "Come chill out with us for a bit. It's the best part of the evening."

For a second, Valentina's expression faltered.

"What about breakfast? I have to be up in three hours if I want to get everything ready."

"We'll help you out." Diana looped an arm over Valentina's

shoulders, gave her a smacking kiss on the cheek. "Right, Rachel?"

"Of course." Diana was already coaxing open her bedroom door, throwing her shoes in a heap before guiding Valentina inside. "We do it for each other all the time. Don't spoil the fun now."

Like a single, choreographed dance move, Diana peeled off her dress, plucked a little plastic baggie from the depths of her bra and threw herself on top of the covers, head sinking into the pillows. She patted the space in front of her, and I saw Valentina hesitating, eyeing up Diana's naked flesh before tentatively moving across the room and sitting gingerly on the edge of the bed. I couldn't help a little flutter of annoyance at the thought of her taking my place, even if only physically, but was rewarded by Diana reaching out the pad of her foot, pressing it into Valentina's thigh.

"Scooch up—make room for Rach."

I nestled in next to Valentina, pressing my back against the wall, and obediently took the bag when Diana handed it to me, tapped the white powder onto the top of my wrist.

I inhaled, passed it to Valentina, but she looked at me aghast: "Please, no."

I eyed Diana, who shrugged—"Fair enough"—and took the bag back herself. "So, you enjoyed yourself tonight, Valentina?" She arched her back, pressing herself more comfortably into the pillows.

Valentina nodded. "Yes."

Diana smiled. "I saw the way you looked, when those men were dancing with you. It felt good, didn't it, to be wanted like that?"

A shadow cast over Valentina's face, lips parting as if hesitant about how to answer.

"I don't know how you mean?"

"You don't have to be shy with us, Valentina—we're friends. It feels good to know that a man desires you and can't have you, doesn't it? To let those men think they have a chance with you, and then walk away—drive them mad—so they want you more. That's what you're doing with Sebastian, isn't it? It's very clever."

From my position on the end of the bed, I was coiled tight, afraid to say anything lest I spoil Diana's serpentine attack.

Valentina looked genuinely horrified. "I don't know what you mean. I'm not playing any games with Sebastian."

"But you're not sleeping with him." Even in the dim light of Diana's room, I could see her cock an eyebrow. "Keeping him panting on his leash. I like it."

"It's not like that." Valentina shook her head vehemently. "I'm not trying to be clever. I can't sleep with him. I want to, but I can't."

To my surprise, I saw a tear escaping from Valentina's right eye, tracing a sorrowful path down her cheek. Diana was already there, wrapping a consoling arm around her shoulder.

"Oh, honey, I didn't mean to upset you."

Valentina sniffed loudly, pressing her palms to her cheeks to mop up the new tears that were starting to fall. "It's okay, it's not your fault. It's just that Sebastian... I... We..." I didn't know if it was the late night or the booze, but she broke down into loud, messy sobs.

Diana pulled her into her chest, made loud shushing sounds in her ear as if she were soothing a baby. "Rachel," she said softly, raising her chin from Valentina's shoulder. "Why don't you get Valentina some tissue from the bathroom?"

When I returned, Valentina had her head on Diana's shoulder, intermittent wails escaping as she tried to speak.

"Here you go," I said gently, handing her a wad of toilet paper before resuming my useless position on the end of the bed.

"We had a fight about it, just before he left for Rome. That was why I was so upset he didn't call. *Grazie*, Rachel." Valentina paused long enough to look up at me, before balling the toilet paper into her right hand and pressing it against her wet cheeks. "He told me if I truly loved him, that I would trust him. He said of course he would marry me, one day, but that first he needed to finish university and get a job, so that he could give me the life I deserved." Her lip trembled. "He says he doesn't understand why it matters—if we're going to be married *one* day, why we can't just get on with it?"

"Well, why don't you?"

Both Valentina and I looked up at Diana in surprise.

In return, she batted her eyelids at us demurely.

"Diana, I *can't*. My father...if my family found out...he would kill me."

"But you love him?" Diana held Valentina's gaze. In the glint in her eye, I could see the predator rising to the surface, poised to strike.

"I love him." Valentina, the defenseless baby deer, widened her eyes imploringly.

"And you want to marry him?" Diana took a strand of Valentina's hair, stroked it tenderly.

Hypnotically, Valentina nodded back. "I want to marry him."

"And you want to sleep with him." It was a statement, not a question.

"I..." The room lapsed into silence. Diana said nothing, just kept on stroking Valentina's hair, the dark ringlets winding methodically in and out of her fingers. Eventually, Valentina blinked, swallowed. "Yes."

Diana bared her teeth.

"I want to make him happy." Like a little singing bird that had just been released from its cage, the words begin flying out of Valentina. "I want to show him how much I love him. And that I trust him. And that I want us to be together, always. And…I want it too." This she said a little quieter, looking down at her fingers as though ashamed to admit it. "Sometimes, when we are kissing, I feel his hands on me, on my body, and I am pushing him away going, 'Stop, stop, stop,' but really, I don't mean it. I don't mean it at all."

I recoiled at the thought of their intimacy. Bile pooled at the base of my throat, but I swallowed it down. I couldn't let the thoughts in, if I wanted this to work.

Instead I edged across the bed, feeling the mattress sigh beneath me, and wrapped an arm around Valentina's shoulders.

"Then what have you got to lose?" I whispered the words into her neck, feeling my own hot breath aspirating back at me, and watched her turn, desperate and hopeful. "What you have with Sebastian—" I braced myself for what I was about to say, trying to separate myself from the words. "What you have with Sebastian is special. If you love him that much, fuck the rules. Fuck what you've been told. If you want to be with him, then that's all that matters."

"Rachel's right, Valentina." On her other side, Diana squeezed in close, her voice low and seductive. "It shouldn't matter what anyone else thinks—this is about you and Sebastian. Just imagine, he'll have spent days away from you, thinking about you, wanting you. Wouldn't it be perfect timing… and just *so* romantic…to show him just what he's been missing?"

Valentina stared straight ahead, barely moving but for the rise and fall of her chest. I could practically see the words reverberating in her mind. A bird chirruped outside the window, and I saw her eyes flicker, awareness of the day ahead taking hold of her.

"I...I should go to bed." She shook us off, her feet padding to the floor with a soft thud as she stood, swaying slightly, the long night and copious alcohol finally taking hold of her. "Thank you, Diana, Rachel. Honestly." She turned back to look at us both, gave us a small, graceful smile. "It means so much, to know I have you as my friends."

I thought Diana would protest, implore Valentina to stay until she was sure we'd got the outcome we were after, but instead she stood herself, drew Valentina into a hug.

"Of course. We girls have got to stick together. We're here for you, anytime...right, Rachel?"

My mind was chaotic, but I scrambled to my feet and heard myself echoing, "Anytime."

Once the door clicked shut and we were alone, I turned to Diana, searching her for answers.

"Now what?"

Diana tilted her chin to the door, a look of serenity blooming across her face.

"Now, we wait."

"And if she doesn't sleep with him?"

"She'll sleep with him." Diana stretched languidly, pale arms looping in the air above her, and then climbed into bed. "She was always going to—she just needed a little push." She yawned dramatically, nestled her head into the pillow. "She'll sleep with him, and then he'll forget about her. It's how boys like that work. He'll see she's no better than the rest of us..." She yawned again, her voice growing slow and soporific. "And she can take that bloody halo she walks around with and shove it up her arse."

I nodded conspiratorially, but I couldn't help a tremble of doubt from flickering in my limbs. I thought all I wanted was for Sebastian to see me; I wasn't sure how driving Valentina into his arms was going to achieve this.

I turned to go, but as soon as my hand touched the door-knob Diana called out to me.

"Rach," she mewled, and when I looked back at her she pulled off the covers, shifted her body to one half of the bed. "Stay with me—I can't sleep."

And I went to her, as I always did when Diana called, allowed her to wrap her arms around my torso and listened as her breathing slowed, grew heavy, as I stared wordlessly up at the ceiling, wondering if it was possible to put the genie back in the lamp.

29

Now

No one is more surprised than me to be ringing the door-bell of 54 Merton Lane at 11:00 a.m. on a Saturday morning.

School breaks up, the tinsel-lined corridors echoing with the dramatic farewells that teenagers do so well. The next day, I wake early and pack a bag, slipping a note under Alex's door on my way out: "I'm sorry." We haven't spoken since the party. I don't know what else to say.

"Rachel." Mum answers the door, blinks at me, then looks down at my suitcase.

"Hi, Mum." I shift my weight from one foot to the other, wonder if I've made a mistake.

"You're staying?"

"It's been a while. I thought it would be nice; I could stay for the holidays. I can cook for you guys, look after Dad for a bit—give you a break." She's still looking at me, not saying anything. My fingers tense involuntarily around my suitcase handle, and I think about jacking it in, changing my mind. "Is that okay?"

Mum hesitates. I can see her taking in my hair, clothes; the myriad unanswered questions she is trying to form into sentences but won't, not yet. Then she opens the front door fully, arm outstretched so that her palm is pressing into the rough, unpainted frame.

"Yes, I suppose that's fine. You'll have to move all the stuff off the bed, though. I've been building a pile, for charity." She turns back inside, and I follow her through the narrow corridor to the bottom of the stairs that lead to the rest of the house. "Dad's in the garden."

She shuffles off toward the kitchen, and I watch her go for a moment, inwardly playing out a different sort of mother-daughter reunion—*Hello, darling, so nice to see you, you look well.* Not really our style, but a hug would have been nice.

I take my suitcase upstairs to the room that was once mine, blue-and-white-striped wallpaper once plastered with posters of Björk and Alanis Morissette, now remodeled in neutrality to serve as a guest room, although I can't imagine who else would be calling in to stay. I stare at the magnolia-painted walls, try to work out exactly where my desk sat against them, where the bookshelf that Dad and I built hung, only for it to come crashing down a few days later in the middle of the night, sending books flying in all directions. I remember stepping in here the day I came back from Italy. How shockingly normal, suburban, it seemed, after the police and the interviews, the reporters. I felt like Alice in the White Rabbit's house, growing too tall to fit the space. When I left for Cambridge a few weeks later, I was convinced I wouldn't be moving back. Doing so was its own sort of penance.

I go out into the garden to find Dad. He's sitting on the wooden bench against the wall at the far end of the garden, where next door's roses have climbed over and wrapped themselves down the fencing, all shriveled and brown in the dank winter air. Dad used to love pottering around the garden, taking a particular pleasure in having the benefit of the neighbors' roses to tend to. When I get closer, I see he has a blanket over his knees, a dark blue plaid, which I think we used a few times as a picnic blanket, and when I get up close, I can hear the chatter of voices, spot the red Roberts radio beside him. Dad had a stroke a few years ago. He used to love reading, but the stroke made his right arm weak and he finds it difficult to turn the pages now. I tried to set him up with an audiobook account when it first happened, but he never got the hang of it. That was probably the last time I stayed over.

He looks up as I walk over, and I see him processing me, the smallest hint of confusion before recognition takes hold. "Rachel!" He sits himself up taller, struggling a little on his right side, and switches the radio off.

"Hi, Dad!" I say cheerfully, although it's difficult, it's always difficult, to see him incapacitated like this. I kiss the top of his head and he pats my arm softly.

"What a nice surprise."

I take a seat next to him on the bench. "Thought it was time I came to say hi. Give you a hand looking after Mum." I raise an eyebrow at him, and he chuckles. It's always been our joke—Mum being a handful—but it's taken on a new resonance now that Dad's the one who needs help.

"You changed your hair." He shifts his weight to get a better look at me. I notice his speech is better than the last time I was here, clearer. I hope that means he's been doing the speech therapy I suggested.

"Yes," I say, touching a hand to the back of my ponytail. "Thought it was time to shake things up."

"Suits you." I shrug. I'm used to it now; I've stopped wondering whether it suits me or not. The layers have started to grow out since that first cut, and I know the roots are beginning to show, but I've paid enough attention to it that it still manages to pass for acceptable. "You look good." I can feel him searching me, his eyes still as sharp as ever as they glide over my face. "Boyfriend?"

"Dad." Silly, how I feel like a teenager again, wanting to curl into myself and avoid making eye contact.

He laughs, three short, outward breaths, and when I look at him, he holds his good arm up in protest.

"Teasing. But I want grandkids."

I take hold of his hand, squeeze it, and we sit in silence, listening to the sound of birdsong and next door's radio playing *The Archers* through the walls, the whoosh of water from the pipes telling us she's running the tap in the kitchen, the whomp of a football being kicked around the garden on the other side. The not exactly calming but altogether familiar sounds of my youth.

Eventually: "Why are you really here, Rachel?"

Dad's hand slackens, and I pull mine away. I knew I couldn't get away from it forever.

"I told you." I glance down at my nails. I try to keep them painted these days, but the polish is already chipping from the upheaval of traveling, and I can't help picking a loose ridge, working a piece free. "It's the holidays."

"I thought you normally stayed in Ascot for the holidays."

When I was a kid, Dad was a master of cryptic crosswords; he even used to send his own ones into the paper, in the hope that they'd be published. I feel that same forensic eye being used on me now, a sharpened 2B pencil testing if the letters fit.

"I wanted to see you." I speak carefully, trying to imbue my voice with extra pleasantry. And it's true, isn't it? I do want to see him; it just isn't my primary reason for being here.

"If you don't want to talk about it, that's fine by me." Dad, clearly not fooled, pulls the blanket up from where it's slipped below his knees.

"There's nothing to talk about."

Dad turns the radio back on. *The Archers* tunes in with next door, but with a second's delay, so for an irritating few moments, we're listening to Ruth and David arguing in echo.

"Mum said that boy got released." He switches it off again, filling the silence instead with what he's been trying to say all along.

"He's a man now."

"Don't be facetious." The word takes a second to come to him, but I can't help a smile when it does. The old man has still got it.

"She's right, though," I say quietly. The chip of nail polish comes loose, flicks off my finger and lands on the grass, a red fleck of confetti against the green.

"Where is he now?"

"I don't know, Dad." It comes out harsher than I intended, but if he takes offence, he doesn't show it.

"You haven't…"

"No, I haven't spoken to him. It's been twenty years." A lie by omission. I know even this morning he was there, in my inbox.

This is your last chance, Rachel. Look, you've got my number now. Day or night, I'll answer. But call me, please.

"Hmm." Dad nods sagely. "And what about that girl… Joanna…?"

"Diana." Even saying her name out loud, I feel prickles of

energy shooting up the backs of my legs, between my shoulder blades. "No, I haven't spoken to her for a long time."

"Shame. I thought you were friends." Dad pauses for a second, looks up toward the house, contemplating. "Probably best, though. Put it all behind you."

I wrestle to say something more—to defend myself or disagree, I can't decide which—when I feel Dad's hand on my knee.

"Rachel." I look into his soft gray eyes, now surrounded by a patchwork of wrinkles and yellowing around the irises but no less keen than ever. "It's good to have you here."

"Thanks. It's good to be here."

"Please don't upset your mum."

"I'm not planning on it." I try to press it down, that little niggle of frustration. Dad: forever Mum's protector.

"It's hard for her, me…" He leaves the sentence dangling, doesn't need to finish it. "She's always just wanted the simple life. She doesn't need any more…disruption."

"It's okay, Dad. I'll be on best behavior."

Dad removes his hand, and I watch a yawn snake through his body, escape silently through his lips.

"That's a good girl."

I smile, wishing it to be true.

30

Then

Diana and I lay in wait, watching for the trap we had set to go off, but nothing we had said to Valentina seemed to have sunk more than skin-deep.

We quizzed her—our newfound friendship giving us the guise of interested pals—but Valentina just shook her head, a serene smile lending her the air of someone far beyond our own base understanding of relationships.

If anything, her resistance served to heighten her bond with Sebastian, brought a sexual tension to their relationship you could practically taste in the air when you were with them.

Diana noticed too. I saw her observing them, the intimacy that seemed deeper than before—bodies closer, skin in constant contact—and as the two of them blossomed, grew, it was as if Diana withered in response.

"I can't believe he's still with her, the prick-tease," she hissed at me as we dusted the living room one afternoon, Sebastian just in sight through the passageway of open doors, swirling a cup of coffee in the palm of his hand and laughing at something Valentina was saying. "She's so boring it must be like trying to fuck an ironing board." I tried to think of some clever retort, an additional insult to sling at Valentina, but my mind was empty. I had wanted to believe so badly in Diana's scheme, had been so convinced that she knew him and his type so much better than I did, but rather than driving them apart, it seemed we had only served to bring them closer together.

The smell of frying onions whispered through the open rooms, and my stomach, in betrayal, grumbled. As if Valentina wasn't untouchable enough, love had aroused in her a sudden magic in the kitchen, her re-creation of her grandmother's ragù recipe so intoxicating that it was now a daily fixture on the menu, much to Carla's displeasure.

"He loves her." I felt my shoulders sag, letting the cushion I was plumping go limp in my arms. "It's not just about sex. We should give up, Di. Let her have him. It was a stupid idea."

Diana scowled, snatched the cushion from my hands and plumped it so vigorously I worried it would burst.

"Rachel, it's always about sex."

And then, one day, it was.

I don't know what changed. I don't know what clever tricks of persuasion Sebastian had discovered, or what vital conclusion Valentina had reached, but she waltzed into the kitchen one morning as Diana and I were taking the cups and saucers down for breakfast, and she didn't have to say anything; I knew. It was there in her gait, a more pronounced slither to her hips. In the way she unconsciously touched her body, as if discovering it for the first time. And it was there in her sappy, sex-drunk smile, a deep contentedness that wasn't there before and screamed, to use one of Diana's favorite expressions, of "a good rogering."

Diana's approach was less subtle than mine. She circled an index finger coaxingly in Valentina's direction.

"You've had sex."

"*Scusi?*" Valentina tried not to look at her as she took a box of croissants out and began arranging them on a platter, but the tops of her ears turned pink.

"You slept with Sebastian, didn't you?"

She paused, and I could see her weighing up her options, deciding whether to let Diana and me in.

"Yes," she conceded, turning to us, her fingers fluttering to either side of her face. "Last night. It was…it was right."

I watched Diana's chest rise and fall as she observed Valentina from across the room, and the smile that spread across her face made me feel both petrified and hopeful in equal measure.

"Good." She licked her lips. "That's good."

Because, whether Diana was some sort of oracle or she just knew the stuff Sebastian was made of so intrinsically it couldn't have played out any differently, from that day onward, we began to see the slow but steady ebbing away of his affections.

It started with his body language, an awkward distance whenever he was with Valentina that wasn't there before, a more avuncular nature to his touch that suggested something was amiss. He was still pleasant to her, absolutely so, but somehow all the mystery, all the expectation and lust, seemed to have dispersed as easily as a bubble pricked with the tip of a needle.

Then pretty quickly it deteriorated further—irritation, exasperation, his presence at the villa a less and less regular occurrence.

I heard them arguing in the walled garden where we hung the laundry, peeked through the kitchen window to see Sebastian with his fists balled, Valentina's face tear-streaked and red.

"It's one fucking night!" he was saying to her, flinging his hands in the air for emphasis. "I never see my friends anymore. I don't see what the big deal is."

"Why don't you want to spend time with me instead?" she wailed in response. "All you want to do is get drunk with your friends."

He huffed a low, infuriated groan, grasped at the hair on either side of his head. "We don't have to be together every sodding minute of every sodding day. Why do you have to be so clingy? It's like you're trying to suffocate me."

"You didn't seem to think that when you were trying to get me to sleep with you."

"Well, maybe you were a lot more interesting then."

As soon as he had said it, it was obvious he knew he'd gone too far. His face paled, and he clamped a hand to his mouth. Valentina, in response, looked like she'd been slapped.

"Val, I'm sorry, that was a horrible thing to say..." He tried to reach out to her, but she wrenched herself away from him.

"Leave me alone."

"No, seriously, I don't know what came over me. It was the heat of the moment, I—"

"Leave me alone." The tears started streaming down her face. I knew I should look away, but I was mesmerized.

"Val, please..."

"Vaffanculo!" she howled into the ether. *Go fuck yourself.* She turned on her heel and stormed off.

I lingered, watching Sebastian standing alone among the billowing tablecloths hanging on the lines, his head shaking from side to side as if he didn't quite know what to do with himself. The sound of hurried footsteps brought me back to the room, and I quickly whipped myself around as Valentina came tumbling in.

"Val, is everything okay?"

She hurried past me out of the kitchen, her voice thick with mucus. "I'm not feeling very well. Would you please tell Silvia I need to take the morning off?"

"Sure…" I called to her retreating back. "Anything."

When I looked back to the garden, Sebastian was gone.

Good little messenger that I was, I couldn't help but report it all to Diana, verbatim. She sat cross-legged on her bed, drinking it in.

"I can't believe it worked." She pressed her fingertips to her mouth, her voice almost vibrato with giddiness.

I wanted to mimic her excitement, wanted to let myself be intoxicated by her good humor, but something about the retelling of it left me strangely flat. The look on Valentina's face as she sped past me, eyes red-rimmed and hollow, seeing our plan formulated in the flesh, literally, made it so much more…real.

"Di." The feeling was ephemeral, a piece of gossamer slipping through my fingers, but I tried to grasp at it. "Maybe we should try and put this right. I think…I think we did something wrong."

A funny look contorted Diana's features, made all her angularities even sharper, and when she spoke, there was almost no expression to her voice at all.

"I thought this was what you wanted."

"What?" My heart twitched.

"This was all your idea, Rachel."

I felt sick. I ran through our initial conversation in my mind.

Yes, I had been angry with Valentina, but it had been Diana who wanted to take her down, hadn't it? Hadn't it?

"What are you talking about?"

"We did all of this for you. If you hadn't been so angry with her for stealing Sebastian from you, I never would have suggested any of this. This was all part of your plan and you've made it work so brilliantly. Don't tell me you're not going to do it now?"

I stilled. "Do what?"

She licked her lips and gave me a patient, parental smile.

"Are you going to sleep with him?"

"What?"

"You heard me."

I swallowed. My throat was dry, my heart quickening with a dull thud that echoed in my ears.

"I can't."

"You have to." Although she spoke quietly, almost tenderly, I could hear the razor-sharp edge to her words, and I had a worrying feeling this wasn't persuasion so much as a command. "You sleeping with him was the whole point. And it's the only way we can make sure they're over and done with for good. Otherwise everything we've done will have been for nothing; all that time spent with Valentina, all that money we spent on her—*I* spent on her—you wouldn't want that to go to waste, would you?" Whether her question was rhetorical or not, I shook my head mechanically. "Good girl. That would have been very ungrateful of you. And besides—" she flicked a loose lock of hair out of her eyes "—isn't this what you wanted, Rachel? Isn't this what you've been waiting for all along? He's finally yours. Take him."

An image of Sebastian bobbed to the surface of my mind. The way the corners of his eyes creased when he squinted in the sunlight and instinctively held a hand to his forehead, like a captain observing the horizon. His habit of doing and undoing the top button of his shirt when he was thinking, thumb and forefingers working almost independently from the rest of his body. The easy smile I always hoped to elicit with some clever phrase or joke. The wide palms I imagined brushing the hair off my neck, squeezing my shoulders, touching the small of my back, my hips, my...

"It is...but..." I thought of Valentina, the way he had looked at her. The way that he had never looked at me. "He's not interested in me. Not like that."

"Rachel." Diana widened her eyes at me, and I saw a glimpse of her old self, cocky and assured, rising to the surface. "Do you understand nothing about men? Sure, he might mope around for a bit, but then he's going to want some... perking up." She gave me a lascivious wink. "All it's going to take is a little *push* and he's yours." She stroked a finger under my chin, her voice suddenly slow, tantalizing. "Don't tell me you haven't been thinking about it."

I went back to that day, the Feast of St. John. I had never told Diana about it, especially after everything that happened with them afterward. It was too humiliating. Instead I looked down at the carpet, inspected the individual loops of ice-cream-colored wool.

"Of course I have. I just don't think it'll happen."

"You haven't *tried*." There was electricity in Diana's voice. Her hands reached for my shoulders and she pulled me down onto the bed, sat beside me. "We need to get Valentina out of the way, and then we need to show him a good time. Remind him what he's been missing since he decided to become a monk. And then, when the moment's right..." She snapped her fingers in my face. I blinked. "You strike."

I tried to picture it, sidling up to Sebastian, leading him

away to a quiet corner, nuzzling at his neck, and felt the palpitation of foolishness beating in my chest.

"I'm not you, Diana. I can't be like that."

"You *can*, Rach." She leaned in so close her forehead was almost touching me, her hair falling around her shoulders and tickling my cheek. "You need to believe in yourself. Have confidence. You know what you want…take it."

I felt like Eve, Diana's serpent tempting me with a shiny red apple. All this time, I had been so fixated on the pure taking down of Valentina, I had thought little of my own gain. But now the path to her destruction had me in it, and what if, *what if*, the result of it was that Sebastian saw what he had been missing, realized it was me he wanted all along?

It took mere hours for Diana to work her powers on Valentina. When they finally emerged together from her room later that evening, she seemed remarkably calm. Her olive skin was still sallow, but it had been overlaid with a slick of makeup, the precise application having Diana's handiwork all over it, her hair neatly brushed and tied in a ponytail at the nape of her neck.

"I'm going to go home for a few days and get some rest." Her tone had a martyr-like inflection, and I had to try very hard to squash my reflexive irritation and cultivate compassion instead. "My *papà* is going to come and collect me now. Diana has offered to speak to Silvia for me and tell her I'm sick. She said…" She looked up at me hopefully. "She said you two wouldn't mind picking up the extra work?"

Diana gave her shoulders a reassuring rub. "Of course we will. What are friends for?"

Valentina couldn't see the ice in her eyes, but I could.

Sebastian was over first thing the next morning, as I knew he would be, long after Valentina had disappeared in a puff of smoke from her father's white Fiat 500. I wondered what she would tell them, at home over dinner that night, whether she would weave the same tale she had told Silvia, shuffle around feigning sickness, or if Catholic guilt would prevent even that.

He came in through the front entrance rather than his usual slide into the kitchen, a telltale sign that he was feeling remorseful. I found him skulking under one of Silvia's portraits as I was carrying a huge vase of dahlias through to the hall. When he saw me in the living room, he ducked his head, a lick of hair flopping over one eyebrow and hiding his eyes from mine.

"Hi," I said from behind the vase. My shoulders tensed, trying to keep it upright. It was heavy—Silvia had complained to the florist last week that he was shortchanging her, and this week the delivery had almost doubled in size—and I had been scuttling through the rooms as fast as I could, terrified that I would drop it. Silvia had mentioned several times that the vase had been a gift from Versace himself.

"Let me take that." He reached out toward the vase. As he did, his fingers grazed mine, sending involuntary shivers up my wrists. He set it down on the wide, gilt-edged coffee table in the center of the room. "Hi."

He allowed himself to look at me, and there was a wan quality to his expression, to the way his eyebrows knitted together and his lower lip dragged at the corners. His polo shirt was slightly crumpled, enhancing his forlorn, little-boy-lost appearance in a way that pulled at something inside me.

Diana's words from the day before came back to me.

All it's going to take is a little push…

I felt dizzy.

"You heard, I assume, about…"

I nodded. "I heard."

He sighed, and I saw his shoulders slump as he dropped down onto the sofa. "She's gone home."

"I know… I'm sorry."

I hesitated, wanting to hug him but not sure if it was the right thing to do. I took a step closer to him, but the creak of the door made me pause.

"Well, hello there." Diana slunk into the room as smoothly as oil poured from a bottle. "If it isn't the heartbreaker."

She was fresh from the shower, smelling of moisturizer and clean hair, and, I could tell by the alertness in her expression, ready for action.

"Di." I spoke sotto voce, expecting him to rise to her, but instead his head sank lower.

"Low blow, Diana."

"Oh, come on…don't be like that." Diana melted into the sofa and wrapped her elbows around the arm of it, so close they were almost touching Sebastian's upper thigh. She looked as though she were posing for a painting. "You're no fun anymore."

"I don't feel much like being fun at the moment." He tucked his hands into the pockets of his shorts, shuffled his feet.

She tutted. "Honestly, Sebastian, what's come over you? You can't go on moping about like this forever. You're young, you're on holiday, you're in the most beautiful city in the world… don't you think you need to blow off some steam?" I didn't know whether Sebastian could read the softening of her voice, saw the slow fluttering of her eyelids, but I could. "Actually…" Her eyes flickered to me and I read the play in them instantly. "Actually…what are you doing tomorrow night?"

He shrugged. "Nothing."

"Now, that's exactly what I mean." She sat herself up. "Honestly, pal, and I mean this with the greatest of affection, you've become such a *bore* recently. You never go out. You never see your friends. Don't you think having some human company and seeing the people who really care about you would make you feel so much better?"

Ice cream wouldn't melt, let alone butter.

His expression didn't change, but he raised his chin, pointing it in her direction. He was listening.

"What did you have in mind?"

"I don't know that I've thought about it a great deal, but...I don't know...why don't you have a party tomorrow night?"

Sebastian was working the idea through in his mind, little crinkles at the edge of his lips as he parsed through the possibilities.

"A party? I'm not sure I—"

"It's been *such* a long time," she lisped.

"It just doesn't seem right."

"Oh, don't be a killjoy!" Diana pouted, throwing everything she could into the seductive possibility of it. "Wouldn't it be nice? The chance to let your hair down? See all the friends you've been ignoring for so long? I am *telling* you, it'll make you feel better. I *promise* you, all you need is a little perspective and you'll feel like a new man. Thirty-day, money back guarantee. Brownie's honor." She held up three fingers on her right hand. "I was a Brownie, you know." She added huskily, "I think I could probably still fit into the uniform."

I could see her game: keep talking, blindside him with reasons until he couldn't say no. Be cute and sexy and lighthearted, to demonstrate the fun he was missing. And for Sebastian, party boy at heart, it was working. I saw the shift in his features: the little glint in the corner of his eye, like a child who has just discovered the treat cupboard and is debating whether he can get away with emptying it.

"I suppose I do have some mates who are over from Milan..." His tongue roved thoughtfully over his bottom lip.

"And Elio's been complaining he never sees me…" Diana nodded sweetly, encouragingly. "I'm not sure how many people I could rustle up for tomorrow. But how about Saturday?"

"Even better!" Now Diana had him in her snare, she wasn't letting go. "Isn't it, Rach?"

She waggled a hand encouragingly toward me, and I looked up at him, at the impending fate he presented before me. "Saturday's great, Sebastian." And then, perking up, "It would just be nice to spend some proper time with you."

"All right." Sebastian bobbed his head, a slow smile spreading over his face. "It's true—it has been ages since I've had a proper blowout. Maybe it's what I need, to clear my head." He raised his hand in the air, coaxed his fingers into a wave before gesturing to go. "Let me make some calls. Speak to some people. I'm going to pop by and see Silvia, but unless you hear otherwise, Saturday it is."

We both remained silent, watching his retreating back, listening to the soft tread of his footsteps on the heavy carpet once he got out of sight, the whine of the front door as it opened and the satisfying clunk as it slammed shut.

When Diana looked back at me, mischief played across every cell of her face.

"Saturday it is, Rachel." She leaned across to the vase on the coffee table and plucked a flower from it—a tight pink one not yet flowered—and in one continuous motion stroked the side of my arm, nestling it in the dimple of my collarbone before letting it rest in front of my lips like a microphone. "Are you ready?"

I thought of Sebastian. Holding me, touching me, finally getting what I'd wanted for so long. I tried to ignore the image of Valentina's face, pressed to the window of her father's car as she drove away.

I leaned toward the flower. "I'm ready."

31

Now

"A run?" Mum puts her hands on her hips, and I try not to rankle at the scathing expression on her face. "But it's Sunday."

I defiantly pull the zipper up on my new Sweaty Betty running top, repeating an interior monologue to myself: *Don't pick a fight, don't pick a fight, don't pick a fight.* "Yes." I pat my stomach. "Health kick. Trying to avoid the onset of middle-age spread."

I imagine this is the sort of thing mothers and daughters who are close would chat about at length, along with who won *Love Island* and what the latest gossip with Aunt Margery is. Instead, Mum makes a nondescript noise and goes back to washing out the mug she's holding, Fairy Liquid foaming over the top of it as she sponges out the tea residue.

"I won't be long." I attempt a smile. "I'll buy something for dinner on my way home."

The walk to Woking Station is about thirty-five minutes and particularly unlovely, down an unremarkable A road and then through a homogeneous high street, and so this bit I do actually run, feeling all the more up for it because it verifies my white lie. I pull my headphones on and break into a pace I am pleased to report no longer leaves me feeling like my lungs are going to combust, watching the familiar scenery whizz by me as Fleetwood Mac reassures me that I can go my own way.

When I get there, I'm glad to see there's a train only a few minutes away—South Western Rail isn't known for its efficiency—and from Waterloo it's only a short hop on the Jubilee Line to Bond Street, so I should have plenty of time before class. I pull my phone out of my pocket and flick to her Instagram page, hoping for verification that she'll be there. Nothing, but also nothing to suggest she won't be there like clockwork: 3:00 p.m. FlashCycle Xpress with Donnie, as she put it in last week's story:

Wouldn't miss it for the world!

I am reassured, at least, that James won't be with her: Daddy day care! a follow-up story announced, flashing up a picture of him on a sofa, buried in children.

The studio's around the corner from Primark, in a basement, which it tries to use in its favor by going all black and moody on the paintwork, the heavy *doof-doof-doof* of the previous class's soundtrack escaping into reception and adding to the club-like vibe. Behind the desk, a girl with lime green nails and a torso so thin it makes her head look like a Chupa Chup, beams at me. "Welcome to FlashCycle. Have you cycled with us before?"

"Yes," I say distractedly, trying to avoid the how-this-works patter. "But not this branch."

"Great!" She gives me a plastic grin. "Are you a member?"

"No, I'm not."

"Would you like to be? The next class doesn't start for half an hour. I can sign you up, and the good news is we're running a special offer right now—no joining fee if you sign up before Christmas."

"No, thank you." I put my hands out firmly, see her smile falter. "I'm not in London very often. It's just a fleeting visit. But I'll sign up for the next class, please."

"Okay, sure." Her fingernails clack on the keyboard in front of her. "There are only a couple of spaces left—I'll book you in." I say a silent thank-you to whoever is on high—a full class will make me far less conspicuous. "It'll be fifteen pounds for the class, plus a five-pound deposit for shoe rental, unless you brought your own cleats?"

I blink at her. I have no idea what she's talking about. "Um, no?"

"Size?"

"Six."

She reaches behind her to what I now notice are rows of little pigeonholes, and pulls out a pair of firm red-and-black shoes which make a metallic clattering sound as she places them on the desk in front of her.

"Cash or card?"

I stare at the shoes, which remind me of the old bowling alley near my house, where kids would throw birthday parties.

"Card."

I tap the card reader and take the shoes gingerly, expecting them to have that funky smell of feet and antibac spray, but they're surprisingly scentless. Posh people obviously don't sweat much.

In the changing room, I stuff my things into the locker and put on the bowling shoes, which have a metal attachment on each of the soles that makes me hobble when I try to walk. I toy with keeping my running top on, hood up, but figure that will make me stand out even more, so I opt instead to screw my hair into a bun and hope to find a corner to hide in. She probably won't recognize me with the hair, I reassure myself. At least, I think I don't want her to recognize me.

Donnie is a short, muscular man with a headset mic, a charcoal tank top and the most LA accent I've ever heard. The studio is as mercilessly black as the rest of the place, so I tuck myself into the far right-hand corner and try to observe what the handful of other people are doing, which seems to be fiddling with the various knobs and screws on the bike to move it into a more comfortable position. I'm confused when I look down at the pedals and see a metallic cage rather than anywhere to rest my foot, but the girl hopping onto the bike next to me leans over and whispers, "You clip your shoe in like this—" she demonstrates with her right foot "—then twist to get it out. A bit like skiing."

"Skiing, sure. Thanks."

I turn my attention to the center of the room, where Donnie's bike is mounted on a platform, demonstrating that I'm not here for the chitchat. I feel my body freezing each time someone walks in the room, but there's still no sign of her, and I start to worry that I'm about to be landed with an hour's spinning class for nothing, when finally, at one minute to three, the door bursts open and in she walks.

The energy in the room shifts—I'm sure it's not just my imagination—as she strides across the space and takes position front and center on a bike I now realize has been left purposely vacant for her. Bringing up the rear like a Lycra-clad handmaiden is one of the women I recognize from her profile—

Melissa or Melanie—a petite but buxom brunette who slides in next to her. They both blow kisses to Donnie, who finger-waves back at them.

"We-ell." He puts his hands on his hips in mock indignation. "Now you two sluts have decided to show up, I guess we can begin."

Most of the class—regulars, I assume—titter. Diana puffs her hair with a hand and gives the room an embarrassed grimace.

"Sorry, folks, childcare issues."

I automatically duck into myself, but I needn't have bothered—the back corner isn't important enough for her gaze to extend to.

The class begins, Donnie lisping into the bike to "saddle up" as Taylor Swift's adolescent whine floods the room, but even though my legs are moving in vague time to the beat, I allow everything to melt into the background as I fix my eyes on Diana.

She is effervescent. Even more lovely than I remembered from the glimpse of her at her home. She is so clearly the class's fearless leader, punching her fist into the air as a new track starts and woo-hooing like she's at a gig when the beat drops. Watching her, my skin feels as though it's on fire, conflicting emotions licking at me like flames: desire—to see her, to touch her, to talk to her—but hatred too, for everything that happened then, and after. Her total obliviousness to what is happening with Sebastian right now. As the two battle it out in me, I give myself over to the ferocity of the class, pushing the pedals harder, faster, as the music beats so loudly inside me I feel it reverberating deep within my core.

When at last Donnie shouts, "Done!" and bids us all to slam our hands down on the stop button on the bike frame,

I am dripping with sweat, my face radiating with such heat I know if I look in a mirror it'll be tomato red.

The class begins to file out but Diana remains, laughing and chatting with Donnie and Melanie/Melissa, so I scuttle out and make a beeline for the changing room water fountain, where I guzzle through ragged breaths. I hobble back to my locker, legs quivering and nerve endings firing off random pulses through my body, and pull out my things, swapping the ridiculous shoes for the safety of my common, or garden, trainers. I hear her voice before I see her—even plummier than I remember it—and quickly turn back to the lockers, pretending to busy myself with my phone. From her relentless stream of consciousness, I can follow her movement with my back turned, through the room and into the showers at the back. She emerges moments later, and I can't help sneaking a peek from just above the safety of my left shoulder, the sight of her naked body and the towel wrapped around her hair reassuring me that nothing has changed in twenty years. I feel her moving closer toward the lockers, and me, so I bury my head deep in the locker, staring with rapt attention at the imaginary notifications on my phone, even though there's no reception down here. My skin prickles as she approaches, and I start to plan myriad excuses for when she inevitably realizes who I am.

At last: "Excuse me." The lightest brush of her skin against my shoulder as she reaches for a locker above mine. I flinch, waiting, not looking, but when I hear nothing more I dare to glance up, find her perched on a bench in the center of the room, a slick black gym bag beside her as she slathers body butter on her calves.

I am invisible to her. And I don't know if I should be relieved about it or not.

She dresses, carrying on a rolling conversation with her

friend and a couple of women she must know from the class, nothing particularly insightful, just mundane chatter about television programs and school trips, and then she leaves. Just like that. The changing room as empty of her presence as if she had never existed.

I feel hollow; all that promise, all that tantalizing proximity, extinguished to nothing.

I sit there in silence for a moment, hands shaking, ears still ringing from the music, the sound of her voice. And then there's noise from the corridor, the changing room springing into life again as the next class arrives.

I give it a breath, then gather my things and leave.

That evening, after Mum has quizzed me on where exactly I ran, and complained that the mash on the fish pie I made was too salty, and managed to shoehorn into the conversation which of my school friends are on to their second or third child, I stand naked in my room, in front of the mirrored wardrobe door. My body is still warm and damp from the shower, smelling of the medicinal Badedas shower gel my parents seem to be the only people still buying. I inspect the skin on my shoulder where Diana's arm grazed it, half expecting to see a mark or discoloration, as if her very touch has reshaped my genetic makeup. No. The skin is smooth, unblemished. And yet it *feels* different; *I* feel different.

I pull on a T-shirt from the pile on the floor and then lie idly on the bed, stretching across the side table for my phone, flick to her profile, to the latest perfect update from perfect Diana's perfect life, when a message flashes up on the screen. It's from Alex.

Saw the Sebastian Hale piece in the *Mail* and thought of you. Apology accepted. Hope you're okay? Call, when you get the chance.

Any residual warmth from the shower evaporates from my body and I am up, instantly out of bed and down the stairs, past my parents' closed bedroom door, from behind which comes the familiar cacophony of Mum's television and Dad's snoring. In the kitchen, I lift the lid of the bin, rifle through the vegetable peelings and plastic containers Mum refuses to recycle, until I get to the wodge of newspapers that she ceremonially scoops off the coffee table, rolls up together and chucks, half-read, each Sunday night before dinner. I tried to suggest once that she'd be better off just getting an online subscription—it would be a hell of a lot less mess and wasted paper—but I was told I was interfering.

I fan out the supplements and flyers for car insurance and wine clubs on the kitchen table, trying telepathically to locate the article Alex is talking about. I start with the newspaper itself, flipping through the pages as quickly as my mind can process them, the ink turning my fingertips resinous. I skim the contents of *Event*, bypassing a four-star review of Hackney's new Ethiopian small-plates restaurant, and advice on how to pull off the season's mustard-scarf trend, and toss it aside. But there he is—in *You*, where else?—dolled up in baby blue cashmere to make the mums swoon. A three-page spread:

Devilishly Handsome or Handsomely Devilish? An Interview with Italy's Most Notorious English Expat

The wooden chair makes a low screech against the tiles as I pull it out, sit, read.

Apart from an introduction to sum up the case, the majority of the interview is about his time in prison—his daily life, his relationship with the guards, friends he made. He's got a degree—political and social studies, which he acknowledges is ironically a damned sight more useful than the BA in his-

tory of art he was studying at the time of his arrest. He's finally learned Italian, which, despite having an Italian mother,
he somehow failed to do previously. He's hoping to do some
work with the Injustice Scheme, a network established to help
overturn wrongful convictions. He is, to quote,

> looking forward to making the most of his freedom and
> the new lease on life he has been granted.

Despite the pleasantries, the playful cat-and-mouse tripping
through the article is palpable, the interviewer gamely steering Sebastian back toward that night, Sebastian politely evad-
ing him, darting away. Their footwork is as neat as a fencing
duo's: never rude, never abrasive, but tense enough that the
white spaces on the page do little to dilute the claustrophobia
of the increasingly pointed questions, and Sebastian's increasingly blunt responses.

Until eventually the interviewer, growing bored of the pretense, decides to go for the jugular.

> "Come on, Sebastian, cut to the chase, tell the readers
> what they want to know: if you didn't do it, what's the
> truth about what happened that night?"

Hale stares me in the face at last, the bright blue eyes
that must have once been full of youth and vitality now
hardened by the life that fate has dealt him. He licks his
lips, brushes back his hair, sighs.

I wait.

"You want to know the truth."

Thoughtfully, he begins to speak. I lean forward, not
wanting to miss a syllable.

"Well, the truth is, there were six of us on that boat—
plus the crew, although being who we were, we didn't

think of them as people at the time—and the only one of us who is able to say what really happened is unable to. I know what people think. I know what people have said. But, as I have maintained over the last, long, twenty-one years, there has never been a single shred of evidence that proves I was anything other than innocent."

Hale hesitates now, and I see that he is weighing something up, determining whether to press forward with a thought or not. I barely breathe. I can't disturb whatever wheels are turning behind those baby blues.

At last, he speaks.

"What happened that night was a tragedy. I like to think it was an accident; an accident that destroyed lives, mine included."

He leaves the thought suspended, and I snatch at it.

"You 'like to think'?"

My heart pounds, my brain moving at sixty miles an hour.

"Sebastian, are you suggesting... Are you implying...?"

At this Hale shifts in his chair, destroying the intimacy of the moment.

"I imply nothing. Unless anyone can prove otherwise."

The interview over, the journalist sums up in a giddy reverie, taking up the battle call he supposes has been laid at his feet.

I dump the paper back in the rubbish, shiver involuntarily as I notice for the first time that my skin is pockmarked with goose pimples. I scan the kitchen, looking for an open window, a gust of wind, but it's just me. I know this hack isn't the "anyone" Sebastian is referring to.

The sand in the hourglass is growing thin. Sebastian promised that he wouldn't contact me again, but I was a fool to think that meant I was forgotten.

Instead, he is offering an invitation. Now is the time to answer it.

32

Then

It felt as though a lifetime had passed since I had first walked the path to Villa Allegria, not a mere matter of months. True, I was a completely different person from the naive schoolgirl I was back in June, but in fairness it wasn't just me: the landscape had shifted too, hedgerows growing fecund with flowers blooming in the late-summer heat, thickening the air with a ripe scent that was almost unpleasantly sweet, the atmosphere heavy with storm clouds that threatened overhead.

I had gone back and forth over how to appear that evening, neither Diana's bombshell makeover nor my own attempts at seductive dress having done much to impress in the past. Diana had offered to help, as she always did—a trip Via Tornabuoni, a rifle through her wardrobe—but I wormed my way out of it, craving for once the comfort of my own company. I thought of Valentina, my reluctant admiration for her graceful femininity, and opted for simplicity: a white cotton shift dress I'd bought on a whim from a stall at the bric-a-brac market near Sant'Ambrogio, a soft sheen of makeup, hair plaited loosely at the nape of my neck. I didn't feel sexy, but somehow I felt confident, secure, and when Diana met me in the corridor outside our rooms, a fog of rose perfume and fresh blow-dry, she gave me one of the most genuine smiles I had seen her make.

"Oh," she breathed, "you look really pretty." Pretty.

We shared a bottle of wine on the walk over, pilfered from the fridge before Carla had a chance to notice, passing it back and forth as the liquid grew warmer, the outside of the bottle slick with condensation, so that by the time we reached the villa my limbs had a pleasant numbness to them, sounds—Diana's voice, birdsong, the rumble of cars—fuzzing through my brain as though through ceiling insulation.

The house was nowhere near as heaving as it was that first night, but all the same we could hear the low thud of music and the babble of voices escaping over the garden walls. When we walked through the open front gates, though, I was surprised to find the entrance hall empty, the sleek whiteness of the place amplifying the effect, and felt a pang of loneliness for Sebastian, roaming this large ivory box on his own. Suddenly his daily visits to Villa Medici, even before Valentina, seemed to make more sense than just the presumed social call.

In the garden, we spotted Sebastian in a circle of about ten bodies, most of them male, seated around the glass dining table. The flagstones surrounding them were studded with empty beer and champagne bottles rolling on their sides, while scattered across the tabletop were most of the contents of a high-end bar: bottles of spirits, a vast crystal ice bucket with a silver rim, champagne coupes, heavy cut-glass tumblers. As we grew closer, I could make out the residue of white powder streaking the surface.

Most of them I recognized—Elio, immaculate in beige chino shorts and an open-necked linen shirt, his arm slung around a boy with full pink lips and soft blond hair so beautiful he could almost be a girl; Cecily, the small brunette who Diana knew, sprawled across the lap of a boy with a neck as thick as an elephant's leg and an equally chunky signet ring weighing down his left little finger; a couple of other faces from Sebastian's convivial expat orbit. The sparseness of the group made me feel naked, exposed. I had envisaged slipping through heaving bodies, leading Sebastian away undetected, but in this coterie I was hardly inconspicuous. They were all so good-looking, so perfect, their wealth woven into the crispness of their clothes, the carelessness of their posture; suddenly I noticed the roughness of my dress's cheap cotton against my skin, the childishness of my silly plait, compared to Cecily's sleek blow-dry. What arrogant part of me had made me refuse Diana's help? What made me think I could do this? I hung back, my old insecurity returning, but Diana grabbed my hand and propelled us both toward them.

"I thought this was supposed to be a party, Hale." She stopped at a far enough distance for all eyes to focus on her, and jutted a hip bone out, wrist placed firmly on it. "Where is everyone?"

"Ah, good, the help is here. Diana, fetch us a drink." Sebastian pivoted toward us, and I recognized the looseness in his eyes, the drawl elongating the ends of his words. Diana stuck her tongue out in response, but I instantly felt a blush creeping across my face, and Sebastian must have sensed it too, because he caught my eye, grimaced. "A joke. Just a joke. Please, ladies, sit down."

Diana pulled a spare chair over from where it rested against the wall, but when I glanced around, the only seats I could see left were the deck chairs over by the pool and I hesitated, frozen in an awkward middle distance between the back door and the table.

"Sit on Sebastian's lap!" she commanded, nestling into her seat at the other side of the table. I knew from the smirk of her lips that her quick-fire brain had assessed the situation moments before I had, already perceived the outcome. She was taking no prisoners tonight.

I waited for Sebastian to vocalize some form of encouragement, but after a second's delay in which I wanted to hurl myself into the swimming pool, I jumped in on his behalf.

"No, no, it's fine. I'll grab a deck chair."

I motioned toward the pool but Diana tutted, loudly. "Don't be ridiculous, you'll be at midget height if you do that. Sebastian doesn't mind, do you, Seb?"

"No, really, I—"

"No, it's fine," Sebastian interjected, and when I looked at him, he smiled, patted his lap. "Pull up a pew."

I eyeballed the chair. It was one of those expensive-looking clear plastic ones that make you look like you're suspended in midair, with two curved armrests Sebastian was leaning the points of his elbows on.

"I'll...perch." I rested myself gingerly on the edge of the armrest, very aware of how close my bottom was to Sebastian's forearm. He was so near I could smell the laundry detergent on his clothes, and something else—herbal and citrusy—which I deduced was from the red liquid in the glass in front of him.

"What are you drinking?"

He shifted his body weight, stretching his arm for the glass, and in doing so, brought it around my waist, tipping my back into his chest in a way that was almost an embrace. He resettled, held the glass up toward me. My skin tingled where we'd touched.

"It's a negroni. Elio introduced us to them. Apparently, it was invented in Florence by the eponymous Count Negroni." This he said with the exaggerated tone of an antiquated British historian. "What's in it again, mate?"

"Campari, gin, vermouth." Elio counted the ingredients off on his fingers.

"Wow, where's the alcohol?" I got a laugh for that. No wonder Sebastian was tipsy.

"Try it." Sebastian held the glass to my mouth, and as I took it from him, his fingers brushed mine. I had to really focus, to stop myself from dropping the glass. What was the matter with me? I scolded myself sharply. I knew I fancied Sebastian, but tonight I felt like I'd never seen another human being, the anticipation of what I was going to attempt later setting my nerves jangling like a bunch of keys left on top of a moving car.

I wetted my lips with the alcohol. "Delicious." It wasn't delicious. It tasted like petrol.

"Ha. There you go, Cecily." A few seats down, Cecily minced and pouted on Elephant Leg's lap. "Cecily said it was horrible, and a man's drink, and that the only reason we were drinking them was because of male bravado. But see, Cecily—" he took the glass from me, swigged deeply and set it back down on the table with a loud clink "—Rachel likes it."

His tone was petulant; I recognized the same giddy childishness in him that he only displayed when he was *really* drunk. I wondered how long he had been drinking for—the others seemed nowhere near on par with him, and there was something particularly reckless about his manner, a sort of rubbedover quality to his hair and clothes, that felt as though he had been quite purposefully making up for lost time. I forced myself to brush any worry aside, focusing instead on the prickle of pleasure I felt at being held up as an example by him.

"It's great. Fix me a strong one, Elio!"

If the wine hadn't already given me my fair share of Dutch courage, the red rocket fuel I was about to drink was surely going to power me through.

Elio grabbed a glass, scooped some ice from the silver bucket in the middle of the table and then shook the bottle of Campari in Diana's direction.

She screwed up her nose. "Gosh, no. I've had that stuff before. It tastes like Calpol—the bad kind." She surveyed the debris on the table, selected a bottle and a clean glass. "I'll stick to champagne."

Elio walked the glass round to me, the liquid sloshing against the sides, and held it out to me as if he were presenting a glass slipper.

"Here you go, *principessa*." I hadn't seen him since the trip to the beach, and now he looked pointedly from me to Sebastian. "It's good to see you again."

"Right, if everyone's settled, let's carry on with the game." Sebastian sloppily banged his free hand on the table for emphasis.

"What game?" I asked, swilling the liquid around in my glass and taking a tiny sip.

"Truth or Dare. It's Elio's go." As soon as he said the words, I felt Diana's eyes on me, penetrating across the distance. When I looked up, a slow smirk was spreading over her face. I met her gaze and she winked. I felt the blood thudding in my ears.

I managed to remain an innocent bystander for longer than I had anticipated. The game batted about the table like a Ping-Pong ball, requests getting lewder and more ridiculous, but somehow I avoided being picked upon. The more I sipped at my drink, the more the flavor of it mellowed, until I was happily requesting a second one, a third, my body relaxing and sinking into its perch. Sebastian too seemed to soften his posture, and to my delight, he even rested his left arm across my lap and let it remain there, pleasantly heavy.

A joint was lit, clouds of its sweet fug filling the air. I sucked deeply on it when it was passed to me, holding the smoke in my mouth until it burned my tongue and it took all I could muster not to choke. My limbs melted, my mouth slackening into a peaceful smile.

The sky darkened overhead, clouds gathering so that the atmosphere felt close, thick, like a lid being set on a pan of simmering water.

And then it was my turn.

Diana, fresh from being dared to demonstrate her best fellatio moves on a neighboring finger, wiped a hand across her mouth and took in the group of people watching her.

"Okay, my go." She pointed a demonstrative finger in the air and then waved it slowly around the table, making a song and dance of where it might land. "Who should I pick? Who… should…I…pick…" But I didn't need to guess who she'd pick. When her finger landed on me, I was ready for it. "Rachel." She beamed at me. "Truth or dare?"

I knew what she was thinking. I knew that she was determined to be the puppet master of this show. Say "dare" and I was in her hands.

"Truth." I looked her square in the eye. "I pick truth." I searched her face, looking for some hint of annoyance, some sign that she had been thrown from the path she was planning. She studiously avoided my gaze.

"Tell Sebastian how much you want to fuck him right now."

The atmosphere shifted. The tone of her voice, the plainness of it, cut through the debauchery of the gathering and silenced the party's inconsequential burbling. Diana had picked up her bow and fired a shot straight at my chest, and I had nowhere to hide.

I felt the heat flare in my cheeks as everyone turned to look at me. Worse, I felt Sebastian's arm stiffen against my lap. Thank goodness, at least, I couldn't see his face. "Diana, that's not a question." My throat felt raw, as though I'd swallowed a length of barbed wire, but I wanted desperately to prove to her that I wasn't shaken, forcing the words to come out steadily.

Diana looked coolly down at her fingernails, and then back at me.

"Fine. On a scale of one to ten, how much do you want to fuck Sebastian right now?"

"Diana, don't mess around." Sebastian's voice surprised me. I wanted to turn my head, but I was too embarrassed to even look at him.

"Why?" She cocked her head, gave him a look of pure malice disguised with a beautiful red bow of a smile. "At least someone wants to."

Sebastian inhaled sharply. People shifted uncomfortably in their seats, everyone pretending to avert their eyes while secretly trying to sneak a glance at Sebastian or Diana.

"Di, don't." I spoke softly, more to myself than Diana, but she heard me instantly, snapping her head to look at me, whippet fast.

"Why not? It's the truth." Her voice beat the air with a staccato rhythm.

"Please." I looked at her imploringly. I wanted Sebastian. I wanted nothing more than to break up him and Valentina. But not like this.

Like a deus ex machina, a streak of lightning cracked through the air, bursting the sky into life. Thunder roared moments later, and then the rain began to fall, thick droplets as big as thousand-lira coins, pinging off glasses and drenching us all in seconds.

Everyone sprang into action, gathering glasses and bottles and half-empty bowls of olives and nuts.

"Inside!" someone yelled. A chair crashed to the ground. Another fizz of lightning struck.

Cecily shrieked and threw her arm over her head. "My hair!"

The rain pounded down, soaking through clothes and plastering our hair to our faces.

Sebastian banged open the garden door, holding it with his back as he ushered people inside. "Quick, quick. Into the kitchen."

We streamed in, and he slammed a fist into the light switch. The lights blared for a second, then there was an electrical pop and the room plunged into darkness.

"Fuck." He tried again: on, off, on, off. *"Fuck."* He ran a hand through his damp hair. "Power cut."

We stood there, dripping on the tiles, smelling of wet dog, as he processed his thoughts.

"Towels. We need towels. There are loads in the bathrooms upstairs. And there are candles in the utility room somewhere, and a torch, I think. Everyone, just…go into the living room. I'll sort it."

"I'll get the towels," I volunteered, not looking at him. I hadn't looked at him, not eye to eye, since Diana had started her tricks. I snatched at the opportunity to be by myself, to have the space to think. Without waiting for an answer, I turned and walked out of the kitchen, holding my hands in front of me to help find my way.

The villa was in near pitch darkness, the lack of any streetlights or nearby houses denying me even the dullest artificial glow. I found my way back to the hall, to the foot of the grand curved staircase leading to the upstairs rooms, removing my sodden sandals before I started my ascent, feet feeling for the thick, deep carpet I remembered was a pristine vanilla white and prayed I wouldn't mark. I stepped tentatively, heel to toe, the palm of my hand pressed against the polished wooden banister to guide my way.

I had never been upstairs before, and my pulse raced a touch faster at the thought of the more intimate, private Sebastian the closed doors secreted. I saw a bathroom immediately—a door was ajar at the end of the wide hallway, and I could see the moon-bathed curve of a bath inside—but I couldn't resist the temptation to draw out my search a little longer as my eyes began to adjust to the dark.

I clasped at the first door handle on my right, the curved brass cool beneath my fingertips as I pulled it down and then pushed. Inside, a guest room, twin beds made up and untouched. I left disappointed, unearthed two more equally uninhabited rooms, then an obvious master bedroom: huge sash windows overlooking the gardens, an en suite bathroom, a vast king-size bed with freshly plumped pillows I had the urge to throw myself on. All of it was sharp, clean, modern, the antithesis of the Villa Medici's odds and-ends Renaissance antiques but, I was sure, not a penny less expensive.

Eventually, I found what I was seeking. The hallway curved around, past the bathroom with towels I had easily spied and now guiltily ignored. The last door but one on the left, already a hairbreadth open.

I knew it was his as soon as I stepped inside. It smelled of him. Of his cologne, of his sweat, of his shampoo, all the other obviously identified scents, and that familiar essence that was so hard to define: a "himness" that even here, divorced of him, made me feel nervous and tongue-tied. The room was strewed with clothes, the bed unmade, duvet balled up and pushed into a corner, and when I edged closer, I could see the depression on the pillow and sheets where his body had lain, bare skin kissing cotton. There was a tranquility to the room that made me want to linger; it was so calm, so still, devoid of the chaos downstairs, and I found myself overcome by a wave of tiredness, a perfect storm of negronis and weed and Diana's machinations. The rainwater had evaporated from my skin, leaving it sticky to the touch, but my dress was still soaking, and without really being aware of what I was doing, I began peeling it off, sinking onto the mattress and pulling the duvet across me.

I lay listening to the rain lashing against the windows, my skin touching where his skin had touched, and replayed the game of Truth or Dare over and over in my mind, wrestling with whether there was any way I could have made the situation better, disarmed Diana and saved myself the humiliation. Motion in the doorway made me look up, and to my horror, I saw a figure there, illuminated by candlelight.

"Rachel?"

It was Sebastian.

I sat up, clutching the duvet to me, agonizingly aware of my half-naked body, my dress tossed on the floor.

"Hi," was all I could think to say.

"What are you doing in here?" He moved fully into the room, and as he got closer, my nostrils burned as the smell of synthetic flowers filled the air, and I realized he was holding a scented candle. "Turns out we don't have that many candles." He held his aloft. "Found this in the downstairs loo. Wild fig and freesia." He sniffed it. "Thought you might be having trouble with the towels—came to find you."

"I…I was tired." It sounded pathetic—even as I said it, I didn't believe it—but for some reason Sebastian didn't challenge it. He stumbled across the room, his movements slow, jerking, and, coupled with the thickness of his voice, I realized quite quickly he was even drunker than I'd thought. He tripped on a pair of jeans, his hand shooting up to steady the candle.

"Whoopsie," he blathered, and then laughed, a low, closed-mouth chuckle. "Whoopsie? Who says that?"

I followed him with my eyes, the rest of me not daring to move, as he made his way to the other side of the bed, set the candle down on the bedside table and then heaved his body onto the bed beside me. Thoughts combusted inside me: panic, pleasure, terror, delight. He was just inches away from my bare skin and I felt my body start to quiver involuntarily, adrenaline coursing through me, as I watched him press his head into the pillow, sigh deeply.

"This is nice." He elided the words together into one hushed, outward breath: *This is nice.* I turned my head, lay listening to his heavy, alcohol-soaked breathing, watched his eyelids fluttering closed.

"Sebastian." I spoke barely above a whisper, but somehow his name filled the silent air of the room.

He opened his eyes. "Mmm?"

"I'm sorry, about earlier. The game."

He shook his head, the sides of his cheeks nestling into the pillow. "Doesn't matter. Don't talk about it." *Don-talkh-aboudit.*

I couldn't help myself; something was urging me to keep going.

"You know what Di is like. She likes to get under people's skin. Push their buttons. I don't think she intentionally means to upset people—it's like she doesn't see the seriousness of it. It's harmless, really." Even I didn't sound convinced. Why was I making excuses for her? Why was I always making excuses for her?

"Why are you making excuses for her?" His response was uncanny.

Cautiously keeping the duvet tight to my body, I turned on my side so we were facing one another. The flickering candle-light rounded the edges of his features, made him even more boyish than usual. We were so close I could hear the whoosh of his breath, in and out, smell the rainwater drying on his hair.

"Because she's my friend. Because she has been kind to me."

"Not always."

I knew what he was referring to. I saw them again, the twisted limbs, the low grunts, the muscles of Sebastian's back flexing, Diana's limbs emerging from the tangle of bedsheets.

"No, but neither have you."

"No." He closed his eyes, turned his face away from me.

"Why?"

He didn't answer. Rolled onto his back so that he was star-ing at the ceiling, his arms curved so that his head rested on his palms.

"I honestly don't know. I was confused. A little drunk." He sighed. "She was there."

That stung.

"*I* was there." I sat up, crossing my arms around me so the duvet was tucked under my arms.

"I'm sorry." And he was beside me, his palms touching my naked shoulders. "I'm sorry I hurt you."

"You said you didn't want to complicate our friendship. But then, her…?"

"I don't know what I want, Rachel," he murmured, slurred. As he said it, I felt him moving closer toward me until his chest was touching my back, so that the clasp of my bra strap bit against my spine.

The energy in the room changed, I felt it; it was almost as though the air itself grew thick. Without him speaking a word, without me daring to utter one, he looped a finger underneath my bra strap, pulled. It slid down my shoulder with little resistance. My body began to tingle, flushing hot and cold in equal measure as my heart began beating a tattoo in my chest, the same rhythmic thought pulsating through my synapses: *This is happening, this is happening, this is happening.* I felt his breath, sticky against my neck, and then his lips, kissing the hollow where neck and shoulder met. His arms came around me, guided me, and I felt my limbs slacken, allowed myself to be entirely malleable to him. He laid me down in the middle of the bed, one hand reaching for his shirt buttons, undoing them with clumsy fingers as he leaned over and kissed me sloppily on the mouth. For the first time, I began to feel scared, frightened by my lack of experience and a growing awareness that *this was it*, the thing that the books and magazines all talked about. I looked up at him, hoping for reassurance, but was met with a surprising vacancy in his eyes.

"I…" I tried to find the right words, the way to tell him it was my first time, hoping for a scene like in the movies where he would sweep me into his arms, tell me he'd be gentle.

Instead he murmured a throaty "Shh," gave me a rough kiss somewhere near my mouth as he threw his shirt to the floor and began to unbutton his shorts. My bra came undone, was pushed aside, and any fear I had at my breasts being exposed to him was overshadowed by the sensation of his hands cupping them, mashing them together.

"You do have great tits." He kissed the space between them as he wrestled off his shorts and boxers in one motion. A surge of panic jolted through me as his naked body came fully into view, the body I had pictured so many times before now literally in the flesh. He touched himself, wrapped a hand around it, and I watched in pure virgin amazement as it grew. And then he reached for my hand, placed it over him, and a low groan erupted from somewhere deep in his chest. I felt a mere witness to his pleasure, following his lead as he rubbed my hand under his—up, down, up, down—my brain bursting with the horror and the fascination of it. Next, my knickers were pulled aside, and I breathed in sharply as his fingers thrust inside me. "Is that good?" he slurred, eyes closed, fingers jabbing. I nodded tentatively, made an "Mmm" sound that vaguely resembled pleasure, hating to offend him. I closed my eyes, my hand limp around him, and he began to clutch it more fervently, jerked it harder, harder, kneeling over me as the stabbing fingers worked rhythmically in time. For a second he paused, and I peeked one eye open: he was leaning over me toward the bedside table, rummaging in the top drawer, and then I saw him pull out a small, square cardboard box—I knew what it was instantaneously, even though I'd never seen them in real life—opened it and swore, tossing the empty packet to the floor. "Are you on the pill?" He kissed into my neck, his hands offering my lower regions respite as they served instead to balance him over the pillows.

"Um, no, sorry," I whispered.

He groaned again into my neck—I wasn't sure if it was pleasure or frustration. "Don't worry, I'll pull out."

And then he was inside me, a rasping, rough pain that made me gasp out loud. I was suddenly aware of my arms, floppy and useless beside me, and tentatively reached them around his back, hoping, I don't know, that perhaps I would be able to guide his motions and lessen the pain. He began to speed up, his chest jammed against mine, and I could feel the sweat pooling between us, the heat of the room closing in. I closed my eyes tight, tried to overlay all the romantic fantasies I had pictured for this moment so many times, so very different from the reality. I focused on the smell of the scented candle, imagining crisp cotton sheets and the Goo Goo Dolls playing in the background, tangled limbs and him murmuring words of love and affection. And then he spasmed quickly, grunted loudly and rolled off me, lying faceup on the pillow beside me.

The room was quiet for what felt like a very long time. I didn't want to be the first to move—to breathe, almost—and so I remained planked in position, skin cooling from our shared heat, my mind strangely numb. "Pffft." Finally, he made something resembling a noise, then pressed his heels into the mattress and hauled himself to sitting, his arms draped over his knees, apelike. "God." He pressed his forehead into his hands, raked his fingers through his sweat-dampened hair. *"God,"* he said again, louder. A tiny part of me wanted to hope, pictured some magical revelation where he prostrated himself at my feet, told me he had known all along how he felt about me, that this was all he needed to realize it.

But if I am telling the truth, I knew in that instant, from his very first sound, that the reality was far crueler than that.

"Rachel," he said, and I swallowed, tasted metal in my mouth from biting the inside of my cheek. I pressed my head into the pillow and turned, very slowly, to face him. And I saw it all there in his eyes. The mistake. "I'm so sorry." He hugged his knees tighter, inadvertently shielding his body away from me—the body that only moments before was so alive in mine. "We shouldn't have done that, should we?" His thoughts picked up speed, and I knew I wasn't required to answer. "God, this was so *stupid.* I'm so, so sorry, Rachel. This was such a terrible mistake. Oh *God*—" He balled a fist, smacked it against his other palm. "How could we have done this? How could we have done it to Valentina? Rachel." He lurched suddenly to face me, eyes wide. "Rachel, we can't tell her—do you understand?" Nausea coursed through me, my body rousing to expect the blow my mind already knew was coming. "Rachel, it would kill her. We can't tell her, we

can't tell anyone—you get it, don't you?" He raised his arms
out toward me as if he was going to touch my shoulders, but
then he stopped himself as if he'd thought better of it. *"Please."*
He looked deep into my eyes, imploring. "Please, don't tell
anyone. I mean *anyone*, not even Diana. Promise me? You
know she'd tell the world, the first chance she got. I fucked
up. This isn't me. I never meant this to happen. I was going
to apologize…as soon as she came back, I was going to go to
Valentina, beg her to take me back. I can't let this ruin that.
We're both just so drunk, and it was the heat of the moment
and…and…you understand, don't you?"

I tried to speak, but my insides felt ripped out.

And I was worried that if I tried to speak, the tears would
fall instead.

Instead, I pressed my lips together, held my breath, nodded. He exhaled deeply, pushed the back of his head into the
headboard. "Oh God, thank you, thank you so much. You
have no idea how much it means to me, Rachel. Honestly,
you know I'd do the same for you." He was speaking rapidly
now, sliding off the bed and moving about the room, pulling
on his shirt and gathering his boxers, socks, as I lay immobile, bile bubbling inside me. "I'll get the towels and go down
now, say I had trouble finding enough, and that you'd fallen
asleep. Wait twenty minutes or so and come down, and then
we'll make a joke of it, huh? They'll believe it, right? Right?"
He was looking in my direction, but it was as though I wasn't
in the room at all. "Okay." He was fully dressed now, and
even as he was talking, he was backing toward the door, plan
already in motion. "Oh." He paused, and then walked back
around to the bedside table, picked up the scented candle.
"Better remember this." He retreated to the doorway, stood as
he had at the beginning, as if he was pressing Rewind on the
videotape, truly erasing the act for good. "Thank you again,

Rachel. I'm sorry it had to be this way." And then he smiled, that wobbly, foppish smile, which in that moment stabbed at my heart like a knife. "We're still friends, right?"

I gathered everything I had left inside me and smiled back. "Of course," I half whispered. "Still friends."

Moments later, he was gone, his smell on my skin the only thing that lingered.

33

Now

It is less challenging than I thought, becoming someone's shadow. Particularly when that someone is so infatuated with their own sense of self that, even if one is not too precise, *even if one is not that careful*, one can quite easily lurk in the background of their life without causing so much as a wrinkle of disturbance. For a week, I become as skilled as a trained investigator while I plan my next step. I loiter in the fruit-and-veg aisle at Waitrose, hand skimming the carrots just moments after hers. I slide into the hairdresser's, dark glasses shielding my face, and make enquiries about the costs of the senior stylists as she sips a Diet Coke and fluffs her blow-dry. I observe the tired nod of the waiter in her favorite Italian, when she confirms again that it's dressing *on the side*, crunch popcorn in the row behind her when she complains loudly to her friend about how "comedies are rarely even funny anymore." *Actually, Diana, I thought it was hilarious.*

I am there when she steps into her Range Rover in the morning, and when her key clicks into the lock of her Farrow & Ball–painted door at night, careful—always so, so careful—to avoid James's detection. I am there when she plumps for the organic nonapplicator tampons in the pharmacy, and when she catches sight of herself in a shop window and artfully flips her hair from one side to the other. I am there when she selects white roses, ivy and berries from the florist—"The annual pre-Christmas soiree!" she tells them, gaily—and later, when she calls to confirm the caterer; when she picks up a green velvet dress from the dry cleaner's, pursing her lips when they tell her they couldn't quite remove the stain on the shoulder. And when the guests arrive, rising out of their lumbering vehicles to be greeted with open arms and a champagne flute by their glamorous hostess, I am there, across the street, watching from the shadows.

Do I imagine it, or does she sense me there, lingering in the doorway as she wafts a batch of guests in ahead of her, sniffs the air, shivers?

Back home, Mum wears her indignation as lightly as a shearling fleece.

"Where do you go all day?"

"Out."

"Out with whom?"

"Out with friends."

She mutters at Dad that it's like living with a teenager all over again.

I concede, mainly because of Dad, who touches me lightly on the arm one morning as I am making my way out the door and says in his quiet way that it would be nice, seeing as I'm home, to see more of me.

On Sunday, I take the day "off," suggest a trip to see the Wisley Gardens Christmas lights—knowing it's one of Mum's favorites—lunch in the pub they like, my treat. I am antsy and distracted all day, wondering where Diana's been, what she's done, and when we finally return home and sink into the living room sofa in front of the latest ITV period drama, Dad promptly falling asleep and Mum escaping upstairs to tidy, I dig out my phone in an instant, finally treat myself to a virtual hit.

Her profile.

Her day summed up in a single shot. She and her daughter, Phoebe, a rose-printed teapot and two pink-frosted cupcakes in front of them.

Their likeness is almost uncanny. Bow-shaped mouths pursed in near-identical pouts, creamy cheeks pressed together to fit into the frame, the doppelgänger joy that lights up their faces.

A day out with my precious baby girl,

the caption reads, and a row of pink hearts.

Life wouldn't be worth living without you.

You can see the uncomplicated joy in both of their eyes. Phoebe's carefree sparkle, Diana's as unsullied as her perfectly applied eyeliner.

And it is this that finally breaks me.

Of all the things that mark Diana out, this—this total, uncompromised joy—curdles in my stomach like sour milk. The life that she is living—the life that she has *created*—palpates so brazenly in the face of the rest of us: Valentina six feet under,

Sebastian caged, me stuttering and stalling from day to day. All of us, in our separate, different ways, are the collateral from Diana having a life worth living. She treads through each shiny, pastel-pink day oblivious, and in her obliviousness, she is cruel.

Dad lets out a whistling snore, shifts position, settles. I feel suffocated by the living room walls, the smell of dried-rose potpourri and the beige shag-pile carpet that dulls the sound. I thud upstairs, close my bedroom door behind me as quietly as I can and sink to the floor, letting the heat rush through my body, breath escaping me as forcefully as a train whistle.

I remain there, trying to collect myself, when an object in the corner of the room catches my eye, something I'm sure wasn't there earlier: a large plastic storage box with a piece of A4 paper sellotaped to the front: Rachel Misc. Resting on top of it, a message scrawled on a piece of ruled paper torn from a notepad:

Rachel, we don't have space in the attic for all this junk anymore. Can you either take it back with you or throw it away?

Typical of her to leave it for me to find like this, rather than mentioning it in person when we're living in the same house. I shuffle the box to the foot of the bed and cross my legs underneath me, opening the lid with a cautious click. I know what's inside: an ode to my youth, the contents neatly stacked, a cacophony of fabric and papers and boxes. I pull out a T-shirt that still has the faint whiff of Body Shop White Musk embedded in it, and the iconic words Spiceworld Tour emblazoned on the front above black-and-white headshots of the five famous faces. I didn't even like the Spice Girls, but a girl in my year had a spare ticket and I was flattered to be asked. I shove it aside. There are my GCSE results, A levels, my offer letter from Cambridge:

Dear Miss Bailey,
I am delighted to inform you…

All useless now, but relics of my youthful sense of self. There's the laminated poster of Alanis Morissette, rolled up and held together with masking tape, but no Björk—I must have gone off her by then—and another for the film *Armageddon* I'd forgotten I possessed, remembering with a hint of revulsion my brief but fervent crush on Billy Bob Thornton.

I keep delving into the treasure trove, distracting myself with my bronze Duke of Edinburgh certificate—never again—birthday cards from classmates whose faces I've forgotten, a nearly evaporated bottle of Clinique Happy I bought on a whim to wear at my Leavers' Ball; all nostalgic and pleasant, but ultimately not the real reason I am looking through this box. Because if I am right, if Mum's offhand giveaway houses within it what I think it does, then I have just discovered the perfect way to get Diana's attention.

And there, right at the bottom, hidden beneath the T-shirts and the trinkets, I find it.

The jewelry box is mink colored, white stitching running around the perimeter, with a silver clasp that bears my initials in punctuated capitals. Doing a good approximation of leather despite it being one hundred percent polyurethane. Dad bought it for me: a reward for straight As which Mum had met with, "Raymond, don't overindulge her." He hadn't totally; he'd seen me looking at one in the Smythson shop window when we'd gone into town to see the Christmas lights being switched on—dove gray French calfskin with a baby-soft nubuck interior—and I guess this was the runner-up prize. I don't know if he ever realized that I'd left it behind when I left home, and if he did, whether he was hurt, but at the time, my embarrassment at the idea of someone spotting the tawdry synthetic thing in my room was far worse than upsetting him. I feel a bit ashamed at the thought of it now.

To the naked eye, there's nothing left in it—I still wear Gran's pearls on occasion, and the costume jewelry I've worn and discarded over the years has lived clustered in the top drawer of the bedside table wherever I've lived in the intervening years. But the naked eye may not think to pull up the top tray, have a look at what is hidden underneath.

I do this now, pinch the middle of one of the dividers, exposing the cavity underneath.

Inside: a single object, kept impervious to the erosion of time by the box's sarcophagus-like seal. A navy pouch tied tightly at the neck in a double knot. The pouch itself is unconnected, belonging to some long-forgotten pair of earrings I hastily tossed aside, but it was useful at the time, its inconspicuousness serving its purpose ever since. Because, really, it was what was inside that was important.

I roll the pouch between my palm and fingertips, overwhelmed by its corporeal reality, so long has it been hidden, forgotten, and then the memory breathes into me with a force that makes me gasp, inhale a wave of iodine seawater, salt spray whipping my face, the susurrant hiss of lapping waves. A strangled cry erupts from me, and reflexively I fling the pouch from my hands to where it lands with a soundless thud in the corner of the room, mocking me.

I don't want to, but I know I have to look.

I gather myself, stretch across the carpet for it and unlace the cord, first using the point of my nail and then my teeth to release the knot. I hold out my left palm and the object slinks out, cold and tangled but unchanged since the last time I looked at it.

The necklace.

A thin gold chain, punctuated with a simple, diamond-studded pendant, shaping out the letter *V*. She wore it for a relatively short time, and yet I can picture it on her so distinctly, looped around her delicate throat, fingers teasing it, rotating the letter around the chain.

V for Valentina: Sebastian's peace offering. Diana smirked that it certainly couldn't stand for *virgin*. Afterward, of course, it also stood for *victim*.

I flick back to the photograph of Diana and Phoebe, the symbol of all the things she won, that we have lost. It was supposed to make things better, this necklace.

But perhaps, now, it finally will.

34

Then

I kept my word to Sebastian. I said nothing to anyone. But that didn't mean Diana believed me.

After the door to his bedroom clicked shut behind him, I did as he asked: lay rumpled in the sheets, listening to my breathing steady and slow, and then allowed myself to rise, gather my clothes from where Sebastian had tossed them, unthinking, during the act, just as he had done with me now. I dressed slowly, ignoring the stickiness on my thighs, the ache between them, set my tangled hair loose from its braid, running fingers through the matted sections and replaiting it as best I could. And then I went downstairs. Most of the party had left, but the remainder sat huddled around the white marble coffee table, nursing glasses of Sebastian's dad's imported single malt whiskey and chatting in low, drink-drugged voices.

I gave an exaggerated yawn, arms outstretched, for the full effect.

"Whoops, sorry about that. Fell asleep upstairs. You managed to get the towels, though? Good."

I curled around myself as the conversation resumed, ignored Diana's penetrating gaze, as any interest in my disappearance gradually sank into the backdrop.

The power came back on; a metallic crackle like a fly too close to a bulb, and then a low whir and we were plunged into light. I didn't want to go home, was dreading being alone, alone with Diana and her inevitable poking and prodding, but the electricity had the effect of dunking everyone into cold water, making us sober up and remember reality.

When we stepped into the open air—now clean and fresh and quiet—I was surprised to see it was almost light, a hint of daylight blinking into view on the horizon. We picked our way along the silent path, the atmosphere still ripe with the smell of rain, and I waited, unspeaking, for Diana to make her move.

"Did you have fun?"

We had barely rounded the first corner before she spoke. I was surprised; I should had given her more credit.

"Yes. It was a fun evening. Shame about the weather." I looked straight ahead, concentrated on the individual nodules of stone that paved my view.

"Ha, ha. I meant with Seb."

I paused, swallowed. "I don't know what you're talking about." An ache was beginning to pulsate at the corners of my temples, and I instinctively reached a hand to my forehead, pressed the pads of my fingertips into the pressure points.

"Don't play about—you had sex."

The bluntness of it shocked me—the word, unleashed into the open air, seemed to echo in the empty fields—and I had the distinct urge to grab her and press my hand against her mouth.

Instead I balled my fists, kept walking at a steady pace.

"No, we just talked. It got quite deep—life, all that. He didn't want me to say anything to the others. Didn't want to seem 'soppy.' Boys...you know what they're like."

I attempted an eye roll I couldn't quite bring myself to follow through on. I was suddenly exhausted, dreaming of a shower, of cold, fresh water to wash the evening off my skin.

"No, you didn't. Why are you lying?"

"I'm not." Villa Medici was creeping into view, its buttercup-colored stonework the promise of salvation.

"You are. I can tell from the way you look. I can even smell it on you."

There was a tease in Diana's voice, a playful singsong in the rising inflection of each phrase. She leaned over and gave me a slow, lascivious sniff.

"Diana, stop."

"Come on, out with it—what was it like?"

"Please. Leave it."

"Oh, don't be a bore. We're penis pals now—I want to compare notes."

She reached out to tickle me, witchy fingers digging into the soft tissue between my ribs. I instinctively wrenched myself away, wrapped my arms around my torso, stormed ahead.

"Shut the fuck up, Diana."

It startled her. Momentarily knocked her off her axis. I could tell, even though she tried to hide it, to smooth over the shock on her face and repaint the expression of calm control.

"No need to be a bitch about it. I'll pretend I never asked."

She folded her arms, looking into the distance, and instantly I felt bad, wanted to apologize. It's amazing how she always had that effect on me, even when I was the wronged party.

"Sorry," I mumbled, touching an arm to her shoulder. "I shouldn't have snapped. I'm really tired. Would you mind, please, if we didn't talk about it? I just want to go to bed."

For a moment she didn't speak, toying with me as I waited, ever patient, for her to show me grace.

"If you're going to be like that about it, I won't mention it again. Although I thought a thank-you would have been in order, at least." She tossed her hair and started toward the villa, leaving me standing uselessly in her wake. But before she got too far, she turned back. Just her head—I wasn't worthy of the full body turn. "Don't forget—you need me, Rachel. I know you'll want to talk, eventually. And when you do, you'll know where to find me."

In the depths of myself, I knew that she was right.

And so, I said nothing. I said nothing when Valentina returned the following morning, cutting a more withdrawn figure than previously, but at least calmer and more resolute than the day she had left.

She didn't ask about Sebastian, although I could tell from the hunger in her eyes when she asked Diana and I how we were that she wanted to. The question lingered in the sauce-scented air of the kitchen, carving around the sweating onions and browning mince. But she said nothing. And I said nothing.

To his credit, Sebastian waited until late that afternoon to try his luck. I saw him skulking outside the kitchen window, all the nonchalance knocked out of him. He at least gave me the courtesy of looking embarrassed when he saw me.

She saw him too, the color draining out of her, the wooden spoon she had been holding going limp in her hand.

"I have to…" she panted, eyes round and panicked. "I need to…"

Her body spasmed as she turned in the direction of the

door, jerking limbs moving across the room like a windup toy running out of power.

There was movement from the kitchen window, then a hand on the French doors.

"Val!" Sebastian called, seizing the moment. "Val, wait!"

"*No!*" she growled, not looking back. "*Vai via.*" She flung an arm out behind her, batting the air. "Leave me alone."

"Please, Val, just let me talk to you for one second..." Their darting footsteps echoed into silence.

It went on like this for days, their operatic lovers' quarrel: his hangdog expression at the kitchen door, her fleeing the room, him running after her. I began to feel like I was trapped in the midst of some sort of Sisyphean loop.

But gradually the points of their swords were sanded down, the troops battle weary. The pace of her kitchen retreat weakened, the sound of his desperation ebbing to a low hum. The shy smiles returned. Fingers found each other once more. And then hands. And then mouths. And in the end, with a sickness that spread through me like a slow-release poison, I realized that the war had been won. And I was not its victor.

The necklace really cemented it, though.

He arrived in the morning, all pink and pleased with himself, holding a white cardboard bag with a name stamped on in gold: Fratelli Piccini, Ponte Vecchio.

I thought for one heart-stopping moment that this was actually it—a ring—and was relieved to see the flat navy velvet box arguing to the contrary, although her dramatic gasp when she drew out the loop of gold and glistening diamonds gave me a soupçon of what her reaction would be if it had been.

Valentina, blissful, adoring Valentina, flew into his arms, nearly knocking over the mixing bowl she had been holding, and clung to him, giddy as a toddler, covering his face in kisses.

"Amore, amore!" She nestled her head in his chest.

He caught my eye watching them and swiftly averted his gaze. We both did.

This had been the pattern since their reunion: no matter how hard I tried to avoid him, he was always there, his presence a cruel reminder of what we had done, what I had promised.

Why he chose this, why he didn't try to construct these little moments with more privacy, I will never understand, but I couldn't bring myself to believe it was pure cruelty and told myself, with all the ignorant hope of a wounded heart, that he was doing me a kindness: demonstrating the worth of the love I had been tossed aside for. But it didn't make me any less miserable.

"I hope you like it." He had the courtesy of speaking softly, pulling her into him in an attempt to effect privacy.

For my part, I focused intently on the rosemary I was stripping, its resinous scent cloying, making the room close and claustrophobic.

"I love it! Rachel—" to my horror she called to me "—look!"

"Very pretty," I agreed absently, roughly chopping and then folding the rosemary into the lumpen pork mince with my hands, ready to be turned into *polpette*, enjoying the gluey resistance as I attacked it.

"No, Rachel, you're not looking—*ma dai*, come on!" Ever since Diana and I had struck up this supposed friendship with her, she seemed to have cast herself in the role of annoying little sister. Which, I gathered, bumped me up to awkward middle child.

I fixed a smile so bluntly on my face it could have been carved with a spoon.

"It really is lovely." I turned my head to Sebastian but didn't meet his eyes. "Well done, Sebastian. Great taste."

"It's from a shop on the Ponte Vecchio we walked past when we first met." She burbled on, oblivious. "I told Sebastian it was where my grandfather got my grandmother's engagement ring from. I can't believe you remembered." She mooned at him.

"How romantic." I turned my attention back to the meatballs.

"Would you?"

"Sorry?" When I looked up, she was holding the necklace out to me by the open clasp. "Oh..." After swallowing down bile, I held up my flesh-smeared hands in defence. "Better not."

"Oh, come on, Rachel! You know boys are useless at these things. I want to try it on." She pouted. *"Please?"*

Summoning everything I had within me, I stalked silently to the sink and rinsed off my hands, raw fat melting in the warm water and greasing my palms. I dried them on a tea towel and beckoned her toward me.

"Vieni."

She brushed her hair away from her neck, exposing its elegant curve as I laced the chain around it, and I couldn't help thinking, just for a second, about the meat I had been kneading only seconds before.

The clasp secured, I released my fingers from her skin, springing back as though I had been stung.

"There. Done."

"Thank you." She touched the three points of the *V* into her clavicle and coiled herself into Sebastian once more. "I'll never take it off—*ti prometto.*" She stood on her tiptoes to kiss his cheek.

"Ugh, get a room."

Diana, saving me as ever, swept into the room with an armful of laundry, the fresh, powdery smell as much of a balm as her presence.

"Hi, Diana," Sebastian said wearily, but jovially. I saw his shoulders relax with the release in tension and couldn't help a prickle of jealousy at the ease of their friendship, an ease I wasn't sure we would ever be able to rediscover.

Diana set the laundry down in a basket, ready for me to hang up shortly, and then reached behind Sebastian to where a bowl of greengages sat ripening in the sun. She pinched one, wiped the small, green ball on her skirt and then bit into its taut skin, releasing the sweet yellow flesh with a burst of juice that dribbled down her chin.

"Oops." She wiped the back of her hand across her mouth, gave him a vigorous grin. "I would ask what you're here for, but I assume it's not to see me." She looked teasingly toward where Sebastian's arm was coiled around Valentina's waist.

"*Actually*, I was also coming to ask what you were planning to do for Ferragosto." He cleared his throat and turned his body to face me, even though he couldn't quite bring himself to meet my gaze. "All of you."

Ferragosto, the Italian August holiday where the majority of the country shuts down or goes off to the coast for anywhere from a few days to the entire month, was a couple of days away. Silvia, true to form, was closing the villa and flying to Costa Smeralda for a week with her elusive family, giving us the time off to do with as we pleased. I had already imagined spending the week finally able to catch up on my pre-term reading list, hoping perhaps to even tick off some of the museums I was yet to visit, if I could get Diana in a particularly compliant mood, and generally give myself the space to forget whatever last petty feeling I had for Sebastian, but this sounded worryingly like the universe had other intentions.

"I was going to fly back home." Sebastian released Valentina's waist and relaxed against the kitchen counter, crossing his ankles for balance. "Florence is awful in August—all the good stuff is shut, and it's overrun with Americans. But Mum's in the flat in Zurich, Dad's working and everyone interesting is away, plus, of course, Val…" He reached across to stroke her upper arm, a light, unthinking act of affection that made my heart involuntarily squeeze. "So, I spoke to Elio, and he's invited everyone to go on his boat."

"What boat?" A million thoughts instantly pounded away inside my brain, but before I could even begin to sort them, Diana leaned across the counter, her interest piqued.

"Well, calling it a boat is modest." I could hear a degree of relief in Sebastian's voice, that his initial bait had been picked up so easily. "It's a yacht. Beautiful thing—I went on it a few summers ago. It's a Riva, they're like the Ferrari of yachts, and it's got about five cabins, a couple of crew. We'd pick it up in Portofino, pootle along the Italian Riviera, see Cinque Terre, maybe even head up to the South of France if there's time… What do you think?" He was technically addressing all of us, but I could tell it was mainly for Valentina's benefit. His fingers found hers, clasped them gently, and I heard the softening of his voice as he said, "I thought it sounded quite romantic."

To my surprise, Valentina loosened her grip on Sebastian, and I saw two little spots of pink forming on her cheeks

"It sounds lovely…" She swallowed, her voice small. "But I can't swim."

"What?" Sebastian tried to hide the laughter in his voice, but I could hear it there, crinkling around the edges. "How do you not know how to swim?"

Her eyes flickered first to Diana, then to me, and I could tell she was embarrassed, having to make this revelation in front of us both. Diana's barely concealed snicker didn't help.

"My mother and father both worked. We didn't live anywhere near a pool, and they didn't teach us at school. I never learned." She turned away from us. "And now I feel like a…I don't know what the English word is…*una guasta festa*. A party spoiler."

"Oh, Val." He threaded an arm around her, pulled her close. "You're not a party pooper. It's not your fault you never learned. You don't have to swim, but it would be a shame to miss out—it's going to be such a lovely trip. You won't even have to touch the water, and I promise to look after you. But say you'll come, please?" He furrowed his eyebrows at her, gave her his best heart-melting, puppy-dog expression. "For me?"

She touched a hand to his chin. "You really want to go, don't you?"

He nodded his head hopefully.

"*Allora.*" She nodded, brave soul. "I wouldn't want you to miss out because of me. If you really promise to look after me then yes, okay, I'll go."

"Yes, yes!" Sebastian punched a fist into the air, picked her up underneath the armpits and twirled her in the air. She giggled, delighting in his delight. "It's going to be *fan-bloody-tastic*. We'll pootle around the coast, moor for lunch and wander around the little towns, dinner and nightcaps on the boat… It's gorgeous, I'm telling you. It's going to be the best trip."

He set her down and she wrapped her arms around his shoulders, gave him a long, slow kiss. I realized that I had been observing them as if they were actors on a television screen, as if I didn't know who they were, but that kiss… I had to look away, the memory of his lips on mine coming back to me fresh and raw. My insides contracted, fit to burst. It was all I could do to restrain myself from shouting out, "Stop!"

"You'll come too, won't you, girls?" Sebastian broke away from her, ran an awkward hand through his hair. And how I hated him in that moment: his nonchalance, his cavalier disregard for anyone but himself, and what he wanted. I looked down at my hands, saw that I had been balling my fists together so hard the knuckles had turned white.

"I'll think about it," I breathed, feeling his eyes searching but refusing to let their gaze catch mine. "I might be busy."

"Doing what?"

Suddenly the heat of the kitchen was overwhelming. My skin crawled with the humidity, made me want to dig my nails into it, scratch until I bled.

"Sorry, I'll have to come back to you." I reached blindly for the pile of linen tablecloths, taking comfort in their soft whiteness. "I need to get the washing on the line or Silvia's going to have a fit. I have to go. I'll...I'll speak to you later."

I stumbled backward out of the kitchen doors and dragged myself around the corner to the small courtyard where the washing lines hung, tripping on a loose cloth just as I reached the first line and falling, arms full and unable to balance me, onto the hard flagstones. My right knee connected with the ground with a hard crack, sending a shooting pain up my leg, and I cried out, reaching for it, as the rest of the laundry went flying from my grasp. I lay tangled in it, the laundry ruined, covered in dirt and shoe marks, and now a trickle of blood from my grazed knee, wishing I had never come here, that I had just stayed in England and got a job over the summer like Mum wanted. It had all been a stupid fantasy, and now the cracks of reality were beginning to show.

"Rachel?"

Diana's voice made my breath catch in my throat. She appeared around the garden wall, a surprising smoothness to her features, as if she wasn't surprised to find me like this in the slightest.

"I can't go on that boat." I stared up at the sky, forcing the tears back.

"Why?" Her tone was probing. She knew the answer; she just wanted me to say it myself.

I shook my head. "I just can't, Di."

"Something happened with Sebastian the other night, didn't it? Are you ready to talk about it now?"

The tears were threatening to fall, and I blinked them back sharply.

"I said I don't want to."

"Come on, Rach. Why won't you tell me? Why are you protecting him?"

"I'm not protecting him. I told you, nothing happened." The weakness of my lie was obvious, even to me. "Don't play me for a fool. I know something happened, so you might as well tell me."

"I can't."

"Tell me."

"I *can't*." I was losing control; I could feel it, my voice teetering on the edge of breaking.

"Rachel."

"I—" I tried to fight it, but snatches of that night flashed into my head as viscerally as if it were happening all over again. I could feel his hands on me, the touch of his lips on my neck, the pain, both emotional and physical, and when he left.

The tears fell.

"It wasn't how it was meant to be." I collapsed into the now-dirty linen, sobbing deep, hacking cries that I knew Diana would find undignified but couldn't hold back. "It wasn't how it was meant to be—if anything, I've made it worse, practically thrown him toward her. I have to watch them *mooning* over each other like Romeo and Juliet, tying that fucking necklace around her like the maid of honor at her fucking wedding. There's no escape. And now I'm expected to be on a boat with them? Surrounded by them car-

rying on like that every day for a week? How can I do it, Di?
I can't bear it."

She said nothing. Just stood watching me, not a finger
touching me, until I cried myself out. Only then, when there
was nothing left in me but infrequent snatched breaths, did I
feel her arms under my shoulders, hauling me up to standing.

She brushed the stray hairs away from my face as tenderly
as a mother with a child, rubbed her thumbs over my cheeks
to wipe away the mascara-streaked tears that lined them, and
then she pulled me into a hug.

"I'm sorry, my love. Sex is never how it's meant to be. But
it feels better now, to let it out, doesn't it?"

She pressed the back of my head into her shoulder with
her palm and rocked us both in a gentle side-to-side sway. I
let myself be comforted by her, by the familiar press of her
body against mine, the kindness of her touch, so different
from Sebastian's.

"I don't know why you even cared about him so much in
the first place, Rach. You're so much better than him," Diana
began as my breathing steadied. "He's a child. He's arrogant.
He's self-obsessed. He picks people up and puts them down
wherever he fancies, without any concern for them or their
feelings. He did it to me. He did it to you. I have no doubt
he'll do it to Valentina. Forget him—he's not worth it…he's
certainly not worth us fighting over him. Our friendship is so
much more important than some stupid boy. I'd rather Valentina had him a thousand times over than ruin that."

Like a flower after rain, I was nourished by her words, the
promise of her friendship the elixir I needed after the drought
of Sebastian's rejection. And as I let my body calm and slacken
in her arms, I began to think: *This is what it's about.* Not some
silly, one-sided romance, but this friendship, this girl, all the
love and kindness she had shown me ten times more real than

the fleeting glimpses of affection Sebastian had offered me. I breathed in the evaporating notes of her rose perfume and I thought about Sebastian, really thought about him, and I began to even wonder why I cared about him so much in the first place. Perhaps the act of sleeping with him would cast out the remnants of any feelings I had for him, and I would be able to enjoy the last of the summer in peace.

"Forget him, Rach. Come on the boat. Show him you don't give a damn about him or that idiot Valentina. Show him he can't stop you having a good time." Diana held me apart from her, gave my shoulders a squeeze. "And if he does anything to hurt either of us again…" She looked into my eyes with a steely determination. "I promise we'll make him pay."

35

Now

The tube pauses just shy of Holland Park Station, and a metallic screech of gears whines in protest. Outside, nothing but endless black tunnel. It makes me nervous, this unannounced stopping—memories of the London bombings, the phrase "suspicious package"—or maybe I am already nervous and the noise is just exacerbating it. I glance at the other passengers, looking for mirrored signs of fear, or worse, that one of them could have terrorist leanings. A voice on the loudspeaker— shirty, irritated—asks if they can *please* remind passengers to make sure all items are well clear of the closing doors, and then we're off again. No one else in the carriage even blinks.

My hand moves to my jeans pocket. The necklace is still there, cushioned in its pouch, pressed down into the deepest crevice where I secreted it away this morning. I'm relieved it hasn't slipped out and fallen into the hands of some commuter, to be stolen or thrown away or handed in to the cavernous vaults of Lost Property, but its presence means I have no excuse not to carry on.

The nursery isn't far from the boys' school, on a residential road just back from Holland Park, and I almost miss it—it looks more like a house than a school: a graveled carriage drive, abundant ivy winding around the drainpipes, glossy black front door—until I see the sign above the door in neat, precise lettering: Madame Beaumont's, est. 1971.

I check the Facebook post from a couple of months ago, just to be sure.

Phoebe's first day at nursery—SOB! When did my baby get so grown-up?

Underneath, a flurry of missives from fellow yummy mummies:

They grow up so fast!

Blink of an eye!

Next stop: teenagers!

The child is wearing a blue tartan pinafore, her red curls pulled into low bunches. With her left hand, she is both clutching a book bag and wedging a thumb into her mouth, her right hand stretched into a wave at the camera. Behind her: the same front door I am staring at now.

The location tag reads "Madame Beaumont's Bilingual Nursery" and I can't help a chuckle at that—Diana's sketchy Italian hardly pegs her as a linguist. One small click on the hyperlink and the location is confirmed in the palm of my hand. I have to praise Diana's lack of discretion—data companies must have a field day with the customer profile they can model on her.

The front door is closed, not a whisper of chalk on a board or children's voices coming from behind it, and for a second I think about pressing the buzzer, waiting for a face to come to the door, and saying…and saying what, exactly?

I hesitate. I thought myself so clever, sleuthing out her location, but really, what is the plan here?

The air is still, barely a bleat from a passing car or chirrup from a bird. I fabricate that this is the sort of place you can pay them off—the cars and the birds—a paltry sum in return for keeping the peace. I shift my weight. The gravel crunches loudly underfoot, and I freeze, half expecting the door to burst open, for someone to demand what I'm doing here, but it remains shut.

I close my eyes, willing an idea to form in my brain—*Think, Rachel, think*—when a sound to the right of the house makes my ears prick up. I edge closer, peer down the shallow path at the side return and see a wooden gate, the unmistakable flicker of bodies behind it. There is a muffled sound of bolts being undone, an almost perceptible tremor in the brickwork, and then they are unleashed: a tiny army of swinging arms and jostling fists. The air explodes with their high-pitched chatter, and in a blind panic, I retreat out of the driveway before they have a chance to reach the top of the path. I take up position in front of the house next door and watch as, two by two, the army snakes around the corner and lines up in perfect formation on the pavement.

"Alors, petits canards." The Marion Cotillard of nursery teachers stands at the front, issuing commands in perfectly unaccented French. "Does everyone have their hats and gloves?" Bringing up the rear, the Audrey Tautou of nursery assistants

straightens the line, checks uniforms, nods. "*Bon*. Then number off, *s'il vous plaît*."

And, in succession, each impeccably dressed child calls out a number.

"*Un*."

"*Deux*."

"*Trois*."

I find her at *dix*, which she pronounces, with relish, *deez*. The pigtails are a good deal more skew-whiff than in the photograph, but that red hair is impossible to miss. The last child hollers into the air, "caaaans," and then the army marches steadily onward.

I loiter for a few minutes, pretend to take a stone out of my shoe for no one's benefit, and then I shuffle after them, just out of sight, as they make their way toward the entrance of Holland Park.

We stroll through the parkland, passing a water feature and a double-height café stuffed to the rafters with mums and strollers, defying the frost for the sake of a latte, and eventually arrive at an adventure playground, where, to my absolute stroke of good luck, the lead teacher holds out a hand to pause the children, claps once, twice, and then gestures toward the requisite twisted metal climbing frames, slides and sandpits.

"*Alors*." She makes a shooing motion. "You have half an hour. *Allez!*"

The kids scatter, utterly delighted, and in an instant, the playground is overrun with clambering bodies and shrieks of joy. Knowing the tightrope I am walking should I be spotted and questioned, I eschew entry into the playground itself and instead edge around the gated periphery, reasoning that the metal fencing is a surefire way of verifying that I "just happened to be passing." I spy her queuing up for the slide, impatiently jiggling from one foot to another. I situate my obstacles: the teacher, currently engaged in disentangling two little girls and a skipping rope; her assistant, shielding herself from flung spades and plastic buckets in the sandpit. Both of them are facing away from me.

I walk around the fence until I am lined up with the slide. The queue shortens.

I edge closer. Check the teachers once more. From this angle, the slide almost blocks me from view.

One by one, the other children mount the stairs, seat themselves at the top of the slide, push off.

Finally, it's Phoebe's turn, last in line.

It's a big slide, high, and from what I can gauge from the other children, she is small for her age, but she grips the handlebars with vigor. I watch her pause, look up, all the way up, and then huff. Her grip falters, then tightens, and I see the tops of her shoulders tense as she readies her right foot to climb.

"Phoebe," I say softly. I remain a little way off, rehearse a line in my head—*Oh yes, how funny. I thought it was her, just saying hello!* The girl freezes, but doesn't turn around. "Phoebe," I say a little louder, but not too loudly.

Her grip loosens. She cocks her head and then pivots fully, squinting at me.

"How do you know my name?"

"I'm a friend of your mum."

She assesses this, takes me in with the wide, watchful brown eyes I know are her father's.

"A friend of Mummy?" She puzzles over it, taking in our surroundings, the unusualness of it. I proceed very, very carefully.

"Yes, that's right. An old friend of your mummy—Diana," I add for reassurance, hoping the name will earn points in my favor.

She's still wary, keeping the frame of the slide within touching distance, but now she regards me with growing interest.

"But what are you doing here?"

I hesitate. I am thinking on my feet, spiraling through options as fast as I can think of them.

I beckon her toward me. "Come over here and I'll tell you."

I know instantly I've said the wrong thing. She backs farther away, and I see a look of panic clutch her fine features.

"I don't know you." She shakes her head, and I curse the nanny-state society that has taught her to be wary of strangers when she's barely out of nappies.

I try to keep my voice light, my smile pretty. "You don't *remember* me, sweetheart. I haven't seen you since you were a little baby—but I remember *you* so, *so* well. Gosh, you're so grown-up!" I can already feel the beginnings of a headache twitching at the corners of my temples, the strain of false jollity. She says nothing, so I keep on. "I'm an *old* friend of Mummy's. We lived together in Italy a long, long time ago… Surely your mummy has mentioned Auntie Rach?" I pout in mock indignation. My talking is easing her, piquing her curiosity, and so I carry on, gentle, coaxing. I look up again at the teachers, note their distraction, take a step forward so that I am now leaning against the fence. "How are Harry and Charlie?" My mind filters through Diana's data points. "Did Charlie find Wobbie the Wabbit?"

Facebook entry from two weeks ago: the younger of the brothers sucking on a mottled gray toy rabbit, one of its eyes dangling loose.

Can we make this message go viral and help poor Charlie find his beloved pal?

"Yes," she says in a small voice, and takes a few steps toward me. I, in turn, retreat. "He was at the Hurlingham Club."

"Good." I am almost in touching distance now, can make out the baby-smoothness of her skin, the little dusting of freckles on her nose and cheeks. I have to hand it to Diana; she is a beautiful child. "I thought that was where he might be. And how was Harry's X-Men party?"

"I wanted to go as Mystique, but Mummy said I'd get blue paint everywhere. And Harry said it was boys only. I had to wear a dress."

"Oh, I'm sorry—maybe you can dress up another time. What do you want to do for your birthday party?"

"Disney princesses." For the first time, there are echoes of a smile on her face. "I want to be Merida. Because she has red hair. And a bow and arrow."

"I think you'd make an excellent Merida." I have no idea what she's talking about. "I'll make sure I can make it."

"You have red hair too." She points to it. "But it's dark, not like me and Mummy."

"That's right." I am edging toward the side of an equipment shed, bent on getting us both out of sight. "Once, when Mummy and I were younger, I tried to color my hair to make it look like your mummy's, but it didn't look nice at all. I think this is a much better color for me, don't you?"

She nods solemnly.

"Does Mummy ever talk about the summer we were in Italy together?" I don't want to ask, guessing what the answer will be, but am compelled to.

She shakes her head. "I don't think so." She lisps the *th*: *fink*. "We went to Sardinia last year, though. I learned snorkeling."

"Well, once upon a time—a very, very long time ago, in fact—your mummy and I lived there together and were the best of friends." As I speak, I fish out my phone, scroll through the images until I find the one I want: a photograph of a photograph, taken from the album in my flat a few weeks ago. Me,

Sebastian and Diana, leaning against a wall overlooking the Arno, a cocktail in each of our hands. It's a shit photograph—Diana and I are looking in different directions, and Sebastian's right arm is cut out—but it's the only one I could find of the three of us together.

I hold the phone up above the bars so Phoebe can see the screen. "Who's that?"

Phoebe leans across me, presses her face close into the phone, and I see her face light up.

"It's Mummy!"

"That's right. A long, long time ago. And there's me." I wait, seeing if she'll take the bait on her own or if I'll have to push her.

"Who's that?"

"Who?" I smile inwardly.

"The boy. The one next to Mummy."

"Oh, that's Sebastian." Saying his name to her feels almost blasphemous, as if I might conjure him up, find him perched at the top of the slide.

"Is he one of Mummy's and your best friends too?"

I swallow. "He was."

"But where is he now?"

"Actually, he just got out of prison."

Her eyes go round as the moon, and I expect a million questions to come bursting out of her, but instead she leans in, looks at me solemnly. "Prison is where bad people go."

I nod carefully. "That's right."

She says nothing more, but I can't help but push just the tiniest bit further.

"Has Mummy…has she ever said anything about him?"

She shakes her head.

"Not even in the last few weeks?"

"No."

"Are you sure, Phoebe? Take another look." I thrust the phone through the gap in the bars, a little bit more vigorously than I intended to. "You haven't seen her reading something about him in the newspaper, or perhaps on TV...?"

"I said *no.*"

I see the caution clouding in her eyes, and am aware my window of opportunity is closing, feel the tension fizzing all the way to the tips of my fingers. The teacher is calling out, "Move away from the slide once you're at the bottom, Isla!" and I assess my position, shift over an inch to the left.

"Sorry, sorry. I just wanted to be sure." I put the phone away, check the assistant, who is now lifting up a small Chinese boy who has landed headfirst in the sandpit. "So, listen." I bend one knee to the ground, feel the imprint of playground tarmac leaving little pockmarks in my flesh. *Just doing up my shoelace.* "I need to ask you something—a favor."

"A favor?" She rolls the word around in her mouth.

"Yes...a very special favor. More like...a secret." I whisper the word conspiratorially and am rewarded with the rounding of her eyes as she regards me with renewed interest. "Are you good at keeping secrets?"

I move my face a fraction of an inch closer to hers, but I know I have her. Kids love secrets.

"Charlie broke Mummy's vase. The one Daddy got her for Christmas. He was playing cricket in the hall and knocked a ball into it. I saw, but he told me if I said that it was Coco he would give me all his leftover sweets from Halloween, even the gobstopper." She looks up at me with all the gravity of a witness in the dock. "I didn't tell." She pauses. "Coco is our dog."

"That is very good secret-keeping." I give her an impressed nod, taking the opportunity to reach through the bars, very gently touch my fingers to the palm of her hand.

For just a second, I imagine keeping hold of that hand, propelling the child over the fence and away from the playground. I imagine the lineup, the numbering off in reverse—"*Quinze, quatorze, treize, douze, onze, dix...dix?* Where's *dix*?"—the frantic searching, and the phone call to Diana, her clipped voice answering, bored at first, and then rising in panic. "Phoebe? Gone? *How?*" I picture myself chivying her back past the yummy mummies in the café and onto the streets, bundling her into a cab and then heading off...heading off...where?

Phoebe squints up at me, impatient. "What's the secret, then?"

The fantasy evaporates.

Instead, I touch the small bulge in the right pocket of my jeans. *Still there.* I'm relieved; this is a far easier way to get Diana's attention than kidnapping.

"Well, it's not so much a secret as a secret object. I need you to keep it very safe for me, and not tell any of your friends at school, or your teachers, and then when you get home, I want you to give it to your mummy when you see her. Can you do that for me?"

She frowns. "Why?"

"Because the thing I want you to give her is a surprise."

"But why can't I tell my teachers?"

I lick my lips. I didn't realize children would have so many questions.

"Because then they'll tell Mummy before you get the chance to, and that'll spoil the surprise, won't it?"

She nods. "Okay."

Satisfied that she has no more questions, I reach into my pocket and pull out the pouch, unlace the knotted ties and hold the chain up by the catch, allowing the pendant to fall in a straight line toward the grass. Phoebe cocks her head, examines it thoughtfully.

"Is that the surprise?"

I smile. "Uh-huh."

She leans closer, reaches out a hand to touch it where it hangs over the fence, but then hesitates, looking at me for reassurance. I nod, and she strokes the letter with the tip of her index finger.

"Vuh," she pronounces, in lower case.

"That's right."

"Vuh for what?"

"An old friend. Someone your mummy and I knew when we were young. I think your mummy might have forgotten her, so I thought it would be nice to remind her. Would you like to try it on?"

"Um…" She stares as if hypnotized at the necklace, mesmerized by it rocking back and forth on my finger. "I don't know if I should… Mummy doesn't like me wearing jewelry. She says it's common."

I huff, glance toward the teacher, who is now holding apart two warring children by the swings. The assistant is sitting on a bench, pressing a tissue against a sobbing boy's exposed knee. I have to finish this before they announce time's up.

"You don't have to wear it." *No need to explain,* I think to myself, *that the clasp is broken anyway.* "You just need to keep it with you, keep it safe."

The gold catches the light, makes the little diamond chips on the *V* sparkle, and I know she is entranced by it. "Pretty," she concludes, touching the tip of her finger to the point of the *V.*

"It is pretty," I agree. "But you can't show anyone until you get home." I look down at her uniform. "Your dress has pockets, doesn't it?"

She folds her hands in them to demonstrate. "Uh-huh."

"Great." I give her a thumbs-up; then, with her watching, I put the necklace back into the pouch and beckon her to come closer, tucking it as far as it can go into the bottom of her right pocket, giving it a little pat for extra security. "It should be nice and safe there, shouldn't it?"

"Uh-huh."

"Good. And you won't take it out, or show it to anyone until you get home, will you?" I look deep into her eyes. "It's a secret...remember?"

She purses her lips. "But what do I say when I get home?"

"You don't have to say anything. In fact—" the idea seizes me, even better than the original "—don't even mention it to her. I know...why don't you put it on your bedside table when you're getting into bed? Wait for her to see it for herself. Can you be a big girl, and do that for me?"

I imagine Diana pulling Phoebe into a hug, her long fingers encountering the keloid scar of the chain beneath her blouse.

Phoebe, what's this? she'd say—lightly, but with an edge of irritation creeping into her voice. *You know I don't like you wearing jewelry.*

Reaching to pick up the object on the nightstand, the gold *V* resting in her palm with searing clarity.

Darling—fear starting to creep into her voice—*darling, where did you get this?* Trying to keep everything calm, jolly, even as ice crystals start to cluster in her veins. *Did a friend give it to you? Tell Mummy where.*

It's so delicious. So perfect. I wish I could be there to see her face.

"I can be a big girl." Phoebe's voice pulls me out of my reverie. I look back into the playground. The teacher has put the swing argument to rights, and is now looking at her watch, about to gather the troops.

"That's excellent. I think you're going to do a really, really good job." I stand back from the fence, absently brush dirt off my knees. "In that case, I should probably go. And you prob-

308

ably need to get back to your teacher. But you'll remember what I said, won't you?" I press my finger to my lips. "Shh."

She widens her eyes, nods proudly with the magnitude of it all and then presses her finger to her lips in return. "Secret," she hisses.

"Good girl." I am about to release her when a pleasing thought enters my head. "Oh, Phoebe?" She lifts her chin. "Before you go…" I reach into my handbag, pull out my phone. "Selfie?"

She automatically pulls her lips into a grin. She is her mother's daughter.

I turn my back to the fence and crouch down so I'm at her level, flip the camera screen and hold out my arm to get both of us in the screen.

"Say 'Selfie!'" I command, and "Selfie" she mouths in return. I snap the picture, then put my phone back in my pocket and reach a hand over the top of the bars, pat the top of a baby-soft bunch. As I do, I hear the telltale clap of the teacher's hands, then snatch my arm away. "Go on, go," I say roughly, stepping swiftly back.

She observes me for a second, and then turns to go, her little legs picking up speed as she sees the teacher starting to re-form the line of students.

When I am a safe enough distance away, I turn back, watching cautiously to see what she does. I see her hand fluttering to her pocket a couple of times, but then she stops herself, standing straighter and slapping her hand down by her side. She is a good girl. Her life hasn't given her cause to be anything else. I don't think she'll sway from what I've told her.

The class marches off, but I hang back, wait until they're fully out of sight before I leave the park.

When I am safely on the tube, I pull out my phone, scroll to the most recent image, our twinned smiles staring back.

Funny: with our red hair, that close-up? It's not impossible that she could be mine.

I don't know what I'll do with it. I don't intend to send it, yet. I shouldn't have to—I'm sure Diana will be in touch soon enough. But knowing that it's there, knowing that I could— should I want to—chill her with just a few clicks of a button, is power enough.

For twenty-one years Diana has had mastery over me.

It's about time I started to take back control.

36

Then

We drove to the coast. Sebastian and Valentina and Diana and Elio and Tomaso, the beautiful blond boy Elio was with at Sebastian's party. And me, of course.

Six of us, dressed in summer whites and sunglasses—a linen dress had appeared hanging on the back of my door, price tag removed. I was rewarded with Diana's approving nod when I emerged wearing it—straight out of a Fellini film.

I didn't even know Sebastian had a car, but when Diana and I arrived at the villa, suitcases in hand, two convertibles were waiting for us in the driveway, roofs down, drivers and shotguns already in position.

"Siete in ritardo!" Elio called, looking back at us in the rear-view through an oversize pair of tortoiseshell shades. *You're late.* *"Veloce, veloce!"*

We dragged our suitcases nearer to the cars and then looked at one another. Sebastian and Valentina were in one car, Elio and Tomaso in the other. It made sense for us to split.

"I'll go with Seb," Diana said demonstratively loudly. "That way I can make sure they don't start going at it and drive over a cliff."

I gave her a grateful smile and steered myself toward Elio.

"Don't mind a third wheel?" I asked, as he climbed out of the car and reached to put my bag in the boot.

"Some less so than others," he muttered quietly, glancing back at Diana. I had been so caught up in Sebastian and Valentina, I had forgotten about Elio's dislike for her. At least she wasn't the only one doing a favor with the seating arrangements.

The car was a stunning vintage Jaguar, bottle green with cream interiors that somehow still smelled of new leather, and when he offered me a hand to climb over the front seat, I saw there was no proper back seat, just a single bench that ran along it.

"Sorry." Elio shrugged as I hugged my knees to fit into the narrow space. "But it's good if you want to lie down."

"Don't apologize. It's beautiful."

I went to a vintage car show with my dad once. He had mentioned it in passing and, feeling sorry for his lack of sons, I offered to go with him. It was largely boring—stalls and beer tents and people dressed up in 1920s clothing—but I loved the cars, all sleek and shiny and colorful, like one of those Victorian wall mounts of insects. I could never have imagined I'd be driven in one myself. I ran my fingers along the spotless upholstery.

Elio tapped his cigarette packet on the open window ledge and put one to his lips.

"A twenty-first-birthday present from my dear *papà*. He

forgot about it for six months, so…" He put his fingers together in a particularly Italianate gesture.

The journey took almost three hours. We wended through the outskirts of Florence, all unattractive cream high-rises and discount furniture shops so at odds with the medieval city center, and then headed onto the autostrada, whizzing past signs for towns straight out of a grand tour guidebook— Prato, Pistoia, Montecatini, Lucca. To his credit, Elio tried hard to include me in the conversation, even as he looped an arm around Tomaso's shoulder, ruffled his hair, but the wind rushed at me so that even at shouting pitch, I lost every other word, exacerbated by trying to keep up with their Italian, and so I resigned myself to the silence, watching the landscape rolling around me.

From my position on the back seat, I found I could just about see the other car, the backs of their heads and tops of their shoulders in clear view if I angled myself just right. Diana, of course, clearly had no intention of being shunned to the back: she had propped herself forward, an elbow resting on each of the front seats, blocking any physical interaction between Sebastian and Valentina in a move I was sure was about more than just the need for inclusion. Sebastian was driving with one hand, the arm resting on the window ledge, and I could see his fingers tapping rhythmically against the wheel, strumming along to whatever Italian pop song they must be listening to on the radio. For a moment, just a moment, I imagined it was me next to him, that we were on some romantic getaway together, listening to a mixtape he'd compiled with me in mind. We'd pull off the autostrada and find a bucolic *pensione* nestled in the hills, shut the door and not open it again until breakfast the next morning, lie naked against crisp cotton sheets…

The fantasy was jarred by the memory of Sebastian's urgent shoving, his monotone grunts as I lay passively beneath him, his pleading tone afterward, as he cast me aside like yesterday's meat. I gave myself a mental shake. *It's not like that. It will never be like that. I have to get over it, over him.*

Instead, I cast my roving eye to the third member of their party: Valentina. Her brown hair was twisted up into a bun, exposing the long curve of her neck and elegantly avoiding the bird's nest the wind was currently forming of my hair. She was staring straight forward, shoulders back, barely moving, and the more I looked at her, the more I noticed it: there was something wrong.

I had spent so much time over the past few weeks observing Valentina, comparing myself to her, finding my faults in every one of her perfections, that I realized I had come to have an intimate knowledge of her physical quirks, and this—this constricted movement, the tension in her shoulders—was a sign that all was not well. My interest piqued, I scooted hungrily forward, imaginary binoculars honing my vision. Diana was talking—I could see the bob of her head, the theatrical arm gestures—and Valentina was making a pretense of listening, giving well-timed nods, but every so often I saw her glancing across to Sebastian, the little tilt of her head. I watched her hand go to her necklace, fingers feeling for the chain round the back of her neck, and she began to play with it restlessly, pulling the *V* right and left across her finger.

When Elio got bored and revved up to overtake them, I seized my chance, twisting my head to observe her head-on, and from that one glimpse, I knew I was right. To the casual observer, it may have looked like nothing, but I *knew* her, practically every inch, and there was a waxiness to her expression, a gray dullness underneath that olive skin, that hinted at an internal unrest. Something was wrong with Valentina.

★ ★ ★

We hit the coast just before Forte dei Marmi, and for a worrying moment I thought we might be breaking the journey there, our previous excursion still leaving a sour taste, but instead Elio slowed so that Sebastian's car pulled up alongside us and called across to him.

"There's this great little place in Pietrasanta I want to show Tomaso—follow me?"

At Sebastian's nod, Elio sped up again, veering right to take us away from the coast and in the direction of the marble-topped Carrara mountains. We stopped in the foothills, where Elio led us through the back streets until we arrived at a jazzed-up *enoteca* where primary-colored wooden chairs and tables spilled out from the wine bar entrance onto the cobblestones. It was filled with Italian families laughing over carafes of wine, forks twirling into plates of pasta. Overhead, suspended from the side of the building, fluoro-pastel-colored parasols hung open as if floating in midair, like a scene from *The Umbrellas of Cherbourg.*

"*Che bello, eh?*" Elio grinned as we sat down. "The town is famous for its artists and sculptors. Every year they put up a new installation like this. Botero has a house in the hills here—this is one of his favorite restaurants."

Everyone looked up in wonder at the floating parasols, but I stole a glance at Valentina. Her head was tilted too, but her eyes were unfocused, and after a second, she turned away, hiding her face in the shoulder of her blouse. We ate—platters of cured meats, cheese served with fragrant, floral honey and walnuts, soft *schiacciata* flatbread studded with grapes—and then wandered through the town's tight cobbled streets, bursting with smart clothes shops, quirky antiques and achingly cool modern art galleries.

It was in one of the latter that I saw Valentina slip off. The gallery had three rooms, all displaying the work of a local sculptor whose latest collection was loosely inspired by Michelangelo: monolithic men cast in bronze, legs dipped in black, eyes covered in bizarre goggle-like objects, their bodies twisted as if trying to escape, mouths half-open in voiceless screams. They unsettled me, these silent soldiers, and I turned away, and in doing so, caught a fleeting glimpse of Valentina's sandaled foot escaping out onto the cobbles.

I looked back at the others, all engrossed in what the gallery owner was explaining, and then slipped out myself, scanning the narrow street until I saw Valentina disappearing through an open archway. I waited, giving myself a decent distance to follow her, and then inched along the street, eyes trained on the archway in case she reappeared and spotted me.

It was a church, I discovered, hugging the brickwork with my back and rotating my body in increments until I could just see inside the entrance. A minuscule chapel, no room even for pews. It was dark, the only light coming from the two stands of votive candles that lined the entrance, casting an eerie flicker across the room, and it was cold; even from the entrance, I could feel the stale air that no sunlight had ever kissed. Taking a chance, I leaned in closer, breathing in dank stone and beeswax, and let my eyes adjust to the light as they narrowed in on Valentina.

She had her back to me and was standing over a small marble font, above which hung an oversize crucifix, the body of Christ picked out in gold. I took a step inside, could just make out her voice, urgent, frenetic whispers interspersed with ragged cries. Another step, and I heard a glassy clink from between her hands—the rosary beads I knew she always kept on her person. One step more, and I could just make out her words.

"Ave Maria, piena di grazia, il Signore è con te. Tu sei bene-
detta fra le donne e benedetto è il frutto del tuo seno, Gesù.
Santa Maria, Madre di Dio, prega per noi peccatori, adesso e
nell'ora della nostra morte. Amen."

I couldn't quite translate the religious specifics, but I caught
enough to recognize the gist of the Hail Mary.

Over and over she recited it, her prayer getting louder, more
desperate, each time.

The louder she became, the closer I got, enough so that I
could smell her shampooed hair, clean and fresh that morning, the talc scent of her clothes. And then, without really
thinking about what I was doing, I reached out and touched
her shoulder.

"Valentina?"

She shrieked, the cry pinging off the stone walls, and the
rosary beads fell from her hands, clattering noisily to the floor.
When I looked into her eyes, I knew that this was something
more serious than whatever petty grumbling I had imagined.

"Val, it's fine—it's only me," I whispered, something about
the hushed setting making me afraid to raise my voice. I lifted
my hands up in submission. "I saw you leave the gallery and
came to look for you. Is everything... Are you okay?"

She nodded fervently, but then I saw the tremble in her
pressed lips, her eyes brimming with stopped-up tears. And
then, slowly, slowly, the nod turned into a shake.

"No."

"What is it? What's the matter?"

She turned away, her head shaking more violently.

"Come on, tell me... I'm your friend." The words stuck
in my throat, but I needed to know. Still she said nothing.
"Valentina..." Kinder now, softer. "Come on, it's me."

She gave a rattled sigh. "If I tell you, you can't tell anyone—you're the only one who will know."

"I won't. I won't say anything."

She squeezed her eyes shut and raised her chin heavenward, drawing a deep breath from the pit of her stomach before she opened them, staring back at me with a mixture of pain and desperation.

"*Sono incinta.*"

I rolled the words around in my head, trying to pick them apart and find their meaning. But then I looked at her hands, pressed against the small of her stomach, and I knew what she was trying to say.

Sono incinta. I'm pregnant.

37

"Mum?" My voice echoes down the empty hallway as I walk through the front door.

"I'm in the lounge."

I cringe at the word, Diana's crystalline laugh in my ears— *Don't say 'lounge.' It's common*—but don't bother correcting her, walk silently in her direction to find her fluffing cushions, those far-too-many throw cushions she seems to take so much pride in rearranging on a daily basis. A pile of them lies in wait for her to pluck, one by one, give a firm bash and place with precision across every soft surface.

"I think I'm going to go back home." It feels weird to call Ascot "home," here in the place I supposedly grew up in. I hover in the doorway, stuffing my hands into my now-empty pockets. I'm scared to look at her, scared she will spy the sheen of sweat across my forehead and know something is up, but I've overestimated her: she is far too concerned with the task at hand to bother looking up herself.

"Oh?" Smack, smack. She moves rhythmically, first whacking each cushion with the palm of her hand and then tapping each side of the square before arranging it against the seat back.

I swallow.

"There's something unexpected I need to take care of back there. I thought I'd be able to sort it here, but…" I can't think of a good enough reason to finish the sentence, so I leave it dangling on her lack of interest. "I'll go pack up and say goodbye before I leave."

I turn to go, but before I've gone three steps into the hallway her voice calls me back.

"Your father will be disappointed. He's barely seen you since you've been back."

Somehow it is this, this above any of her barbed comments, her ill-concealed attempts to demonstrate how unwelcome I am here, that gets me. I stalk back into the room and wrench the cushion from her hand with such vigor that when she is finally forced to look up at me, I see genuine surprise, perhaps even a hint of fear, in her eyes.

"Why do you hate me?"

The words fly from my mouth faster than I can think about it. The question that has lurked in the background of so much of my adult life, too terrifying, too unthinkable to ask. But it is a release, now, to let it loose. If today is a day of finality, I may as well settle all old scores.

"I don't hate you, Rachel." Mum flattens the palms of her hands against the skirt of her dress, purses her lips in a gesture that, oddly, reminds me of myself. "I don't understand you."

I can't think how to answer this. I open and close my

mouth, hoping some clever retort will find its way to me, but nothing comes.

Mum seizes my indecision, sits. She sighs. The sofa wheezes in sympathy.

"We've always been so different, you and me. It scares me. It's always scared me. Do you remember when you were little, when Dad lost his job, and I got a second job as a cleaner for those posh houses in Chelsea?" The question is rhetorical; how could I forget the embarrassment, the knowledge that everyone in our small circle knew and was talking about us? "You used to come with me on the holidays—there was no one else to look after you, and I didn't want to spend the money on childcare. It was that house on Cheyne Walk, right on the river—Amanda Fairfax." She sniffed. "I won't forget that name in a hurry. I hadn't strictly told her I was bringing you with me, but it didn't seem to matter—she was never home, and I didn't see what difference it could make. But she came home early—I think she'd forgotten something she needed to return or get dry-cleaned or some other silly reason—and found you in the library, reading one of the old books from the case. She fired me on the spot."

I remember. I remember Mrs. Fairfax, the clack of her heels with their bloodred soles, the smell of her perfume, vanilla and musk, infusing the room as soon as she entered. Her jacket so beautifully cut it looked as though it were sewn onto her. I remember, too, her clean French manicure, the white tips of it digging into my wrist as she hauled me to my feet and twisted the book out of my hands.

"What are you doing? Those books aren't for reading."

How she had shouted for my mother without even moving an inch, her voice ricocheting off the oak-paneled walls, as if she were calling a dog, and how my mother had *raced* in within seconds, ashen faced, and said nothing to defend herself. I looked at Mrs. Fairfax, and then I looked at my mother, hair sticking up in all directions, her blue-and-white-checked overalls spotted with silver polish and soap suds. And I felt ashamed.

"We got in the car, and you were silent for the whole journey home, over an hour, and so I thought you must have been really shaken up. But then, when my key turned in the ignition, and I reached across you to open the car door, you said with total calm, 'When I grow up, I'm going to live in a house like that.'"

I did. I did say that. I can taste my childhood desire even now: it tastes of expensive leather binding and musty yellow pages, like polished hardwood floors and vaulted ceilings. It wasn't so much the house that I wanted as what the house stood for: the ease of having the things I wanted without having to fight for them, as we, as my parents, always seemed to be fighting for them.

"Nothing was ever good enough for you." Mum picks a cushion up off the floor and hugs it to her chest. It's one she's had for years, burgundy tassels dangling from each corner, a Scottie dog stitched on the front in a pattern of red-and-green tartan, although, as far as I'm aware, she has no interest in either dogs or Scotland. "Your father and I, we did our best. We put food on the table and clothes on our backs, kept this house, the car, the odd holiday here and there. But you always wanted more. You were always so bright…so bright it scared me because I could see that you felt trapped. The life that we had was too small for you. And when you had the chance to go to Italy, I didn't want you to go—I hated the idea that you would finally have your eyes opened to how big and wide the world was, that it would make our own world seem even smaller—but I thought, *Maybe this is what she needs, maybe this will set her free.* But Italy changed you, Rachel, and not for the better. You were always determined, but Italy turned you ugly. You came back from that place and you turned your nose up at all we had done for you—even after that business at Cambridge, even after we brought you home and took care of you and helped you get back on your feet, it was like nothing we did was ever good enough. Whatever happened out there, whatever you did with those people, in that hotel…on that boat…I could tell the moment I saw you again that there was no coming back to us—you were gone. So, in answer to your question, no, I don't hate you, Rachel. I don't even know you."

It isn't until she stops speaking that I realize how still the house is, so still I can hear my own breath, the systematic push and pull of air through my nostrils as I try to still the hurt that has taken root in my body, wrapping itself around my entrails like poison ivy.

"Why…?" I press my lips together, words and thoughts rushing at me simultaneously. "All these years…why did you never ask me what happened?"

Mum stands, still holding the cushion. She plays with one of the tassels thoughtfully, weaving it in and out of her thumb and middle finger before tucking the pillow neatly in position where her back has been resting.

She doesn't look at me, but I can tell she wants to, can see the darting of her eyeballs underneath the lids as she stares fixedly at the sofa.

"I wasn't sure I wanted to know the answer."

38

Then

Sono incinta. The words curdled in my stomach. "Pregnant?"

I searched her face in the dim light, hoping for some sign this could be a joke, but she nodded balefully back at me.

"*Sì.*"

"Does Sebastian—?"

"*No.*" Fresh tears brimmed, splashed down her cheeks in waves. "I don't know how to tell him."

I swallowed. "I see. And would you...? Have you thought about...getting rid of it?"

"*NO!*" She shrank back from me like I had struck her, giving terrified glances at the walls, as if the fresco of the Virgin Mary to our right might be condemning her for even hearing the words.

"Sorry, no, of course not. So...what are you going to do?"

"I don't know." At that, she broke down again into mewling sobs, clutching at her stomach as she collapsed down onto the stone floor and I remained just where I was, standing over her feeling...feeling what, exactly? Pity? Yes, there was some pity there, for her lot, for the misfortune of it. Jealousy? That too, because although I could not imagine what I would do if I were in her shoes, I couldn't avoid the overwhelming understanding that she was carrying Sebastian's child inside her, however mistimed it may be.

But it was disgust I felt most keenly. Disgust at the pathetic state she was in now, a stain on this beautiful town and the glamorous adventure we were having. Disgust at the way she had waded into our lives and systematically ruined *everything*.

Disgust that by my own willfulness, I had ended up as her confidante: that curled my toes and burned inside me and made me ball my fists and lock my jaw, yet also made me reach my hand out to her, help her to her feet, brush down the folds of her skirt and say, "It'll be all right."

I spoke with authority, a calmness that balanced out her hysteria, and she looked back at me with a tiny grain of hope in her eyes.

"How? How do you know?"

"You love each other. I'm sure everything will work out. You should tell him."

"Wh-what?"

Why did I want her to tell him so badly? I had been proved wrong on so many counts during their relationship. There had been so many times I thought that Diana and I had finally cracked them apart, only for them to spring back together, as good as new. Why did I think she wouldn't fall into his embrace and they'd go marching off into the sunset, Sebastian and Valentina and baby makes three?

The memory had been waiting for me, floating under the

surface until just the right time to make its presence known. That very first party—it seemed like a lifetime ago now—stumbling from group to group in search of Diana. Sebastian, his back against the brickwork, drink in hand, flanked by a couple of male friends in identical loose flannel shirts and stonewashed jeans, wearing identical mesmerized expressions as they hung on to whatever words Sebastian was speaking. I had hidden, shrunk back around the corner, slightly tipsy and not ready to face him yet, not ready to feel like the lemon in their conversation. But I had listened.

"Of course she got an abobo—what do you take me for? I have a trust fund waiting for me when I turn twenty-five, but only on the condition that I finish my degree, spend at least a year working for Dad and, most importantly, sire no offspring. There's nothing in hell or on earth that will stop me getting my hands on it."

It took me a while to work out what he meant by "abobo." It sounded at first like it was some type of posh clothing, a hat maybe, or a car. But then I parsed the rest of the sentence, the callous way he had brushed off one of his friends' next questions—"Nah, I didn't see what the point of going with her was. That's all women's business"—and I twigged.

Abobo. Abortion.

I looked at Valentina and saw the hope in her eyes, the desperation to believe that maybe I was right, and that she could have her fairy-tale ending…or perhaps just her desperation to believe that anything I said would make it all go away.

"You should tell him." I held her gaze steady. "You're going to have to, eventually. It's his, after all—he has a right to know. Besides, if you say he loves you and wants to marry you, then maybe you could just see this as a little…fast-forward?"

I remembered our night together, the nonchalant way he had batted away our lack of protection: *I'll pull out.* The possibility had niggled away at me until the relief of my period arrived—I never thought I'd feel grateful for cramps—but I bet he hadn't thought of it once.

Sebastian didn't want a baby. And Valentina didn't want to get rid of one. Could it be, finally, that this was the catalyst to break them apart? Was the world finally falling into place?

Even as I was thinking this, I found myself touching her on the shoulder, coaxing her gently toward the door, none the wiser that my maternal act hid ulterior motives. "Listen, you can't do anything about it now. And we can't stay here— someone is going to come looking for us. Do you really want to have to explain this in front of the whole group?"

She sniffed, her bottom lip threatening to tremble once more.

"No." She pressed the heels of her fists to her eyes. "They're going to ask where we've been, though, and they'll see I've been crying... What will we say?"

"We'll think of something. We'll say...we'll say we went to look at another gallery, and you saw a cat get run over, got upset." I laughed, more to myself than with her. "I'm sure they'll believe that."

She paused, thinking, and then without warning I felt her arms around me, her salt-sticky cheeks burying into my neck.

"Thank you for being such a good friend, Rachel. Whatever happens, at least I have you."

I stuttered, trying to find the right words to answer her, words that didn't choke me.

"Come on. Let's get back."

I patted her on the back, only marginally harder than a friend would do, and pulled myself free.

We arrived at Portofino's tiny, crescent-shaped harbor midafternoon, avoiding the postlunch traffic that snaked bumper-to-bumper along the narrow coastal roads.

The jewel-like *piazzetta* held no attraction for me. I could sense its beauty, taste, vaguely, the lingering scent of honeysuckle in the air, see the faint shimmer of the diamonds dripping from languid, suntanned limbs, but the billion-dollar speedboats, the eye-popping boutiques, the waterside restaurants that echoed with the clink of champagne flutes and the laughter of people permanently on holiday, were merely blurred backgrounds to my myopic view: all I could see was her. Valentina's confession became like an invisible thread that joined the two of us together; wherever she went, I couldn't help but follow, waiting for that unavoidable moment when she lost control and her secret was unleashed.

Even boarding the boat, I did so as though I was surrounded by a thin film of gauze, the ridiculousness of it only penetrating skin-deep. Me, on a yacht: the very idea was laughable. As we stepped onto the sunken platform at the back, where a dining table was already laid with a white tablecloth, fine china and delicate-handled silver cutlery, I forced myself to pay attention and take in every detail, imagining Dad's face, Mum's sneer of contempt, in the retelling.

The exterior was a sleek, gunmetal gray, with a menacing, almost military effect which seemed to tie in with the picture I had of Elio's father. But the interiors were all smooth wood, cream and beige—if they had ever so much as glanced at a stain, they didn't kiss and tell. The liveried crew were waiting to greet us when we arrived, three of them: the captain, in one of those proper white caps that in any other world I would have thought was fancy dress, and two skippers, each in beige chino shorts and shirts with epaulettes, one of them holding a tray of filled champagne flutes, the glass just starting to frost.

Elio boarded first with Tomaso, greeted with deference by the captain, who doffed his cap and called him Signor Agnelli, then Diana, then me, each of us taking a glass and moving farther onto the platform, facing out to see the sun setting over the postcard-perfect marina. For just a moment, I allowed myself to be immersed in it, wondered why this couldn't just be enough, why I couldn't let all the other stuff go, and allow myself the pure pleasure of being in the fantastical world I had somehow found myself a part of. But then a squeal brought me back to reality: Valentina, white-knuckled, gripping on to Sebastian's forearm as she boarded, fear making her legs jittery as he righted her, helped her stumble gratefully to the safety of the back wall.

"Sorry," he said sheepishly, to no one in particular. "She can't swim."

It was later, when we were putting our things away in the cream-washed bedroom we were to share, that Diana, sensing some change in me, pressed me for an answer.

"What's up?" she asked casually, unfolding a silk cardigan that still had the labels on it—a shopping trip she had dragged me on before we left, "to prepare our yachting wardrobes."

"Nothing." I didn't look at her as I shook out the dress she had begged me to let her buy me, a beige satin Valentino slip covered in lace that I still couldn't believe I owned.

"It's not nothing. Something's the matter." She rested the cardigan on the bed and sidled over to me. A little smirk danced at the corners of her mouth as she came close enough that I could smell the biscuity tang of champagne on her breath. "I know there is—when something's worrying you, the vein on your forehead pulsates…" She reached a finger out, stroked down from the tip of my forehead to the bridge of my nose. "This one." I shivered. "You have a secret." She leaned in closer. "What is it?"

I bent over my suitcase, breaking her claustrophobic proximity. "You're imagining things, Di."

Diana folded over the flap of the case, trapping my hands inside. "It's something to do with Valentina, isn't it?" I paused, mouth falling open, blindsided by her perception. "Aha, so I'm right." She seized the opportunity. "Where did you two really go this afternoon?"

"I already told you—we went to look at another gallery, and then Valentina saw a cat being run over and freaked out. You know what she's like."

I tried to free my hands, but Diana pressed down harder.

"Don't be boring, Rachel. Do you expect me to believe for one second that you're all pally-pally with Valentina? That you went skipping off arm in arm to have a look at pictures?"

The teeth of the zipper cut into my wrists. "Ow, Diana, you're hurting me."

"Or maybe I'm right?" She thrust her face toward me, almost daring me to look away. "Maybe you're a little turncoat, and you've been getting cosy with Valentina behind my back? Maybe you'd like to forget everything I've done for you and go off ravioli-stuffing in the village with Valentina and the nuns? Is that it? Maybe you'd rather have Valentina for a friend, and don't care about me at all?"

The low ceilings of the cabin suddenly felt like they were pressing in on us. I had seen this rage in her before, but never directed toward me, not to this extent. It was frightening.

"Diana, you know that's not true."

"*Isn't it?* You mean you haven't been using me this whole time to get what you want? Sebastian, money, *clothes*?" Before I could stop her, she had released the case and snatched the Valentino dress from where I had laid it on the bed.

"Of course not, Di. None of that matters." The lace contorted in her hands.

"I don't believe you."

She pulled at the dress, and with horror, I realized what she was about to do.

"I hate Valentina—you know that. It's you I care about," I pleaded, wanting to reach out for the dress but knowing it would only make things worse.

"Prove it. Tell me what's going on."

"I told you, there's nothing—"

"Prove it."

I heard the sound of stitching tearing, watched in dismay as the top of the dress came apart.

"Diana," I begged pathetically, a tear rolling down my cheek. *It's only a dress*, I told myself. *What are you getting so upset about?* A dress that cost more than my return flights to Italy.

"Tell me."

A wrenching. The dress tore down to the waist. It was ruined.

"She's pregnant, okay?" I gulped back phlegm. She had proved her point.

I waited, expecting a gasp of surprise, but instead an enigmatic smile bloomed across her face.

"I thought so." She tossed the dress to the floor. "But I wanted you to say it." She walked back to her bed and picked up her empty suitcase, stowing it in the corner next to the wardrobe. "Don't keep secrets from me, Rachel," she said without turning her head. "I don't like it."

I tried to catch my breath. How was Diana always two steps ahead of the game?

"How—?"

"Did I know?" she finished for me. "The chalky skin. The way she keeps pressing her hand to her mouth to stop herself from hurling." She shrugged. "I saw enough girls shepherded out of Matron's office to know the signs."

I nodded. There had been a girl in my year who was pregnant. Sandra Jones. She stopped coming to classes, but she showed up at the end, for exams; I remembered watching her waddle across the gym, the glimpse of her engorged belly peeking from under a straining T-shirt as she took her seat. I remember how smug I felt as I turned over my exam paper, thinking of the exciting future that lay at the end of it. Girls like her, I thought, didn't have a future.

"So, what are we going to do about it?" I asked, because the implication was there, in the silence between her words.

And now she did turn around, and she looked at me with an expression that to a bystander would seem perfectly harmless yet chilled me to the core.

"Leave it to me."

39

Now

"Are you sure this is where you want to sit?" The waiter who has led me up to the rooftop of the bar looks back at me uncertainly, shivering through his black puffer gilet as he finishes setting up the table and chairs that he has pulled out from a stack hidden beneath black tarpaulin. "I'm sure we can find you a seat inside."

It's cold up here, by the river. Colder than in Woking, which I left over three hours ago, the taste of Mum's disappointment still bitter in my mouth. The wind kisses the surface of the Thames and sucks in its icy chill, and I clutch my coat tighter at the neck, wish I'd also brought a scarf.

"No," I say dismissively, adopting the sort of brusque tone I imagine Diana using with the help. "As I said to your manager, it's imperative for this meeting that we have use of the rooftop. I trust my deposit was enough to secure complete privacy for the duration?"

He shrugs, obviously used to the quirks of City types who frequent the place. "I just do what I'm told."

I take the seat he holds out for me, wait for him to go, but he hovers. "Yes?"

"Ma'am, when your guest arrives…?"

I appraise the gel in his hair, the diamond stud in his ear. He can't be much more than twenty; I suppose to him, I am a ma'am.

"They'll know where to go."

He nods, but still doesn't leave. All I want is to be left in peace.

"Is there anything else?" I ask.

"Did you…do you want something to drink?"

I pause. Yes, actually, I do fancy a drink.

I reach into my wallet and draw out a fresh fifty-pound note, one of the last from the withdrawal I made on my way over, reducing my bank account to almost zero. New coat, new shoes, new dress—if I am going to see Diana, I am going to do it in style.

"Espresso martini. Two. Keep the change."

I dangle the note between my fingertips, make him reach to take it. He pockets it, chastened.

He's almost out of the door before he turns back. "Oh…"

I huff audibly. "Yes?"

"Be careful near the railings. We normally have the barriers up in front of them, but with no one out here…" He looks back toward the stack of furniture and I see his shoulders sag. "I mean, I could…?"

"We'll be fine." I dismiss him with a wave of my head, and finally, finally, I'm alone.

★ ★ ★

The Vertige rooftop certainly looks less glamorous than in Diana's photograph, now that it is devoid of people. Without the sparkle of heirloom jewelry and designer clothes, the tangle of bodies draped over the furniture and fighting for the best table, it feels mundane, almost ugly. Beige concrete floor surrounded by black iron railings. It's amazing how this city can take any manmade slab, label it cool and get the crowds to flock.

The view is beautiful, though. Although it rained heavily earlier on, the ground still slick with puddles, the sky is clear, allowing for a perfect 360-degree panorama of London's greatest hits. St Paul's, the Shard, Tate Modern; old and new rub up against one another without the slightest concern for hierarchy or status.

I walk over to the railings and look down onto the streets below, at the blur of commuters filling the pavements as the working day ends. It's quiet up here, the blare of traffic and shops and pubs muffled, and somehow that makes the dizzying height of it feel more real. The waiter was right: the railings do feel unsafe, the slats between them easy enough to slip and fall between. Vertigo makes my stomach lurch, and I retreat from them, sit.

When the drink arrives, I drain mine in one gulp, feel the caffeine and vodka jolt through me. Then, on second thought, I drink the other.

"Cheers," I say out loud, holding the martini glass aloft to an imaginary Diana.

What time does a nursery close—five, six? I open my phone and scan robotically through her social media profiles, silent since this morning. Her last update was at 10:00 a.m.: a close-up of a pair of baby blue running shoes, somehow pristine despite the rain, with the caption,

Let's do this! #tenweekstillholibobs #nopainnogain

It gives me a ripple of schadenfreude, picturing the intervening hours, her blissful unawareness of how I have inserted myself back into her life.

Will she collect Phoebe, or will it be the nanny, whisking her out of the cold and into her home, to her mother's waiting arms? Will Phoebe show her the necklace right away? Fingers twitching by her side all afternoon, will she reach into her pocket for her treasure, hardly able to contain her excitement at showing her mother her surprise? Or perhaps she'll wait, bide her time until just the right moment, hide the thing under her pillow until Diana comes to kiss her good-night, and there, in the dark, Phoebe will confront her with it, Diana's past dangling on a fingertip.

My tongue tingles from the vodka, the corners of my mouth burning with a pleasurable pain. I want to order another, but I don't want to draw the waiter's attention, so instead I reach for the little glass ramekin of nuts he brought, crunch down on a smoked almond. My stomach grumbles, and I remember I haven't eaten today and am suddenly ravenous, finishing the rest of the bowl in two handfuls.

The nuts make me think about pesto for some reason, the jar of it I know sits in my fridge, probably the only thing in it that's not off by now. I imagine setting a pan of pasta to boil, the steam on my face as I drain it. And then I laugh. Because pesto was what I ordered, wasn't it, that last evening? Proper Ligurian stuff—the viscous green coating my bowl, the weird mix of green beans and potatoes, and that funny, rolled-up pasta, what was it called? Trofie? Diana laughed at me, spearing a piece off my plate and eyeing it up. *"Darling, it's what you eat here—it's molto tradizionale."* And then I tasted it, flavors bursting in my mouth, peppery basil and crunching pine nuts and garlic so pungent it was almost spicy, and she grinned at my facile pleasure. *"Good girl."* The atmosphere was so awful, by then, that the pasta gave me something to focus on. I ate it all, every piece. It took me years before I could eat it again.

The thought of that pesto congeals in my stomach now, mixing with the vodka that sloshes almost audibly inside me, creates a bubble that rises up my gullet and explodes in a fat, gassy burp. Imagine what Diana would think of that.

As if on cue, my phone vibrates on the table in front of me.

I look at the numbers flashing on the screen and my throat dries. They're unfamiliar—she changed it years ago and I don't have the new one—but they may as well be saying, *Diana, Diana, Diana.* It feels so odd, all the time I have spent searching for her, looking at her, for her to now be the one trying to reach me.

I hesitate—the thought of her voice being on the other end, of *her* being on the other end—but then the fear of her giving up and ringing off gets the better of me and I snatch the phone to my ear.

"Hello?"

My voice rasps. I reach for my glass, realize it's empty.

"Rachel? Is that you? Is this… This is still your number?"

She hisses, almost a whisper, and I imagine her hiding somewhere, in a darkened corridor or the close confines of a bathroom, afraid of letting her husband overhear.

When was the last time she called me? Eight years ago? Ten? Those cutting, final words: "Rachel, what is it you want? How much? How much do you want to stay away?"

So many things I want to say—so many questions, accusations—but I cut through all the noise whirring in my brain and head straight for the jugular.

"So, you got my present."

I can taste her silence. Hear the swallow of saliva down her throat as she collects herself, considers what move to play next. *Oh, Diana, you are always so careful, so conniving, but you forget that I have learned from the best—when it comes to manipulation, I have had an excellent teacher.*

"Why? Why now?"

I am surprised at this, so surprised I laugh.

"You know why. Don't tell me you don't watch the news, read the papers?"

She sighs, the exasperated sigh of an older sister tired of her naughty younger sibling, and the sound makes the anger bubble up inside me. I clench the phone tighter, wait for her to speak.

"That was a long time ago, Rachel. My life is... That's not a part of it anymore."

"Oh, I know all about your life." The anger rises now, makes my cheeks hot, my eyes smart. "About your drinks with the girls and your fancy exercise classes. I know about your huge house and your gorgeous husband and your beautiful children. But you can't just layer all that fancy stuff over you and pretend that what happened, didn't. You can't just think ignoring me will make me go away. Make *him* go away."

I hear her sharp intake of breath. Spittle flecks my lips. I wipe it away with the back of my hand. I wait.

Finally: "What do you want?"

She attempts her signature cold calm, but I can hear the quiver underneath it—a crisp, white shirt edged in Chantilly lace.

I mash the phone into my ear. My cheek is wet—from sweat, from tears—and the glass slides against it. After all these years, after all that has happened, finally, finally, I have Diana where I want her. I close my eyes, breathe deeply and form the words I have been rehearsing for so long, that I knew were inevitable since the moment I touched her sweet daughter's fingertips.

"I just want to see you, Diana. Is that so bad? I just want to talk."

"I don't want to talk to you, Rachel. I thought I made that perfectly clear."

"You have to."

"Why should I do what you say?"

I consider telling her. Sharing some of the paranoia I have felt for the past few months. The emails. Sebastian's veiled, televised threats. But I know that whatever menace Sebastian poses for me, she will find a way to frame it as mine and mine alone. If I am going to get to her, I need to cut to her core.

"It was easy enough to find Phoebe," I say, hating myself for using her as bait, but knowing there is no other way. "I told her all about our time in Italy, how we used to be such good friends. She was so trusting, so amenable. I thought about taking her home with me. A sleepover with Auntie Rachel—wouldn't that be nice? Perhaps I'll come again. Or the boys—their school wasn't hard to track down either. I'm sure I could find another gift for each of them. Or maybe I'll pop into James's office—30 Fenchurch Street, isn't it? 'Congratulations to the boys at Spirex Capital on a successful fundraise! Wins for hubby means wins for me!'" I quote a Facebook post verbatim, picturing the looping video clip, the clinking champagne glass, Diana's wrist just in shot, agitating a diamond bracelet shimmering on her wrist. "I'm sure he'd love to meet one of Diana's oldest friends, hear all about what she was like as a teen. Or perhaps I won't even tell him who I am at first. I could just…stumble across him one night after work in a tight skirt and high heels, fuck him first, explain later." I begin to relish this fantasy, picturing, as I did with the boys, an alternate history of my visit to James. He wasn't bad-looking, after all. "I could do it, Diana—I learned the art of seduction from his wife, after all. And then, when we're lying in bed, tangled in the sheets and his seed in my cunt, I'll tell him just how angelic his wife *really* is."

"Stop it, Rachel." And there she is, the old Diana I know so well. The command that can stop you in your tracks with a single, well-timed imperative. "Stop being a child. I know you saw him. Did you really believe he wouldn't tell me? I thought you would just give up, like always. God, now this, with Phoebe? He wanted to call the police. I had to practically beg him not to. I said I was giving you one more chance—*one more chance, Rachel*. Do you understand?"

The threat of the police doesn't spook me, not yet. I know Diana would do anything to avoid that.

"I just want to talk to you, Diana. Please. After all this time, can't you just give me that?"

I can hear nothing from the other end, and for a moment, my heart stills, and I wonder if she's even there, if she's given up, rung off.

But then I hear her huff, and know she is ruffling her hand through her hair, pressing her lips together in familiar, haughty displeasure.

"Okay, okay. Where do you want me to go?"

I end the call.

It could have been enough. To see her, to talk. She could have helped me find a solution.

But instead I let the blue light glow once more, scroll through my contacts, pause on one, click.

"Hello?"

The voice answers on the third ring, jolting through me so clearly that I almost toss the phone aside, but I don't. I need to finish what I started. What we started.

"Hello?"

I swallow.

"Sebastian? It's me. It's Rachel."

40

Then

We survived that first day, motoring up the Italian Riviera, stopping on occasion to dive into the azure waters while Valentina cowered belowdecks, any implication of her being mysteriously unwell conveniently manifesting as seasickness. Dinner in Santa Margherita Ligure, a traditional trattoria beloved by Elio's mother, a serious sort of place where there was no background music to obscure the clink of glasses, and people really did groan through the full Italian meal of *aperitivi, antipasti, primi, secondi, dolci*. Everyone seemed tired, and rather dazed, from the food and the traveling and the salt-spiked sea air, slinking off to their cabins once we got back on the boat with promises of a "proper one" the next night. Diana hurled herself into bed and quickly fell into a red-wine snore-sleep, but despite the fact that I felt drained to the point of exhaustion, I couldn't switch off, tossing restlessly in the dark until sleep finally claimed me in what must have been the early hours of the morning.

When I woke with a start from the depths of a dreamless sleep, sunlight was streaming through the portholes and Diana's bed was empty. I dressed nervously, following the sound of voices on deck to find the rest of the party eating breakfast on the back platform: orange juice, steaming *cafetières* of coffee, intricately arranged fruit salads and cream-filled *cornetti* that were so fresh the crew must have fetched them that morning. I took a breath when I saw Diana seated next to Valentina, tearing a pastry to pieces and putting one out of every three pieces somewhere near her mouth. She beamed when she saw me, though, and even with her sunglasses on, I could sense the tease in her eyes.

"Morning, sleepyhead, grab a seat." Valentina instinctively started to rise to make room, but Diana patted her forearm indulgently. "No, no, Val, no need for you to move."

The downward inflection on that "you" was minuscule, certainly not noticeable to anyone else at the table, but the way she left her hand to linger on Valentina's as she watched me sit down made me think she meant it. I saw Valentina pause, look hesitantly from me to Diana, eyes wide, but without missing a beat, Diana was already passing me the basket of croissants—"Try one. They're delicious"—so that neither of us had the time to dwell on whether the intention was real or imagined.

She played with me like this all day, little hints or phrases that sounded like something might be coming, then subsided into nothing. It was like sleeping with a mosquito in the room: hearing the low hum and knowing the inevitable bite is on its way, fixing you in a state of constant awareness.

But when she did eventually strike, like everything with Diana, I didn't see it coming.

We reached Monterosso al Mare, the first of the five towns that make up the Cinque Terre, in the early afternoon. Elio had talked in radiant terms about this string of coastal towns, recently made a World Heritage site, but nothing quite prepared me for the living, breathing sight of them: pastel-colored houses piled cheek by jowl on the craggy coastline, tumbling into the turquoise waters below. All the glitz and glamour of Portofino paled in comparison with the rugged beauty of these lively little villages.

We planned to flit between the first three towns—Monterosso, Vernazza, Corniglia, each one named like characters from a Petrarchan sonnet—and then walk the Sentiero Azzurro, the "blue path" coastal hiking trail that runs from Corniglia to Riomaggiore, have dinner and then pick the boat up there. But when we arrived in Corniglia, Diana, dressed in a wide-brimmed straw hat and mammoth tortoiseshell sunglasses, announced that she had no intention of hiking anywhere.

"I'm taking a taxi to Riomaggiore. It's too hot, and *these* certainly aren't hiking anywhere." She pointed to the soft pair of gold leather sandals that had emerged this morning from a box labelled Salvatore Ferragamo. "I have the name of the restaurant. I'll meet you at supper." Finally, I felt like I could breathe again, the suffocating threat of Diana's presence momentarily lifted. The walk was fairly easy and flat, a gently winding path that wrapped along the coastline, studded with scraggy plants, agave and prickly pear and pine, as well as bushes of rosemary, thyme, lavender and honeysuckle. Their clean scents mingled in the air, almost medicinal, reminding me of the little Santa Maria Novella pharmacy back in Florence. We fell into a relaxed silence, all of us admiring the breathtaking views of the sea, and for once, I didn't mind that I was so obviously alone, bringing up the rear behind

Elio and Tomaso, Sebastian and Valentina, falling naturally into two by two.

When we reached the start of Manarola, the fourth of the towns, Elio pointed to a sign attached to the cliff wall. "This stretch is called the Via dell'Amore—the lovers' path. Legend has it, it was created in the 1920s and became a meeting place for lovers between the two towns. Before that, villagers rarely ever married anyone outside their own town."

We stood in silence, looking at the trail extending before us, the sea air clinging to our skin. It wasn't difficult to imagine the place inspiring romance. I watched Sebastian squeeze Valentina's hand, saw the tensing of her shoulders in response, even as she left her hand in his. She and I hadn't spoken properly since her revelation in the chapel, but it was clear she hadn't said anything to him yet, and that the burden of the secret was beginning to weigh on her.

The restaurant was located at the southern tip of Riomaggiore, a clifftop perch that led us through the narrow, cobbled paths of the town and back up into the hills. I could just imagine Diana's irritation at having to make her journey up there on foot. There was no way a taxi would or could pass through.

She was waiting for us when we arrived, though, her back to the panoramic views of the sun setting over the sea, basked in a deep golden glow, and smiling.

"The weary travelers arrive!" She stood up to greet us, kissing us one by one on both cheeks. The hat and sunglasses had been discarded and, Diana-like, she had changed outfits, the bikini and sundress of earlier replaced by a white dress with a deep V which showed the grooves of her rib cage. I hadn't noticed it properly until now, but she'd lost weight somewhere in the past few weeks, her already thin figure now angular and gaunt.

"Before you sit down, I've been making a seating plan while I was waiting. I think we should mix things up a bit."

Without waiting for protest, Diana proceeded to maneuver us into position, she and I taking up the heads, Tomaso and Elio flanking me, Sebastian and Valentina either side of her.

"We're even numbers...shouldn't we do boy, girl?" I asked weakly, sensing a ruse.

"Don't be so old-fashioned, Rachel. Gender is a construct... right, Elio?"

He raised his eyebrows at her, irritated, but took his place.

Her manner was skittish, tense, and I think all of us felt it. My blood began to itch beneath my skin.

"I thought," she began, still standing as the rest of us sat, hands pressed onto the tabletop, arms hyperextended, "that it was high time we had a little celebration for this lovely gathering, don't you agree?" She didn't pause for an answer. "Rachel, I ordered a bottle of wine—it's in the decanter on the table behind you... Would you mind doing the honors?"

I widened my eyes at her, but she stared pointedly across the table at me and I stood, turned to the small wooden table behind me, picked up the bulbous glass decanter without protest.

"Me first, please," she commanded. I made my way toward her, the liquid sloshing heavily against the glass. Balancing the weight of the base with my right hand, I leaned over her shoulder to pour the wine into her waiting glass. Unlike me, caked in sea spray and dried sweat, she smelled as though she was fresh from the shower, and that smell—her shampoo, roses, clothes that had never seen a tumble dryer—made me long for the old Diana, the two of us gallivanting around the center of Florence as if we owned it.

She picked the glass up from the stem, agitated the wine and took a slow, steady sip.

"Mmm…" She breathed out, taking in the eyes that were all on her. "Perfect."

She nodded to me as though I were the waiter, and then turned to her right.

"Sebastian?"

I scanned the order of the seating, saw the path that led round to Valentina, and my palms began to sweat against the glass.

"Di?"

"What?" Her voice was high, sweet, challenging. I wanted to lean into her, ask her what she was planning, but there was no way of doing it without being overheard.

"Nothing."

I dutifully circled the table, pouring the wine as Diana briefed us on what we were drinking.

"It's a super-Tuscan—Tignanello, 1985. On me, of course. You know the Antinori family, I think, don't you, Tomaso?"

I didn't know what any of these words meant, but from the look on the others' faces, I didn't need to; they were all code for "very expensive."

I would have given anything not to reach Valentina—even as I was pouring Elio's glass, I tried to think of something I could do to avoid it—but soon I was standing behind her, waiting for some word or deed from Diana to blow the whole thing up.

Instead: "Go on, Rachel, Val's waiting." A hand reached to Valentina's forearm. "Valentina, darling, you'll have a glass, won't you?"

To her credit, Valentina matched Diana's gaze, but in that moment, I saw the realization sweep over her. She turned to look at me, a mixture of hurt and fear trembling in her features.

I poured, tipping the decanter until the last drop had been

emptied, receiving a satisfied nod from Diana as I set it back down on the wooden table and took my place.

"And so—" Diana rose from her seat, glass in hand, her voice rising in volume to address us all "—I thought it fitting, on this beautiful night, to make a toast to you all, coming together for what has already been such a *wonderful* holiday. Elio—" she raised her glass to him "—it goes without saying, but *what* a magnificent boat. I'm sure I speak for all of us when I say a hearty thank-you for inviting us all—to you, and to your father, and to whatever Mafia money he used to buy it." She let out a sparkling laugh that covered most, not all, of the discomfort. "Tomaso!" She fluttered her eyelashes to the other side of the table. "To friendships new. Thank you, for making our Elio so happy. Rachel—" she turned to me "—*amore mio*. My soul sister. My partner in crime. We've known each other for a relatively short amount of time, but already you are one of the most important people in my life. We're a team, you and I. Don't forget it. *Salute*."

"And finally—" and here my throat tightened "—to Sebastian...and to Valentina."

All thoughts of myself flew from my mind as Diana looked to either side of her. This was it, I realized, the last act she was building up to, and there was nothing I could do to stop it.

"Our very own Romeo and Juliet. A testament to the world's great love stories—you two have shown us what true happiness is made of. Congratulations on finding one another. You make the rest of us goddamned sick, but congratulations nonetheless." She paused, and for a moment I thought it was over, that the threat was merely that, but then she leaned across to Valentina and clinked her glass, and I knew it wasn't over in the slightest, not with Diana. "And of course, it would be remiss of me—" she rose again, addressing the whole table, her voice growing stately and sonorous "—not to say a final congratulations to you two lucky, lucky people. Sure, it's going to be tough, I know you're only young—gosh, some may say you're just kids—but if anyone can make it work, it's you two. *Salute!*"

Throughout Diana's speech, Valentina's face had been visibly draining of color, waiting, with as much inevitability as me, for Diana to have her moment. Now, she was as white as the tablecloth in front of her, pale and lifeless as one of the weathered statues in Piazza della Signoria.

Sebastian's brow furrowed as the rest of us looked awkwardly down at our empty place settings.

"What are you on about, Di? What's going to be tough?"

She placed a reedy hand on his shoulder and giggled, as freely as though he had told a joke.

"Don't pretend you didn't know." She smiled indulgently at him. "Valentina's pregnant, silly! You're going to be a daddy! Hooray!"

She stared down the table at me as though through the barrel of a gun.

And she winked.

41

Now

The door to the roof terrace bounces on its metal hinges, bangs loudly against the concrete wall. I see her just before she sees me, allow myself in that tiny second to drink her in. Her pointed features are taut—almost too taut, I notice, smooth and entirely ageless, not a hairbreadth of a wrinkle on her forehead or at the corners of her eyes. Without too much difficulty, I picture the prick of a needle piercing her porcelain skin, erasing the months and years, as she has tried to do, less effectively, with me.

"Your hair." The first two words she says to me, as she approaches, her voice crisp as a Granny Smith and lacking any discernible emotion.

I put a hand to it, having almost forgotten its ruddy hue,

and find myself aping my sheepish teenage shrug, winding back two decades with no help from a doctor's needle.

"Remember when we tried to dye it in Florence? What a disaster." I attempt to catch her eye, desperate, always so desperate, to rekindle the rosy glow of that time.

She looks away.

"I've done what you asked, Rachel, I'm here. Are we going to keep on standing in the cold reminiscing about a holiday, or are you going to tell me what this is about?"

I breathe in all of her in one split second, the flesh made real in a way none of her digital images, none of my recent covert glances, could ever quite glimpse.

In many ways she is entirely unchanged: still pale, still beautiful, still erring on the side of too thin. Like Shakespeare's Hermione, it is as if she had been turned to stone that last night in Italy, only restored to life by my missive. But she is no Shakespearean heroine. Her coldness reminds me of that, makes me snap back to reality.

"Is that how you remember it? A holiday?"

Ignoring my previous dread, I walk to the edge of the building and run a hand across the top of the railings, cold and slippery with rainwater. The rooftop extends right out over the riverbank, and through the railings' open slats I stare directly into the black Thames, water whipping up in the wind.

The Thames is precisely nothing like the Arno, but I appreciate the river's simulacrum all the same.

The chill in the air becomes a bite, and I notice Diana pulling her coat tighter around her throat, navy, with the signature Burberry beige checked collar. The gesture makes her look vulnerable, and I can't help feeling pleased at this, at for once having the upper hand.

"Do you remember the day we threw the keys into the Arno?" I tilt my chin to look at her.

The memory comes back to me, richer now for having looked at the photograph so recently: the feel of her arm across my shoulder, the talc smell of her deodorant, the tickle of her hair on my cheek. A pain clenches at the top of my chest, makes my eyes sting; how is this the same woman I now can't envisage allowing me to shake her hand?

"Yes." She sighs, seems hesitant to come closer, but eventually walks a few steps toward me, not touching, but still. Do I imagine it, or can I hear a softening in her voice? "You were convinced we were going to get arrested. Every time we saw the carabinieri the next week, you'd duck into an alleyway to avoid them."

"Ironic, isn't it? Thinking that *that* was the thing we could get arrested for."

"Rachel."

The memory vanishes, and I fall silent, watching the little breaths of movement on the water's surface. The river seems angry here, churned up, and I feel another lurch of vertigo as I stare into its depths, remembering yet another body of water Diana's and my history seem bound by. What was it like, that night? I try to picture any peaks of white, or the shush of waves lapping at the boat's edges, but all I remember is its inky blackness, how different it looked from in the azure daylight. How much more dangerous.

"You must know he's been released?" I didn't mean to mention him so soon. I meant to hold him back, dangle the promise of his presence over her as she dangled it over me, for very different reasons, all those years ago, but now that he is out there, I feel a sense of relief.

"Yes."

I swallow.

"Did you know that he's writing a book?"

"I heard."

I am surprised at this. Surprised at how matter-of-fact she sounds, barely a flicker of movement rippling across her body. I turn to her, searching her smooth features for an emotion, a flutter, a hint, anything, *anything* to show that she is alive in there, is hearing what we're saying.

"Diana…" I try to put my feelings into words, try desperately to overcome my dumb incredulity that she is actually here in front of me, and form years' worth of things unsaid into coherent sentences.

"What, Rachel, *what?*" And finally, her features erupt, displaying the scorching flipside to the queen of fire and ice.

"I…I…I…" I stumble backward, spine pressing into the railings. "I just wanted to talk about it."

"Talk about it?" Color floods her face. "You come to London, you stalk my husband, you go to my daughter's school—*my daughter*—fill her head with nonsense and tell her to give me your little 'gift' because you want to *talk?"* She reaches into her coat pocket, takes out a curled fist and hurls an object from it. The necklace skitters to the ground, stops just before falling over the edge. I snatch at it, secrete it into the depths of my pocket, and with a flash of memory so strong it takes my breath away, I can remember holding it. Not now, but then. The three points of the *V* pressing into my palm. The tug and then release as it came free from its owner. The cool wetness of the chain against my skin as I begged Diana, as ever, for an answer.

"I thought I had made it perfectly clear to you many years ago that I didn't want to talk." The ice queen replaces her crown. "I had thought, from your eventual silence, that you finally understood that. So, I heard your message, and I have done what you asked—you got me here, I have done your bidding. But now this has got to stop. I won't have you threatening me or my family because of your pathetic little obsession with the past. So, go on, tell me." She turns, arms folded, eyes narrowed. "How much?"

I know, I know exactly what she means, but I can't help myself: it comes out involuntarily, like an itch.

"What?"

"How much do you want, to make this go away?"

"Diana, I—"

She huffs, and it is amazing to me how transactional she becomes, her voice turning clipped and formal in an instant. "You obviously feel that the stipend I've been arranging for you isn't enough, so name your price and I'll call Coutts right now and amend it."

She is already reaching into her handbag, pulling out her phone.

I look down at the water below us and feel sick, my palms sweaty despite the cold.

Those payments. The third day of the month, like clock-work.

I spend every day leading up to it vowing that this'll be the month I tell her to stop. But then I balk, every time, unable to sever that last remaining tie to her.

"Or maybe it's not money you want?" She pauses, finger on the screen. "Is it a particular teaching position, perhaps? Head of department? Assistant head? I'm sure there's an art studio that needs building, a tennis court in poor repair. Just say the word and I'm sure Ms. Graybridge would be happy to have another one of our little chats."

I press my lips together, shame radiating through me. She knows what she is doing; I can sense the tease in her voice, the needling of her eyes as they try to catch mine. Reminding me just how firmly I have been in her pocket, how much I need her, even when she's not there.

"Come on, Rach, name your price," she cajoles. "You could

take a nice holiday. Help out your parents. Fuck, you could buy a house, retire. Spend all your days…reading books? I remember how much you used to enjoy that."

She taps a toe against mine, the first point of physical contact we have had, and I flinch. Surprisingly, however much I have longed for Diana's touch, now it makes me feel sick.

Money. It all comes down to money with her. "Stupid money," as the Diana of the past once dismissed it. Only here it is, being used to keep me under her thumb once more, not so stupid after all.

"It's not about the money," I mutter, staring at the shiny, sharp point of her boot.

She tuts. "Don't be a fool."

"It's not about the money," I say again, louder, heat rising at my collar, making the tips of my earlobes tingle.

"You say that now, but it's not like it's the first time, and I'm sure it won't be the last. So stop playing with me, name your price and then we can both—"

"It's not about the fucking money." The words rip from me. So loud, I am sure someone will hear me, come running to find out what the commotion is. But the sky is dark and the streets below are too far down. Diana and I are alone.

"Well, what, then?" Diana matches my heat with sobriety, turning the tip of her patent leather boot outward in an impatient tap.

"I don't want your money. I don't want your connections. I just want to know… I only want to know…" I steel myself, try to distance myself from the hurt of what I am about to ask. "Why did you leave me?"

"Leave you?" Diana cocks her head to the side. "Rachel, what are you talking about?"

"Don't do that." I breathe in, let the sharp bite of the winter air invigorate me. "Don't use that fake 'concerned therapist' voice on me. You know what I'm talking about." I look into her eyes, trying to reflect into them even the smallest understanding of my life over the past twenty years. "I needed you, Di. During the trial, after. All these years. I was drowning in it all, and you just…let me go." A sob threatens. I swallow it down. "I could feel you pulling away from me. Every phone call I made, every letter I wrote, I felt your rejection getting stronger every day. But I couldn't stop—I didn't *want* to stop. Because I kept hoping that one day you would remember everything we had, all the promises we made, all the things you said to me—*the things you said to me that night*—and you'd come back to me. You promised me that we would always be friends. I kept hoping you would remember that. It was all I ever wanted, to be your friend. But when I needed your friendship the most, you paid me to disappear."

My voice cracks, and I feel like I am cracking too, the hurt that has built up over two decades now finally breaking free. She says nothing. I turn away, look hard at the yellow squares of office lights blinking in the tower blocks over the river until their colors start to merge.

Finally: "You were never my friend."

I try to look back at her, but I can't—it's too painful, like staring straight into an eclipse. Her words sear into me, the words I have always feared to be true now undeniable.

"You were never my friend, Rachel." Diana walks behind me, close, making the skin on the backs of my arms prickle. "It was fun, Florence, but it's *over*. What happened out there— all I wanted to do was forget about it. But you couldn't let it go, could you? You kept writing, and calling, and emailing. Home, university, for years, wherever I went. I wanted to be nice, but for God's sake, Rachel, you didn't get the bloody message! Calling my house in the middle of the night, showing up at my wedding—*yes, I saw you*—Jesus, do you realize how crazy that all was? My family, James, my parents; they all wanted to get the police involved, get a restraining order, but I told them I'd handle it myself. And I tried to be nice—I *did* try to be nice, didn't I? You stopped calling. I could finally hear the beep of my phone and not feel that little clench of dread that it would be you. I could finally walk out the door without glancing both ways to see if you would show up, unannounced. Don't you see how nuts this all looks? Twenty-one years, Rachel. I mean, *get over it*."

Each word is like a blow to the chest. I brace myself as she hurls the insults my way, and every time they strike me as viscerally as a new wound.

"You're pathetic, Rachel." I can hear the sneer in her voice, even if I can't bear to look at her. "You were pathetic back then and you're pathetic now. I'll admit I enjoyed it, molding you, getting you to do what I wanted. It was like having a little plaything, a pet. But seriously, friends?" She snorts. "I would never be friends with someone like you, any more than I would be friends with poor, dead Valentina."

"But you said…you said…" I grip the railings. They wobble at my touch, making my stomach lurch—or is it her?

"I said, I said!" Diana mimics in a nasal baby voice. "I was *using* you, you idiot. God, it's so pathetic that you didn't even realize that. I knew you'd listen to anything I said. I had to keep you on my side, to stop you going off and saying something stupid. I was doing it for both of us! And it worked, didn't it? You've had a good life, haven't you? A nice job, cash, freedom." And then she's right behind me, close enough to smell her perfume, spicier and richer than her teenage florals. "So, I will say this once, and only once—leave me alone." Her breath on my neck. "Leave my family alone. In two minutes, I am going to turn around and walk away, and then I am never going to hear from you again. And if I do—if I so much as hear a *whisper* from you, online or in the papers or anywhere else, believe me when I say I have the resources to make your life *very* difficult."

"I hate you." I turn to her, speak through gritted teeth, spittle flecking my lips.

She reaches out to touch my chin, tips my face so that I can look nowhere but at her.

"You don't hate me, Rachel." She smiles with her mouth, but her eyes are hard. "You love me."

"No." I shake my head, try to tear my face from her, but she presses her fingers into me, gripping my jaw so tightly I think she might crack a tooth.

"Admit it, Rachel. Whatever you think, whatever little stunt you may think about pulling, you won't do any of it. Because you love me."

For the first time tonight, I look at her. Really look at her. This hardened woman with her sleek hairdo and her smart coat.

I think of those teenage girls folded into one another on the banks of the Arno. Holding hands as they sprinted down the Ponte Vecchio, dodging the carabinieri after attaching the Lovers' Locks. The *bambole*, always a two, surviving lazy, hazy nights and early-morning starts at Villa Medici together.

All my adult life, I have longed for that time, that girl. Seeking something I have never managed to recapture. But I see nothing of that girl in the woman who stands before me now. I don't know either of them anymore. I realize that it is finally time for me to set the past to rest. *"No!"* With the full force of my complicated, competing emotions, I jam my arms out toward her, hands connecting with her shoulders, bony even through the woollen coat. The feeling of something falling distracts me—Valentina's necklace. I forgot I have been holding it. It slips from my grasp and I bend down, snatch it between my fingers and tuck it into my coat pocket just as the sound of the terrace door jerks me upright.

I look toward it. Both of us look toward it. To the figure illuminated in the frame.

A figure in a dark woollen overcoat, wisps of sandy hair just visible from beneath a gray cashmere beanie.

A figure who has never felt more real and more surreal to me than at this very moment.

Sebastian.

42

Then

I didn't realize silence could be so loud. It ricocheted off the walls surrounding our table, echoing in the scrape of Diana's chair as she pulled it back, sat down. Valentina fixed her place setting. Sebastian concentrated on the cement between the brickwork on the wall behind him. Elio, Tomaso and I looked nowhere and everywhere. The waiter came over, heavyset with a bristling mustache, like a cliché of an Italian uncle, bustling around us with blissful ignorance as he prized monosyllabic orders out of us.

When he left, Sebastian raised his glass to his lips, drained it.

"I'll order another bottle."

His dismissal laid down an unspoken rule that we weren't to talk about it, but, unsure what else we could possibly say, we fell into a restless quiet.

Tomaso, in a dismal attempt to defuse the atmosphere, tried to ask me questions about my course at Cambridge, which was now, unbelievably, just a few weeks away. But I couldn't think of the answers, responding in stumbling, barely formed sentences until he stopped asking.

The food arrived, the smell of it intrusive, acid, salt and fat rising over us like a storm cloud. I'd ordered pesto pasta but it wasn't how I'd had it before, arriving with potatoes and green beans and weird twirled pasta shapes, and Diana had to explain that was how it came here.

Diana ordered steak. It was the first time I saw her finish her plate.

Another bottle came, then another, and another. Which seemed odd when I was sure I hadn't had more than a couple of glasses, until I looked over at Sebastian and saw him filling his almost to the brim.

And then there was the sound of a chair being pushed back, scraping through the silence. Valentina flew from the room, a hand pressed to her mouth. The chair toppled backward, hit the ground with a jolting clack.

Moments later, Sebastian followed.

We attempted to finish the meal as if nothing had happened. Diana, alone at the end of the table, tried to move next to Elio, but he gave her a look of such disgust that she actually flinched. She huffed, tried Tomaso, who acquiesced with a pained smile.

We boarded the boat without them, asked the crew to take the tender back to shore to collect them while we stayed on deck, waiting. Someone brought out cards. Elio mixed drinks. But then the hours got later and the attempts at conversation began to stick in our throats like rough, unsalted pieces of Tuscan bread, and we escaped the suspenseful atmosphere for our cabins, making an unlikely attempt at sleep.

★ ★ ★

Shouting jolted me awake. I knew immediately it was very late—not even a hint of light crept through the cracks of the curtains and when I turned to the clock on the stand between the beds, the sharp red numbers flashed up at me: 03:38.

I raised myself up on my elbows, noticing for the first time that Diana's bed was empty. My eyes adjusted to the dark as I scanned the room, spotted the outline of her body pressed against the door, holding it open by the smallest crack.

"Di?" I croaked, my throat dry from too much alcohol and the stale cabin air.

"*Shh,*" she hissed, but then inched the door open another centimeter and nodded her head toward the outside world. "They're back."

I trained my ear to the open doorway, only just able to make out the difference between Valentina's high-pitched sobs and Sebastian's angry rumble, but then Diana widened the gap farther and beckoned me over.

"*Come on.*"

"What?" I looked from Diana to the open doorway and clutched my sheets to my skin.

She crossed the room and wrenched the bedclothes from me, snatching me by the wrist and giving it a sharp tug. "*Let's go.*"

She tried to coerce me toward the door, but I pulled back, wanting at least a moment to collect myself.

"Di, we can't just…"

She slammed a finger to her lips, shook her head vehemently and opened the door fully.

The boat had five levels, the bowels of which we crept through now, pressing our palms against the wood-paneled walls to feel our way. We passed the other guest rooms, all with their own minimalist gray marble en suite bathrooms.

OUT OF HER DEPTH

Beyond us, reached via a separate entrance, slept the crew. A
narrow staircase reached the main deck, which featured a large
dining room and living area, and a separate lobby which led to
the spacious master suite comprising a study, living room and
en suite, out of bounds even to Elio. At the stern of the yacht
and accessed via another set of stairs was the platform where
we had breakfast each morning, and where a hatch allowed
us to come and go easily from the ship's speedboat, as we had
done earlier that night. High above the main deck and jutting
out past the cockpit, a sundeck was kitted out with lounge
furniture and sunbeds, and had quickly become the favored
spot from which the more daring among our party jumped,
aquiline bodies diving into the water beneath.

The voices were louder as we reached the main deck, looked
upward to spot Sebastian's form on the sundeck above us. Valentina couldn't be seen, but her catlike cries were unmistakable.

"Please, Val, please be reasonable here," he was saying,
throwing his arms aloft. She let out a strangled string of
sounds, and he responded with an infuriated growl, kicked
one of the metal bars surrounding the deck so loudly I heard
his shoe make contact. "Just stop fucking crying. I can't fucking think."

I was staggered by the viciousness of his tone, and she must
have been too, because she gasped and fell into a low whimper instead.

"I just don't understand why it's such a big issue," he continued, and I heard the creak of his feet moving on the wooden
deck once more. "This is going to ruin our lives. If you deal
with it, everything can go back to normal."

A squawk from Valentina. "Why do you keep saying that—
'deal with it'? What am I supposed to do?"

"You know what I mean. For God's sake—it can barely be more than a bundle of cells."

"How can you say that about our baby?" This set her off again, erupting into messy sobs.

Diana squeezed my hand to get my attention, pointed toward the rear of the ship.

"The platform," she whispered into my ear, pulling me close to her. "They won't see us there."

Despite myself I followed her, the burning desire to see this played out trumping any respect for their privacy.

Keeping a close watch on Sebastian's back, we hugged the periphery of the boat, toeing the floors as lightly as we could for fear of alerting them to our presence. We reached the stairwell and slunk down it onto the sunken platform below, flanking either side of the entrance so that we could just get a clear view of the sundeck through the gap in the stairs.

The platform was empty, I noticed, the breakfast table and chairs stowed against one side, but the boarding hatch was still fully open, leaving the stern of the boat exposed to the sea, the occasional spurt of water spilling over the side as the yacht rocked. The crew must have forgotten to draw the hatch up after collecting Sebastian and Valentina.

We should close it, I started to think, *or the platform is going to be soaked.* But then the voices upstairs rose again, and I looked up, distracted.

"What do you want me to do, Val?" Sebastian continued, pacing the length of the deck. "What other option is there?" Valentina said something unintelligible to which he lurched forward, bending down to where, I assumed, he was looming over her. "What?"

"I said..." She gave a ragged sigh, trying to gather herself. "I said...I don't understand why we can't get married."

"What?" Sebastian's cry of astonishment wavered between a laugh and a choke.

"You said… You told me…" And then Valentina came into view, fists balled. "It was a lie, wasn't it? Everything you told me…all the promises you made…did you mean any of them at all?"

"Aaaaargh." Sebastian stumbled away from her, hands clutching at his hair. "Don't start this again, Val. I honestly can't deal with this bullshit right now."

He swayed, reached for something on the floor of the deck, and then I saw him raise a bottle thirstily to his lips.

"Will you stop drinking?!" Without warning, Valentina lunged at him, and the bottle escaped from his grip, flying backward off the sundeck and landing with an almighty shatter on the floor of the main deck below, a few feet away from the steps where we were hiding. We both instinctively jerked backward, pressing ourselves against the wall of the platform. When we looked again, a dark stain of red wine was pooling on the wood, looking a little bit too much like blood.

"Are you happy now?" he hissed, raising his hands aloft. "You're going to wake the whole fucking boat." He paused, and I heard him sigh heavily. When he spoke, his voice was softer, as though attempting a compromise. "Enough now. Let's go to bed. I can't talk about this anymore. I'm exhausted and apparently I've run out of alcohol."

He reached for her, but Valentina wrenched her arm out of his grasp.

"No. I'm not going to bed with you. I'm not going anywhere with you. I can't even look at you."

He tutted. "What are you going to do, sleep out here?"

"I don't care. I don't want to sleep. Just leave me alone."

"Don't be ridiculous. Come to bed. We can talk about this in the morning." He tried to move toward her, but she raised both palms and pushed so forcefully that he faltered, teetering warily, close to the edge of the deck. "Jesus fucking Christ, woman. Are you trying to get me killed?"

She said nothing, jerked away from him so that she was looking out over the vast, black sea.

"Fine." He turned to go, starting for the steps that led down to the main deck. "Sleep where you like. Drown yourself for all I fucking care. I'm going to bed."

He left, not looking back. Diana and I watched him until he reached the bottom step, disappeared into the depths of the cabins below, and then we pulled back, both of us sinking to the floor. Diana beckoned me over and I crawled beside her, both of us resting our backs against the platform wall.

"*W-o-w*," Diana mouthed, opening her lips wide to enunciate each letter. I nodded in agreement. Both of us fell still, listening to the sound of Sebastian's footsteps fading to nothing. An eerie silence fell over the boat, underscored by the persistent shushing of the sea. There was no sound at all from the deck above, and when Diana pressed a finger to her lips, motioned for us to have a look, Valentina was just standing there, hands pressed against the metal railings, staring out into the waves.

We watched her for a while, the soft glow of the moonlight outlining her figure so that we could just make out the rise and fall of her shoulders as her breathing slowed, the gentle waft of the sea breeze agitating her hair. It was almost peaceful.

"Valentina." With no warning, Diana crawled over me and launched herself to the base of the platform steps.

"Di, what are you doing?" I scrambled after her and tried to pull her back, but she brushed me off with a backward flick of her wrist.

"Valentina," she hissed, louder.

From my hiding place behind Diana's back, I saw Valentina's head whip around and then down, to focus on us standing at the opening of the platform.

I don't know what I expected, not a friendly wave exactly, but certainly not the venom I saw emanating even across the distance: her features morphing, shoulders rising to a definite hunch, and a hiss, the fury of it carrying across the breeze.

"*You.*"

Valentina charged into motion, darting down between the decks until she was standing at the entrance of the platform. All trace of the innocent, sweet young girl had vanished. In her place: a woman, spitting with rage.

"Why did you do it?"

A nervous energy began to creep over me, but Diana was as cool as ever, straightening her back, feet planted firmly on the floor as she spoke in crystalline received pronunciation.

"I don't believe *I* did anything. I'm sure that that was all you and Sebastian."

Without warning, Valentina launched herself down the stairs and was on Diana, the slap she gave to her cheek echoing into the night air.

"*Puttana!*" she spit. "You *bitch!*"

"Are you fucking crazy?" Diana's hands flung out in response, grabbing a fistful of Valentina's hair and pulling so hard Valentina yelped in pain.

"No, you're the crazy one." Valentina's body contorted as she tried to free herself from Diana's grasp. "What was this, some kind of…revenge? Because you didn't get your own way? You're *obsessed.* Obsessed with Sebastian. It's so obvious— everyone can tell, even him."

"You don't know what you're talking about." Diana faltered. Her grip slackened, and Valentina used the opportunity to wrench herself free.

"I do." Noticing Diana's hesitation, Valentina gave her a

taunting smile. "Don't think I don't know the truth. That you…you only were…pretending—*che innocente*—that you were telling me that you slept with him because you were doing me a favor. I'm not stupid—I know. I *know* it was all you. He told me. How you…how you *dragged* him into bed with you. How you pushed…no, *forced* yourself on him, even when he said no. And after, how he tried to explain that it had been a mistake, and you begged him, *begged* him to be with you." She pressed her hands to her face, her English stumbling and becoming more erratic the more impassioned she became. "You hated it, no. When it became me he loved, not you. *Io, non te.* You hate that he doesn't want you. You…you with your education *aristocratica*, your expensive clothes. You think you deserve everything, just, *perché!*" She snaps at the air near Diana's face. "But you don't know…you don't realize that all your money…all the clothes…all the perfume in the world can't cover up the truth. You're nothing but a *puta*, a cheap, lying *whore*."

"You fucking bitch!" Diana hurled herself toward Valentina, arms outstretched. "You know that's not what happened. You're making it up. *You're* the fucking liar." Their bodies intertwined, hands clutching at faces, hair, limbs twisting and turning, and all the while my own mind was twisting and turning, trying to make sense of what Valentina was saying. I recalled Diana's cool detachment toward Sebastian after the Feast of St. John, how I assumed the feeling was mutual. The boat bobbed on a wave and seawater splashed onto the open deck.

"I'm not a liar!" They knocked into the wall, connecting with wood in an angry clash. "You'll see! You can't stop us. When Sebastian realizes the truth, everything will be okay. We love each other. This is all just…*cosa hai detto*—how did you say, Rachel?—a little fast-forward."

I had thought that my presence had been forgotten, but in that moment, they both turned to me, Valentina imploringly, Diana with amusement, lips curled into a sardonic smile.

"Is that what you said, Rachel?" she asked, laughter tickling the edges of each word.

"I…" Forced into the present, I looked from one to the other. It couldn't be right, could it, that Diana had forced herself on Sebastian and been rejected? That was certainly not how she had framed it to me. And yet, she had seemed so determined to take him down, take both of them down. Why would she have cared so much if it had just been a drunken mistake?

"It *is*, Rachel…*per favore*, it is." My intrusion on the scene had broken them apart, and now Valentina came toward me, hands clasped as though in prayer. "You *said*, no? You said everything would be all right. And it will be, yes? It *has* to be. Please. Be my friend, tell her."

Her friend. My mind was a mess of confusion. I had thought that *Diana* was my friend. But she knew how I felt about Sebastian. If she really did have feelings for him, why didn't she just tell me? And Valentina… I hated her, didn't I? If she hadn't arrived, Sebastian and me…I would have had a chance, wouldn't I? I feel the weight of both their eyes on me. The breeze had picked up, pulling at my hair and making me shiver through my thin T-shirt. We were so exposed, the three of us on that empty platform. Surrounded by nothing but sea, no light, no sound but the lapping of the waves, the scent of salt and seaweed blanketing us; the sensory deprivation enhanced their twinned figures, made obvious the boy who tied them, tied all of us.

"Diana, is it true, what she said? About you and Sebastian? Because I thought…I thought…"

"*No.*" Diana shook her head vehemently. "God, Rach, I

would never do that to you. It was a mistake, just like I told you. I'm sorry, I'm so sorry for what happened between me and Seb, but he was yours—he was always yours." I wanted to believe her. I willed myself to believe her. I looked at her and she smiled sweetly, encouragingly. "You're my friend, Rachel. My *best* friend. What we have—it's special. It'll last far longer than this trip, than Italy. We have a *lifetime* of friendship ahead of us. No boy is worth ruining that for. I swear to you that I will never do anything to hurt you like that, ever again. You believe me, don't you?" She reached a hand to me, pulled me into her, the taut hardness of her body beneath her cotton top so familiar, so hard to ignore.

Her best friend. All at once, I felt the glow of Diana's attention cast over me. I was hungry for it. Needed it. I had hated her being angry with me. I felt myself being won over.

"I liked him first." I turned to Valentina, knowing, as I said it, that it sounded pathetic. But the idea began to grab hold of me and I found myself clenching my fists, stepping toward her. "*I liked him first.* Him and me...it was going to happen, I know it. Diana... It was a mistake, a drunken mistake. But me and him... It was finally going to happen. And then *you* showed up and everything went wrong."

Valentina pressed her hands to her chest, shaking her head at me, eyes round and wide as the moon overhead.

"I...I don't understand, Rachel. You...and Sebastian...? How? How could you do that to me?"

"Don't play dumb, Valentina." Diana took a creeping step toward her, her voice low and steady. Totally in control. "Don't pretend you couldn't see what was going on, from the moment you set foot inside the hotel. Acting so sweet and innocent when really you knew exactly what you were doing, didn't you?" Diana was right next to Valentina now, and it scared her—I could see it: the quiver in her lips, the tremble that ran through her body and made her clasp her arms around herself for protection. "I know girls like you. You never really liked Sebastian. You took one look at him, and knew what he was. You saw your opportunity."

I felt the energy of it, fizzing through the salty air. I was drunk on it. Drunk on Diana, powerful and beautiful, finally putting Valentina in her place. Finally putting things back to where they belonged.

Another wave splashed on the deck. A wind was picking up, whipping the surface of the sea.

Valentina blinked from one of us to the other.

"I don't know what you're talking about. What opportunity could I have seen?"

"Oh, give up. You never loved him, did you? You just wanted him for his money." Diana poked a finger to Valentina's chest. Valentina backed away, hugging her body to the yacht's smooth sides.

"How can you think that? I don't care about Sebastian's money. I wouldn't care if he was penniless. I just want him."

"I don't believe you." From the other side, I began to move toward her, barely feeling the deck beneath my feet. "From the moment you arrived at Villa Medici, it was obvious what you were. All that batting eyelids at the guests, lingering after service, trying it on. You knew exactly what you were after, and with Sebastian, you got it."

"No, no." Valentina shook her head, tears streaming down her cheeks faster than the wind could dry them. "It's not true! I love him! I love Sebastian!"

"*Liar,*" Diana sneered. I felt giddy. "Admit it. Admit you're a fucking little liar."

Valentina tried to swerve out of her way but stumbled on the wet wood, feet slipping out from under her as she fell to the deck.

"No, no, no." She scrambled to get up as a high wave crashed over the side, soaking her back.

"Admit it."

Grounded, Valentina began a backward crawl away from Diana—toward, I suddenly realized—the edge of the open platform.

"Diana…"

I spoke low, motioning toward it, but Diana thrust an arm out to stop me, and I froze in my tracks.

"Tell the truth, Valentina." She took a step toward her.

"I…I…I don't know what you want me to say."

"Diana." I tried to get her attention. Valentina was perilously close now, her hands slipping on the slick deck as the waves lapped over the platform. The wind whistled in my ears as Diana ignored me, moved closer.

"Say you're a liar. You don't love Sebastian. You never did. You were just using him for his money."

"No, no, it's not true!"

"Say it, and we'll leave you alone."

"I can't, I can't!" Valentina turned her face away, a mess of sobs.

"You're probably not even pregnant, are you?"

"I…I…"

"Say it."

A flurry of movement. Diana's form over Valentina. I flinched, turned away—the briefest of seconds—looked up to see Valentina tumbling backward over the side of the platform.

"Valentina!"

In that instant, it was as though whatever spell had been cast over us was broken. I raced to the edge and flung myself down, reaching over the side to catch one of Valentina's thrashing limbs.

"Valentina!" I cried into the blackness, as one of her arms

after the other reached haphazardly for the side and then sank uselessly under again. "Diana, help me!"

I leaned over farther, fearing that I too might go overboard. Her face emerged, gasped for air before sinking once again, her flailing body pulling her down.

"Diana! For fuck's sake, help me! Diana, she can't swim!"

I turned, briefly, not wanting to take my eyes off Valentina. Diana was stock-still, motionless, her face as expressionless as a stone.

"Diana!" I hissed once more, and then plunged my arms back into the sea, searching the waters for any part of Valentina I could find.

Her head bobbed more and more urgently in and out of the water, lips searching the breaking waves for air, the image searing itself into my brain. I tried her wrist, but she was thrashing so hard I lost my grip. I caught hold of her dress, but the material was too loose to pull her close.

Finally, finally, my slippery fingers caught the chain of her necklace and I pulled with all my might. I felt it, felt the weight of her rising up out of the sea, could picture her landing, terrified but unharmed, on the deck beside me.

A second too late, I felt the release, my body forced backward from the shift in weight.

With a cool horror that spread from the tips of my toes up to the crown of my head, I unfurled my gripped hand. In it, Valentina's necklace, the clasp broken.

Valentina was gone.

"No, no, no!" I lurched my upper body over the side, reaching uselessly into the empty water to feel for some sign of her. Nothing. "Valentina!" I cried into the sea. "Valentina, no, I'm sorry!"

"Rachel." All at once, Diana was beside me, hissing furiously. "Shut up. You're going to wake up the whole boat."

And then she took me by the wrist, fingers pressing into the flesh. "It's no use, all this carrying on. She's gone."

"No!" I turned into her, burying my face into her stiff, unmoving body. "Diana, oh God, what have we done? We have to do something. We have to wake them up, tell someone, I—"

"Stop it!" Diana shook me so hard I thought I would break. When I looked up, her eyes were boring into mine. "Listen to me—we were never here."

"I—"

"No." She pressed a finger to my lips. "We. Were. Never. Here. Do you understand me? You're going to toss that necklace back into the sea, and then we're going to go to bed, and when we wake up, we're going to look for Valentina just like everyone else. Got it?"

Sickness grabbed hold of my stomach, my insides twisting and turning like I'd eaten something rotten.

"How can we just…leave her…?"

Diana sighed, but then she pulled me toward her, her body slackening as her arms enveloped me.

"Rachel, my sweet, sweet Rachel. We can't do anything for her now, my darling. You realize that, don't you?" My body prickled at this sudden warmth, and I turned my chin, trying to read her face. "Love, if we told people what happened, you understand what that would mean, don't you? There would be an investigation, a trial. We'd go to prison. Both of us. The lawyers' fees, the expense. You know I don't like talking about money, but your poor parents… Could you do that to them? And all that studying…your place at Cambridge. Our whole future. Our lives would be over. Do you really want to let that go…for her?"

I thought of who I was at the start of this all. Everything

I'd worked so hard for, everything I'd dreamed of. Gone, in an instant.

I shook my head. "No."

"Good girl." Diana drew an arm around me. "Sebastian and Valentina had an argument. Valentina was very upset. She was very unhappy. Who knows what would have happened if her family had found out about her and Sebastian? She was out here on her own. The platform hatch was down. She doesn't know how to swim. Maybe it was an accident—maybe, I don't know... Maybe she couldn't take it anymore. Do you see what I'm saying?"

I swallowed. "I do."

I felt Diana's shoulders relax against my own. She loosened her grip on me. Sighed.

"We have to protect each other, you and me. That's what friends are for. We can't tell anyone what happened tonight, ever. But we can be there for one another, and as long as we have that, everything's going to be all right. You trust me, don't you?"

Numbly, I agreed.

"You're my best friend, Rachel. I'd never do anything to hurt you. I love you—you know that, don't you?"

And then she turned her face toward me, and she kissed me. Not quite on the cheek, not on the lips exactly, but at an odd, indefinite midpoint above my jawline. And for some reason, it was this that made me pause, raise my eyes to look into hers, search their murky, brown depths for some hint of remorse, fear, sadness, horror.

The mouth smiled. The eyes didn't flicker.

"We should go to bed, Rachel." She stroked my cheek. "Throw the necklace away now, and then let's go."

My heart skittered. I ignored it. "Okay."

She nodded. "Good girl."

I walked to the edge of the platform. It was still wet from the seawater that only moments before Valentina's arms had splashed across the surface. I imagined her body, gradually sinking to the seabed, tangling with the weeds and pecked at by curious fish. Or pulled along by the tide, caught up in a fisherman's net, emerging, arms outstretched, eyes wide, unblinking as birds cawed at it in horror and the cry for help rose in the air.

A wave of nausea washed over me, exacerbated by the swell of the boat on the water's surface. I doubled over, fists pressed against my stomach. And then I stretched out my right arm, fingers opening like petals.

The gold *V* lay faceup in the center of my palm. It felt hot, as if, once released from my grip, it would have left its mark, branded me. I clenched my fist, drew my arm back in anticipation, and then just before I was ready to throw, I turned back to see...to see...

No one.

Diana had gone. Left me to finish the deed, alone. My arm fell to my side.

I stood alone on the silent platform, gazing up at the fading stars, gradually being claimed by the breaking day.

Diana was right. Protection was what we needed. But there was no harm in protecting myself.

Without another thought, I slipped the necklace into the pocket of my pyjama shorts.

And then I followed her inside.

They didn't find her body for a week. Almost as I had envisaged, it had been pulled along by the tide, got caught among the rocks of Cinque Terre's craggy coastline and remained wedged, hidden in the arteries of a nondescript cave, until some tourists—Germans, I think they were—got a bad handle on a rental boat and had to be rescued. Suffice to say, they didn't go back home raving about the Italian Riviera.

She was pregnant, though. Diana had been wrong about that. And once the prosecutors got hold of that…well, it was game over.

The story wrote itself. Posh playboy, Catholic schoolgirl. Sex, sea, sun, scandal.

You may call me foolish, or just plain stupid, but at the time, I swear to you, I honestly didn't think it would go that way. It seemed so obvious to me, standing on that platform that night, listening to Diana's solid assurance, that it would be taken as an accident, suicide at the worst. Any other option didn't even enter my head, and once it did, once it all started spiraling, it was too late, and I was too scared to stop it.

A couple on a nearby boat testified to the fact that they had heard arguing, shouting, a man and a woman's voice. The sound of screaming. The crew confirmed that the couple had been fighting when they picked them up; even Elio and Tomaso agreed. And there was the broken bottle, the testimony from everyone about how much Sebastian had drunk that night.

The necklace, it turned out, was a key piece of evidence. Faint ligature marks on the back of her water-bloated neck to suggest a struggle. She never took it off. Who else would care enough about it to want to remove it, fight for it? "Where is that necklace, Mr. Hale?"

It made me sick when I heard that. In trying to save Valentina, I had damned Sebastian.

But.

Cambridge. My whole future, everything I had worked so hard for. My life would be over.

Diana may have been absent throughout the trial, but her words lived in me every day of it.

And besides, I thought, it wasn't as though he was entirely blameless in all this. Playing with us, using us, pitting us against one another... No, no, not deliberately, I agree, but you'd have to be two crayons short of a pack not to recognize what was going on. Blameless in the act, but not necessarily the cause.

And so, for a while, I let my conscience rest. Because I had something far more important to gain: I had Diana.

And then I didn't.

I tried so hard. I clung on to that friendship so tightly I thought I would never let it go. But her silence wore me down. And over time, my grip loosened, just like it did that night on poor Valentina. And I let another body slip through my fingers.

But I kept the necklace.

43

Now

"Sebastian!"

We speak in chorus, living up to our twinned reputation of old.

"Rachel." He remains frozen in the doorway, his features masked by the backlight. But then he clocks her, his eyes squinting as they adjust from light to dark. *"Diana?"*

"Hello," she offers, her voice betraying nothing.

For a moment, no one speaks, and I allow myself to take in the strangeness of it: Sebastian, Diana and me, together at last. The dull sounds of the city below, the wind whistling around us, the blank concrete of the rooftop... Up here, it is as though only the three of us exist, have ever existed. And I can't help but allow myself a flicker of a fantasy, the thought of a different life, in which meeting these people at a rooftop bar is just a normal, quotidian occurrence.

But then he moves toward us, and I see for the first time what the papers and the interviews couldn't capture. Sebastian is still good-looking—those features can't be weathered—and I have grown accustomed to the way his face has morphed with age and circumstance. But finally, now I see fully who Sebastian has become: the shadow lingering in the blue of his irises, a hunch to his gait, which was always so relaxed and confident, a silver scar seared across his right eyebrow that the cameras haven't picked up. *Oh, Sebastian, what did we do to you?* "What's going on, Rachel?" he asks at last, his voice blisteringly real. "Why am I here?"

And it is like an avalanche, that question: the memories flooding my system as though I have slipped on loose ice and am falling uncontrollably into an abyss.

A naked Diana, extending a hand the day we met.

Sebastian, tanned and nonchalant on Silvia's kitchen counter.

The smell of midnight air in Villa Medici, and people, and parties, and dancing. Sweat slick on our skin and alcohol hot on our breath.

Sebastian and Diana. Sebastian and Valentina. Sebastian and me.

The boat. That dinner. That night. Diana's hands on Valentina.

Mine, reaching blindly into the swirling sea. Valentina's, as she slipped under.

The images make my head whir, and through the fog of it, I look at Diana, standing cold and impervious beside me. What has it all been for? What was the point of any of it if I am still left with nothing? Who am I trying to protect?

"We did it, Sebastian," I breathe.

And for the first time, perhaps since the night it happened, I feel lightness flood my body.

I don't know how I manage it, but I force myself to look at Sebastian. When I do, I expect to see hatred, disgust, shock. But instead his face is surprisingly calm. "She did it, Sebastian. She killed Valentina." The words are surprisingly easy to emit, and I continue, spurred on by his silence. "We heard you shouting and sneaked out to the lower deck to hear. When you left, Diana called Valentina onto the back deck. There was an argument. The platform at the stern was left down, and Valentina slipped and...and..." I take a breath.

"I never meant for things to end up like they did. I never thought anything would happen to you—I promise you, I didn't. I don't know what to say to you, Sebastian. I thought of telling you so many times. I've been a coward. And a liar. But it is time you knew the truth. I know I am not blameless in this either. And it's time we paid for what we did. I can't give you your past back, but if I can, I want to give you your future."

Tears blind me. A sound escapes from me as though I have been punched in the gut, and I double over at the imaginary pain, a pounding ache beginning to form at my temples.

Silence.

"Sebastian?" I look up. My whole body is trembling now, the cold feeling of the wind's icy fingers across my exposed skin. "Say something."

Slowly, Sebastian turns his gaze from me to Diana. "Diana." His voice is low, his face expressionless. "Is it true?"

"It's over, Di. Tell him it's true." And I realize, now, it is over. There is nothing she can hold over me anymore. Diana's spell is broken.

Diana and I lock eyes, and in that single, solitary moment, I see exactly what she thinks of me, how she has really thought of me all along. She smiles, and I am surprised to see that there is some glimmer of pity in her eyes—perhaps the closest thing to a genuine expression I have ever seen. But then she breaks our gaze, and before she even speaks, I know what she is going to say. "No." She shakes her head lightly, flicking me away as easily as a ladybird on a leaf. "Of course it's not true."

The Thames whooshes below us. I look at Diana, her expression impervious, and realize that this is how Valentina must have felt, right at the end. At Diana's mercy. "I'm sorry, Sebastian, I don't know what to say." She stalks toward him so that they are both in profile, and I can't help but notice, even here, even now, how fine they are, both of them, their beautiful features etched out by the starlight. "I know you always cared for Rachel, that you thought she was a good person, but all I can tell you is what I know for sure. I was asleep in the cabin—"

"No." The blood begins to drain from my body.

"I'd drunk so much that night I didn't hear a thing. I didn't know she'd left. But then I woke in a start to find her standing over my bed, just...staring..." I shake my head, knowing where this is going, but lured by some sick fascination into hearing what she is going to say. "It was the middle of the night. The room was pitch-black. She was soaked in water and sweat, and icy cold—gosh, I remember her hands were like blocks of ice. She didn't tell me what happened, but it wasn't hard to guess."

"*No...*"

But Diana carries on, the lies tripping easily from her tongue.

"Sebastian, I am so sorry for how I behaved that night. I've never forgotten it. I was a horrible person back then, childish and jealous, and just plain *awful*. But her..." She turns her head in my direction but doesn't bother to look at me. "She was something else. She *adored* you, Sebastian. You know that. We talked about it all the time, didn't we? You said how you felt sorry for her, that she was like a little sister, that you felt bad about letting her down."

And among these lies, among these sickening, lurid untruths, I can't help but feel something else: humiliation. Sebastian talked about me. To her. Pitied me. Was I ever anything to these people but a joke?

"And then you slept with her, didn't you? You cad," Diana mews, sounding suddenly so much like her teenage, seductive self. She is owning the stage now, strutting about the rooftop with both our eyes on her. "You must have known, didn't you, how much Rachel hated Valentina? You rejected her and took Valentina back, and then you went and got Valentina pregnant—God, it must have made her sick. So, you can only imagine, for her to kill Valentina and make you take the blame...it must have been the ultimate revenge."

"*No*, don't listen to her," I moan, trembling with horror as Diana spools out the story as easily as if it were the truth. But it was true, partly, wasn't it? He did reject me. I did hate her. And really, although it wasn't me who gave the final push, did I do anything, truly, to stop it?

I see Diana moving toward him, reach an arm out as if she's about to touch him, but she pulls back, perfectly timed. And then, for the first time—the *only* time, in all the years I've known her, apart from the day after she slept with Sebastian—I hear Diana start to cry.

"I should have said something, Sebastian. I know that," she wails, and if I didn't know her better, yes, I suppose I would be taken in by it. "At the time, I was so young—I just wanted it all to go away. I was even too scared of coming to the trial—scared of what she'd do to me if I said the wrong thing. After what she did to Valentina, can you blame me? And then she blackmailed me, for years. Stalked me—ask my parents, they'll remember. Extorted money from me, made me use my connections to get her a job. Did you know she left Cambridge because she had a psychotic break? She made me come here tonight—threatened my family if I didn't. But I had no idea you would be here, that she would try to frame me for... *gosh*." Diana presses a hand to her cheek, and I have to hand it to her; her act is impeccable. Even I am in her thrall. "We were arguing, before you got here—I was convincing her to tell you the truth. *Fuck*, Sebastian, if you hadn't turned up, I think she could have pushed me over the side."

I can see what she is doing. Everything she's saying—there's no denying the facts as they are. But what proof—what proof do I have over her but my word?

"Surely you know she's lying?" I ask desperately. "I would never... I couldn't..."

I try to form sentences, but my thoughts are like marbles scattering across a stone floor.

"I don't know what to believe." He shakes his head, turns away from me. "All the letters I wrote to you, all the chances I gave you, to tell me the truth. If you were innocent, how could you have let me just...?"

"I—I wish I could explain it," I stutter. "I wish that there was some way that I could make you believe me. I know it was wrong, Sebastian. You don't know how many times I wished I could... But she told me... She said... I thought..."

"Oh my God...what's this?"

Diana's voice cuts across my plea as I tear my eyes unwillingly from Sebastian just in time to see her swooping toward me, reaching into my pocket. All too late, I realize what she has.

When she rises, the diamond *V* is dangling from her palm.

"*Oh...*" Her voice is low, the sound steady as a perfect note on an oboe. "Sebastian, come here. You won't believe this. Isn't this…? Wasn't this…?"

"*No!*" A strangled cry rips from me.

"She must have brought it here tonight, to show us," Diana continues, her voice surprisingly calm. "Look, she must have kept it all these years, carrying it around like some sort of sick trophy."

"*No. It's not true*," I try to explain, pathetically, squeezing my eyes to clear them from the tears that fall freely now. "Can't you see she's lying? That she…that she…"

"That I *what*?" Diana looms over me, spitting acid. "That I planted it there? That I'm some sort of magician that made it suddenly appear in your pocket? Sebastian, you've been standing here the whole time—was there any way I could have possibly put it there before seeing it, just now?"

"Her necklace." He takes it from Diana's outstretched palm, stares at it, mesmerized. When he turns to me, his face is snarled with hatred. And I know the game has been won. "You never liked her, did you?" He sighs, voice heavy. "I remember your face when she asked you to put it on her. It was stupid, giving it to her in front of you. As a kid, I thought I was giving you a message, trying to demonstrate to you, in some misguided way I couldn't put into words, how important Valentina was to me. I can see now how hurtful that must have been, but I never thought… Rachel, how could you have done this? To Valentina? To *me*. All these years. All those times I begged you to say something, to tell me the truth. I thought there was something you might have seen, something that would have proved it was an accident. But I never… I couldn't have guessed…this. I never knew you hated me this much."

"*No, no, no.*" The horror of it grips hold of me, and I am overwhelmed with a sudden sense of vertigo, a nausea that

LIZZY BARBER

makes my head swirl, my stomach feel as though the bottom
has fallen out of it.

"For fuck's sake, Rachel." Sebastian is angry now, his voice
morphing into something hard and full of force. "If you're so
innocent, why didn't you say something? If you're *so innocent*,
why do you have it? Why do you have Valentina's necklace?"

"It's complicated." My mind is chaos. It has started rain-
ing again, icy sheets that make my coat heavy. "I was there
that night too."

"Valentina," I called into the deep. "Valentina!"

"I didn't do anything to her, I promise. But I tried to save
her." I carry on, tears hitting my cheeks and freezing to salt
from the wind and the cold. "I honestly did, but it was too
late."

The necklace, the pull and release as it broke off in my hand.

"Diana, help me!"

"Are you listening to her, Sebastian?" Diana inserts herself back into the narrative, flings an arm in my direction.
"She's deranged. What, first I'm this solo murderess, hellbent on destruction—now suddenly she was there too, some
white knight? She's just making it up as she goes along. She's
dangerous. Insane. She's been stalking my husband, my children. I'll show you the bank statements. It's been going on
for years. She's—"

"Sebastian, don't—"

I flail wildly, take a step in Sebastian's direction. As I do,
I feel my foot connect with something hard. A flash of black
patent. Pain shooting from my ankle. I stumble, lose purchase
on the wet ground and feel myself falling against the railings,
the shudder as they rebound against my weight and then the
shock of open air surrounding my legs as I feel myself slipping underneath.

The scream that rips from me is inhuman, loud as a crack

of lightning, but by some mercy of God, my hands connect with one of the slats, take hold.

Just as I feel myself rebalancing, icy fingers wrap themselves around my right wrist, and I see Diana, staring at me.

"It's okay!" she shouts back to Sebastian. "I've got her!"

I am paralyzed with fear, legs knocking against the side of the building. I try to haul myself up, but the slightest movement makes the railing quiver and my body lurch, and I grip hold anew.

"Sebastian, stay back!" she calls to him, and from my position I can just make out Sebastian freezing on the spot. "The railings aren't stable—too much weight could make them break!"

The rain lashes at my face but I can't wipe it away. My body is shaking from the cold and the fear and the adrenaline. But I force myself to look up, to stare into Diana's eyes.

"Tell him the truth," I spit. "Please."

"Enough now, Rachel." Diana leans over the railing to look down at me, and her voice is gentle, almost sweet. "It's time to finally put this to rest. All these years, all these secrets... You've hurt a lot of people in the past, but what I really think you need...is *help*."

"Diana, please."

"You need help, Rachel," Diana coos. "But it's okay; I'm going to see to it that you get it. You've wronged a lot of people, but now is the time you can make it right." She leans over, adjusts her grip so that one of her hands is holding my coat, the other extending toward mine on the railing. "We're going to get you safe. Just grab hold of my hand, and this will all be over."

I look up at her long fingers, the pale perfection of her skin evident even in the dank city glow. Each nail the exact same length, smooth and round, painted a baby-soft pale pink, not a chip in sight. Like Diana, the hand is spotless. Like Diana, no one will ever know the cruelty it is capable of.

In an instant I picture how this moment will play out. Finally, I will pay for my part in our story. And there is some justice in that. For Valentina, for Sebastian. I am not entirely innocent in all this; I have always known that. And there is something comforting to that, about finally relieving some of the guilt that has sat with me for so long. Isn't some justice better than none at all?

Slowly, I ease the fingers of my right hand off the railing, the sight of my own damaged, dirt-stained nails not escaping me. I feel the shift of my weight, the traction of my hand in hers. Take hold.

"Easy now," she coaxes. "Good girl."

And it is possible, perhaps, that if she hadn't used that phrase, things would be different.

Yes, it is possible that there could be a world in which I am Diana's "good girl" once more, keep her secret, just as I did on that night, all those years ago.

But hearing that phrase, I know I can't be Diana's good girl any longer.

She has won, I know. Perhaps I have always known she would.

Because when it comes down to it, people like her will always find a way to win.

But just because she may have won, it doesn't mean I should give her the satisfaction of making me see her victory.

And so, for once in my long, long history with Diana, I make a decision that is my own.

I look into her eyes. And I let go.

44

After

Diana checks her smile in the long oval mirror in the entrance hall.

They'll be arriving soon. A small team, they said: producer, cameraman, lighting and sound. The bubbly host of the show whose speech is always peppered with Americanisms, and whose hair color always screams "bottle." No, she won't need hair and makeup. No, her husband and children will not be in.

They were paying handsomely—not that she needed the money, not like Sebastian. Even the official pardon from the Italian courts couldn't unwind his family's two decades of lawyers' fees, and he was hardly going to be putting himself on the job market.

She'd heard there was already a second book in the offing.

Some hot, new streaming service had snapped up the rights to a film. Heard, because it turned out that she and Sebastian had very little left to say to one another, particularly once a few donations to the right hands had managed to extricate her from any messy implications.

She had hired an agent, a northern woman with a sharp gray bob and a penchant for trouser suits, to manage the overwhelming enquiries and draft the appropriate statements:

"Please respect our family's privacy at this difficult time."

But they had both agreed that one interview, one carefully worded tell-all, with a strictly adhered-to list of caveats, would be no bad thing. Plus, she looked excellent on camera.

She scrutinizes herself in the mirror once more, removes a stray hair from her face. Wonders if she should have worn the green shirt, not the cream. Rachel always liked her in green.

The name floods her with cold adrenaline, as if she has accidentally turned the wrong tap in the shower. Instantly she pushes the feeling back, observes herself, practicing: a flutter of the eyelids, a wobble of the lip—*years of blackmail, fears for her safety, her children's lives.*

And it's not exactly a lie, is it?

True, some minuscule fraction of herself, some tiny, carefully filed away diary entry of a thought feels bad for the way things ended with Rachel. Yet, it is truer still that her first major, overwhelming feeling was relief.

All those years. All those messages, and missives. All those times that Rachel had pleaded with Diana; made Diana feel like she was the sole villain, Rachel nothing more than collateral damage.

But that wasn't the truth, was it, Rachel? The adrenaline surfaces again, and she has to fight to press it down. *I may have made the first move, but it was you who delivered the final blow.*

It may have been over twenty years ago now, but she still knows what she saw that night.

"Diana, help me! Diana, she can't swim!"

The sound of water sloshing onto the deck. The sight of Rachel crouched over the edge.

She might have gone to her. She might have snapped out of her cold, white anger. Who knows—Valentina might have been alive today, the whole thing blown over in a bout of silly, teenage jealousy.

But for Rachel.

Rachel's arm reaching into the water—no, not reaching, pressing—muscles flexed to hold Valentina down. A second arm, joining it, one single, deliberate pull to free the necklace from Valentina's failing body. The necklace Rachel had always so despised.

Did she feel Valentina slacken? Did she know what she had done? Did she enjoy it?

Diana meant what she said at the time—how it would look, their futures. She knew even in that moment that it would be the case of preserving both of them...or neither of them. Which was why she had done what she had to do. And when the necklace resurfaced, the poisonous thing clutched in her daughter's little hand, ready to infect all that she had secured, she had done what she had to do once more. It could be both of them...or one of them.

The doorbell rings. It blares through the last of her thoughts, and she snaps to attention, summoning the best of the woman she has worked so hard to hone and perfect for the past twenty-one years.

She smooths her collar. Fixes her smile a little higher.

Opens the door to allow them their first precious glimpse of her beautiful home, her beautiful life.

"Please," she beams, every inch Diana. "Come inside."

* * * * *

ACKNOWLEDGMENTS

At the "eyes-wide" age of eighteen, I spent the summer in Florence studying Italian and generally stomping through Tuscany, falling in love with one beautiful town after another. As I had a fairly sheltered childhood, it was my first taste of independence, my first experience of living alone and pretending at being an adult. I made lifelong friends and developed a lifelong love of the city, whose narrow streets and myriad piazzas I still visit year after year. So first and foremost, thank you to beautiful Florence for inspiring in me the same joy that grasps Rachel so wholeheartedly. I hope you feel I did you justice.

This book would be nowhere without my marvelous agent, Luigi Bonomi, and his wife and colleague, Alison. Luigi, your constant encouragement and belief in me kept me writing, even through messy rewrites and when everything seemed as tangled as Rachel, Diana and Sebastian's love life. Our shared love of Italy shaped many wonderful and wistful conversations, and I hope to be able to toast with you over a glass of prosecco in the shade of a pine tree soon. *Saluti e abbracci!*

To Wayne Brookes, my fearless editor at Pan Macmillan—thank you for seeing so clearly and precisely the vision for this book, and for having such enthusiasm for it. You absolutely nailed what was going on in my head from day one and it has been pure joy working with you—I can't wait for the next chapter. And to Emily Ohanjanians, my editor at MIRA—you have such an infectious delight for my characters (even the ones we love to hate). I have been thrilled to work with you again, along with Greg Stephenson and everyone at MIRA.

And thank you, too, to Charlotte Wright and the team at Pan Macmillan, and the rest of the team at MIRA, for all the work you have done to get *Out of Her Depth* into paper form. A book is so much more than the words on the page: you have brought them to life.

Friends and family, as ever, have been the backbone I have needed to man up and finish this thing. Special shout-out to Emma Hughes, my "book sister," for constant words of encouragement and for seeing something working in the mangled chunks you read, and to Ferdy, my brother-in-law, for fielding constant Italian-language questions. Mummy, as always, my primary reader, thank you for reading drafts over and over, even when I wasn't sure what I was writing. I couldn't wish for a more enthusiastic beta reader. Jamie, I'm sorry there are still no aliens. Maybe next time?

And finally, to my husband, George, thank you for your constant support, for carving out writing space for me from a wailing newborn and for indulging my stream of consciousness over this and subsequent plots, even when what you really want to talk about is the cricket. It means a lot. And you mean even more.